The Dover Café *at* War

Ginny Bell

ZAFFRE

First published in the UK in 2020 by
ZAFFRE
An imprint of Bonnier Books UK
80–81 Wimpole St, London W1G 9RE
Owned by Bonnier Books
Sveavägen 56, Stockholm, Sweden

Copyright © Gillian Holmes, 2020

A CIP catalogue record for this book is
available from the British Library.

ISBN: 978-1-83877-143-0

Also available as an ebook

1 3 5 7 9 10 8 6 4 2

Typeset by IDSUK (Data Connection) Ltd
Printed and bound in Great Britain by Clays Ltd, Elcograf S.p.A.

MIX
Paper from
responsible sources
FSC® C018072

Zaffre is an imprint of Bonnier Books UK
www.bonnierbooks.co.uk

Prologue

Marianne leant wearily on the wooden counter at the back of the café. The tables were crowded and the hum of conversation and clink of cutlery on plates was making her head ache. Her older brother, Rodney, was skirting carefully down the narrow aisle between the tables for four holding some dirty plates. It was always a bit of a squeeze when the tables were full, but he was an old hand and his tall, slim frame twisted nimbly towards her, the plates held high over the customers' heads. He'd just finished his final exams at school so was helping out for the summer before leaving Dover to join the navy. He'd always been the clever one, unlike Marianne who'd been working in the café for three years, since she'd left school at fourteen to help look after her four younger brothers and sisters and help her mother with the cooking. Sometimes she wondered if she'd ever leave. There had been a time when she thought she might ... She shook her head, unwilling to think about the man who'd left her broken-hearted the previous winter.

1

She pulled the cloth of her blue cotton dress away from her back, suddenly aware that the sweat was trickling between her shoulder blades. Despite leaving the door open, the café was hot, and the smell of sausages and cabbage filled the steamy air, combining unpleasantly with the cigarette smoke rising from almost every table. Usually she would have been in the kitchen preparing the meals, but today she'd begged to be allowed to stay out front as she was feeling so unwell. The heat of the kitchen in summer could be punishing, and she'd thought that being out in the main room would be cooler. She'd been wrong. If anything, it was worse.

She gasped quietly as a jolt of pain radiated out from her back, around her stomach and then ran through her entire body. She grabbed the edge of the counter, her knees buckling slightly.

'Marianne! When you've finished daydreaming, take this over to Mrs Reynolds.'

Her mother's harsh voice brought her back to her senses. Nellie thumped a plate of sausage and mash on the ledge of the hatch between the kitchen and the café and wiped her brow. She was angry with Marianne for not being in the kitchen, and when Nellie was angry, everyone knew about it.

'I don't know what's wrong with you today, girl, but you better sort yourself out. There's no room for laggards in this family. Now get on with it.'

Behind her mother, her thirteen-year-old brother, Jimmy – a head taller than their mother now, she suddenly realised – crossed his eyes and stuck his tongue out at her. He knew she was feeling ill and, ever the joker, he was trying to cheer her up. But it wasn't working today. She shook her head at him warningly. If Nellie saw him, she'd give him a clip around the ear.

'Sorry, Mum.' Marianne obediently picked up the plate, wincing as her stomach tightened again. God, would it never stop? She'd have to tell her mother she was sick at this rate. She shuddered at the thought. Unless you were throwing up or unconscious, her mother didn't believe in illness.

Rodney took the plate from her. 'Don't worry, I'll do it.' He looked at her with concern. 'You don't look too good, sis.'

Marianne forced a smile to her lips. 'Thanks, Rod.' She glanced back at the hatch where her mother was still standing, an impatient look on her face, the brightly coloured yellow and green scarf tied around her chest-nut hair damp with sweat, her round cheeks shiny and red. Today, her apron was an iridescent orange, the cotton dress underneath puce green. Marianne blinked. Her mother was loud in every way: her voice, her opinions and the clothes she wore. Normally it didn't bother her, but today just looking at Nellie made her head ache even more.

'I don't care who does it, just get it done.' Nellie turned away with a grunt, taking a swipe at Jimmy with a tea towel when she saw his expression, and picking up a spatula from the large table in the centre of the kitchen before hurriedly turning back to the sausages frying on the black range that took up the entire right-hand wall of the kitchen.

Rodney hastily collected the plate and weaved his way back through the tables; each one had a small white porcelain vase on it, containing a bunch of sweet peas. Her mother liked to make sure the place looked nice. 'We are a café not a caff,' she frequently reminded them. 'And I don't want anyone forgetting it.'

Marianne stared towards the large plate-glass window at the front of the room. The good weather always brought more customers as people lingered over their shopping in the market square, chatting to their neighbours, and then more often than not deciding to pop into Castle's for a cup of tea and a rock cake. The sun was streaming through the window, causing the dust motes to dance in its rays. Her stomach churned. Staying as still as she could, she focused on the writing on the window and the tall, white buildings opposite. The word 'Castle's' was written in large, gold block letters on the outside, arching over smaller black letters rimmed with gold that read: 'Hot Food, Tea, Cake'.

'Seltsac,' she murmured, trying to distract herself by reading the words backwards. Then moving her eyes down, she said, 'Toh doof.' She gasped then, as another pain gripped her.

'Marianne!' Gladys, one of their regulars who ran the flower stall in the market, shouted over to her. 'You couldn't get us another cuppa, could you, love?'

Marianne started and picked a clean cup from the shelf beneath the counter. Going over to the large tea urn that stood by the wall next to the cash register, she poured out a cup for Gladys, adding a splash of milk and four sugars, as she knew the other woman liked it. But as she walked towards Gladys's table, a pain so sharp and so devastating rushed through her and she doubled over. The cup and saucer dropped to the black-and-white tiled floor. The woman seated at the table nearest to her shrieked and jumped up, dabbing at the splashes of hot tea on her blouse. Suddenly, a warm flood of water ran down Marianne's legs and she gasped in shock and humiliation as the liquid splashed on to the floor. The woman screamed louder.

'You disgusting girl! You've only gawn and wet yerself!'

The low murmur in the café came to a halt and a deathly silence descended as everyone looked at her. If she hadn't been in so much pain, Marianne would have fled; she'd never been so embarrassed in her life. But she couldn't move. All she could do was stand bent over, her hands braced on the dark wood of the table in front of her, and pant as the pain roared through her.

Nellie came bustling out from the kitchen. 'What the hell is going on?' she shouted. She looked down at the floor, and then at Marianne. If this hadn't been her slim, shy, seventeen-year-old daughter, she'd have thought . . . But she couldn't be. Surely not. Not her Marianne. She'd always been such a good girl.

She grabbed Marianne's arm and dragged her through to the kitchen, opening a door on her left where a staircase led up to the apartment above.

'Rodney!' she shouted over her shoulder. 'You're in charge! Jim!' Jimmy stepped forward, his mouth hanging open in shock. 'Get a mop and clean up that mess! Glad, you couldn't help our Rod, could you?'

Gladys nodded and ran to the kitchen to get an apron.

The woman who had been splashed was still complaining loudly. 'If that girl's not having a baby, then I'm the pope's daughter!' she declared. 'It's a disgrace. Young girl her age getting up to all sorts. Well, I'm not staying in a place like this.' She marched out with her nose in the air. A few of the other customers were muttering, their faces registering disbelief. Most of them had known Marianne all her life. They liked her. She was a sweet, pretty girl, who never had a bad word to say about anyone.

'. . . Just shows you never can tell.' An old woman got up from her table with difficulty and picked up her shopping bag. 'Nellie Castle won't be so high and mighty now.' She sniffed and walked out, making a beeline for the crowded stalls set up in the market square, each one covered with a colourful striped awning, to spread the news.

One by one the customers left, while Rodney watched helplessly, his mind in turmoil. He knew his sister better than anyone. Marianne always followed the rules – just as he did. But if she'd been hiding this secret all these months . . . He shook his head in disbelief.

Suddenly, from upstairs, they heard Nellie's scream of disbelief. 'Jesus Christ! Marianne Castle, you're only having a bloody baby!'

She hadn't considered that the window was open, that the market square was packed – and that everyone could hear her.

∽

Just two hours later, Marianne drifted in and out of sleep. At some point during the last nightmarish hours, her mother had forced her up the stairs to the bedroom she shared with her sisters on the second floor. It had been a difficult climb as she'd had to stop frequently, her pain-wracked body barely able to move. But her mother had pushed her on, and now, at last, the pain had gone and her mind had taken her far, far away from the memory of the panting and straining, the sheer agony. When she thought at all, only two questions occurred to her: How could she not have known? And how on earth had this happened?

She closed her eyes in despair as her mind took her back to a winter's day when a beautiful man had convinced her that she was the most wonderful girl he'd ever met. That he'd never felt like this before ... So handsome and charming, she couldn't believe he'd picked *her*. His attention had come at a price, though, and she'd paid it willingly, convinced that she'd met the love of her life. She was sure they'd be married soon and she'd finally get away from the café and out from under her mother's thumb. What an idiot she was. After that day, he'd disappeared from her life and she'd never seen him again. She'd not considered, not even for a second, that her constant crying and occasional sickness had been anything other than due to the heartbreak. She'd been taken for a fool and felt so ashamed. Her only consolation at the time had been that at least no one else had known. But now everyone would know. And they would never forget.

A sharp cry brought her out of her doze and she opened her eyes reluctantly as her mother came over and placed a small, towel-wrapped bundle on to her chest with surprising gentleness, considering her towering rage. 'Here. Looks like you've got a son,' she said. 'And soon you're going to tell me exactly where he came from!'

Marianne gazed at the baby, speechless with shock and fear. She looked up at her mother, tears welling in her eyes. 'What should I do?'

'If you're old enough to get yourself knocked up, you're old enough to look after it,' Nellie spat, then walked out of the room, leaving Marianne staring at the creature in her arms. His dark hair was matted, and one tuft at the front curled back from his forehead, stubbornly refusing to stay down. His tiny rosebud mouth emitted soft, mewling cries and he was wriggling in distress. She had no idea what she was meant to do with him.

How was this even possible? Then another thought came to her: what if her mother threw her out? Where would she go? And what about her friends? Would they ever speak to her again? Tears dripped down her face and on to her baby's soft cheeks, until she couldn't hold in her sobs any longer and she started to cry in earnest; huge gulping sobs that shook her entire body, while her baby, shocked by the noise, escalated his cries to match hers.

'For God's sake, Marianne. Feed the bloody baby!' Nellie said as she strode back into the room.

'I don't know how!'

Nellie sighed and, roughly unbuttoning Marianne's dress, she pulled down her Liberty bodice and pushed the baby's face into Marianne's breast. His little mouth clamped down hard on her nipple and she shrieked. 'Ow! It hurts, Mum! Everything hurts!'

In the doorway she could see the bewildered faces of her brothers and sisters. They were only young themselves: Lily was seven and Edie nine, Bert and Jimmy eleven and thirteen. They'd always been her and Rodney's responsibility, and she knew they looked up to her. That would be gone now, too. And as for Rodney? She couldn't imagine him forgiving her for this.

Chapter 1

6 August 1939

Marianne placed a plate of freshly-baked sausage rolls on the table and looked around the café. She just needed to lay out the plates and cups and everything would be ready for Donny's birthday party. Rodney was due any minute, and the rest of their friends would be coming in an hour or so. As for her younger brothers, Bert and Jimmy, who knew? They said they'd try to get the afternoon off from their barracks in Canterbury, but she wasn't sure they would. She hoped so, though; they hadn't been home once since they'd joined up in March.

Through the large plate-glass window at the front of the café, she could see Donny and his best friend, Freddie, kicking a football around. As always, Donny was looking on the scruffy side. The smart shorts she'd persuaded him to wear for his party were slipping down his skinny hips, his blue shirt, with only two buttons done up, was untucked and his socks were around his ankles. She stepped out of the door and raised her face to the sun, enjoying the warmth and breathing in the scent of the sea that was blowing in on the soft breeze. Castle's Café sat on the corner of the market square and Castle Street. On an ordinary day, the place would be buzzing with activity, and the covered market across the road would be full of shoppers, but Sundays were always quiet, and Marianne savoured the peace of the afternoon.

A wolf whistle startled her from her thoughts and she glanced up and smiled as she saw her friend Reenie – one of only three friends who had stood by her following Donny's scandalous birth – hands on hips, standing outside her uncle and aunt's grocery shop directly opposite the café on the corner of King Street.

'Look at you in your glad rags! You look the spit of that Olivia de whatsit!'

Marianne laughed and looked down at the rose-pink shirt-waister she was wearing. It certainly made a change from her usual baggy skirt and blouse. 'Yeah right. And my mum's Vivien Leigh!' Marianne ran her eyes over her friend. She was wearing her customary slacks, with a red and blue checked short-sleeved shirt. Her curly blonde hair was hidden under a scarf and on her feet were sturdy lace-up shoes. Reenie was clearly on her way to the allotment where she grew vegetables to sell in the shop.

'Are you coming over later, Auntie Reenie?' Donny called out to her, as though reading his mother's thoughts.

Reenie opened her mouth to answer then stopped as a group of planes whined above them. Instinctively they all looked up. Over the past few weeks, the sight of the Spitfires and Hurricanes flying out on exercise had become all too common, and though she'd been determined to put any thought of war out of her mind today, Marianne felt a shiver of apprehension sweep over her as she wondered what would be happening this time next year. Would they be celebrating Donny's birthday with their customary tea party, or would they be too busy trying to survive? She found it impossible to envisage what life might be like, though preparations for war were all around them with blackout curtains being hung at every window, air raid sirens wailing out for practices at regular intervals, and bomb shelters being dug in Pencester Gardens. She prayed her little boy didn't have to grow up in a world at war, would never know the terror of a bomb falling on his town, but with every day that passed, it seemed less and less certain that her prayers would be answered.

'Try keeping me away from your mum's cakes. I'll be there and so will the others,' Reenie replied, as soon as the noise from the planes had abated.

Just then, Nellie came out, resplendent in her party outfit of a bright green summer dress printed with large red flowers. Her short, greying chestnut hair was curled tightly around her head, and she was carrying a chair. She set it down at the edge of the square and opened the red and white polka-dot parasol that had been tucked under her arm.

'Come on, Lily,' she called. 'We ain't got all day!'

The loud sound of metal scraping against paving stones presaged her sister's arrival as she struggled around the corner carrying a stepladder. She was wearing one of their brother's old shirts and a pair of shorts and had tied one of their mother's gaudy pink scarves round her bright-blonde hair. At seventeen, Lily was the beauty of the family, but today her pretty face was set in a scowl. She propped the stepladder up beside the window and then went back to the side gate that led into the small concrete yard at the back of the café, returning shortly with a bucket full of soapy water. She then proceeded to climb the ladder, one hand on the side-rail, the other carefully holding the bucket of water.

Marianne grimaced at her sympathetically and retreated back inside. Her mother and Lily, though they looked nothing like each other, were very similar in personality – and sparks inevitably flew.

'Get on with it, girl, or you'll still be at it when everyone arrives!'

'Mum, for gawd's sake give it a rest! If you think you can do it any quicker, you should bloody do the job yourself.'

Nellie snorted. 'I've served my time cleaning those windows. Anyway, look at me! I can hardly do the job in my best frock.'

14

'And you can stop your smirking, Edie. It's your turn next week.'

Marianne turned her head and noticed her other sister had crept up behind her and was pulling faces at Lily through the window. Edie laughed. 'And I'll make a better job of it than you. Washing all those cars up at the garage has honed my skills.'

Edie worked as an apprentice at Pearson's Garage near the castle. It was a job that raised more than a few eyebrows among the market community, but it seemed to suit her.

'You look nice, love,' Marianne remarked, noting the pretty blue and white striped cotton dress her sister was wearing. She'd left her dark hair loose and clipped it behind her ears, and her green eyes were sparkling. And was that lipstick? Her sister was a bit of a tomboy so she wasn't used to seeing her dressed up. 'What's this all in aid of?'

'Can't I dress up for my nephew's birthday party?' Edie snapped.

Marianne was surprised by her tone.

'Anyway, thought I'd pop out for a bit of a walk before the party. See you soon.'

Edie hurried out of the café and turned left towards the seafront.

'Where you off to?' Nellie called after her.

'Just a bit of a walk. Not that it's any of your business!'

15

She flounced off and Marianne stepped out on to the pavement again, staring after her. Strange, she thought. All dressed up and going for a walk could only mean one thing – she was meeting someone.

'What's that all about, Lil?' She looked up at her sister.

Lily shrugged. 'She's been acting strange for a while. There's definitely a bloke involved. Why don't you follow and find out?'

'I can't do that!'

'Huh! If I wasn't stuck up here, I'd go. You don't fancy swapping places, do you?'

Marianne was saved from answering by a whoop of excitement from Donny.

'On yer head, Davey!'

'Happy birthday, Don!' A small brown-haired boy wearing glasses came bounding into the square.

'Here, you want to come to my tea party later? Can he, Mum?'

Marianne looked at Donny's hopeful expression and her stomach sank. Davey was a sweet boy but . . . She cast a furtive look around for his parents. If they saw their son playing with Donny, there'd be hell to pay and she didn't want anything to ruin Donny's birthday.

'Course he can,' Nellie said stridently, before Marianne could reply.

The boys started kicking the ball again, while Marianne looked right up Cannon Street and there, just as she'd feared, was Davey's father. She let out a breath as she tried to work out how best to deal with what was sure to be coming next.

'Davey!' the man boomed.

The three boys froze and watched as a middle-aged man wearing a suit and tie strode towards them, his glasses glinting in the sunshine and his thin black moustache twitching in annoyance. His timid wife remained a few steps behind, refusing to look at any of them. Nellie folded her parasol and got up to stand beside the boys as Marianne inched forward. Behind her Lily got down from the stepladder and went to stand beside her sister, her arms folded across her chest.

Davey took one step towards the man, head bowed. 'Yes, Father?'

'Come away from there this instant!' Horace Smith grabbed his son's arm.

'But it's Donny's birthday and they said I could go to the tea party.'

The man looked around at the little group and sneered. 'What have I told you about the sins of the parents?'

Davey glanced at Donny, then looked down in shame as he muttered something.

'Speak up, boy!'

He shook his head miserably.

Nellie sighed loudly. 'Horace Smith! Have you ever heard the expression: "Let he who is without sin cast the first stone"?'

Horace glared at Nellie. 'Mrs Castle, permit me to know what's best for my son.'

'Permit you, eh? You know, I don't think I will, you self-righteous little God-mutterer. You think I don't know all about you and that Hester Erskine? One minute you two were walking out together then suddenly off she goes, never to be seen again.' Nellie looked up at the sky, as if deep in thought. 'Last I saw of Hester, she'd gotten strangely fat. And then *poof*, she was gone. Did she lose all that weight, do you know?'

Horace spluttered in indignation while Marianne smiled inwardly. Sometimes it seemed that Nellie knew everything about everyone in town.

'Mrs Castle, I will bring up my son as I see fit. And I do not want him mixing with the likes of ...' He stopped and looked around at the family group then threw a contemptuous glare at Marianne.

Though she tried hard to hide it, Marianne felt tears spring to her eyes. Would it never end? she thought in despair. Ten years she'd lived with the scorn of some of the townsfolk and on the tenth anniversary of the day that had been simultaneously the best and worst of her life, she was still seen by some as a scarlet woman, when the reality was she'd been a stupid, naïve girl who'd been betrayed by a man.

Lily marched over to Donny and put a protective arm around his shoulders, looking at Horace with hatred in her eyes. 'Oh bugger off, you miserable old sod,' she said through gritted teeth.

Horace's face was flushed. 'And *that* is precisely the sort of language I need to protect my son from. It wouldn't surprise me if we didn't have another little Castle bastard running around soon.'

For a moment, Nellie stiffened, then, her face set, she thrust the tip of her parasol towards the man's stomach. 'Get off with you, you revolting little man! Go on, git!'

Horace whirled around, Davey's arm still gripped tightly in his hand, and started striding back towards Cannon Street, dragging his son behind him. But Nellie was far from finished with him, and moving swiftly after him, she poked his behind hard with her parasol.

Horace let out a yell of indignation and turned around, his hand raised. 'Why you . . .'

'Go on, Horace, I dare you.' Nellie's chest was heaving with fury. 'Why not add hitting old women to your list of despicable actions – that's on top of insulting children and knocking up young girls! You can wear your knobbly knees out praying as much as you like, but it's not going to take away from the fact that you are a nasty, vindictive little hypocrite.'

Horace opened his mouth but before he could say anything, a tall figure wearing naval uniform came running towards him, his cap under his arm.

'Oy! That's enough!' Marianne breathed a sigh of relief as her older brother Rodney came and stood beside his mother, arms folded across his chest. 'I think you'd better leave, Mr Smith,' he said icily.

Horace spluttered briefly, then turned and started to stomp away.

Nellie stabbed him again, harder this time. 'And by the way, you're not welcome in the café again!' she screamed.

At these words, Davey looked around, tears cascading down his cheeks.

'Not you, Davey, love,' Nellie said in a softer tone. 'So long as your father's nowhere near, you'll always be welcome. Now get off with you and I'll have a special bun waiting for you when you come by next time, all right?'

With a sniff, Davey nodded tearfully as he was dragged away.

'If I hear you've been within ten feet of that place, then you'll get the hiding of your life, boy!' Horace's words drifted back to them, and Marianne's heart contracted with pity for the poor little boy.

Nellie sat down on her chair with a huff. 'Bloody bastard bugger!'

Marianne watched as Horace stormed up Cannon Street, shoulder-bumping into a tall, rotund figure with a large grey moustache and a bushy head of grey hair coming the other way. The man stared after the Smiths for a moment before turning back and jogging over to them.

'What was all that about? Old Horace the Horrible giving you trouble again?'

'Nice of you to make it, Jasper!' Nellie said scathingly.

Jasper ignored her and instead went over to Donny. 'Hey, Don. Happy birthday, mate!'

Donny took one look at the huge man and threw his arms around him.

'Jasper, Davey told us that his dad said he couldn't play with me cause I don't have a dad,' Donny said. 'But I do, somewhere, don't I?' He looked over at Marianne.

Marianne hesitated and her mother gave her a meaningful look. Donny had started to become far more inquisitive about his father lately and she didn't know what to say.

'Donny, love. You did have a dad. It's just he . . . well, he died before we could get married, I've told you that before.' This was the story that Nellie had insisted upon. Though few believed it – before Donny was born, Marianne had never been seen with a boy. So she'd stopped saying it, hoping people would forget, but Horace Smith would never let anyone forget. For some reason he seemed to hate her family with a passion, and she was sure it went deeper than just her own mistakes. Maybe it had something to do with this Hester Erskine.

'You've nothing to be ashamed of, love. Here, why don't you go in and get a sausage roll and forget all about him.' Nellie's tone was jovial as she tried to distract her grandson. But it didn't work.

'Are you sure, Mum? Are you sure he's dead? If you tell me who his mum is, I can go and check to see.'

Marianne shook her head and looked over at her mother, her eyes pleading.

'Don, love, they've left town and we don't know where they are.' Nellie helped her out.

Donny thought about this for a while, then said in a hopeful tone, 'What if you found a man that wasn't dead and married him, do you think Davey could play with me then?'

Marianne sighed. She was used to the insults, but she hated that Donny had to suffer too.

'It's not quite that simple.'

'Anyway, Don,' Jasper interjected. 'What would you prefer? Three uncles who are a million times better than one dad, or someone like Mr Smith? If you think about it, you're a very lucky boy.'

Donny's shoulders slumped and he kicked the pavement. 'I suppose,' he huffed.

'Hey, Don,' Rodney said. 'Wanna play some more?' Rodney tossed the football over to Donny, who didn't even try to catch it.

Jasper came to his rescue. Bending down to pick up the ball, he bounced it on the boy's head. 'Come on,

Don! You and me against Uncle Rod and Freddie. What do you say? Do you think we can do some damage?'

Donny grinned reluctantly and, grabbing the ball, he dribbled it across the square before kicking it through the makeshift goal he and Freddie had made with their jumpers.

'Goal!' he shouted.

'That's the spirit,' Jasper laughed as he swooped over to the boy and raised his hand above his head. 'Show us all who's champ, eh?'

Freddie rushed over then and kicked the ball to Rodney. 'Shoot, Uncle Rodney!' he screamed.

Marianne let out a relieved sigh. Beside her Lily shook her head. 'You know, Marianne, one day you'll just have to tell everyone the truth.' She looked over at her sister. 'And don't give me that innocent look. We're not stupid. You're hiding something, and Mum seems to be the only one who can't see it.' She turned and started to pack away the stepladder.

Marianne stared at her sister aghast. Was that true? Maybe she should just confess. Now she was older, she realised it wasn't such a terrible crime not to know the full name of the man who'd seduced her, but at the time she'd been in shock and certain that if she confessed she had slept with a man she barely knew, she would forever be seen as a trollop. But it was too late now. If her mother ever found out she'd lied, she really would hate her.

She walked back into the café, her mind in turmoil as she thought back to the terrible, interminable days after Donny was born. Days when she'd lain in bed staring helplessly at the snuffling little creature who lay in a drawer beside her bed, praying that she would wake from this nightmare soon.

Aside from showing her how to change and feed the baby, her mother had left her alone and instructed her brothers and sisters to stay away. Even so, they'd snuck in every so often to see the baby, but she'd always refused to talk to them. She wasn't sure she'd ever be able to look any of them in the eye again.

Finally, after two days, her mother had flung open the bedroom door. 'Right, I've been patient long enough, young lady. It's time you told me who is responsible for this. And when I find out, I'm going to give him the hiding of his life, and then you'll marry him! No grandchild of mine will be brought up a bastard!'

Marianne had looked at her mother with dull eyes. How could she tell her she'd barely known him? Her mother would think she was even more of a hussy than she did already. But unless she told her something, Nellie would never stop pestering her. So, taking a deep breath, she'd started to talk. Her tears of grief and humiliation were genuine, even if the story she told wasn't.

She'd never forget her mother's reaction. Rather than berating her further, Nellie had put her arms around her and pushed Marianne's head against her ample chest. 'Oh, love. Oh, my poor girl. Why didn't you tell me?'

'I just wanted to forget,' Marianne wailed.

'And you swear, Marianne, that he is the father? That he forced himself on you? I'd never have thought it of him. He always seemed such a nice lad. I even went to his funeral!'

'I wouldn't lie about that!' Marianne kept her head down, her cheeks burning with shame.

'That little weasel. If he wasn't already dead, I'd kill him myself,' Nellie exclaimed, her face red with anger as she thumped her clenched fist on the chest of drawers beside the bed.

'So, you . . . you're not going to send me away?' Marianne's lips quivered and she felt sick with guilt.

'Send you away? Oh, love, as if I'd let a daughter of mine starve on the street, let alone my grandson.' Nellie took hold of Marianne's shoulders and stared intently into her eyes. 'Fate has dealt with that boy, and it'll be over my dead body that that family has anything to do with my grandson. Now, I never want you to speak of him or what he did to you again. Not even to Rodney, and definitely not the children. It would upset them too much. If they ask, say the father died and the family moved away. But Marianne' – Nellie sighed deeply – 'it's not fair and it's not right, but life is not going to be easy for you and this little boy.' She glanced at the baby who was fast asleep in a drawer on the floor by the bed. 'I'll do my best to protect you but you need to be strong, love.'

The baby started to stir, making small snuffling sounds. Nellie picked him up and cradled him gently, staring down at his little face. 'None of this is his fault and he's going to need his mum to protect him, just as I will try to protect you.' She looked up at Marianne. 'Do you understand what I'm saying, love?'

Marianne nodded, though she didn't, really. All she knew was that her life had changed irrevocably and any dreams she'd had for her future – a husband, a home of her own – were gone. Who would want her now?

'Life is unkind. *People* are unkind. Especially to unmarried girls with babies. Be prepared for that and keep your mind on the baby.' She had handed the tiny bundle to her. 'Don't you think it's time you gave my grandson a name?'

Marianne had stared at the little red face of her son and thought of her own father, dead for nearly two years now, his mind and body destroyed by the war.

'Donald,' she'd said decisively. 'For Dad. But let's call him Donny. He looks like a Donny, don't you think?'

At that moment, Donny had opened his blue eyes and stared at her, and for the first time since she'd had him, Marianne felt a flicker of love for the little creature in her arms.

'Oh, love. Your dad would have liked that.'

Marianne glanced up at her mother and noticed the tears in her eyes. Nellie so rarely showed emotion. With her quick temper and strong opinions, she ruled the café and her children with a rod of iron, but Marianne saw now, finally, that beneath her bluster, she truly loved them. She swallowed back her guilt at the lie she'd told. She'd had to do it. And if Nellie never told anyone, then surely no harm could come of it.

∽

Coming back into the present, Marianne realised she'd wandered into the kitchen. As Nellie had insisted, they had never spoken about Donny's father again, and there had been times over the years when she'd managed to forget that she'd lied. But recently, as Donny's questions became more insistent, she realised that she had no choice but to stick to the story she and her mother had agreed upon. If she didn't, Nellie would never forgive her.

Chapter 2

Edie stood on the edge of the cliff, the grey majestic castle walls rising up behind her, and gazed out to sea. She liked to call this *their* place as it was where she always met Robert. The note he'd delivered to the garage yesterday had said to meet him at two, but it was three o'clock now and he still wasn't here.

She sighed heavily as she looked out over the sparkling blue water of the Channel. It was a beautiful clear day and the coast of France was visible in the distance. It was funny how close it was, and yet it seemed as far away as the moon. Although she'd lived all her life in Dover, she'd never been to France, despite the fact Jimmy had worked on the ferries before he joined up.

Staring over to the Western Docks, she watched idly as a car was winched on to a waiting ferry. When she was younger, after her father had died, she'd sit for hours on Western Heights and watch the comings and goings in the docks below. She thought back over the years. It had been twelve since he'd died and ten since she'd stood in the doorway of the bedroom she shared with her sisters, staring in bewilderment as Marianne cradled a tiny, squawking bundle, crying as if her heart would break. It had been a terrifying moment. Marianne was the one she relied on whenever she needed sanctuary, either from her mother or from the teasing of her more rambunctious siblings, and to see her like that had shaken them all.

The five of them had stood there, speechless, until Rodney, his face pale, had put a protective arm around them all and ushered them downstairs to the living room where they'd sat in silence, listening to Nellie's shouts, Marianne's sobs and the baby's screams. Lily had started to cry as well then, and Rodney had sat her on his knee and told her everything would be all right, and that she had a brand-new baby brother.

'B-b-but *Mum's* not had a baby.'

'Well, you can think of him as your new baby brother. Cos that's what he'll be. And the five of us' – he'd looked around at them all – 'we need to help Marianne because people might not be kind. So, let's all promise now that we will never let anything bad happen to that little baby, or to Marianne.'

'But Rod . . .' Jimmy, at thirteen, was more aware of the bomb that had just been dropped into the centre of their family. 'Won't she get in trouble cos she's not married? That's what happened to Colin's auntie. She got sent away and he's never seen her again.' Jimmy's voice began to rise as he thought about the possibility of his beloved oldest sister being sent away from home.

'No one will send her away,' Rodney had said firmly. 'And if Mum tries, then we have to stop her, don't we? Now, hands out, everyone, this is a solemn oath I want you to make. Repeat after me: "I, Rodney Castle ..."' They had dutifully repeated his name and he'd sighed. 'No, say your own names. "I, Rodney Castle, do solemnly swear that we will never allow harm to come to Marianne or her baby. And if Mum tries to send her away, then we will take action."'

Edie smiled to herself. Funny how she was remembering that now. But then Donny's birthday always brought back memories. And also served as a reminder of the unbreakable bond her family shared. Rodney could be stuffy, but she would never ever forget his words that day.

Her head tilted back as yet another squadron of Spitfires flew over, and she stared up into the sky until the vapour trails started to dissipate, blown away on the soft breeze. A shiver ran through her. With her brothers already in uniform, she realised it would only be a matter of time before Robert joined up too.

Which brought her back to her earlier thoughts. Where was he? Had he changed his mind about her? Especially now she'd been to bed with him. Didn't her mother always say that you should 'never give a man what he wants until he puts a ring on your finger'? Edie shook her head. Maybe her mother was right. Maybe that was all Robert had been after and now she'd given it to him he'd lost interest. After all, she'd always wondered what a man like him saw in a girl like her.

Staring down at the large tankers and warships beneath her, she fought back tears and straightened her shoulders. Well, whatever would be would be. She could deal with this; she'd dealt with far worse, after all.

∞

Hidden by the pillars of the covered market, a man sat smoking a cigarette, idly watching the lively game of football that was taking place in the square between two small boys and a couple of men. It had been a bad day, what with his father cutting off his allowance and threatening to write him out of his will, and his wife's demands becoming ever more insistent now she was pregnant. Still, it wasn't all bad. As soon as the baby was born, he knew he'd be able to change his dad's mind about his will *and* his allowance – especially if it was the longed-for grandson. It bloody better be a boy, he thought darkly. Not only would it secure his money but he'd be able to get one over on his smug brother, who so far had only managed to produce a couple of daughters.

He looked at his watch. Just an hour more to kill before he was due at a private party at one of the naval officer's digs. Hopefully he'd be able to recoup some of the losses he'd had at the tables recently, and once he'd done that, who knew what other entertainment he might find?

There was a holler of delight from the square drawing the man's attention back to the scene in front of him. The group had been joined by two khaki-clad soldiers who had thrown off their caps and jackets and were energetically chasing after the boys. That reminded him. Ever since the government had passed the Military Training Act a few months before, he'd been meaning to sort out a medical certificate to keep him out of the line of fire. No way was he going to allow himself to end up as cannon fodder like those poor saps.

His gaze wandered over the square again and settled on the café that was housed in a tall white building on the corner opposite. A memory stirred as he tried to remember when he'd last been there. His thoughts were interrupted as a football thumped against his leg and he looked down.

'Sorry, mister.' The dark-haired boy, his hair sticking up around his head, ran over and picked up the ball, grinning up at him as he straightened. The man took in the grey eyes and wide mouth, and a strange feeling of familiarity came over him. It was unsettling and he shook his head slightly, confused.

He was about to answer when a voice shouted across the square. 'Donny!'

The boy looked around.

'Party time!'

'Coming, Mum!' The boy grinned at him. 'Gotta go.'

The man stood up and looked around the pillar that blocked his view of the door. A small woman with chestnut hair pulled back in a bun was standing with her hands on her hips. He assessed her idly, noting the ample curves beneath the bodice of her pink dress. Then his breath caught in his throat as the woman turned her face away. Good God! He straightened, his eyes flicking between the boy and his mother.

He watched curiously as one of the soldiers ran over to the woman, scooping her up and twirling her around while she shrieked in protest. Just then, a girl came down Castle Street and rounded the corner. Her long dark hair was loose around her shoulders and she was wearing a blue and white dress. His eyes sharpened.

The boy kicked the ball at her, hitting her squarely in the chest. With a shout she ran over and grabbed him in a stranglehold.

The woman in the pink dress was standing alone outside the door now. 'Don't encourage him, Edie!'

'Your son needs to learn some respect for his aunt!' she called, laughing as she walked over, dragging the boy with her.

Well, well, well. He grinned to himself. This was all very interesting. Very interesting indeed. And as for the boy . . . Well, what did it matter, anyway? But he could have some fun with this.

Taking one last long, considering look at the café, the man threw down his cigarette and sauntered towards the seafront, grinning.

Chapter 3

Marianne had just finished laying out the crockery on the tables when she heard a loud cheer outside.

Glancing up she saw two tall, dark-haired figures in khaki running into the square. She grinned. At last! Her brothers were here.

She ran to the door and flung it open, causing the bell to tinkle wildly.

'Donny!'

Her son looked over to her. He seemed to be speaking to someone on the steps of the covered market. She squinted, trying to see who it was, and just for a moment a tall man with wheat-gold hair stepped out from behind a pillar. Her eyes narrowed momentarily, wondering who Donny could be talking to, but then he disappeared from view again and she dismissed him.

'Party time!'

At the sound of her voice, Bert and Jimmy jogged over to her and, laughing, her youngest brother picked her up and swung her around before setting her on her feet again.

Marianne gazed up into his face affectionately. 'Dear God, Bert, you must be beating them off with a stick – what with the uniform and all.'

Bert's bright blue eyes sparkled as he grinned at her, carving deep dimples into his cheeks. 'I don't do too bad.' One lock of dark hair had fallen over his forehead and Marianne smoothed it back. He was far too handsome for his own good.

Pulling away from him, she turned and reached up to put her arms around Jimmy's neck. 'And how are you, Jimmy Castle? Everything all right?' She stared intently into his eyes.

'Course it is.' He smiled reassuringly before setting her gently aside and striding through the door.

Marianne stayed where she was, waiting for Donny as the others followed her brothers in. Donny was looking over to the side of the café and, smiling wickedly, he drop-kicked the ball just as Edie bounded around the corner and grabbed him in a stranglehold.

'Don't encourage him, Edie!'

Edie's reply was drowned out by Nellie's loud voice behind her.

'Where the hell have you two been? We were expecting you ages ago!'

'Sorry, Mum.' Jimmy sounded guilty. 'You know what the buses can be like.'

Nellie sniffed the air suspiciously. 'Hmm. Started stopping at every pub between Canterbury and Dover, have they? Get on with you and sit down.' Nellie shooed them to the table.

Edie walked towards her and Marianne saw that though her mouth was smiling as she nudged Donny with her shoulder, her eyes were red-rimmed. She put her hand out to touch her arm. 'You all right, love?'

Edie evaded her gaze. 'Why wouldn't I be?' she said dismissively as she brushed past.

Marianne stared after her. She knew her sister, and clearly something had upset her. Well, Edie would tell her in her own good time, she thought as she walked through to the kitchen and took Donny's cake from the pantry. Just a few finishing touches and it would be ready.

'Oy, Marianne, where are the girls?' Nellie called through to her.

Marianne stuck her head through the hatch. 'Any minute now. I told them six.'

As if on cue, Reenie clumped through the door.' Afternoon all. 'Scuse the scruffy clothes. Been at the allotment. Bloody slugs have been decimating the lettuces.'

Behind her sauntered Marge, looking tall and elegant in her new Wrens uniform, her red hair rolled up under her hat and a cigarette between her fingers.

'Where's the birthday boy, then?' she rasped in her throaty voice.

Donny ran up and gave her a kiss on the cheek, but his eyes were fixed on the door.

'Don't worry, she's bringing up the rear.' Marge smiled without rancour.

Daisy came in then, looking flushed and beautiful.

'Auntie Daisy!' Daisy was the favourite of his adopted aunts. She looked like a tiny fairy with her long, shiny, white-blonde hair, forget-me-not blue eyes and rose-petal complexion, and Donny worshipped her. 'I'm nearly as tall as you now!'

'A little way to go yet, but give it a year. Mind you, most people are taller than me.'

'How's Stan getting on, Dais?' Bert asked.

Daisy's husband had joined up not long after Bert and Jimmy. 'Not too bad, I think. Hopefully he'll get leave once his training's finished.'

Daisy and Stan were rather unkindly known as Beauty and the Beast. Daisy could have had any boy she chose, but it was always Stan for her, with his bright red hair, gappy smile and kind, freckled face.

Nellie clapped her hands. 'Right everyone, sit down! Marianne is about to unveil *the cake*!' She gestured at the table, now laid out with plates of sandwiches, sausage rolls, a fruit loaf and biscuits.

While Marianne put the candles on the cake, the rest of the group sat around the table singing 'Why are we waiting?' accompanied by a drumming of feet.

Laughing, Marianne poked her head out through the hatch behind the counter.

'If you lot don't shut up, I'm going to give the cake to the gulls,' she yelled over the racket.

'Mum, if the gulls eat chocolate cake will their poo turn brown?' Donny called back before bursting into peals of uncontrollable laughter.

Rolling her eyes, Marianne withdrew her head and carefully lit the candles, then she picked up the tray, holding it high in front of her, and marched out singing 'Happy Birthday'. Donny was standing at the head of the table, hopping from foot to foot, his face aglow with excitement.

'Let's see, let's see!' Marianne's cakes were always a work of art.

She placed the tray on the table and there was a gasp. It was a large chocolate cake on top of which Marianne had created a beach using blue and yellow icing, and right in the middle of the cake, two small figures were playing leap-frog. The one representing blonde-haired Freddie was bent over at the waist, a grin on his face, while a tiny marzipan replica of Donny, one hand on his friend's back, flew over the top of him, legs akimbo, his dark hair standing up on end.

Donny ran over to his mother and flung his arms around her neck. 'It's us, Mum! It's me and Fred! You're the best and cleverest mother in the entire world.'

Marianne hugged him back tightly. 'And you are the best and most perfect boy in the entire world. Now blow out the candles and make a wish. But don't tell anyone what it is or else it won't come true.'

'But I want to tell you, cos you need to know.' Donny stood up on tiptoe and whispered in her ear, 'I'm going to wish for a dad so next year Davey can come to the party.'

Marianne drew in a breath. Donny was nothing if not persistent. To cover her unease, she gave him another hug, whispering, 'You do that, Don. But now you've told me, you know it won't come true, don't you?'

Donny's eyes turned serious and Marianne hated herself for manipulating him.

'We'll see,' Donny said, using his mother's favourite phrase, before turning away to blow out his candles.

An hour later, the party was still in full swing and Nellie sat back with a sigh of contentment. The evening sun was streaming through the window, casting a halo of light over the table. Donny and Fred, their faces smeared with chocolate and mouths too full to talk, were eating their second slices of cake. Rodney was bickering with Marge – nothing new there. She wondered if Marge had told him yet that now her training was over, she was being posted to the castle. She smiled to herself; she wasn't sure he'd welcome the news. Reenie and Daisy

were having a heart to heart while Daisy absentmindedly handed a napkin to Donny so he could wipe his
face. It was a shame she didn't have a child of her own
yet. Still, there was plenty of time, but who'd want to
bring a child into the world right now, as it teetered on
the brink of war?

Her four youngest children were ribbing Jasper mercilessly about his moustache, which was covered with
crumbs. She smiled at that, noting how Jasper had no
blonde left in his hair now. When had they both got so
old? she wondered. She'd known him for longer than she
cared to remember. He'd been Donald's best man at their
wedding, and had been a fixture at the café even before
Donald had died. In fact, if it hadn't been for Jasper, she
wasn't sure how she would have coped when the children
were young. Jasper's wife had died of influenza shortly
after the war and he'd taken to coming to the café for all
his meals, unable to bear the quiet of his own house. But,
Nellie reflected, though she'd never say it to him, he'd
helped her just as much – if not more – than she had him.

As if sensing she was watching him, Jasper put his
hand over Nellie's and gave it a squeeze. 'All right,
old girl?' he murmered quietly, a twinkle in his warm
brown eyes.

'Less of the old, if you don't mind,' she replied tartly,
but her words were softened with a smile.

He nodded at Marianne, who was sitting on Nellie's
other side watching Donny, a faraway look in her eyes.

'She's done a grand job, don't you think? Today must always be a strange day for her.'

He was right, Nellie reflected. Against the odds, somehow her daughter had managed to rise above the insults and hold her head high.

She put her hand on Marianne's arm and leant towards her. 'These last ten years haven't been easy for you, Marianne, but look at him.' She glanced over at Donny. 'He's been worth the price. I know I don't say it often, but I'm proud of you and how you've handled yourself.'

Marianne smiled at her mother, tears in her eyes. 'Thanks, Mum. You know I couldn't have managed without you.'

Nellie patted her arm. 'Course you would have. Now, where's the sherry? I'm parched. Want one, Jasper?'

Jasper shook his head. 'Not for me, love. I've got ARP training later.'

Nellie rolled her eyes. 'Training, my foot. Bunch of old men playing soldiers, more like.'

'You won't be saying that when I'm dragging you out of a burning building.'

Nellie wrinkled her nose at him. 'I can drag myself out, thank you very much. I don't need a grizzled old man to do it for me.'

Jasper sat back in his chair, clutching his chest. 'You wound me, Nell. You really do.'

Lily stood and walked over to Jasper, putting her arms around his huge shoulders from behind and dropping a kiss on his bushy head. 'Never mind, Jasper. She loves you really.'

Jasper looked up at the girl affectionately. 'Thanks, love. But at this rate, she'll only realise it when I'm six feet under.' He grinned and nudged Nellie's shoulder. 'Still, better late than never, eh?'

Nellie snorted, but her eyes were smiling.

Chapter 4

The following day, Edie yawned as she walked up Castle Hill, the trees providing a green canopy above her and the smell of grass cuttings mixed with the briny scent of the sea filling the air. The party hadn't gone on late, but she hadn't been able to sleep. It had been hard, pretending she was happy all evening, and once in bed, her thoughts had been consumed with Robert. Something must have happened, surely? Or maybe her first thought was right and now that she'd slept with him he'd decided he could do better than her. She cringed as she thought of it now. She shouldn't have allowed herself to be seduced, she thought, but how could she resist when he'd seemed to want her so desperately?

She wiped a bead of sweat from her forehead. It wasn't yet seven thirty, but even so the sun had been up for a couple of hours and the air was warm. She had always loved this walk and the way the tree-covered hill wound around and around, until suddenly, there was the castle, its grey turrets rising magnificently from the top of the steep bank, glaring out to sea on one side, as if daring anybody to get too close, and gazing benignly down on Dover on the other.

It was her frequent walks up to the castle when she was younger that had led her to Pearson's. When she'd first seen it, she'd been enchanted. Even though it was a garage, Mr Pearson had tried to make it look pretty by hanging baskets of flowers outside the door of the whitewashed office building and tubs of them had stood all around the perimeter of the concrete forecourt. The sight of the flowers and the cars had drawn her over, and she'd watched in fascination as Mr Pearson and his mechanic worked on an engine.

In the months following her father's death, Mr Pearson had taken the grieving girl under his wing, always happy to show her the workings of an engine, or ask her to help him. By the time she left school, she'd become an accomplished mechanic and he'd been more than happy to take her on as his apprentice, despite the raised eyebrows of many of the customers.

As the road plateaued, the garage came into sight and Edie could see Mr Pearson through the open doors of the workshop, bent over the bonnet of a large truck. Next to it was a sleek black Humber with a man's blue-clad legs sticking out from beneath its chassis.

Her eyes eagerly searched the forecourt and her heart leapt. There it was: Robert's beautiful motorcycle. He'd come back! Eyes shining and a smile on her lips, she floated into the office, where she stashed her lunch and changed into her overalls before walking into the workshop.

'I see Mr Stafford's motorbike's back,' she said cheerfully. 'That thing is cursed. I promise you it was fine when he took it back last time.'

Mr Pearson withdrew his head from under the truck's bonnet and gave her a disapproving look. 'There's nothing wrong with it now, but I found it here this morning with a note addressed to you.'

He reached into the pocket of his blue overalls and pulled out a crumpled envelope.

'Probably just instructions about what's wrong with it,' she stammered awkwardly, well aware that her face was flaming.

The man underneath the chassis of the car wheeled out on his trolley and looked up at Edie curiously.

'Bill, you remember Edie, don't you?'

Bill stood up, wiped his hand down his overalls and held it out to her. 'The little girl with pigtails who used to loiter around the garage. Nice to see you again.'

Edie blushed. She remembered him very well. Bill was Mr Pearson's nephew and he used to tease her for being a tomboy. At the time she'd been embarrassed and had started to stay away when she knew he'd be there. Well, she wasn't that little girl anymore and if he tried to tease her now she was more than happy to give as good as she got. She gave him a challenging look. He looked like a younger version of Mr Pearson – tall, with light brown hair and brown eyes. Good-looking, she supposed, but nothing compared to Robert's golden beauty.

'Where's Bates?'

'Joined up. You're gonna have to step it up cos Bill's only here for a couple of days and then it'll be just the two of us.' Mr Pearson took a pipe from his top pocket and started to fill it with tobacco. 'Before you start, love, you couldn't make us all a cuppa, eh? Bill takes it with milk and two sugars. There's a good girl.'

Edie sighed, but bit her tongue. She could count on one hand the number of times he'd asked Bates to make the tea, and she was willing to bet that Bill would never be asked. But she didn't mind really; Mr Pearson had shown her kindness when she'd needed it most, and had thought nothing of teaching a girl everything he knew about engines. Plus she'd be able to read Robert's note in private.

In the small kitchen she turned on the electric kettle and got out the tin mugs, before tearing open the envelope. Her face broke into a wide grin as she scanned the single page.

My darling,

I am so sorry I let you down today. I'm afraid my poor father wasn't too well, so I needed to stay with him. I hope you didn't wait for me for too long. Surely you would have guessed that only the most urgent of problems would have kept me away from you. To make it up to you I've arranged somewhere we can be properly alone tonight. Please say you'll come. I just want to be able to hold you and kiss you without anyone interrupting.

Robert xx

At his last words, Edie blushed again.

'What's keeping you, girl? Me and Bill are parched.'

Edie jumped as Mr Pearson came into the kitchen, and quickly stuffed the letter into her pocket.

Her boss raised his eyebrows at her. 'What does that oily so-and-so have to say for himself?'

'Oh, nothing. Just instructions about the bike,' she said, grabbing the kettle's white Bakelite handle and pouring water into the teapot.

Mr Pearson grunted. 'Well, get a move on. We haven't got all day.'

For the rest of the morning she and Bill worked on the Humber, and she soon realised how much she still had to learn as Bill showed her how to fit a new engine. Luckily, he was a patient teacher who was happy to share his knowledge. She was concentrating so hard that she managed to forget about Robert's letter, until at midday, Bill threw down his tools and suggested they have lunch. After washing their hands, they took their sandwiches to a patch of grass beside the fore-court.

'So what are you doing now, Bill?' she asked him.

'I'm an erk.'

She looked at him, puzzled. 'You seem all right to me.'

He laughed. 'That means I'm a plane mechanic. I service the planes at Hawkinge airbase.'

She was impressed in spite of herself. 'Isn't that difficult?'

He shrugged. 'Once you know your way around an engine you can pretty much work on anything. But I've been training to be a pilot, and it won't be long until I get to fly them rather than service them.'

As he said this, a group of Hurricanes whined over-head on yet another practice run. It had been non-stop over the summer. Edie looked up at them. 'You must have been pretty busy recently.'

'Yes. And we'll be getting busier when war breaks out.'

'When?'

'Come on, you must know that it's going to happen sooner rather than later. And judging by the news it could only be a matter of weeks.'

She sighed. 'Mum says we haven't a hope in hell of winning with Chamberlain in charge. What do you think?'

'I have no idea. But I do know we're all going to have to do everything we can. And I reckon the RAF will be crucial.'

Edie lay back on her elbows and squinted at Bill. When he'd worked here with his uncle, she'd been too shy to speak to him much, but now she was surprised at how comfortable she felt in his presence.

'But it's so dangerous. Don't you think you'll be frightened?'

He shrugged. 'Maybe. But what choice do any of us have? Our parents had to go through this last time, now it's our turn.'

Edie looked away. She didn't want to think about the damage war could do. She'd grown up with it, and spent every day since her father died fighting to bury those memories.

'I'm not sure I'm ready,' she whispered, tearing at the grass.

'Of course you are. You have to be.'

She shook her head, unable to speak past the lump that had suddenly appeared in her throat.

'Hey.' Bill touched her arm. 'I'm sorry if I've upset you.'

'No, it's not you. It's just the thought of it. Of everything. Of my brothers, and my friends . . .' She stood up abruptly. 'Anyway, we should get back to work. I still have Mr Stafford's motorbike to see to.'

Bill stood too. 'Ahh. The mystery motorbike man. Uncle Sid seems to think he only brings it here so he can see you.'

Edie laughed, embarrassed. 'I doubt he'd be interested in a grease monkey like me!'

'Oh, I don't know. I think grease monkeys like you are very interesting.' He smiled at her, and Edie, cheeks burning, turned away, hurrying across the road to the forecourt.

∽

By five o'clock, Edie had lovingly polished the Silver Hawk until there wasn't a speck of dirt on it and it now stood on the forecourt, gleaming in the sunlight, and every time she looked at it her stomach churned with excitement as she thought of the evening to come.

'Pass us the large spanner, girl.' Mr Pearson's voice wafted out from beneath a van, shocking her into action. Hastily she handed the tool to his waiting hand, but in her distraction she missed, dropping it on to his wrist.

He yelped and wheeled himself out. 'Gawd's sake! What's got into you all of a sudden? You've been standing over that motorbike, mooning for most of the afternoon. You're no use to anyone in your current state. You may as well get on home.'

Ordinarily, Edie would have been mortified at his words, but she leapt at the chance to go and wash before she was due to meet Robert. 'I'm sorry. I'll be better tomorrow. I promise.'

Bill was in the office going over some paperwork when she entered. 'Off already?'

'Your uncle's had enough of me, so I'm just going to . . .' She indicated the tiny bathroom where there was a sink and a mirror, and hurried inside. She washed her hands carefully, scrubbing at her nails with a brush to try to get rid of the oil. Then she let her long, dark hair out of its plait and combed it with her fingers. She stared at herself critically. Her face was slightly pink from the sun and her thickly lashed green eyes stood out in contrast. Her hair hung in shiny waves halfway down her back, but it looked as if she'd let a ten-year-old loose on it with the crimping tongs. She'd have to plait it again, but then that made her look like a schoolgirl. She wished she'd brought some lipstick with her to try to make herself look a little more sophisticated.

Outside the door, she heard a couple of male voices and her stomach swooped. He was here! But what should she do? Should she go out and leave with him – which Robert would not like; he'd always insisted on discretion, saying he didn't want anyone to think badly of her – or should she wait until he'd gone, then go to the agreed meeting spot? She dithered for a moment, before deciding it was stupid to hide away. She'd just say a polite hello, then walk off to their usual spot.

Stepping into the office, her breath caught, as it did every time she saw Robert. Today his blond hair fell over his broad forehead and his open-necked blue shirt was tucked into baggy, high-waisted, tan-coloured trousers, with a leather jacket slung casually over one shoulder. He looked up as she entered, pushing his sunglasses on to the back of his head.

'Well, hello there, Miss Castle. Bill here tells me you've been polishing my bike for half the afternoon and I was just wondering how on earth I could show you my gratitude.'

Edie smiled. 'She's so lovely, I find it hard to stop.'

'Oh, I know exactly what you mean,' Robert said, one eyebrow raised in amusement.

Bill gave a cough and looked between the two of them with a dawning realisation.

Edie coloured. 'I mean . . . the Silver Hawk is a beautiful motorbike, and it's the only one I've ever seen, so . . .' She trailed off as she saw Robert's amused smile broaden into a grin, while Bill's lips had tightened.

'I have to be off now,' she said brightly. 'Bye, Bill. Good luck with the flying.' Head down, she hurried towards the front door, closely followed by Robert.

'Miss Castle, I'd be delighted to run you home on the bike, if you'd like?'

With a nervous glance back towards Bill, she opened her mouth to refuse, but noticing the look of disapproval on Bill's face, she felt a surge of anger. Why shouldn't she leave with him? She had nothing to hide, and what she did was none of Bill Pearson's business.

She gave Robert her sunniest smile. 'Thank you, Mr Stafford. I really do appreciate it.'

He gave her an encouraging wink and offered her his arm.

Chapter 5

It was Tuesday evening and Marianne stood at the large range, frying pork cubes for the pasties she would be making the following day. Her sisters stood at the scrubbed oak table that dominated the centre of the kitchen preparing the veg. They'd brought the radio down and were singing along to 'Pennies From Heaven' on Radio Luxembourg – a radio station Nellie heartily disapproved of, but they welcomed the relief of not having gloomy news bulletins talking about the threat of war and the dire situation in Europe.

Suddenly the back door burst open and Nellie stormed in and slumped into a chair. 'I have no confidence that this government has a clue how to win a war,' Nellie snarled to no one in particular.

'Council meeting not go well, then?' Marianne asked after a pause, when it was clear her mother was expecting an answer.

'It's as if they have no memory of the last one. Of all places in the country, they want to evacuate children here. To Dover! Have they forgotten about the bombs that fell in the town last time around? Do they think it'll be any different this time? Bunch of pompous fools!'

'Surely it won't come to that, though, Mum.' The thought of having to evacuate Donny filled Marianne with dread.

Nellie snorted in disgust. 'That lot in London couldn't organise a game of tiddly-winks, let alone win a war. And as for Chamberlain and his flimsy piece of paper . . .' She kicked the table with her sturdy black lace-up shoe. 'And listen to this – they've removed the stained-glass window from the hall and stashed it in a tunnel. I ask you! They think it's safe enough for kids, but God forbid the pretty window gets damaged.' She huffed loudly.

Marianne looked up in alarm. 'What? But why?'

'War, my girl. War's got no regard for art or beauty, nor people neither.'

'I'm sure you told them what you thought,' Edie remarked with a smirk.

'Too right. I said, "And where do you propose to put the little tykes?"' She chuckled as she remembered. '"Perhaps you could stick 'em in the tunnel with the glass, and then you can cut a nice window into the side so the kids can look through it while the town burns."'

Lily laughed. 'I've got to hand it to you, Mum, you know how to get your point across.'

'Someone's got to talk sense. And I'm not the only one who thinks that – the mayor agrees an' all. Sent that fool from the government packing with his tail between his legs. I reckon the only people we'll be seeing coming into Dover are soldiers, while everyone else leaves. Well, with soldiers comes business, but I don't mind telling you I've got a bad feeling. What with air raid shelters, gas masks, bloody tunnels being dug . . .' She sighed heavily. 'Things'll never be the same around here.'

Marianne turned from the stove, spatula waving in the air. 'Come on, Mum, don't talk like that. Surely things won't be as bad as that.' But in her heart she didn't believe what she was saying. She'd watched the increased activity and preparation with a growing dread. Would they even be able to keep the café open?

'But if things are gonna be that bad, maybe we should think about leaving too. For Donny's sake,' Edie suggested.

'Leave? Why would we do that?' Nellie squawked.

'Because if what you say is true, we'll be in the firing line. Is it really worth risking our lives to stay?'

Nellie's eyes sparked with fury. 'The problem with you, Edith Castle, is that you have no gumption! Leave Dover? Close the café, after I've worked my fingers to the bone to keep the place going all these years? While your dad was away fighting in the last war, and I was surrounded by babies, I still carried on. Then when he came back, neither use nor ornament, did I give up? With six children and your dad upstairs smoking himself to death

57

and rocking backwards and forwards ... Did I sell up and move somewhere else? No, I did not! I could have, mind you. But here I stayed. And here I intend to stay. There have been Castles in the market square for three generations, and unless we all get blown to smithereens, there will be Castles here for three generations more, or my name's not Nellie Castle.'

With that she yanked up her bag and stomped up the stairs, grumbling under her breath. 'Leave the café indeed. No bloody backbone, that's the younger generation's problem. How we're going to win this war with a bunch of cowards and numbskulls is beyond me!'

Marianne looked at her sister, whose cheeks had flushed. 'Ignore her, love. She doesn't mean anything by it.'

'I was only asking the question! Why did she have to go off in a tizzy like that!' A tear started to trickle down Edie's face and she dashed it away. 'I am *not* upset. I don't even know why I'm crying, I'm just so angry! I swear, soon as I get the chance, I'm moving out.'

Marianne put an arm around her shoulders. 'Edie, it's all right. Just sit down for a moment, I'll make you a cup of tea.'

Edie gave a short bark of laughter. 'Always with the tea and sympathy, aren't you? Perfect Marianne with her perfect cakes and her perfect boy! I mean, even when you had a baby after sleeping with God knows who, she still stuck up for you. Bet if it had been me, I'd have been out on my ear.'

Marianne gasped. Is that really how her sister thought of her?

'Edie!' Lily turned sharply and waved the potato peeler at her. 'You can be an evil cow sometimes, you know that? You're up and down like a yo-yo at the moment. Yesterday you were all sunshine and smiles, and today you're being a complete bitch! Has this got something to do with that mystery man that we *know* you've been seeing?'

Edie flushed with mortification. 'For your information, Lil, not all of us are man-mad like you. But I'm sorry, Marianne.' Edie planted a swift kiss on her sister's cheek. 'I didn't mean that. I've just had a really bad day.'

'Did something happen at work?' Marianne patted her hand to show she'd forgiven her.

'Bloody Roger,' Edie grumbled. 'The police car's exhaust was broken and when Mr P. told him I'd fix it, Roger said he'd rather take the police's business elsewhere. His words were, "I'm not sure I should entrust a service vehicle to a young female."' Edie's impression of the pompous policeman was so accurate that the others couldn't help but laugh.

But even so Marianne shuddered at the thought of Roger. He'd spent the last ten years asking her to marry him – to save her from scandal, he said. His proviso was that she had to leave Donny with Nellie. When she was at her lowest ebb, when Donny was a baby, she'd almost considered it. But Nellie had put her straight. 'I'd rather have a bastard running around the place than have him as a son-in-law, so don't even think about it. As if he's good enough for you, even if you are used goods.'

She gave a rueful smile at the memory. That was her mother for you. She gave with one hand and took away with the other.

Lily threw her knife on to the table with a clatter, startling Marianne from her thoughts. 'That little—! Did he really say that? Next time I see him I'm going to give him a piece of my mind! I hope Mr P. told him where to get off! The cheek of him! You know Mr P. told Mum that you're the best apprentice he's ever had.'

'Did he? What, even better than Bill?'

'Who's Bill?'

'Mr P.'s nephew.'

'Is he the mystery man you disappeared off to see the other day? You came back from your *walk* miserable as sin, then yesterday you come in late with starry eyes,' Lily said archly.

'There is no mystery man!' But Edie's red cheeks belied her words. 'And why is it that all I have to do is *mention* a man and you think I'm having an affair?'

'All right, all right. Keep your hair on. But there *is* a man, isn't there?'

Edie sniffed and turned back to the vegetables. 'That is none of your business, Lily Castle.'

'Suit yourself. But I reckon you're lucky, Edie. You're doing the job you love – like you are, Marianne – so that only leaves me to get top grades in my matric next year and start my nursing training and all will be well in the Castle household.'

'Apart from the threat of war, you mean,' Marianne said sardonically. 'And a crotchety mother, two brothers in the army and another living in a tunnel at the castle.'

'Oh yes, apart from that.' Lily grinned and winked at her.

Chapter 6

'Oh my poor feet!' Gladys exclaimed for the umpteenth time as she collected a plate of bacon and eggs from the hatch the following morning. It was seven thirty and breakfast was in full swing with every table full. The air in the café was steamy and the smell of frying bacon mixed with cigarette smoke wafted around the room.

'Glad, if I hear about your bloody bunions one more time, I swear I'll chop them off for you meself.' Nellie was threading her way between the tables carrying a tray of dirty plates. Today she was sporting her most colourful apron – bright orange with yellow and green swirls – and her hair was still in curlers and covered with a purple and red scarf.

'Better be careful wearing that outfit if war breaks out, Mrs C.,' Sam Corner from the hardware store in the market remarked, puffing on a cigarette, not caring that the ash fell onto his plate.

'Eh? What you talking about?' Nellie dumped the plates on the hatch and turned back to look at him, hands on hips. After the drama of the council meeting the night before, Nellie's mood was still dark.

'Was just thinkin', in that get-up the Luftwaffe would be able to spot you from Germany, blackout or not.' A rumble of laughter spread around the room, and Sam stood up to take a bow.

Nellie looked at him in silence, her expression contemplative.

The other customers went quiet, their eyes fixed on Nellie expectantly, waiting for the inevitable explosion. In the kitchen, Marianne, noticing the lull, went to the hatch, whispering over to Lily, who was at the sink in the scullery washing up.

'Uh oh, Sam. You're for it now.' Jasper was sitting at his usual table near the kitchen door, demolishing a bacon buttie before starting work at his forge.

'You can keep your thoughts to yourself, Jasper Cane.' Nellie shut him up with a scowl, then turned her gaze back to Sam. 'You jealous, are you, Sam? Need a bit of colour in your life? Well, never let it be said that I'm not a generous woman.' She squeezed her way between the tables, causing the people she passed to lean back and grab their cups of tea before Nellie's generous hips knocked them over. Reaching her target, Nellie whipped off her apron and quick as a flash dropped it over Sam's head. A roar of laughter went around the room as Nellie grabbed his arm, pulled him off his seat and, spinning him around, tied the apron behind him. Then, picking up his plate, cup and saucer, she shoved them into his hands. 'There now, don't you look a picture. Into the kitchen with you.' She pushed him towards the back. 'If I'm going to give you my favourite pinny, you need to be sure to put it to good use. Marianne, we've got a volunteer to help with the washing up,' she called out.

'Leave it out, Nell . . .' Sam finally found his voice.

Nellie held up her hand. 'You come into my café, you insult my clothes and make me a laughing-stock, and you think I'll just let it pass? You should know me better than that by now.' She looked him up and down, and a smile started to spread across her face. 'By God, that colour looks good on you! Now chop chop. Those dishes won't wash themselves.' She shoved him into the kitchen, then looked around at the tables full of laughing people.

'What are you lot looking at? Got plenty more pinnies for any who'd like to help Sam out.'

A soldier sitting at the table in front of her stood up and, wiping his eyes, came over and shook Nellie's hand. 'Biggest laugh we've had in ages, missus. They told us this was the place to come in Dover for the best food, but it's better than the Hippodrome in here for entertainment too.'

'We aim to please, gentlemen. Just spread the word. Monday to Saturday, seven till five, there'll always be a warm welcome for our servicemen at Castle's. Right'

– she clapped her hands – 'show's over, everyone, so you can stop gawking and get back to your breakfasts. The sooner you finish, the sooner you can leave.'

Marianne and Lily ducked back into the kitchen, chuckling. Sam was in the process of taking off the apron.

'What do you think you're doing?' Lily chided.

'I've got to open the shop.'

'Better get on with it then.' She picked up a stack of plates from the hatch and carried them into the scullery, dumping them in the sink. 'There's plenty more where these came from.' As she spun around, her eyes fell on an envelope that had clearly been pushed under the back door. Curious, she bent down to pick it up. 'Here, Marianne, I think this is for you. It says, "To the Lady Who Bakes the Cakes".'

Marianne was breaking eggs into a frying pan and looked up in surprise. Nobody ever wrote to her. Why would they? Everyone she knew lived within a few miles' radius. She handed the spatula to Lily and snatching the envelope she tore it open. Inside was a folded sheet of notepaper. She opened it and frowned, trying to make sense of the words.

Lovely to see you again. We need to talk. It's been too long. xx

'Who's it from?'

'I don't know.' Marianne felt her stomach tighten with anxiety. With no name and no address, the

65

note felt almost like a threat. But why would anyone threaten her?

'Ooh. A secret admirer.' Lily took the paper from her hand and scanned it. 'You must know who it's from.'

'I really don't.' Marianne racked her brains but she couldn't think of anyone who would write. Her world was small, her social group even smaller, so why would anyone slip a note under the door when all they had to do was pop in to speak to her?

She thought about the people she'd baked cakes for recently, but she knew them all personally and couldn't think of a single reason why they'd write such a cryptic note to her. She thought back over the last few days and an image popped into her mind. A shadowy figure talking to Donny by the covered market. She hadn't seen him properly, but just for a moment, she'd thought she recognised him. She shivered again, feeling unsettled, but not at all sure why.

∽

Later, when the café had quietened and poor Sam had been released from the scullery, Marianne showed Nellie the note. 'I don't understand what this means, Mum. Who could have sent it?'

Nellie looked at it. 'Probably just someone having a joke with you. Or maybe someone wants to order another cake. Just throw it away.'

'I think it's a secret admirer. They ate one of your cakes and instantly fell in love with you.' Lily put the last of the breakfast dishes away and took off her apron, joining her mother at the table.

Marianne wrinkled her brow. 'Hardly.' She thought for a moment. 'There was a man in the square the other day talking to Donny . . . Did either of you see him?'

'I see a lot of men hanging around the square. Can you be a bit more specific?' Nellie said sceptically.

'I didn't really see him. He was behind one of the pillars on the steps of the market.'

Nellie shrugged.

'Hey, maybe he wants to recruit you to be a spy. Like in *The Thirty Nine Steps*.' Lily laughed at her own joke.

Marianne ignored her. 'You're right, I'm probably just imagining it, but I thought I knew him from somewhere.'

Nellie tossed the paper into the bin. 'You worry too much. Now, you couldn't make us a quick cuppa, could you? You want one, Glad?' Nellie called through to the café where Gladys was sweeping the floor.

'Ooh, I could murder one. Any chance to get off me feet is welcome.'

Nellie rolled her eyes at Marianne. 'Don't even think of mentioning the B word,' she called over her shoulder.

There was an indignant squawk from Gladys and Marianne laughed and went to fill the kettle for the hundredth time that day, dismissing the note from her mind. Her mother was probably right, she thought. It was just someone having a joke with her. After all, she wasn't exactly a catch.

⁓

The sound of a motorbike brought Edie's head up from underneath the bonnet of the Ford Model Y she was working on and her heart skipped a beat as she saw the Silver Hawk pull on to the forecourt. It had only been a couple of days since she'd seen Robert, and here he was again. She smiled to herself, all her worries about her wanton behaviour putting him off dissipating.

Robert sauntered towards her, looking impossibly handsome and glamorous, his hair gleaming in the sun, his eyes hidden behind sunglasses.

'Hello, there, Mr Pearson, Miss Castle. I know I was only in the other day, but the old bike has developed a rattle. Think I've been pushing her too hard.' He chuckled and gave Edie a knowing smile as he held the keys out to her. 'I'll be back at six,' he said with a meaningful look. 'Do you think she'll be ready?'

'Oh, y-yes,' Edie stammered, flustered. 'I'll have her ready for you by then.'

'That's the spirit!' He grinned. 'Best be off.' Raising his hand he walked away down Castle Hill towards the town, leaving Edie staring after him, her stomach fluttering with anticipation.

⁓

On the dot of six, Robert came to pick up his bike. While Mr Pearson took him into the office to get his invoice, Edie waited impatiently by the bike. Finally he came out of the office.

'Usual place, half an hour?' he said with a smirk.

'I'll be there,' she murmured, conscious of Mr Pearson watching her.

'Good girl. I'm taking you somewhere special tonight.' And with a wink, he swung his leg over the bike, started the engine and drove off without a backward glance.

Edie rushed to the bathroom to get ready. 'Somewhere special,' he'd said. Maybe today was the day that he'd finally say the words she was so desperate to hear? Brushing out her hair, she stared at herself in the mirror for a moment, then shrugged, and swinging her canvas bag with her overalls inside onto her shoulder, she strode out of the little bathroom. Mr Pearson gave her a disapproving look as she came out but said nothing.

As soon she saw Robert standing in their usual spot, she hurried towards him and threw her arms around his neck.

'I didn't expect to see you so soon,' she said, hoping he'd hear the hint of a question in her voice.

'And what, after our last meeting, would make you think that?' he asked softly, looping his hands around her waist and pulling her closer. 'I found it hard enough staying away for just those few days. And to prove how much I've missed you, I've spent all day preparing a special supper at my house.'

Her heart melted. He'd gone to the trouble of making food and was taking her to his home? Usually they found a secluded spot in the countryside, or occasionally he'd taken her to a small hotel.

He grabbed her hand and urged her towards the bike. 'Come on, you know what an impatient man I am!'

Giggling, she followed him and soon they were speeding through the countryside, Edie clinging tightly to Robert's waist while the green verges, dotted with wildflowers, and the fields of yellow corn raced past.

Finally, they came to a pretty little village and Robert stopped outside a tall white townhouse with wide stone steps leading up to a blue front door flanked by windows on each side. It was one of only eight houses set around a garden square, two on each side.

They hopped off the bike and Edie looked up at the house in admiration. 'This is your house?'

He unlocked the door and ushered her into the hallway, where she dropped her canvas bag by the stairs leading to the first floor. Another flight of stairs led down.

'Well, Miss Castle, what's it to be? Downstairs to the kitchen for food? Or' – he raised his eyes to the ceiling above him – 'upstairs for an altogether different type of refreshment?' He tugged her towards him, making no secret of his preferred choice.

Edie put her arms around his neck and pulled his face down, kissing him on the lips. She felt his mouth curve against hers as he deepened the kiss.

He pulled back and looked deep into her eyes, his expression intense. 'So a different type of refreshment?'

'Most definitely.' She smiled shyly up at him.

'I always knew you were a clever woman, Miss Castle.' Robert took her hand and led her swiftly up the stairs to his bedroom, where a brass-framed double bed covered with a thick, blue eiderdown stood against a whitewashed wall. Then he turned and kissed her again, pushing her gently on to the bed and unbuttoning her blouse.

∞

Later, Edie lay back on the pillows, a dreamy smile on her face. Beside her Robert was stroking her hair.

'Are you all right?'

She turned to him. 'Mmm. Perfect,' she murmured, opening her eyes and gazing sleepily at him.

Robert kissed her on the nose. 'You are a very special woman, Edie. I hope you know that.'

'And you, Robert, are a very special man. I wonder . . .' She hesitated, still a little uncertain of how he felt. 'Would you like to meet my family?'

He grinned. 'There is nothing I'd like more, darling.'

'Really? My mother can be a bit fierce, but I reckon she'd love you.'

'And do you have any brothers and sisters?' he asked, his hand stroking her neck.

Delighted at his interest, Edie told him about her brothers and sisters and nephew. 'Although my brothers aren't around. They've all joined up.' She paused for a moment. 'If war comes, will you be joining up too?' she asked fearfully.

'Of course. We all have to do our duty. And I'd hate to be considered a coward.'

'I can't imagine you're a coward, Robert. I've never met anyone like you.'

Just then the sound of the front door closing made her jump and she looked at Robert in alarm. 'What was that?'

Robert's face had paled and he motioned her to be quiet.

'Do you think you should go and check?' she whispered.

He nodded. 'Probably just my daily. Maybe she left something when she was here earlier. Get dressed while I go down to check. I know you don't want anyone to see you.'

He gave her a deep kiss then threw back the covers.

Robert returned five minutes later with a grin. 'Coast's clear. I think I should take you home.'

Within half an hour, they were racing down Castle Hill towards the market square, narrowly missing a man on a bicycle as they crossed over Laureston Place and pulled in by the side of the café.

Robert stopped the bike and turned to Edie. 'Better let you off here. Much as I want to tell all the world about you, today's not the day. I need to go and see my dad, check he's all right.'

Edie smiled. One of the things she loved about him was how devoted he was to his father. She nodded and got off the bike, looking around furtively to check there was no one she knew in sight before giving him a quick kiss on the cheek.

'Will I see you next week?' she asked tentatively.

He ruffled her hair and grinned, almost as if she was a child rather than a woman who he'd just been to bed with, she thought. 'Wild horses wouldn't keep me away. Maybe I'll surprise you and come to the café? I really would love to meet your family.'

'Really?' She hadn't thought he'd meant it when he'd said it earlier.

'Absolutely! I can't wait, in fact.' With a last wave, Robert turned the bike around and sped off up the hill.

Marianne frowned as she looked at the cake she had just finished decorating for Daisy's parents-in-law's anniversary. It wasn't quite as elaborate in terms of decoration as she'd have liked, but she'd run out of time and Daisy was collecting it for Mavis and Derek tomorrow. Still, it did look pretty. It was a rich fruit cake with three tiers, much like a wedding cake, which she'd been feeding for weeks with little tots of brandy. As it was their pearl anniversary, she'd iced it in white and wound strings of little edible pearls, painstakingly crafted from sugar, around the entire cake. On the top, she'd created a large oak tree out of marzipan to represent their pub – the Royal Oak.

'Marianne! Dinner's ready.' Lily's yell down the stairs startled her and she glanced at the clock. It was gone seven! Where was Don? A vague memory came to her of Donny telling her he was going across the road to Freddie's grandparents. She'd been so absorbed in her task, she'd barely heard him.

She was just walking across the square when the loud roar of a motorcycle made her glance around. She paused and watched as Edie climbed off and leant over to kiss the man sitting with his hands on the handlebars. So there *was* a man. She squinted, wishing he would take off his helmet so she could get a good look at him. Hesitating for a moment, she wondered whether she should go over, but knew Edie would have a fit if she did. Her mind was made up for her when an exuberant voice called to her across the square.

'Mum! Mrs Perkins says I can stay the night. Can I?' Donny ran across the cobbles, Freddie close on his heels, forcing her to turn her attention away from the intriguing scene.

'You know he's welcome to stop over, love.' Phyllis Perkins, Freddie's grandmother, came up behind

74

Donny. 'Wilf's out fishing all night, and one more's no bother.'

Marianne smiled at her warmly. Phyllis had been such a support ten years before when Donny had been born. While so many had shunned her, Phyllis had come to visit with her baby grandson, declaring that the babies may as well get to know each other seeing as they were the same age. Freddie's mother – Reenie's sister, June – had not been happy about it, but Phyllis had done it regardless. Ever since, the boys had been inseparable and, after June died of cancer and Wilf had moved back in with his parents, they had spent most of their time running between each other's houses.

'Thanks, Phyllis. Maybe tomorrow, though? This one looks like he needs a good wash.'

Donny hopped up and down at this. 'Oh, can I, Mrs Perkins? Can I stay tomorrow?'

Phyllis suddenly looked uncomfortable. 'Well ... Maybe not tomorrow, but perhaps the next night?'

'But why not, Gran? Davey'll be here and it'll be more fun with three!' Freddie protested.

Phyllis's cheeks reddened and she looked at Marianne guiltily. 'Sorry, love. I promised to look after Davey for Katherine and ...' She trailed off and stared down at the floor.

Marianne swallowed and forced a smile. 'I understand, Phyllis. Really. It's not your fault.'

Donny was staring between the two women, his eyes wide. 'But why can't I stay too? I won't be naughty.'

Phyllis put an arm around his shoulder and hugged him to her. 'Oh, Donny, I know you won't. But, well, it'll just be a bit crowded tomorrow night. I promise you can come the next night. How's that?'

Donny stared at her, tears shimmering in his eyes as understanding dawned, then without another word he ran across the square. Throwing an apologetic look at Phyllis, Marianne followed after him, her fists clenched in fury at Horace Smith ruining her son's day once again. She'd like to wring his scrawny neck!

She noticed idly that the man on the motorbike was no longer there. Time enough for questions once she'd calmed Donny down. As she reached the door to the stairs, she winced as she heard Donny's bedroom door slam above her.

Ignoring the astonished looks from her sisters and mother, who were sitting at the table in the living room with plates of cold meat, bread and cheese in front of them, she knocked on the door of the little cubby hole that Jasper had built for Donny when he was a baby.

'Don? Can I come in?'

She could hear his muffled sobbing.

'Go away!'

Marianne opened the door and went to sit on the bed beside his prostrate form. 'Donny, love,' she whispered, stroking his back.

He shrugged her hand off angrily. 'I said go away!' Turning over he gave her a fierce look. 'It's all your fault. If I had a dad, then I could stay at Freddie's house and Davey's dad wouldn't call me a . . . a . . . 'bomination. I hate you!' His face was red with fury.

Marianne grabbed his shoulders and pulled him up. Donny tried to resist, but in the end he collapsed against her shoulder, burying his hot little face in her neck as she rubbed his back soothingly and kissed his head, rubbing her cheek against his damp hair.

'What the devil is going on?'

Marianne looked up to see her mother standing in the doorway, flanked by Lily and Edie.

Shaking her head, she mouthed, 'I'll tell you later.' Then she buried her face back into her son's hair.

'Why don't I have a dad, Mum? Everyone else has one.'

'Well, I don't have one either, my love.'

'Yes you do. Your dad is Grandpa Donald. I don't even know who mine is. But if I did, then maybe I could be friends with Davey and . . . and some of the others wouldn't make fun of me.'

'Do they make fun of you?'

He nodded against her neck and Marianne closed her eyes.

'Did you tell the teacher?'

He shook his head again. 'I'm not a snitch. Anyway, me and Fred and Davey made them sorry.'

Marianne sighed. 'When was this?'

He shook his head again.

Gently she pushed him away from her shoulder and looked him in the eye. 'Donny, just because you don't have a father living here, it does *not* make you a bad boy.'

'No. They say it's *you* who's bad. And you are! Go away! I don't want to talk to you!'

'Donny . . .'

'I said GO AWAY!' Angrily he wiped his runny nose on his sleeve.

'But Don—'

'LEAVE ME ALONE!' He pushed away from her and flung himself face down on the blue candlewick bedspread.

Nellie was still standing at the door, staring at her grandson sympathetically. 'Leave him for now, Marianne. Let him calm down. Then, Donny, my lad, you and your gran are going to have a chat about how you speak to your mother, all right?'

Donny sat up angrily and was about to shout at his grandmother, but seeing the stern expression on her face, he closed his mouth.

'I should think so too,' she harrumphed. 'You might get away with that sort of talk with your mother, but your gran won't stand for it. Now,' she said in a softer tone, 'you take a bit of time to think, Donny, and when you come out, I'll have your tea waiting for you. All right?'

'I'm not hungry.'

'Course you are. You're always hungry. And if you promise to say sorry to your mum, maybe I can find you a little treat. How does that sound?'

Donny paused for a moment, thinking about the offer. 'Can I have one of your chocolate bars?'

Marianne smiled. For as long as she could remember, Nellie had kept a supply of chocolate bars in a cupboard in her bedroom as rewards for good behaviour. They were doled out so infrequently that the chocolate had usually turned white by the time anyone got to eat one, but that didn't take away from the triumph of being awarded one. Poor Bert, she remembered, had never earned one in his life.

'We'll see.' Nellie looked at Marianne and nodded at the door, indicating that she should leave. Marianne kissed Donny's cheek, ignoring the fact that he flinched away from her, and rose to follow her mother.

Lily and Edie were sitting at the little table in the corner of the living room near the window that looked out on the square. Edie was hungrily stuffing bread and cheese into her mouth.

'What was all that about? Or shouldn't I ask?' Lily said.

Marianne shook her head wearily. 'Don't ask.'

'If he's getting bullied, then you need to talk to his teacher,' Edie said, waving a piece of bread at her sister.

Marianne stared at her angrily, noticing that Edie's cheeks looked unusually flushed and her eyes were sparkling. But even more mysteriously, her thick, dark hair, usually tied tightly back in a plait, was hanging in luxuriant waves down her back. Edie had always been pretty, but right now she looked beautiful; glowing. Obviously this had something to do with the man on the motorbike. She glanced at Lily, who shrugged. Clearly she'd noticed too.

Edie looked at Marianne challengingly. 'Well? Can't you at least tell him about his dad's family?'

Marianne shook her head. 'I can't.'

'But why? Why have you always been so secretive about it? Marianne, the poor boy is *suffering*, and he's right, it is your fault.'

'It's not that easy . . .'

'Of course it is! Open your mouth and tell us. Unless you don't know who it is?' Lily said slyly. 'Perhaps there's more than one man who could be the father?'

'How can you say that? Don't you understand what the last few years have been like for me?' Marianne's voice rose. 'I . . . I . . . Look, he's dead, so what's the point of even talking about him?'

'But . . . surely he had a family?' Edie persisted. 'Can't you at least allow the boy to know his other family?'

Marianne slumped down into one of the garish armchairs that sat either side of the small fireplace and put her hand to her head.

'Enough, you two,' Nellie said impatiently. 'It might come as a surprise to you, but life doesn't always go to plan. Now, what Marianne's said is good enough for me, so it should be good enough for you! Haven't you ever thought that there might be a very good reason why she doesn't want you to know?' She gave her two younger daughters a hard glare and they looked away in shame. 'Good. Now let that be the last I hear of this. Your sister has many faults, but one thing I can say for sure, she's never been a liar!'

Marianne kept her head bent, guilt washing over her. But then, even if she knew where he was, she didn't think she'd want the man to come back into her life. The more she'd thought about what had happened when she was sixteen, the more she'd realised how he had taken advantage of her youth and inexperience. Donny didn't need a man like that in his life.

Lily huffed. 'Oh, are you saying *we*' – she gestured towards Edie – 'are?'

'And are you saying you've never lied to me? Or you, Edie?'

They didn't reply.

'As I thought.' She leant over and switched on the wireless. 'Now be quiet, the news'll be on in a minute.'

After a tense pause, Lily turned her attention to Edie. 'All right then, seeing as we're talking about lies. Where have you been this evening, Edie?'

Edie blushed. 'If you must know, I was working late. It's busy at the garage at the moment.'

'Oh really? And you worked for so long that your hair just fell out of its plait, did it? And' – she reached over to run a finger over Edie's mouth – 'is that lipstick?'

Edie batted her hand away. 'Oh, leave me alone and mind your own business!'

Nellie sighed. 'Will you two stop bickering! Listen . . .'

The girls stopped talking as the newsreader began to read out Chamberlain's speech to parliament that day: 'The issue of peace or war is still undecided, and we still will hope, and still will work, for peace; but we will abate no jot of our resolution to hold fast to the line which we have laid down for ourselves.'

Nellie grunted. 'Is he just saying that to make us feel better? Peace, my foot. There'll be no peace here for a long while. And the worst of it is that poor Donny won't be the only one left without a father.' She got up and went into her room beside the stairs.

Marianne watched her go, her stomach in knots. It felt like the country was standing on the brink now, and it would take only one small push to topple them over the edge. Her mother was right: the issue of Donny's father might well get swallowed up with more pressing matters. She knew it was wrong, but she hoped so. She hadn't realised how difficult it would be to keep the lie going, and to know that her mother trusted her made it all so much worse. She wouldn't be without Donny for the world, but the pain and anguish his birth had caused her and her family was sometimes too much. How she longed to be married with a little house of her own and a husband who loved her. But that was never going to happen now. Instead, she had to deceive her son, just as she'd deceived her mother for all these years, and the thought left a bitter taste in her mouth.

Chapter 7

Any hope that war might be avoided evaporated completely over the next couple of weeks, and Nellie watched grim-faced as yet more stalls shut in the market.

''Ere, Nellie, did you hear the Clarks off the whelks stall are packing up?' Gladys said one morning as she placed bowls of porridge in front of a group of servicemen.

'What? But they've run that stall forever! What's wrong with everyone? How the hell can the town survive if everyone leaves?'

'The kids are all going soon an' all,' Gladys agreed sadly.

Donny, who was sitting having his breakfast in the kitchen, heard this last remark.

'Mum, you promise you won't send me away?' It was the hundredth time he'd checked. So many of his friends were due to leave for Wales in the next couple of days that he'd become convinced she'd sneak him onto a train as well.

'Not unless it becomes too dangerous to stay here. All right?'

He'd have to be satisfied with that for now.

But just a couple of days later, as the family sat listening to the news about the German invasion of Poland that had started the day before, Marianne wondered whether she might have to send Donny sooner rather than later after all when the newsreader announced that the prime minister would make a special announcement the following day.

Nellie sighed. 'And we all know what that will be, don't we?'

'Perhaps we'll get to see the boys again soon then,' Lily remarked. 'They'd not send them to war without letting them see their families first, surely?'

'Small consolation,' Nellie said. 'Especially if it's the last time we ever see them.' She shook her head. 'This is a time when we all need to stick together, instead of scurrying away like rats.' Suddenly she sat up straight, a determined look on her face. 'Tell you what, how do you feel about a bit of late-night baking, girls?'

'I don't mind,' Marianne said. 'What are you thinking?'

'I'm thinking we open the café for tea and cake so folk around here can listen to the announcement together.' Nellie turned to her grandson. 'Don, get Fred and go knock on a few doors and let people know to come here tomorrow morning. Just the market folk, mind. I've nothing against anyone else, but we need to be with our neighbours. They need to remember we're a community.'

∞

The third of September dawned bright and sunny. And after the efforts of the previous evening, an array of currant buns, fruit cake and a beautiful Victoria sponge, bursting with cream and Marianne's home-made strawberry jam, sat on the kitchen table.

Donny and Fred had done their job well, and as the clock struck ten, the café started to fill up.

'Help yourselves to tea, everyone,' Nellie called above the hubbub. 'Milk and sugar on the tray. Cake and buns for those who can stomach the thought of food. Oh, and leave a donation in the bowl by the urn. We're collecting for the war effort. Gawd knows we're going to need all the help we can get.'

Soon a fog of smoke was hanging in the air and Marianne glanced around the room. The Perkins were here, sitting with the Turners from the grocery store. Reenie sat beside Daisy, while Derek and Mavis, Daisy's parents-in-law, chatted to Ben and Sam Corner from the hardware stall. Marianne looked out of the front window, now criss-crossed with tape in case of bombing. Donny and his friends were playing football in the square, under strict instructions not to go out of sight of the café windows.

Jasper came blundering in then and Marianne sighed with relief. Nellie would need his comforting presence today. Her heart swelled with affection for him as she took in his large figure and the ARP badge displayed proudly on his front.

'Land's sake, Jasper. War hasn't been declared yet,' Nellie shouted as she went over to him.

'Market Square is my patch, so I intend to be ready for anything. And, of course, ready to save your pretty behind should you require it.' He patted her backside and chuckled, earning himself a slap on the arm.

'For that you can get your own tea, you cheeky bugger,' Nellie responded. But Marianne caught a little twinkle in her eye as she walked away from him and shook her head. Even today Jasper could make her mother smile.

The door opened again and Wilf rushed in apologising, his face bright red, and took the last remaining chair next to Reenie. Marianne glanced at the clock. Still thirteen minutes to go. Desperate to distract herself, she checked the urn, then went into the kitchen and busied herself putting more water on to boil and refilling the plates of buns that had been picked bare by their friends.

It was a quiet, grim-faced group that greeted her when she re-emerged. The only sound was the clink of the kettle on the side of the urn and the splash of water as she poured it in. Most of these people had known each other all their lives: they'd worked alongside each other, celebrated weddings and births, and mourned deaths. They knew almost everything about each other and when they got together there was usually a steady hum of chatter and laughter. But today they were quiet as they waited, smoking and drinking their tea, barely looking at the people sitting next to them, each lost in their own thoughts.

At last, a voice boomed from the radio: 'This is London. You will now hear a statement by the prime minister.'

Everyone sat up straighter, their eyes alert. Barely one minute later, a gasp went around the room. Marianne felt her stomach drop as the reality finally hit home: they were at war. No matter that it had been expected, hearing the words felt like a punch in the gut. Gladys put her hand over her eyes, while Phyllis Perkins collapsed forward onto the table, her head on her arms, sobbing softly. Marianne glanced over to her mother, who was standing by the kitchen door, her face paper white. Jasper was looking at her too, and he went over and put a comforting arm around her. For once Nellie didn't push him away, instead she turned her face into his chest, her shoulders shaking before she remembered herself and pulled away, standing tall, her chin jutting, her mouth a grim line.

It was a moment none of them would ever forget. One of fear, but also determination. They had done it before, they would do it again.

As Chamberlain finished speaking and the announcer started to read a list of instructions, everyone listened attentively.

Lily was the first to break the silence. 'They can't shut the cinemas!' she wailed. 'I was meant to be going tomorrow!'

'Lily Castle, if that's the worst that's going to happen to you because of this war, then you will be getting down on your knees and thanking God!' Nellie snapped at her, wiping her eyes surreptitiously.

'Shh, please,' Gladys protested. Then she nodded in satisfaction. 'Good. Churches will remain open. Prayers will be needed at this terrible time.' Gladys had a tendency to be what Nellie called a 'God-mutterer', but despite this, the two still managed to be good friends.

Nellie snorted. 'Fat lot of good that will do us!'

'Mum, please, we need to hear this,' Marianne tried to soothe her mother, while listening to the confusing instructions about the air raid sirens.

'Hand rattles for poison gas!' Nellie was not to be silenced. 'And who the hell will be waving the rattles? The grim reaper!'

The door burst open and the children rushed in, just as the radio announcer said, 'All day schools in evacuation and neutral areas are to be closed for at least a week.'

A loud whoop went up. They'd been due to go back to school the following day, so this was the best news they'd heard in ages.

Jasper took them in hand by giving a loud whistle. 'All right, all right, girls and boys, that's enough. Get out of here and let us finish listening to the broadcast. But stay in the square where we can see you. Go on. Git!' He stomped over to the door, holding it open as the children trooped out in silence. The minute they were outside, though, they erupted again, running around the square, hollering at the tops of their voices.

The National Anthem started to play as Jasper shut the door, and as one, everyone rose to their feet, their loud voices filling the room as they sang the words with more fervour than they had for many years.

As she sang, Marianne watched the children, care-free and happy; for them, life had taken a turn for the better as their summer holiday was extended. But for the rest of them . . . She looked around the room at all the dear faces she'd known her entire life and prayed that no harm would come to them.

As if someone was reading her thoughts, a terrible wailing split the air. Everyone froze, as the children in the square stood staring at each other in consternation. They had heard the siren before during the many drills over the previous month, but this was the first time it had gone off when they were actually at war. They turned as one and ran back into the café.

'Mum! The Germans are coming! The Germans are coming!' one of the little girls cried, running over to her mother. At the sound of her voice, the adults collected themselves.

'Everyone down to the basement!' Nellie called out. They had been clearing it out for weeks now so they could use it as a shelter, and there was ample space for everyone. Nellie had kitted it out with a couple of oil lamps, a table, and the old café chairs that had been down there for years were now back in service. There were also some games to keep Donny entertained. Marianne ran through the kitchen and opened the door at the back by the scullery, then everyone filed down.

∽

Later, after the all-clear had sounded and everyone had gone home, the sisters began to clean up the cellar in silence. Even Donny, who was busy collecting up the discarded playing cards and putting away the board games, was quiet.

Finally, he said, 'Mum, now that there's definitely going to be a war, do you still promise you won't send me away?'

Marianne sighed. 'How many times have I told you, love? I'll only do it if it's too dangerous to stay.'

'Not even then. If it's dangerous and you die, I'll be all alone.' His voice rose in pitch as he spoke. 'Especially as I don't have a dad.'

Marianne knelt in front of him and took him in her arms. 'Donny,' she said softly. 'None of us are going to die, and for now you are staying right here where I can keep an eye on you.'

'You promise, Mum? I swear I'll be good and won't get into any more trouble. I won't even ask about my dad anymore, just don't send me away.'

'Oh, Don, let's just see what happens. It might all be over before even one bomb drops, so try not to think about it, all right?'

Donny nodded and sniffed, wiping his nose on his mother's shoulder, leaving a damp trail.

Lily and Edie had been watching the exchange in silence, and they came over, putting their arms around the two of them.

'Hey, Don,' Lily whispered into his hair.

'What?'

'You've just left snot all over your mum's dress, so if you don't want to be sent away I'd go and get a cloth if I were you.'

Donny giggled and wiped a grimy hand across his mother's shoulder, leaving a smudge of dirt. Then, looking at his hand and wrinkling his nose, he wiped it on his shorts. 'There, all gone.' He kissed Marianne's cheek. 'I'm hungry, Mum. Can I have some more cake?'

Before his mother could answer, he turned and ran up the stairs laughing.

'No! You'll ruin your lunch,' Marianne shouted automatically. But she knew by the time she got back upstairs Donny would be covered in crumbs. She sighed and smiled ruefully at her sisters. 'Ah well, at least not everything's changed,' she said, and the three sisters burst out laughing, keeping hold of each other in a tight huddle, worried that if they let go, they might burst into tears.

Chapter 8

Up at the castle, Marge grabbed a quick sandwich and a cup of tea in the canteen, then made her way along the corridors, trailing her hand along the smooth white board that had been placed over the rough-hewn chalk walls of the tunnel. After nearly three weeks, she was finally coming to terms with living underground. When she'd first arrived, she'd found she had to make her way up to the surface at every opportunity, desperate for fresh air and a glimpse of the sky.

It wouldn't have been so bad if they didn't work such long hours; sometimes they didn't see daylight for days on end. She hadn't expected the work to be easy, but recently, as war drew ever closer, she and the other women in the communications room had been working twelve- to fourteen-hour shifts, sitting on uncomfortable wooden chairs, wearing headphones and with a black telephone and typewriter on the desk in front of them. Their job was to type out the messages being relayed to them before handing them to the supervisor, who would ensure they were distributed to the correct people. Although not difficult in itself, the sheer volume of calls and telegraphs meant there was rarely a quiet time, and any inaccuracy in the message could have serious consequences, so they needed to concentrate at all times.

Still, the other girls were fun, and though the food was bad, they still managed to get out once in a while and there had been plenty of opportunity for flirtation with some of the navy men, although her favourite game was teasing Rodney whenever she saw him. He had begun working with the admiral, and needed taking down a peg or two in her opinion. God knew what they did in there, but she imagined Rodney was well-suited to organising ship movements and making sure everything was in the right place at the right time.

But since the declaration of war, everything seemed more urgent. She had worked for fourteen hours yesterday, flopping into bed, exhausted, at six o'clock that morning. Now, just six hours later, she was on duty again, and not expecting to be back in bed until midnight at the earliest.

As Marge opened the door to the communications room, her supervisor, Carol Molloy, gave her a hard stare. 'You're late, Atkinson.' She looked pointedly at her watch.

She was a fierce-looking woman in her fifties and with her small, round glasses perched on the end of a large nose, and grey hair scraped back in a bun, she struck terror into all the girls. Marge had to admit she was fair and she could be kind, but tardiness and sloppiness were not tolerated.

'Sorry, Miss Molloy. I overslept because I worked until six.'

'I don't want excuses, Atkinson. We are on a war footing, and that means every minute counts. Hitler's not going to wait for everyone to be at their desks before he launches an attack. Now go and relieve Woods.' She dismissed her with a wave of her hand.

Marge went to the desk, pleased to see that she'd be working next to Jeanie today. Jeanie had joined on the same day as her, and they had quickly become friends. She was a petite brunette who, though she looked delicate, could swear like a trooper and had a filthy sense of humour. Marge had warmed to her immediately, and they were almost constantly together. They had been nicknamed 'Little and Large', which Marge thought a bit unfair – she wasn't *that* tall, but for some reason her closest friends always seemed to be the size of gnats, although describing Daisy as a gnat was probably a stretch as she was more like a fairy, whereas Jeanie was most definitely a naughty pixie.

'Where were you last night, Jeanie?' Marge whispered as soon as she sat down. 'I got back at six this morning and your bed was all neat and tidy, and you most definitely weren't working. Seeing Cyril again, were you?'

Jeanie had been meeting a lieutenant in the navy covertly, sneaking through the tunnels that led to the Eastern Docks whenever she could.

'It was our last chance,' she said. 'His minesweeper's been ordered on patrol around the Channel, and God knows when I'll see him again. It's our patriotic duty to keep the troops happy.'

Although Jeanie's tone was jaunty, she looked sad, and Marge reached over and patted her hand. 'He'll be back. Don't worry.'

'Yes, well, if he's not, at least he'll go down happy.' She gave a cheeky wink.

'God, don't say that.' Marge shuddered.

Jeanie became more serious. 'Life's uncertain, especially now. And I for one intend to make the most of any time we have left. And if I can spread a little happiness in the process, well, I can't see the harm.'

'Atkinson! Merchant! Stop chattering and get to work. This is your final warning.' Miss Molloy had fixed the pair of them with a gimlet eye.

Marge hastily put on her headphones and positioned her fingers over the keys of her typewriter.

∽

It was nearly six in the evening before Marge was able to take a break and her fingers ached from typing. In the cramped canteen she collected a plate of greasy-looking stew and dumplings and an apple for dessert, then looked around for a table. Over in the far corner, Marge spotted a familiar face. She grinned.

'Hello there, Rodders,' she said, plonking her tray on the table opposite him.

Rodney looked up and frowned. 'Oh, it's you.'

She raised her eyebrows at him. 'Any more enthusiasm and people will start to talk.' She examined him closely. He looked exhausted. He was still handsome, in a stiff, buttoned-up sort of way, with his dark hair and eyes, but his face looked pale and drawn, and there were shadows under his eyes.

'Look, I'm not in the mood today, Marge. I just want to eat my meal in peace and then go to bed.'

Marge held up her hands. 'I come in peace, Rodney. Promise. How are things your end?'

He sighed deeply, looking troubled. 'The truth? It's chaos. Trying to sort out where fourteen hundred ships should be when no one has a bloody clue how this is all going to play out isn't for the fainthearted.' He rubbed his eyes. 'We've been at it non-stop since yesterday. This is the first break I've had since breakfast.'

She smiled sympathetically, abandoning her plans to tease him. Taking a mouthful of stew, she pulled a face. 'Ugh. They need to get your mum up here to sort out the food. Better yet, Marianne.'

'That would certainly make life here a bit more bearable. I've been trying to get down to see them, but there hasn't been the time. When I'm not working I'm sleeping, and frankly, I'm so tired I'm not sure I could cope with my mother at the moment.'

'Good old Nellie. If it needs to be said, you can guarantee she'll say it. Come to that, she'll say it if it doesn't need to be said too.'

Rodney gave a short bark of laughter. 'A bit like someone else I could mention.' He gave her a pointed look.

'I'm not that bad.'

'Aren't you?'

'Well, only sometimes,' she conceded. 'Have you heard from the boys?'

'Yup, they're coming home any day. A quick leave and then I expect they'll be packed off to France. I'm going to try to get down to see them, but not sure when they'll be there. You want to come?'

Marge put her hand over her heart. 'Rodders! Are you asking me out?'

'Would you like me to?' he asked with a glimmer of a smile.

She bent her head over her plate so she didn't have to look at him. 'What do you think?'

There was a pause before Rodney pushed his chair back. 'I think you have more than enough men asking you out,' he said shortly. 'Anyway, the offer's there. Let me know.' Then he picked up his tray and walked off without a backward glance.

Marge stared after him and shook her head. That man really needs a woman to help him relax, she reflected.

Chapter 9

The week after war was declared saw the streets of Dover overrun with servicemen, with many of them billeted in the town as they waited to be transported to France. This meant the café became even busier than usual.

Every day Nellie expected to see her sons, and every day she was disappointed. Finally, though, one afternoon, just as lunch service had finished, the door burst open, and Nellie let out a cry of excitement.

'Marianne! Lily!'

Lily came out of the scullery, drying her hands on a tea towel, and looked at her sister enquiringly. Marianne shrugged and together they went to the kitchen door, where Lily squealed with delight. For there, looking tall and handsome in their khaki uniforms, were Jimmy, Bert and, of course, Jimmy's best friend, Colin. Jimmy and Colin had been inseparable since their school days so it had been no surprise that when Jimmy joined up, Colin had too.

Marianne hurried towards them. 'You're here! Why didn't you say it would be today?'

'Well, we didn't know, did we?' Jimmy planted a kiss on her head. Behind him, Nellie was fussing over Bert, while Lily had her arms around Colin's neck and was giving him a heartfelt kiss on the lips.

Marianne's eyes were drawn to two men standing just behind her brothers, both smiling and holding their caps.

Bert ushered them through the door. 'John, Alfie, this is my mum. The famous Nellie Castle herself. Hope you don't mind, Mum, but we brought a couple of friends with us. They don't have anywhere else to go and I thought they could do with some of your grub, Marianne. You wouldn't believe the pigswill they serve us.'

Nellie grinned at the two men. 'Course I don't mind. Everyone's welcome here. Go and sit yourselves down and we'll get you some food.'

Bert went over to Marianne and put his arm around her waist. 'And here is the woman herself. The best cook in the land. Marianne, this is John.' He gestured towards the shorter of the two men, who stepped forward and held out his hand. Marianne took it and smiled shyly. The man really was quite handsome with his dark hair and tanned complexion.

'At last,' he said, squeezing just a little too tightly. 'The mythical kitchen goddess.' He stared at her intently. 'And if your food is as delicious as your face then I can't wait to try it.'

102

Marianne blushed and looked away, straight into a pair of merry brown eyes. 'Leave it out, John,' the other man said good-naturedly. 'Any more cheese and you'll ruin the food for all of us. Alfie Lomax.' He bowed his head slightly, the sunlight streaming in through the windows glinting off the red highlights in his dark blond hair.

He was taller than his friend, and though not as good-looking, with a large mouth and a nose that was just a little too big, he had such a warm expression that Marianne felt herself smiling in return as she pulled her hand away from John and held it out to him.

'I'm very happy to meet you. And if you're hungry, would chicken and bacon pie, mash and veg do? And perhaps some apple pie and custard for afters?'

'Sounds like a feast fit for a king.' Alfie grinned and Marianne noticed how his front two teeth overlapped slightly, while his eyes crinkled at the corners. Her stomach swooped. Then, realising she was staring, she dropped her eyes. What was she doing, staring at a man like that? If she wasn't careful, she'd be giving him ideas, and that was the last thing she needed. She pulled her hand away and turned to Colin, reaching up to put her arms around his neck as she kissed him affectionately on the cheek.

'How are you, Colin? Everything all right at the barracks?'

He smiled at her reassuringly, showing deep dimples at the corners of his mouth. 'Of course it is. Stop worrying.'

'Good. Have you seen your mum yet?' Colin's parents ran the bakery on High Street.

'No, I'm just on my way now, so I won't stop to eat, just looked in to say a quick hello.' He put his hat back on, gave her a grin and a wink, and turned to push through the crowd at the door. 'See you later, everyone. Pint at the Oak this evening, Jim?'

'We'll be there.' Jimmy grinned and slapped him on the shoulder.

'Sit down, sit down, all of you.' Nellie clapped her hands and waved to a table, recently vacated by a bunch of very messy soldiers. 'Lily! For God's sake wipe that table.'

'Take it easy, Ma,' Bert admonished. 'It's only us.'

'It's not about you, Albert. It's about keeping our standards up. Go on, Lily, chop chop.'

'Mum, in case you've forgotten, I am your daughter and if you want to treat me like a servant, then I suggest you pay me a bit more.'

John laughed, then, catching Nellie's expression, quickly wiped the smile from his face. But his eyes followed Lily's slim back as she flounced away.

'I'd better get back to the kitchen too.' Marianne smiled briefly, her gaze drawn back to Alfie, who looked straight back at her. Flushing, she turned quickly, tripping over a chair in her haste to get away.

In the kitchen, Lily was protesting loudly to Gladys about Nellie's treatment of them. 'Just because she's our mother doesn't mean she can talk to us like that. I think it's time she learnt a lesson. What do you say we go on strike, Glad? Let's refuse to work for a day and see how she likes it.'

'Hey!' Marianne was alarmed. 'What would I do without you?'

'Oh, you'll manage, Marianne, you always do. Well, Glad?'

'Steady on, Lily. You can't walk out now. Anyway, you'll be back to school next week, so it won't be as bad.'

'It's all right for you. She's not your mother.'

'Lily, please don't walk out now. I've got too much to do as it is. And anyway, what about the boys?' Marianne said.

'What about them? I saw them last month, and they'll still be here later. Sorry, sis, enough is enough and I'm due an afternoon off. I wasn't going to go cos of how busy we are, but' – she pulled her apron over her head and threw it on to the chair – 'I reckon you can do without me for a couple of hours. And it'll teach *her* a lesson.' She winked at them both and sashayed out of the back door.

Marianne and Gladys stared at each other with open mouths.

'Oh bleeding heck! What are we gonna do now?'

Marianne sighed deeply and shrugged. Between the pair of them, her mother and sister were going to drive her to an early grave.

A deep voice behind her made her whirl around in surprise. 'Sorry.' It was Alfie.

Marianne blushed and stammered, 'Oh . . . can I . . . can I get you anything?'

'No, I was just coming in to see if I could help. And to apologise for me and John giving you more work. Especially as . . . er . . .' He nodded at the back door through which Lily had just disappeared.

Marianne looked at Gladys desperately, trying to communicate with her eyes that she wanted her to answer.

Gladys was staring at Alfie with interest, but finally catching Marianne's glance, she smiled at him. 'Get on with you. You're our guest. If anyone should be helping it's those two Castle boys.' She flapped her tea towel at him. 'Go and sit down, me and Marianne can manage just fine.'

While Alfie's attention was distracted, Marianne swiftly turned her back and bent down to open the door of the range to check on the apple pie.

'All right, you can get up now. He's gone.' Gladys's voice brought her head around.

'What do you mean?' she said, hoping the heat from the oven would disguise the fact that her cheeks were burning with embarrassment.

'I think you know very well, missy.' Gladys nodded over to the door with a sly grin. 'I think he's taken a bit of a shine to you. He could hardly take his eyes off you.'

Marianne snorted. 'Well, he'd better not get any ideas about me. You know as well as I do that's not going to happen.'

'About time you stopped thinking like that, girl, or it never will,' Gladys admonished.

Marianne was saved from answering by her mother appearing in the doorway. 'That table won't clean itself, you know. Where the devil is Lily?'

∽

After finishing their meal, the men had sauntered off to the pub, while Nellie, furious at Lily for walking out, was standing at the counter glowering.

There was a knock at the back door. 'Anyone in?'

A familiar blonde head poked through and Marianne's face broke into a grin. 'Daisy! What are you doing here? Shouldn't you be manning the stall?'

'Closed for the day. Soldiers don't seem very interested in my dresses and blouses. Nor do they seem to care for my skirts. And everyone else is so busy worrying about money they're not even buying second-hand at the moment. Especially as the dances have been cancelled, so I've been helping out at the pub.'

Marianne held the kettle up and raised her eyebrows.

Daisy rushed over and took the kettle from her. 'I'll do it. You look done in. Have you eaten?'

Marianne shook her head and dropped gratefully onto the kitchen chair. 'No time. Lily's walked out on strike.'

Daisy tutted, grabbed a plate and loaded it with a piece of pie and the last of the mashed potato and some peas. She sniffed at the plate appreciatively. 'Mmm. Now eat that while I make you some tea. Anyway, speaking of cancelled dances, I just saw your Bert and Jimmy with a couple of very nice-looking men who say they used to be in a band. Mavis asked them if she held a going-away bash for who-ever wanted to come, would they play at it, and they agreed. So, Saturday's the day. Thought I'd come and tell you. I'll make some posters so your mum can put one up in the café.'

Marianne smiled. Mavis was a force of nature who loved nothing better than a party. She was also a canny businesswoman and, as their pub was so large, she laid on the odd event to bring in some extra cash. Which was why the Royal Oak was one of the busiest pubs in Dover.

'But aren't large public gatherings banned?'

'Not banned, just advised against. And since when has Mavis ever taken orders from anyone? Anyway, we can't stop enjoying ourselves just cos there's a war on. What do you say?'

'Sounds like fun. I'll tell Lily to let everyone know. And I'll try to persuade Edie to go.'

'How's she getting on at Pearson's?' Daisy asked, taking a sip of tea.

'In her element. Never seen her so happy. And' – Marianne lowered her voice – 'she's got some mysterious man. I saw her kissing him the other day. He was on a motorbike.'

Daisy frowned briefly. 'Oh, that's who it is! I've seen a man on a motorbike loitering about a few times recently. I've been wondering who it was and why he was around.'

Marianne sat back, surprised. 'Really? You've seen him around here before? Strange.'

'Anyway' – Daisy dismissed the man from her mind – 'you'll be coming too, won't you?'

'I haven't been to a dance in years. Plus, I've got nothing to wear.' She never felt comfortable in a room full of men.

Daisy waved her hand. 'I'll sort you something from the stall. In fact, I know just the thing. Reckon I've got something for Edie and Lily too.' She finished her cup of tea and got up. 'Better get back. Promised Mavis I'd only be a few minutes. Bye, Mrs C.,' she said as Nellie walked through the door with a tray of dirty cups and saucers.

'Bye, love.' Nellie dumped the tray on the table, then went back into the café, staring around her in dissatisfaction. 'Wait till I get my hands on Lily,' she grumbled. 'I'll teach her a lesson she won't forget.' She sighed. 'What did Daisy want?'

Marianne explained about the dance.

'What, and you're going?' Nellie raised her eyebrows in surprise.

'I'd rather not, to be honest.'

Nellie nodded. 'Probably for the best, love. After last time.'

It was exactly what Marianne had been thinking. She had been to only one dance in her life, and it had been a disaster. A year after Donny was born, Daisy had just got engaged to Stan, and Reenie and Marge had decided that the four of them should go to one last dance together as single girls. Marianne had gone for Daisy's sake, but she'd spent most of the time feeling self-conscious, convinced everyone was whispering about her. She'd managed to keep herself to herself since Donny had been born, hiding in the kitchen, but at the dance she'd felt exposed. She'd been considering going home when a boy she'd been at school with had cornered her and said, quite casually, as if he was asking if she'd like a drink, 'How about you and me go outside and have a bit of fun?' He'd raised his eyebrows at her meaningfully.

She'd been so shocked she'd not known what to say. He'd taken her silence for assent and grabbed her hand in his sweaty one, leaning in further and whispering gruffly, 'There'll be no more accidents, I promise.'

Mortified, Marianne had whacked him on the side of the head, then pushed him in the chest. He'd stumbled back briefly, then come in close and sneered into her face, his breath stinking of beer, 'Don't act so shocked. Everyone knows you're a whore.' Then he'd spat at her feet and sauntered off.

Marianne had stood frozen in horror for a moment, then turned and fled. The four girls had spent the rest of the evening in the café drinking tea. It wasn't quite the celebration they'd anticipated, and Marianne had always felt guilty for ruining Daisy's night.

Since then, Marianne had resolved not to give anyone the chance to treat her like that again, and she'd stayed away from men. But even though she felt stronger and more confident now, her mother's comment confirmed that she should probably stay away. Anyway, the boys had invited John and Alfie to dinner tomorrow night, so that would be more than enough socialising for her.

Chapter 10

By seven o'clock the following evening, Marianne was feeling a little flustered. The shepherd's pie and spotted dick were in the oven and she had just enough time to wash and change before their guests arrived. Poking her head through the hatch, she shouted over to Donny, who was laying the table. 'Don, if you smell burning give me a shout. I'm just off to—'

The door opened behind him and John and Alfie walked in. Alfie was carrying a box of chocolates and a black leather case, while John held a bunch of flowers wrapped in newspaper.

Alfie sniffed appreciatively. 'Something smells good.' He grinned at her. 'Sorry if we're early, but we couldn't wait. From what the others have said about your shepherd's pie, seems we're in for a treat.'

Marianne blushed. 'I, um, was just . . .'

'Mum's going to get changed,' Donny piped up. 'What's in the case?'

'This is my trumpet. I thought as you've all been so kind to us, we could maybe provide you with a bit of entertainment.'

'Can I see?'

Alfie put the case on the table. 'Go ahead, I'm just going to give these to your mum, then I'll show you how to put it together and you can have a go.'

'Gosh, thanks, Mr Lomax.'

Marianne ducked back into the kitchen and hastily smoothed her hair, sniffing under her armpits and grimacing: after a long, hot day in the kitchen, she was in need of a wash.

Alfie followed Marianne into the kitchen and held out the box, looking straight into her eyes. 'These are for you.'

'Th-thank you,' she said. 'You really didn't have to.'

'From what the others have said, you're the one who's always giving out the treats, so I thought it would be nice for someone to give you a treat for a change.'

Marianne stared at the box in consternation. What did he want? Men didn't give something for nothing, she knew that for a fact. Had he decided to try his luck because he knew about her situation with Donny?

'They won't bite, you know.' He grinned at her.

She shook herself inwardly and reached out to take the box from him. 'Thank you. That's very kind,' she said primly, keeping her eyes averted. If he thought that she was the kind of girl who could be won over by a box of chocolates, then he could think again.

Her discomfort seemed to rub off on Alfie, and he shifted from foot to foot. 'You do like them, don't you?' he asked. 'I just thought . . .' He shrugged uncertainly.

Marianne softened and gave him a slight smile. 'Of course I do. I don't think anyone's given me chocolates before so I was surprised, that's all.'

Before she could say any more, a strange screech made Marianne jump, and Alfie laughed, turning to go back into the café. 'You're an impatient one, aren't you?' he called out to Donny. 'Here, let me show you.' Alfie glanced back at Marianne. 'If that's all right?'

'Yes, yes. I'll just . . .' She gestured awkwardly to the stairs and hastily turned before she could make more of a fool of herself. She was twenty-seven years old and she didn't have a clue how to speak to an attractive man. Shaking her head, she took the stairs two at a time.

'Your friends are here,' she yelled through the boys' bedroom door when she got up to the second floor. 'Go and entertain them, will you?'

Once in her own bedroom, Marianne noticed Lily was wearing her best blouse and skirt. 'You look nice.' She raised her eyebrows at her. 'If you want to see them, they're downstairs.'

'What, already? But I haven't done my hair!'

'It looks fine. You and Edie go down, I need to wash. I'm all sweaty.'

Edie looked at her, considering. 'Course you do. Like you do every evening before dinner. Seems these two men must be quite something.'

Lily giggled. 'They're not bad at all, if you must know. Even you might be interested – that is if you're not too tied up with your mystery man. But John's mine. You can have Alfie. Lucky for us Marianne has no interest in men, so there won't be any arguments. Come on.' She grabbed her sister's arm, while Edie looked over her shoulder at Marianne and rolled her eyes.

Suddenly Marianne felt foolish. Her sisters were beautiful and young and didn't have children. Whereas she . . . well, she wasn't old, but she certainly wasn't beautiful. And she had Donny. Proof of the lesson she'd learnt long ago, and could not afford to forget.

∽

The meal was a lively one and Marianne sat quietly watching as Alfie and John charmed her sisters and Nellie. Lily and John flirted outrageously, and Marianne watched Alfie out of the corner of her eye to see if he paid special attention to Edie. He didn't. In fact, he seemed to speak to Donny more than anyone else.

As soon as dinner was finished, Marianne rose and took the dirty dishes through to the scullery to get started on the washing up. As she washed she listened to John and Alfie entertaining everyone. John was singing while Alfie played the trumpet. She smiled to herself as she swayed slightly to the music. They were good. Maybe she should go and join them. She went to the hatch to take a look and her heart melted at the sight of Donny, who was watching Alfie avidly. Alfie had noticed too, and he gave the boy a wink, taking his hand off the trumpet momentarily to ruffle his hair. Marianne swallowed and went back to the scullery. The sight of Alfie and Donny had touched her more than she cared to admit.

A few minutes later, Lily and Edie joined her.

'Why did you disappear?' Lily said. 'You should see them, Marianne. They're brilliant.'

Marianne was about to answer when she heard Alfie's voice say, 'Hopefully see you tomorrow, girls. Bring your dancing shoes. And Marianne, thank you. That was possibly the most delicious meal I've ever eaten. Even the Ritz doesn't compare.'

Marianne kept her back turned, her hands deep in the soapy water.

'You've eaten at the Ritz?' Lily gasped.

'Well, strictly speaking it was in the staff kitchen.' He grinned. 'Sounds good, though, doesn't it? But I promise you the food wasn't a patch on yours, Marianne.'

Why was he trying to flatter her? Marianne thought with annoyance. It was only shepherd's pie and spotted dick. Lily nudged her in the side then, so she turned around reluctantly.

'I'm glad you enjoyed it,' she said stiffly. 'And thank you for your entertainment and being so patient with Donny's questions.'

Alfie grinned at her. 'That was my pleasure.'

Unsure what else to say, Marianne nodded slightly and turned back to the sink.

Lily filled the awkward silence. 'See you tomorrow then, Alfie. We can't wait.'

Marianne listened intently as his footsteps died away.

'Marianne!' Edie whispered dramatically. 'I think he likes you.'

'Don't be ridiculous.'

'Hmm.' Lily looked over at Edie and they smiled at each other knowingly.

'And don't give each other that look,' Marianne said, her back turned to them.

'What look?' Edie said innocently.

'You know what I mean. And I'd thank you to stay out of my business.'

'Whatever you want, sis,' Lily said breezily as she stacked a plate on to the shelf. 'You know us – we wouldn't dream of interfering.'

'You'd better not,' Marianne muttered, while Edie and Lily broke into peals of laughter.

∽

As Marianne cleaned the kitchen at the end of the following day, she tried to keep her mind off the evening to come. Reenie and Daisy had been over earlier and had nagged her mercilessly about coming to the dance, and in the end she'd given in. But she was dreading seeing Alfie again. The way he looked at her so intently unsettled her and she wished he'd just stop.

Lily stomped through to the scullery and dumped a pile of dirty plates into the sink where Edie was washing up. She was in a foul mood after a particularly tempestuous argument with her mother that morning, brought on by Nellie's harsh punishment for her act of rebellion during the week. She'd spent the day cleaning the entire house from top to bottom, as well as the privy outside, and once the washing up was done Nellie had demanded she scrub the floor in the café. 'And I mean *scrub*, mind. None of that mop business today. On your hands and knees, if you please.'

Marianne stifled a grin at the memory of Lily's response to *that* particular demand and glanced at her watch. Reenie and Marge – who had come down for the dance, along with her friend Jeanie – were meeting them here before they all walked over to the pub, although Marianne suspected it was more to make sure she didn't chicken out of going.

'Right, I'm going for my bath,' she announced to her sisters. 'Don't be too much longer, will you? The others will be here soon.'

'It's not fair,' Lily moaned. 'I need to wash my hair, but there's no way I've got time now. Who's going to want to dance with a girl who stinks of fags, fat and bleach?'

Edie rolled her eyes at Marianne, who merely smiled and ran up the stairs.

∞

Wearing the violet chiffon dress that Daisy had picked out for her, Marianne stood in front of the full-length mirror and examined herself, smoothing the dress down over her hips and swishing the skirt around her legs. She'd washed her hair the night before, and now it hung straight and shiny to halfway down her back, curling slightly at the ends and somehow looking more red against the violet colour. It was the first time she'd looked at herself like this for years. Since Donny's birth, she tended only to use the small mirror that hung on the wall above the chest of drawers to make sure her hair was tidy.

Her eyes ran down her reflection. The dress fastened at the front with a line of tiny buttons down to her waist, which was cinched in by a silver belt, and the full skirt fell in soft folds to mid-calf. She'd wear her sandals, she decided. They had a slight heel and were a lot more elegant than her everyday shoes. Was her waist really that small? She peered closer, surprised. Her eyes moved to the scooped neckline and she grimaced, pulling it up to try to hide her cleavage. She sighed. If only she was a little taller like her sisters, and wasn't quite so *round* in places, then she'd feel a lot more comfortable. She normally wore baggy jumpers and blouses that disguised her shape, so the dress made her feel exposed. She went to the chest of drawers and pulled out a crocheted shawl her mother had given her a few Christmases ago. If she tied it carefully, then her chest was nicely hidden. Satisfied, she sat on her bed and started to brush her hair.

∽

As Edie and Lily made their way upstairs from the kitchen, Lily looked back at her sister. 'So, is your mystery man going to be there tonight?' she asked slyly.

'For goodness' sake, will you stop going on about this mystery man? There *is* no mystery man.'

'I don't know why you keep lying.'

'I'm not lying and no, obviously there isn't a man coming with me tonight. Because I don't have a boyfriend.' Which was true, she thought sadly. Since the day he'd said he'd like to meet her family, Edie hadn't heard from Robert, and suddenly, once again, she was wondering where she stood with him. Why couldn't they be like other couples and go to dances and the cinema? Why did they always have to meet in private?

She was so lost in her thoughts that she bumped into Lily's back as her sister stopped abruptly in the doorway.

'Crikey! Just look at you!' Lily exclaimed. 'Leave your hair down, Marianne. I've got some clips and you could just fasten it behind your ears.'

'No way! It's too long. Maybe I'll get it cut.' Marianne ran her fingers through her hair, pulling the tangles loose.

Edie pushed Lily out of the way so she could get a look. 'I'll do it for you, but not tonight.' Edie was talented with the scissors and cut all their hair. 'Stand up, let's see you.' Thoughts of Robert faded slightly as she stared at her sister. She was beautiful. How was it she'd never noticed before? Suddenly she began to understand how much Marianne had lost when she'd had Donny. She'd been too young to understand much about it at the time, but Marianne had never had the chance to have fun and be frivolous. To dress up and go to dances. To feel special . . . It made Edie realise what she was risking with Robert. And unless he agreed to make a proper commitment to her, maybe she shouldn't see him again. The thought made her chest ache, so she pushed it to the back of her mind.

Bashfully, Marianne rose from the bed, holding the shawl over her chest.

Lily gave her a wolf whistle. 'I see you every single day of my life – how come I didn't know you had a figure like that? Please don't tell me you're going to wear that old shawl. It makes you look like a cross between

121

old Mother Hubbard and Rita Hayworth.' She reached over and tried to pull it off while Marianne gripped it tighter and slapped at Lily's hand.

Edie giggled at them. 'You do look beautiful, Marianne. But Lily's right. Take that horrid thing off.'

'But look!' She removed the offending garment.

They both stared at her in bemusement. 'What?'

Marianne gestured to her chest. 'I need to hide these. They make me look loose!'

Her sisters burst out laughing and Lily rushed over and put her arm around her. 'If there is one woman who *cannot* be called loose it's you. Edie, don't you think she looks entirely respectable?'

'You do. Respectable and a little bit alluring.'

'I don't want to look alluring. Alluring gets you in trouble.'

'Stuff and nonsense. Alluring means you can have fun!' Lily said, pushing Marianne back down on to the bed. 'Now, sit. I'm going to put a bit of rouge and lipstick on you while Edie has her bath.'

Downstairs, the small living room was crowded. Marge and Jeanie were keeping everyone entertained with their account of underground life at the castle, while Bert, Jimmy and Colin sat squashed on the sofa drinking beer and smoking. Reenie was sitting in the armchair opposite Nellie.

Bert let out a loud wolf whistle as his three sisters walked in. 'Wowee, Marianne. I'm going to have my work cut out for me tonight keeping the men away from you!'

Marianne blushed while Jimmy came over and gave her a kiss. 'You look stunning!' He looked over at his other sisters: Edie was wearing a slim-fitting red dress with white piping and big buttons down the front, complementing her dark hair and beautiful green eyes, while Lily, her blonde hair loose around her shoulders, was wearing a green form-fitting dress that showed off her figure. 'In fact, we're going to have a very busy night.' He gestured at Marge, Reenie and Jeanie. Marge was looking very glamorous in a white lacy blouse and a bright blue skirt patterned with small flowers, while even Reenie, who hated dressing up, had made the effort and put on her best skirt and jacket, although the look was ruined slightly as she was also wearing her clumpy lace-ups. As for Jeanie, she was wearing high-heeled sandals and a tight navy blue dress with a peplum skirt.

'You need to cover those up,' Nellie said disapprovingly, waving her hand vaguely at Marianne.

Marianne put her hand to her chest. 'The girls thought it was all right, but maybe I should wear that shawl.'

'Don't you dare!' Lily glared at her mother. 'Honestly, Mum, when was the last time you saw Marianne looking like this? Can you remember?'

'What I remember is that men – particularly those about to go to war – cannot be trusted to behave themselves when a girl puts herself on display like that. And we have the messy and noisy evidence to prove it!'

Marianne usually let these sort of remarks wash over her, but right now, they hit the mark and she turned abruptly, intending to get the shawl.

Marge stepped forward and grabbed Marianne's arm before she could leave. 'Why are we the ones who are always told not to give men the wrong idea when *they* are the ones who need to control themselves. It seems that just by *being* a woman you're giving men the wrong idea! And don't try to deny it, Mrs C. You know I'm right.'

'Doesn't matter what I think, though, does it? It's a fact of life and those' – she gestured again to Marianne's chest – 'will give men all sorts of wrong ideas. And added to the fact that she has Donny . . . Well, I'm sure you understand my meaning.'

'Leave it out, Mum. When I see a beautiful woman, I don't feel the urge to go and rip her clothes off. Generally, I wait till she gives me permission.' Bert sniggered and looked over at Jeanie.

'I'm sure you don't have to wait too long for that,' Jeanie said with a seductive smile.

Nellie threw Jeanie a contemptuous glance and wagged a finger at her son. 'Are you trying to deny that when you see a woman showing herself off you don't make certain assumptions, Albert Castle? If you are, you're a liar.'

Bert looked away uncomfortably.

'I thought as much. And what about you two?' She looked over at Colin and Jimmy, who were smirking at Bert.

Jimmy coloured slightly. 'No, Mum. I don't. We're not all savages, you know.'

Reenie, who had been listening quietly, her eyes darting between them all, decided to put an end to it. 'Well, I think she looks gorgeous. As do you two,' she said to Lily and Edie. 'But we've got to go, so thanks for the tea, Mrs C., and we'll see you later.'

Donny appeared from his cubby hole then and peered into the room, his eyes round with wonder.

'Mum! You look like a princess!'

Marianne turned to him gratefully, although noticing his grubby hands and face, she merely dropped a kiss on his head. 'Thank you, love.'

'There you go. Out of the mouths of babes.' Marge was still holding on to Marianne's arm, and quickly hustled her out.

As they clattered down the stairs, Nellie shouted down after them, 'You lot, behave! Boys, I expect you to look out for them. As for you, Lily Castle, just cos I didn't say anything doesn't mean I approve of that dress! It's too tight.' She paused, then added, 'Edie, I think you look very nice. Enjoy your evening.'

As they emerged into the kitchen, Edie grimaced. 'I don't know whether to be insulted that she thinks I look nice or not.'

Jimmy laughed. 'I think you look beautiful. Does that help? Who's got the torches?'

Once the torches were produced, the nine young people stepped out into the night. It wasn't fully dark yet, so there was just enough light to see by, but even so, the market square was mostly in shadow.

'Oy!' A figure was walking towards them. 'For gawd's sake turn that light off *before* you open the door, or next time you'll be fined. Alternatively, tell your mum to get another curtain up at the door.'

Lily laughed at that. 'I suggest you tell her yourself, Jasper. I'd rather face the entire German army than tell Mum she needs to put up another curtain.'

Jasper chuckled. 'I don't blame you, love. But I'm serious. You all better get used to it if you don't want those Nazis zeroing in on our little patch.'

Edie, who was last to emerge, hastily shut the door, plunging the square into shadow again. Lily squealed as Marge exclaimed, 'Bloody hell! It's going to be darker than Hades out here later. Let's all hold hands so we don't lose anyone.' And in a long chain they made their way gingerly along the shadowy pavement.

Chapter 11

Even though they all knew Dover like the backs of their hands, it was a surreal experience stumbling down the roads in the semi-darkness. It was the first time Marianne had ventured out at night since the blackout, and even though the evening was quiet, it made her anxious.

Finally, the group arrived at the Royal Oak on the corner of New Bridge and Cambridge Road near the seafront. Like most of the buildings in the area it was a tall three-storey, white stucco building, with a spacious bar on the ground floor that was separated into sections. The quiet section to the left of the door was where many of Mavis's friends would sit, having a port and lemon and gossiping about their neighbours. The men meanwhile would congregate in the public bar on the right-hand side. Tonight it was packed with soldiers and sailors, all relishing one of their last nights out before going to war.

As the group walked in, the noise abated slightly, as dozens of heads turned to watch the progress of the women. Marianne blushed and pressed into Colin's back, clutching her jacket to her chest.

Colin pulled her to his side and put a protective arm around her. 'Hey, ignore them. They don't mean any harm, it's just because you look so pretty.'

She gave him a grateful look, wishing she was sitting snugly with Nellie in their little living room listening to the wireless while Donny did a puzzle on the floor. She knew she shouldn't have come.

At the back of the pub was a larger, more open room with tables and chairs, where people could get some simple food – generally sandwiches or a pint of cockles. This too was crowded with servicemen who exuded a frenetic energy, as if they were determined to squeeze every last bit of fun from the evening.

As the group made their way down the stairs to the large function room, Marianne could hear a trumpet playing 'Jeepers Creepers'.

'Sounds like John and Alfie have started already,' Colin whispered to her as they descended.

'They're good, aren't they? Shame you couldn't be at dinner last night, they put on a fabulous concert for us.'

'Oh well, I've heard them before and you'll see John playing the piano tonight. I think the band had seven members before they all decided to join up. The others have all gone their separate ways but Alfie and John wanted to stay together.'

Getting to the bottom of the stairs, Marianne paused and looked around. It was packed, and the air was blue with cigarette smoke. Mavis and Daisy had spent the day decorating the walls with Union Jack bunting, and had also hung a sign over the stage, which read: *Good luck to all our brave troops. Give them hell!*

Marianne grinned at that, pointing it out to Edie. 'Typical Mavis!' she said. 'Never one to mince her words.'

Edie giggled. 'No wonder she and Mum are such good friends.'

Up on the stage, Marianne couldn't help noticing how handsome Alfie looked. Like so many of the other men, he was dressed in khaki, but somehow he carried his uniform off with panache, as if he was born to wear it. As he played a particularly high and long note, he bent over backwards, pointing the trumpet straight up to the ceiling, causing his cap to fall off. He didn't seem to notice, though, so lost was he in the music. At the piano, John was playing up a storm, bouncing up and down on the stool in excitement, grinning at the audience and winking at every pretty girl who caught his eye. Or rather, Marianne thought, they were trying to catch *his* attention. She noticed a group of girls who she sort of knew standing at the front, ignoring most of the other men in the room and dancing with each other, their eyes glued to the stage.

Just then, Alfie took the trumpet from his lips and started to sing. His voice was gruff and deep, and his dark blond hair gleamed under the light. Marianne was transfixed.

'There's a table over there. Go and sit down and I'll get you girls a drink,' Colin shouted in her ear, directing her to a table against the wall to the side of the stage. He disappeared into the throng, pushing his way to the bar at the back of the room where Daisy, Mavis and another girl were rushed off their feet serving the clamouring servicemen.

Marianne looked at the table nervously. She wanted to sit down, but it felt a little too exposed. Glancing around for Edie, she grabbed her hand. 'Come on. Let's sit down.'

Edie followed her obediently, her eyes fixed on the stage.

Reenie and Lily, Marianne could see, had already been pounced on and were dancing with a soldier and a sailor respectively. Bert was dancing with Jeanie, a little too closely, Marianne thought, considering the tempo of the song, and Marge, too, had found a very tall sailor who was twirling her around and grinning at her broadly.

Sitting down on the stool, Marianne looked up at the stage once more. Alfie and John were obviously in their element. Dover did get the occasional famous per-former, but she could tell these two were in a different class from most.

Suddenly Alfie's eyes locked with hers and he grinned and gave a little wave as he continued to sing. Several of the women who had been watching him looked around to see who had got this special attention, and glared at Marianne before turning away.

A sailor came over to the table, his eyes fixed on Edie, and held out his hand. 'You wannae dance?' he said in a broad Scots accent.

Edie glanced at Marianne, her eyebrows raised.

'Go on, enjoy yourself. Colin will be back soon.'

Edie rose, feeling, however wrongly, disloyal to Robert as she was whirled into the throng. Marianne pulled her jacket closer around her and tried to disappear into the wall, praying that no one would ask her to dance. Her prayers weren't to be answered, though, as a large, rough-looking soldier came over and tried to pull her out of her seat.

'Oh no, sorry. I'm waiting for my . . . my boyfriend,' she stammered.

'Ah weel,' he said, his eyes running over her admiringly. 'I shodae known a bonny girl like you would be taken. He's a lucky man. Make sure he treats you right.'

He had such a friendly face that Marianne suddenly felt bad. 'But . . . I'm sure he wouldn't mind . . .' she said tentatively, holding out her hand.

He waved it away. 'Ach, no, love. I wouldn'a want to steal another man's girl. With me being such a fine specimen an' everything.' He grinned self-deprecatingly.

She withdrew her hand with some relief. 'You're right,' she said with a smile. 'He'd be horribly jealous because you're so much better looking than him.'

'Aye, it's a constant problem.' He sighed comically. 'Ah weel, ne'er mind, eh.' He gave her a friendly salute and disappeared back into the crowd.

Marianne giggled to herself. If she hadn't been so nervous, she would have danced with him. He seemed nice. Perhaps now she was older, she shouldn't be so afraid of men. If anyone else asked her, she'd say yes, she decided.

Her eyes wandered to the stage again and she saw that Alfie had noticed the exchange. He winked at her, then turned away to execute a little twirl. He was a good dancer as well. Was there nothing he couldn't do?

Colin and Jimmy returned and set a tray of glasses down on the table. Jimmy looked around and, spotting Reenie as she was coming off the dance floor, he grabbed her. 'Come on, Reens, let's show them how it's done!'

Laughing with delight, Reenie went with him. They were both good dancers and they were soon waltzing through the crowds.

Colin sat down. He wasn't much of a dancer and was happy to keep Marianne company, although his eyes followed the pair until they were lost in the crowd, a wistful smile on his face. He looked over at Marianne. 'You going to take your jacket off? It's hot as hell in here.'

He was right, it was baking. There were doors at the back beside the bar and usually these would be open on to the garden outside. But with the blackout, they were now covered in heavy black curtains and remained firmly shut.

Reluctantly, Marianne unbuttoned her jacket and hung it on the back of the chair. She put her hands to her chest self-consciously, then brought them down again, thinking she would only be drawing more attention to herself.

'Seems you've got an admirer,' Colin remarked, nodding up at the stage.

She glanced up and saw that Alfie was looking over at her again, his grin wider than before.

'Don't be silly!' She blushed and looked away.

'Hmm. You be careful, Marianne. He's one of the best blokes I've met, but you know what these musicians are like.'

'Not really. What are they like?'

'Well ... girl in every town they play in, more than likely.'

'Like sailors? Different girl in every port?'

'Yeah, something like that.'

'And did he have a girl in the town you were in when you were doing your training?'

Colin looked thoughtful for a moment. 'Now you mention it, I don't think he did. They did a few little impromptu performances in a couple of pubs when we got the chance, but though John and Bert took advantage of all the girls swarming around them, I don't think I ever saw Alfie sneak out with any of them.'

Marianne wasn't sure why this pleased her, but she put the thought from her mind as Marge plopped down on the stool beside her, fanning her face with her hand. 'Jesus wept, it's hot. I can't keep up.' She grabbed a glass of lemonade and drank it down in one go, then scanned the room, looking for her next victim. 'Shame Rodney can't be here,' she said. 'I'd like to see him loosen up a bit on the dance floor. Ah well. Plenty more fish, as they say.'

Spotting a good-looking soldier who was staring at her with admiration, she gave him a sultry smile. He was at the table in a flash and Marge gave him her hand, winking briefly at Colin and Marianne before disappearing again.

'Can you see Lily?' Marianne suddenly remembered she was meant to be keeping an eye on her sister. Colin stood and scanned the dance floor, then sat down and grinned at her. 'Seems some poor lad is so overcome he's trodden on her toe. She looks cross. Don't worry about her, she can look after herself.'

'She's only seventeen, Colin. But she thinks she's a lot older, and that is a very dangerous combination.'

He put his hand over hers on the table reassuringly. 'You had it rough, I know, but honestly, I can't see Lily letting anyone get the better of her. She's like your mum. There's not many that will be able to take advantage of her. You should look out more for Edie.' He stood up again. 'But she's fine. Dancing with Bert.' Still standing, Colin held his hand down to Marianne. 'What do you say you and I have a little whirl? I'm not much of a dancer, but seems a shame not to take advantage of the music.'

Reluctantly Marianne put her hand in his and gave him a weak smile. 'All right. But don't be surprised if I fall over. I've got two left feet.'

'That makes two of us.'

He pulled her up and they made their way through the crowds until they found Jimmy, who was still dancing with Reenie. Without warning Colin whirled her around, and Marianne stumbled, treading on his toe and bashing her head on his chin.

'Ow!' Colin yelped. 'You weren't kidding, were you?'

'Sorry, sorry, are you hurt?'

Colin rubbed his chin gingerly. 'I'll live. But let's make a deal: I promise I won't try to spin you, and you keep your feet to yourself.'

She laughed. 'All right.'

She glanced up at the stage, and saw to her mortification that Alfie had seen the entire incident. He was clearly struggling to play the trumpet because he was laughing.

Colin followed her gaze and saluted his friend, who nodded back at him.

It felt to Marianne that the song went on far too long. She managed, just, to avoid injuring poor Colin again, but he'd had to hold her up more than once as she'd tripped over or stumbled into another couple. Finally, he led her back to the table. 'Thanks, Marianne.' He laughed. 'But I think I need another drink to recover.' He looked at the glasses on the table. 'I'll get another round in.'

Alone at the table, Marianne's eyes wandered around the crowd. It was such a joyful scene she could almost forget they were at war. She looked at the men laughing and dancing as if it was their last day on earth. And, she thought with a shiver, it might not be far off for some of them. It was awful to think that some of these happy faces might never return to England. She should make more effort to be friendly, she decided. If this was to be their last taste of home, then she should try to make it a good one.

Suddenly she realised that the trumpet had stopped. Looking up she saw that John was now alone on stage, playing some very intricate music on the piano, while Alfie had come down from the stage and was dancing in the centre of a circle of girls. He spun around, then grabbed the nearest woman around the waist and waltzed off with her, laughing, while the crowd around them broke into couples. She watched him wistfully. He was so confident and talented; if it had been her he'd grabbed, they'd no doubt be on the floor in a heap by now. Then again, she couldn't imagine why he would want to dance with her, when almost every woman in the room – most of them a lot more attractive, younger, and without a child at home – was clamouring for his attention. She looked away and started as she realised a large figure was looming over her.

'You can stand on my toe anytime, love,' a man said in a broad cockney accent.

She looked up at him; he was huge, with a rough, weather-beaten face and dark stubble on his chin. He gave her a leering smile and she noticed that his teeth were yellow from cigarettes and he was missing a tooth. His eyes were fixed on her chest.

She shuddered, all her previous resolve to dance with the next man who asked melting away. What was she doing here? she wondered. She didn't belong at a dance and the longer she stayed the more likely she was to make a fool of herself.

Hastily she grabbed her jacket from the back of the chair and shrugged it on, then, standing up, she gave the man a polite smile. 'I'm sorry, I was just leaving.'

Turning, she blindly made her way to the stairs, pushing her way through the crowds and keeping her head down. Finally she made it to the front door and breathed a sigh of relief as she stepped outside. It was blissfully quiet out here, apart from the sound of the sea swishing gently in the background and the muffled sounds from the pub, and in the darkness it was impossible to tell that just a few steps away dozens and dozens of ships lay at anchor, waiting to take the men off to France in the next few days. She shivered slightly in the evening chill and pulled her jacket closer.

Before she could take another step the door behind her opened and a hand grabbed her arm.

'Come on, love. I just want to have some fun before I leave.' The man with the cockney accent had obviously followed her and Marianne's heart started to beat fast in alarm as he pulled her around and planted his lips on hers.

Shuddering with disgust, she managed to shove him away with some difficulty. 'Stop it! I told you I was leaving.'

She turned to run down the steps, but she didn't get far before she felt her arm grabbed in a punishing hold. Keeping hold of her, he started to pull her down the stairs. With a yelp of alarm, she tried to get away, but his grip tightened painfully.

'Shut up and stop making such a fuss,' he growled. 'I got it on good authority that you're the girl to go to when a man needs a bit o' relief.'

Panting with fear, she frantically tried to free herself as they neared the bottom of the steps. The pub door burst open and Colin's tall figure was illuminated briefly before it shut again.

'Marianne!'

'Colin!'

She heard footsteps and suddenly the man was gone.

'Get your filthy hands off her!' In the darkness she heard a thwack and a grunt, and the soldier went crashing to the ground, cursing.

Another arm came around her shoulders and she gasped as she tried to pull away.

'Shh. It's all right, it's just me, Alfie.'

Sagging with relief, Marianne turned her face into Alfie's jacket, ashamed and embarrassed beyond measure that he should have been witness to this scene.

Jimmy joined Colin then, and the two of them dragged the protesting man off towards the alleyway. 'Can you take her home, Alf?' Jimmy called over his shoulder. 'We'll deal with this piece of filth.'

'Will do,' Alfie called back, his arm still around Marianne's shoulders. 'Come on,' he said gently, urging her forward.

Straightening, Marianne tried to pull herself together. 'It's fine. I can get back by myself.'

'Marianne, you've had a shock. Let me help you. I promise you're perfectly safe with me.'

She couldn't see Alfie's expression in the darkness, but his voice was deep and sincere, and despite what had just happened, she instinctively trusted him.

Suddenly a torch beam waved over them, and Marianne gripped Alfie's arm in shock as it lit up her face.

'Marianne? Are you all right?'

Marianne groaned inwardly. Of all the policemen who could have been patrolling, Roger Humphries was the very last one she wanted to see right now. 'Hello, Roger. Yes, I'm fine. This man is just taking me home.'

'I heard there was a disturbance at the party, so I've come to investigate. When you put a group of servicemen, particularly the lower ranks, in a room with too much beer, trouble always follows. I would have thought you'd have had more sense than to attend.'

Marianne could feel the mixture of frustration and fury that she so often felt around Roger rising within her, but she bit back her sharp retort. 'No, no, I'm fine. But please could you get that light out of my eyes.'

The torch beam moved over to rest on Alfie's face. 'And you are?'

'Private Alfie Lomax, officer,' Alfie replied, squinting in the light. 'And everything is fine in there now.'

'What happened?' The beam moved back to Marianne's face.

'Roger! Please get that light out of my eyes!' Marianne wished the man would just leave them alone. 'You didn't see Jimmy or Colin on your way here, did you?' she asked. She didn't want them to get into trouble if they were caught fighting.

'No, I haven't seen them. And thank you, Private Lomax, but I can look after Marianne from here. The Castles are *very* old and dear friends of mine.'

Marianne's hand squeezed Alfie's arm tighter. She did *not* want Roger to walk her home. Alfie seemed to get the message.

'No need for that. Marianne's safe with me – Jimmy and Bert would punch my lights out if I let anything happen to her.'

Roger grunted and swung the beam around the streets again. As the light moved over the buildings, Marianne gasped quietly as she spotted two tall figures just inside the alleyway. They had their arms around each other and seemed oblivious to all around them. The light rested there for a moment longer and Roger started to walk towards them.

Alfie had also spotted the couple and he moved to follow, but before he could say anything more, Marianne said quickly, 'On second thoughts, Roger, I would love you to escort me home. It's so kind of you to offer. And Alfie really should get back to the party as he's meant to be playing his trumpet.'

She gave Alfie a little shove away from her, looking up at him, hoping he could see that she needed him to leave. But aside from the slight gleam from the whites of his eyes, she couldn't tell if he'd got the message.

The beam came back to him briefly, as Roger said, 'You're a performer?' There was a condescending tone to his voice, and no sooner had he said this than he swung the torch back to the alleyway where the figures still stood.

141

'Oh yes, I'm due to sing my next number any minute.' He started to do a little dance and sang loudly, his voice echoing in the darkness. 'I'm putting on my top hat, tyin' up my white tie, brushing off my tails.' He did a little spin, ending up right in front of Roger, blocking his view of the figures, the torch beam shining directly into his grinning face. 'Do you know that one, officer? You should come in and join us.'

Marianne watched him in astonishment. What on earth was he doing? Then she realised: he was trying to distract Roger as well as warn the people in the alleyway that they had been spotted. She felt a surge of warmth and gratitude towards him.

Roger cleared his throat. 'I don't think that would be appropriate for someone in my position, and anyway, I'm on duty.' The damn torch beam swung back to the alleyway, but the couple had gone.

Marianne walked over to Alfie and squeezed his arm again, hoping to convey how grateful she was. The burden of this secret and the worry it caused was one she often wished she could share with someone. To know that her brother and Colin had an ally in the regiment was a huge comfort.

Behind them the pub door was thrust open and a group of men stumbled out, shouting loudly. In the darkness it was hard to see what was happening, but Roger swung his trusty torch towards the noise and

Marianne could see that a fight had broken out between some soldiers and sailors.

Roger ran over to them, shouting behind him, 'Apologies, Marianne, duty calls. If you wait there, I will escort you as soon as I've sorted this lot out.'

'No need, officer,' Alfie called. 'I'll see her home safely.' Then he dragged her off. 'I hope you've got a bloody torch because I've got no idea where I'm going,' he said, laughing.

Marianne pulled one from the pocket of her jacket and switched it on. Then she looked up at him and said softly, 'You know?'

He looked back and smiled faintly. 'Of course I do. I'm not blind, you know.'

'Well, no one else seems to have cottoned on. Not even Bert.'

'Are you certain about that? Anyway, in my line of work, it's hardly unusual.'

'Do you think worse of them?' Aside from the threat of prison, one of the things that tortured Marianne was the thought of Jimmy and Colin being bullied and ostracised, because God knew she understood how that felt.

'Why on earth would I? Love is love and you need to grab it where you can, because if you turn it away you might live with regret for the rest of your life.'

Marianne pondered his words. She'd known for years that Colin and Jimmy were more than just friends. She had discovered it one evening when she, Rodney and Jimmy had been sitting with their mother in the living room. Nellie had read out an item from the local paper about a man she'd been at school with who had been convicted of sodomy and was now in jail. Her final remark on the matter had been, 'And quite right too. It's disgusting, unnatural. I always knew there was something odd about that boy. And if we let this sort of thing carry on, what will become of us all? Men marrying men?' Then she'd paused, before adding, 'And if women were allowed to marry women, the population would die out! Can't see why any of us would bother with a man if there was an alternative.' She'd cackled to herself at the thought.

'Mum, you're being ridiculous. But you're right. It's totally against the natural order of things,' Rodney had replied.

'What do you reckon, Jim?' Nellie asked Jim.

'I reckon people should mind their own business!' he'd said aggressively. Then he'd stood up, grabbed his jacket and left without another word.

Nellie had lowered the paper, staring after him in consternation. 'Who's put a bee up his arse?' she'd said, before shrugging and going back to her reading.

Marianne, however, had noted the expression on her brother's face. It was one she recognised from when he was small: he was genuinely upset, and she needed to know why. So she had sat at the kitchen table downstairs after everyone had gone to bed and waited. When Jimmy had crept in, drunk, she'd waylaid him and demanded to know what was wrong.

He'd looked at her for a moment, then dropped into a chair, putting his head on the table, knocking it against the wood.

'That's enough, Jim,' she'd said sharply as she placed a cup of tea in front of him. 'Drink this and tell me what's going on.'

And it had all come pouring out. How he'd known since he was thirteen that he liked boys more than girls, and though he'd had the odd girlfriend, none of them made him as happy as Colin.

Marianne had gasped at that. 'So you and Colin . . . ?'

He'd nodded miserably, staring down at the table. 'Do you hate me, Marianne? Do you think I'm unnatural?'

Though she was shocked because she'd never encountered anything like this before, she'd rested a comforting hand on his shoulder. 'Oh, Jim, of course I don't. And anyway, look at me: pregnant at sixteen, bringing up a baby out of wedlock. Who am I to judge?'

He'd grabbed her hand and sobbed. 'I couldn't bear it if my family turned against me. As for Mum . . . I don't want her to hate me.'

Marianne had pulled him into a hug. 'She could never hate you. She'd bluster and curse and call you all the names under the sun, but you know as well as I do that she loves you no matter what. As for Rodney, he just finds it impossible to imagine anyone living outside the rules. But he'd accept it eventually, it just might take some time.'

'You can't tell anyone!' Jim had said desperately.

She'd put her arm around his shoulders, resting her head on his hair. 'You know I won't. And if Colin makes you happy, then that's enough for me.'

He'd stood and hugged her, and they'd stayed like that for a long time. Finally she'd pulled away and put her hand on his cheek. 'You have grown into a good and wonderful man, but promise me that you'll be careful, Jim. I couldn't bear it if it was your name in the newspaper with everyone making horrible comments about you.'

'I promise, sis. I promise. Thank you for accepting me as I am.'

∽

Marianne had been so lost in her thoughts that she jumped when Alfie said, 'It's been quite a night, hasn't it? Are you really all right? That man didn't hurt you?'

She smiled up at him. 'I'm fine. He didn't hurt me, just my pride, but then I never had much of that anyway.'

'You know, me and John have become great pals with your brothers and Colin. Please know that I will look out for them all – and I don't just mean about Colin and Jim's relationship. But I don't think you should worry about that. They aren't the only ones, you know. And some of the other men are married. It seems that as long as the army needs men, then they're willing to turn a blind eye. Funny, huh?'

'Some of them are *married*? I don't understand.'

He laughed. 'Well, I'm not the one to explain it to you.'

They didn't say anything for a while, but finally Marianne said, 'And what about you?'

'Are you asking if I'm like Jimmy and Colin?'

Marianne blushed, grateful for the darkness. 'Oh gosh, no ... I didn't mean ... I mean, I just meant, well, are you married? I don't know anything about you.'

'No, I'm not married. I've spent the last few years travelling with the band, so I haven't been able to settle down.'

Marianne refused to acknowledge how relieved that made her feel. 'Have you always played the trumpet?'

'Since I was about ten. My parents both died of the flu after the last war, and there was no other family, so I was put in an orphanage and that's where I met John. We became each other's family.'

'Oh, I'm so sorry.'

'Don't be. It could have been a lot worse. But I was nine when they died and a bit of a handful. Got into a lot of trouble: setting fires, smashing things. They were going to move me on, but I was lucky. There was this music teacher at the school who gave me a choice about what I wanted to learn. I chose the trumpet, mostly because I liked the shape and it was shiny.'

Marianne couldn't bear to think of the grieving little boy desperately trying to get some attention in a house full of strangers.

'Anyway, turned out I was good at it. And it made me popular. So as soon as I was fourteen, I left school and joined a band, then another, then another, until a few years ago I formed my own. Now I'm Alfie Lomax and His Band, and we've been doing all right. Even played the Café de Paris a few times.'

They had reached the market square, and Marianne stopped outside the door. 'Goodness, that all sounds terribly glamorous.'

'Not really. I spend most of my life staying in nasty little rented rooms.'

'Do you not have a home?'

'I bought a small flat in London when I had made enough money and John and I live there when we're not touring the country. But then this all blew up in our faces, so we joined up.'

They were standing face to face now, and though Marianne couldn't see his expression in the dark, his tone was wistful, and she realised that he must get lonely sometimes, despite having John.

'I'm glad you've found some more brothers, then.'

'So am I. And through them, I've found your family. They're pretty special, you know.'

She hesitated for a moment, unsure whether to say what had just come into her head. But the darkness gave her confidence – as long as she couldn't see his face, she could pretend it was one of her brothers she was talking to.

'Alfie, if you have nowhere to go when you have leave, you know you'll always find a welcome here. My mother would love it. So would Donny.'

Alfie touched her hand. 'And what about you?' he said quietly.

She flinched away from his touch, and he stepped back slightly, giving her some space.

'Sorry,' he said gently. 'I didn't mean to scare you.'

'No, you didn't, it's just . . .' She looked away. She would never admit to him that every occasion she had been touched by a man in the last ten years had been painful and humiliating. Taking a deep breath, she continued, 'But I . . . I wouldn't mind if you came to visit,' she whispered. And she really wouldn't, she realised. He'd shown her nothing but kindness and she hated the thought that he had no one to look after him.

'Thank you.' He bent and brushed his lips briefly over hers, and Marianne froze. This was nothing like when the loathsome soldier had forced his mouth onto hers earlier, and the sensations it caused unsettled her. Did he think she'd just offered him more than a place to stay? She pulled away in confusion and Alfie took her hand, stroking the back of it as if to soothe her worries.

'Will you write to me, Marianne?' he asked softly. 'I don't want to sound like a poor little orphan, but I don't get many letters.' He laughed shortly. 'Well, I don't get *any* letters.' When she didn't answer, he said quickly, 'And perhaps you can write to John too. Or get Lily to? And just a short note would do.'

'If you want me to then of course I will.'

'Thank you.' He handed her the torch. 'Anyway, I better get back to it. Poor John'll be exhausted.'

'Oh no, keep it, you'll never find your way back otherwise. Mum's been stockpiling them for months so we've got plenty of spares.' She paused uncomfortably.

He seemed to catch her uncertainty, and after squeezing her hand briefly, he said, 'I'll see you again soon, Marianne.'

'Please take care of yourself, Alfie.'

'I always do. And don't worry about the others. We'll stick together and get through this somehow.'

He walked off, whistling in the darkness, leaving Marianne staring after him until the little beam of torchlight disappeared around the corner. She turned and went inside. She was exhausted, but she didn't think she'd be able to sleep after everything that had happened this evening. The memory of the hateful man and his words, and the knowledge that people were *still* talking about her behind her back, had cut her to the quick, but somehow with Alfie it was different, and the brief touch of his lips had made her feel . . . How had it made her feel? Happy. Safe. Had she felt like this with Donny's father? No. That had been different. Then she had been excited. Dizzy. But with Alfie, she had felt not just excitement, but tenderness. She shook her head. What was she thinking? The last thing she needed was some man in her life making demands on her. She was probably reading too much into it anyway. He was being nice to her for her brothers' sake and now he would go off to war and forget all about her. Or, worse, he might never come back. The thought made her feel sick.

Nellie was still up when Marianne got in, listening to some big band music on the wireless and sipping her sherry, a cigarette burning in the ashtray beside her. She looked at the clock. 'You're back early,' she said. 'Didn't enjoy it, eh? Well, that's how it is, I suppose. No matter how you dress up, you'll always be you.'

Usually Marianne let Nellie's tactless remarks wash off her, but right now, she was feeling fragile. 'What do you mean?'

'Well, going out looking like that won't change the fact that you'll always be the girl who got herself knocked up at sixteen, will it?'

Marianne's cheeks flushed in anger. 'That's a dreadful thing to say, Mum. And anyway, you wouldn't be without Donny any more than I would.'

'Maybe not, but are you telling me that you decided to come home cos the men were too nice to you?'

'You know, Mum, I can see you've had a few too many sherries, but don't take your bad temper out on me. And you have no idea how I feel about anything because you never bother to ask me. And maybe if, when I was sixteen, I hadn't been running around after *your* kids and cooking for *your* customers, I might not have been so eager to go with the first man who showed me a bit of affection.'

She turned and stormed out of the room, stopping short when she saw a small figure wearing stripy pyjamas huddled on the stairs. Donny had clearly heard every word Nellie had said, and she cursed her mother all the more.

'Donny?'

He looked up at her, his eyes swimming with tears. 'Do you wish I wasn't here, Mum?'

She plumped down beside him on the stairs and hugged her boy tight into her and inhaled: his hair needed a wash and smelt faintly of the sea mixed with the sausages he'd eaten that evening, and his pyjamas smelt of Oxydol soap powder, but underneath all that was the heady scent of her baby boy.

'Listen to me, you daft ha'p'orth. There is not one day goes by when I don't thank God for you. Not one day, Donny, do you understand?'

Donny lay his head on her shoulder and yawned. 'I heard you say to Gran about a man showing you 'fection. Was that my dad? Was he nice? Was he clever and good and handsome?'

Marianne's heart stopped at his words. 'He was all of those things and more, love. Now, come on, sleepy head, off to bed with you.' She helped him to his feet and shuffled him to his bed.

'Mum, will you stay with me tonight?'

She was surprised by his request. 'Of course, if you want me to, but what's brought this on?'

'I keep thinking of Uncle Bert and Uncle Jimmy and Uncle Colin on those big ships. And now Mr Lomax and his friend ...' He trailed off. 'They'll be coming home, won't they?'

'Course they will.'

'But when we were listening to the wireless tonight, they were talking about the soldiers going to France and Gran said if it was anything like the last time we'd be lucky to see half of them again.'

Marianne sighed angrily. What did her mother think she was doing, sharing her fears with a ten-year-old boy?

'Well, this isn't the last time, so I expect it'll be very different. And anyway, your gran's not right about everything, you know.'

He giggled. 'She always says she is.'

'Doesn't mean she is, though.' She pulled back the sheets. 'Now slip into there, and I'll just go and change out of my glad rags, all right?'

Donny lay down, his eyes blinking rapidly as he tried to stay awake. 'I was right earlier, you know. You really do look like a princess.'

She laughed and kissed his forehead. 'Well, if I am a princess, then you must be a little prince. Close your eyes and I'll be right back.'

Marianne tiptoed out, stopping briefly when she saw her mother waiting in the corridor. Ignoring her, she brushed past her as she made her way to the stairs.

'Marianne . . .' Nellie held out her hand.

Marianne turned, eyebrows raised.

'I'm sorry, love. I let my mouth run away with me sometimes. It's just . . .' She paused, her hands knotted in front of her. 'I'm scared, and I took it out on you. You know I wouldn't hurt that boy for the world.'

'That's as may be, Mum, yet you did just that. But why would you change the habit of a lifetime? You've been hurting all of us our whole lives. With Donny, though, I thought maybe you'd learnt your lesson. Seems I was wrong.'

Marianne found it hard, turning away from her mother when she looked so upset. Usually she would accept the apology and soothe her temper. But not tonight. Tonight, she just wanted to cuddle up with her boy, and try not to think about the beautiful man who had walked her home. She'd been made a fool of before, and she was determined not to let that happen again.

Chapter 12

The day after the dance, Edie crept down to the kitchen shortly after eight to make herself some toast. The house was quiet and she didn't want to wake anyone after their late night, but she'd promised Mr Pearson she'd go in today to help out with the backlog of vehicles. It was so busy at the moment that even working seven days a week probably wouldn't clear it. They needed some more mechanics. But with all the young men joining up, there weren't many available.

Slicing some bread and putting it under the grill, she filled the large black kettle in the scullery and set it on the range. Once she was at the table with toast and dripping and a cup of tea, she allowed the thoughts that had been troubling her all night to come to the surface. The evening had been fun, but she'd wished Robert had been there. She could have left a message at his house, but even if she had, she doubted he'd have come. She sighed. How she would have loved to have his strong arms around her as they danced. They'd never danced together, she realised. In fact, when she thought about it, they'd never done anything that courting couples usually do together. All they'd ever really done was ride his motorbike and go to bed.

Was he using her? No. He loved her, she was sure. He was so sweet and funny when they were in bed together, and hadn't he said he'd like to meet her family? She should have more faith in him. If all he'd wanted was to get her into bed, then he wouldn't have come back after the first time, would he? He'd be in touch before long, she was sure.

Footsteps on the stairs brought her out of her reverie as Marianne came into the kitchen wearing a blue quilted dressing gown, her hair hanging in a long plait down her back. 'Where are you off to?' she asked.

'Work. Mr Pearson needs me. As well as the army vehicles, there's been a rush of accidents in the blackout. So it looks like seven days a week for the foreseeable. Still, can't complain, at least I'll be earning more.'

Marianne yawned and went into the pantry where she extracted a large pork joint, which she put on the table, before going back to collect salt, pepper and some fresh herbs. 'You will be back for lunch, won't you?' she asked, rubbing salt into the joint. 'You haven't forgotten that Rodney's coming over?'

Edie swallowed the last of her tea and stood up. 'I won't forget. In fact, me and Rod can walk down together. I'll leave a note with one of the soldiers at the castle. You know, I have to show ID just to go to work now. They've shut all the roads up there. Speaking of walks, Jim told me what happened last night. Are you all right? He said Alfie walked you home?'

'Yes. He was very kind.'

'I think he was being a bit more than kind. I saw how he was looking at you while he was up on that stage.' Edie made kissing noises and Marianne threw a tea towel at her.

Edie laughed. 'You can tell me about it later. Gotta go.' She slung her canvas bag with her overalls in onto her shoulder and disappeared through the back door.

✺

Once Marianne had finished preparing the pork, she glanced up at the clock. Nine o'clock. Wiping her hands, she went upstairs to get dressed. As she reached the top floor, Jimmy was just coming out of the bathroom.

'Morning,' he said, smiling sheepishly as he attempted to slope past her back into the bedroom he shared with his brothers.

She'd almost forgotten about Jimmy and Colin in the excitement of her conversation with Alfie and then the argument with her mother.

'Not so fast, you,' she said, using the same voice she used with Donny when he was being naughty. 'You and I are going for a little walk, so get dressed and meet me downstairs in fifteen minutes. We need to talk.'

'What about?'

'You know very well what about,' Marianne said over her shoulder as she went into the bathroom.

∽∾

Outside the café, a tall figure holding a large bunch of flowers in one hand and a cigarette in the other watched the man and woman come out of the back gate. He ducked around the corner as they walked towards him. Surely this couldn't be her husband? If she'd got married it could ruin his plans. But no, he'd been watching on and off for weeks and there'd been no hint of another man.

He threw his cigarette away, watching as the couple turned left down King Street towards the seafront. Well, time would tell. He walked to the gate that he knew led to the backyard behind the café and slipped inside, peering through the window curiously. It seemed to be a scullery. A blonde girl walked in and he ducked out of sight. Another sister? He grinned at the thought and sneaked a peek through the window again. This one was definitely the pick of the bunch. Maybe . . . He shook his head. No, he couldn't risk it, no matter how tempting. Placing the flowers on the ground outside the door, he knocked hard, then left swiftly, shutting the back gate quietly behind him, wishing he could see the look of confusion on the woman's face when she saw them. He grinned. This little game was proving to be surprisingly entertaining, and now things had gone so wrong at home, hopefully he could dig himself out of the hole he found himself in. It would certainly prove his father wrong. And teach his bloody careless wife a lesson she wouldn't forget. Stupid cow should never have got drunk, then she might not have fallen down the stairs and lost the baby. Still, when one door closes another one opens, and it seemed like he had the perfect solution to his little problem.

Brother and sister walked in silence as they made their way up to Western Heights. Jimmy seemed reluctant to speak and Marianne didn't know where to start. It was a cloudy, drizzly day, and from their vantage point above the docks, the sea looked grey and unfriendly, made worse by the looming tankers and ships that were crouching low in the water around the harbour like sea monsters, their tall turrets silhouetted against the dark sky, guns pointing towards France. Just the sight of them made Marianne feel sick with anxiety for the men who would soon be sailing off to confront an enemy who had proved ruthlessly efficient up until now, as they slowly crept across Europe like the Black Death.

She shook her head. It was unlike her to be so morbid and fanciful, but the day matched the mood of the nation: dark, gloomy and buzzing with anxiety, despite the bravado of the newspaper headlines.

Finally, Jimmy broke the silence. 'I'm sorry about last night,' he said quietly, staring out across the sea. 'We were a little reckless.'

'A little reckless? You must have known that Roger would be lurking around there like he always does, waiting to catch people out. He loves nothing better than an act of "public indecency". God, if it hadn't been for Alfie . . .' She trailed off.

'I know. But what are we supposed to do? There's nowhere for us to go where we can be like any other couple. Where we can just kiss each other on the cheek even, hold hands . . . It's not illegal, you know, to be like me.'

'But it is illegal to be caught in the act, and you know it, so don't try to plead innocent.'

'You have no idea. No idea at all what it's like to be me.' Jimmy's eyes sparked with fury and frustration. 'Tell me, how was Donny conceived? Was that an act of public indecency? Somewhere in the fields, hidden by the long grass? Because if so, then you have no right to lecture me.'

Marianne coloured. He was far too close to the truth, and the memory made her feel dirty. She turned her head away, allowing the wind to cool her suddenly hot cheeks. If she was honest, she'd never considered this; never equated her experience with Jimmy's.

'That's not fair, Jim! And anyway, look what happened to me! It didn't end well, did it? And what I've

161

been through is nothing compared to what might happen to you if you get caught!'

Jimmy sighed. 'I'm sorry, sis. You're right. That was below the belt. But you shouldn't worry about us, you know. No one seems to care anymore. Things are changing.'

'Are they really, Jim? Or is that wishful thinking?'

'You think we're the only ones? You'd be surprised. Anyway, I don't want to argue on my last day here, so if I promise to be careful, will you promise to stop worrying?'

'How can I? If you got found out . . .' She looked away, her shoulders slumping. She didn't want to argue either. 'I'm sorry too. I shouldn't have got angry with you. But I can't help thinking about that article Mum was reading that day, and it scares me. Have things really changed that much?'

He shrugged. 'I don't know. You know, when I was young, when Colin and I . . . well, we had no idea it was considered wrong. We didn't even think it would mean we wouldn't get married. It was just fun . . . curiosity.'

Marianne wasn't sure she wanted to picture this, but she forced herself to keep listening, looking at him steadily.

'But then . . . well, I tried to feel the same way with girls, I really did. But I just don't. That's all there is to it. I just don't. And neither does Colin.'

Marianne put her arm around him. 'I don't care either way, Jim, and if you say you'll be careful, then that's going to have to be enough.'

Jimmy grinned. 'Anyway, enough about my love life. I want to know what went on between you and Alfie. The man couldn't take his eyes off you all evening.'

'There's nothing going on with me and Alfie! He walked me home because he's nice, that's all. And he saved your bacon with a very impressive little dance in the pitch dark.'

'Hmm, well, I think there's more to it than that. Never seen him walk out on a performance before. Shame we're all leaving. I always thought he might be just the man for you – someone to bring you out of your shell, show you some fun. And as for him, I don't think he's had much gentleness in his life.' He smiled down at her. 'He needs someone to look after him.'

She nodded sadly. 'It sounds like he had a horrible time.'

'Really? What did he tell you?'

'You know, about his parents, the orphanage, John, the music . . .' She trailed off, noticing his expression of astonishment.

'He's never said anything to us! I just assumed because he said he didn't have anywhere to go on his leave this week . . . He must really like you.'

'If he's not told you he probably doesn't want people to know. Then again, you men don't really speak to each other, do you? If you put a roomful of girls together, before the day was out, we'd know every detail about each other's lives.'

'That's because we men have more important things on our minds – you know, like ridding the world of an evil dictator while you girls sit around at home drinking tea and gossiping.' He dodged away, laughing, before she could whack him.

'Well, maybe you men could learn a thing or two from us; maybe if Hitler was more interested in gossiping we wouldn't be in this mess. Anyway, I told Alfie he was welcome to come to us when he has leave. I wonder if he'll take me up on it, though.'

'I'll make sure he does. Like I said, he needs someone like you in his life.'

'Oh, stop it! The man was absolutely surrounded by women last night, he could take his pick. And none of them have a child. Plus, they're younger.'

Jimmy rolled his eyes and put his arm around her. 'I'd say Donny gives you a distinct advantage. Weeds out the scoundrels.' He winked.

'Weeds out all the others as well,' she said ruefully.

'Oh, I don't know. There's always Roger . . .' This time he didn't dodge away quickly enough as she hit him on the arm. He laughed. 'Come on, sis, let's get back. I spotted a very raw-looking joint of pork on the table, and I'm no expert, but I think it needs a couple of hours in the oven before we can eat it.'

'Hell's bells. I forgot. I told Rodney we'd be eating at one and you know what he's like when he's hungry and behind schedule!'

'Oh no!' Jimmy squealed, throwing his arms up in mock horror. 'What are we going to do?'

'Oh, shut up! Come on.' She grabbed his hand and started to jog down the hill.

He pulled her back. 'Tell you what, jump on my back and I'll show you how fit and strong the army's made me.'

'I'll crush you!'

'I think I'll manage.' He bent down slightly, his arms held back, ready to catch her legs. 'Come on! If you don't want to incur the wrath of Rodney, jump on!'

So she did, and Jimmy stumbled theatrically down the hill, moaning about her weight, while she clung on, tears of laughter rolling down her cheeks. How she would miss Jimmy. She loved all her brothers and sisters, but she and Jimmy shared a special bond, probably because, in their different ways, they were both outsiders.

Coming back into the kitchen through the back door, Marianne was pleased to see that Lily had made a start on the lunch. A large pan of potatoes was on top of the range and she was now busily peeling carrots. But her eye was caught by a splash of colour on the small table by the wall.

'Who are those for?' She pointed at the bunch of yellow roses, their stems wrapped in newspaper.

Lily grinned at her. 'Well, the note just said . . .' She hunted around on the table until she found a scrap of paper and held it out to her.

'"For the lady in the kitchen. Hope to see you soon",' Marianne read. Then she looked up, perplexed. 'But who are they from?'

Lily shrugged. 'There was a knock on the back door and when I opened it, these were on the doorstep.' She held her hand over her heart and sighed. 'It's so romantic.'

'Didn't you see who left them?'

'Nope. Just the flowers. I told you Alfie was interested.'

Jimmy snatched the note and looked at it with a frown. 'Well, well. The man clearly knows what he wants.'

Marianne studied the scrap of paper and the memory of another anonymous note came back to her. She couldn't remember what the writing had looked like, but the same feeling of anxiety and unease she'd felt then stirred within her again.

'I don't think they're from Alfie,' Marianne said. 'I mean, why wouldn't he just bring them himself?'

'Of *course* they're from Alfie! Anyone could see that he fancies you. I hope you invited him to lunch.'

Marianne shook her head distractedly. It was the only explanation, but it was strange that he didn't feel able to deliver them personally. Maybe he was shyer than he seemed.

∽

Despite Marianne's worries, lunch was ready on time, and as they always used to on a Sunday, the family gathered in the café. Looking around, Marianne wondered when, or even if, they ever would again.

Throughout the lunch, Donny questioned the men minutely about army life, but he was particularly fascinated by Rodney's job in the castle.

'Uncle Rodney, do you really live in a tunnel?'

'Yes, I share a room with a few others, we sleep in bunks. Very uncomfortable, and I miss having a window.'

'But what do you do there?'

'If I told you that, Don, then the war could be lost. Haven't you heard: "Be like Dad, keep Mum"?'

Donny looked confused for a moment. 'But I don't have a dad to be like. He's dead.'

'You've got three dads, Donny, and they're all sitting here,' Marianne said, hoping to divert yet another conversation about his father.

'You know what I mean. Last night Mum told me he was handsome and clever and that I was just like him. Do you think I am?' He looked around the table at the rest of the family.

Marianne cleared her throat. 'They never met him, love. So they don't know.'

'But if you were going to get married to him, how come they never met him?'

Marianne looked down at her plate, aware of everyone's questioning gaze.

'I hope you're not suggesting your mum's telling porkies, young man,' Nellie admonished her grandson. 'I met him once or twice, and I'd say you're much more handsome. In fact, you're almost as handsome as your uncles, who have been better dads to you than most.'

'Was that a compliment, Mum?' Bert put his hand over his heart. 'Does that mean we can have a chocolate bar each?'

Nellie smirked at him. 'Don't let it go to your head, son. It's about the only good thing I can say.'

Bert laughed and raised his glass. 'Cheers, Mum. For a moment there I thought you were going soft.'

'Huh. Not likely.'

'But they're not any good cos they can't marry Mum. So unless she finds me a dad she *can* marry, me and Davey will always have to play in secret.'

Marianne put her hand on Donny's. 'But you're forgetting that first I'd have to meet someone who wanted to marry me.'

'But why wouldn't they want to marry you? You're soft and cuddly and bake the best cakes in the world.'

She laughed and kissed him on the cheek. 'Ah, if only it was that easy, they'd be queueing out the door. But if

I were to marry, it'd have to be someone special enough to be your dad.'

Lily came to her rescue then. 'Sometimes dads aren't all they're cracked up to be, Don.'

There was an awkward silence, as the memory of their own father reared its head. It wasn't something they needed reminding about just before Jimmy and Bert were sent off to fight in France – as their father had been twenty-five years before.

Realising what she'd done, Lily jumped up from her seat and raised her glass of water in the air. 'Anyway, enough of all that. Edie, Marianne, Mum, Donny, stand up, and let's raise a toast to our men.'

The others rose obediently.

'I just want to say, before you two go off to who knows where to do who knows what, that like Mum said, you three have been the best dads a boy could wish for. Eh, Don?'

Donny nodded and sighed. 'I suppose they're better than nothing.' He sounded so like Nellie that everyone chuckled.

'But not only that, you are the best brothers we girls could have wished for. Even you, Rodney.' She grinned cheekily at him, and he grinned back. 'And Mum might deny it, but you're also the best of sons. Right, Mum?'

Nellie nodded wordlessly, so Lily continued, 'Come home quick, boys. Life's too quiet without you.'

The men stood up then, and they clinked their glasses together over the middle of the table.

Seeming to have recovered his spirits after making everyone laugh, Donny piped up, 'You better get home soon cos life's not easy when you live in a house full of women.'

The table erupted with laughter again. Marianne tried to join in, but her throat felt tight. Lily's words had inadvertently brought the danger her brothers faced home to her. She glanced at them, glad they were smiling, but wondering if they, too, were hiding their fears. Finally her gaze rested on her mother. Nellie was smiling bravely, but her cheeks were wet with tears.

On the other side of the road, hidden in the shadows of the covered market, a man watched the family scene through the large café window. How touching, he thought with a smirk. It would be a shame to break up the family, but still, there were enough of them that they wouldn't notice if one was missing.

Chapter 13

The following morning breakfast service was in full swing, and, as there simply wasn't enough room to fit everyone in, Nellie had decided to offer sandwiches to go. This meant there was a queue of people at the counter that went back all the way to the door, causing much grumbling from those lucky enough to get a seat as their tables were knocked by the people queuing. Nellie had tried to persuade Edie to stay for an hour or two to help out, but she had left the minute she was dressed, not even stopping for breakfast. As for Lily, she was in the scullery trying to keep up with the washing up while Donny dried. Jimmy and Bert, who were due to get an early train back to Canterbury to re-join their regiment, were sitting at the small table in the corner of the kitchen demolishing plates of eggs, bacon, fried bread and tomato, while Marianne stood at her usual spot by the stove with five skillets on the go. It was only eight o'clock and already the sweat was pouring down her back, but for many of the men, this would be their last breakfast in England, so she wanted to make sure they went off with a good meal inside them.

'Knock knock!' a voice called through the kitchen door. 'Blimey, talk about dog eat dog! Have you seen it out there?' It was Alfie, carrying his kit bag in one hand and his trumpet case in the other.

'Mate!' Bert got up from the small table by the wall and clapped him on the shoulder. 'Yup. It's the last supper – or should I say breakfast. Let's get out from under everyone's feet and go and have a cup of tea and a fag upstairs. Train doesn't leave for a couple of hours, so plenty of time. You coming too, John?'

Without waiting to be asked, John had slipped through to the scullery and out of the corner of her eye Marianne could see him put his arm around Lily's waist and plant a kiss on her cheek. Lily slapped him on the chest with a soapy hand. 'If you want to make yourself useful, I reckon Donny could find you a clean tea towel!' she told him sharply.

Laughing, John backed away to the stairs. 'Sorry, darlin'. Some of us have a war to fight.' He looked at Alfie. 'You coming?'

'Be right there.' He hovered behind Marianne, jumping out of the way when she turned to slide food on to some waiting plates, before dumping them on the hatch.

'Sorry, Alfie. Just a bit busy. I meant to say, thanks ever so for the flowers.' She was relieved she couldn't look at him because now, in the cold light of day and after what Jim had said to her, she felt mortified about Saturday night.

He looked puzzled. 'Flowers?'

Marianne turned back to the stove, using one hand to crack more eggs, and another to flip the fried bread. 'You know, the roses. I just thought . . .' She turned her head to look at him. 'Oh. It wasn't you.' Her cheeks flamed with embarrassment. Of course they weren't from him. What was she thinking? But overriding her embarrassment, she felt the anxiety she'd pushed aside return, sitting like a hard ball of lead in her stomach.

'Marianne! Today, if you don't mind! We've got hungry soldiers waiting for their sarnies, and they can't fight that raving lunatic on empty stomachs!' At Nellie's words, a cheer went up from the queue, and, flustered, Marianne loaded up a baking tray with more bacon and stuck it in the oven. What else could she do? With only five rings, she couldn't perform miracles.

'Can I do anything?' Alfie's voice made her jump.

'Here, Mr Lomax, you couldn't help us with the washing up?' Donny was holding a dry tea towel out to him. He eyed the trumpet case that Alfie had set down by the scullery. 'Are you going to play?' he asked hopefully.

'No. I was going to ask you a very big favour. Do you reckon you could keep her safe for me while I'm away?'

Donny nodded eagerly.

'Take good care of her, mind.'

'I promise.' Donny snatched up the case and took it down to the basement.

Meanwhile, Alfie took off his jacket, rolled up his sleeves and went into the scullery, where he started to dry a plate.

Marianne watched in disbelief. He'd really meant it when he offered to help? Even her own brothers had ducked out of service. Her heart warmed towards him. Who needed flowers when a man helped with the washing up? But if Alfie hadn't left the flowers, then who?

∞

At nine o'clock, Marianne collapsed into the kitchen chair with a groan. Gladys came through with some more plates and dumped them in the sink in the scullery and sank into the chair next to her. She looked at Alfie, who was still drying up. 'Alfie Lomax, you are a prince among men. Look at 'im, Nellie,' she called through the kitchen door.

Nellie poked her head through the hatch. 'Marianne, how can you let one of our serving boys do the washing up? Where are Lily and Donny?'

'School, Mum, remember? And before you start, you're the one who insisted she stay on to take her final exams.'

Nellie huffed. 'The sacrifices I've made for that girl's education. Thank God you weren't that way inclined. Started cooking for the punters at fourteen, Alfie. Couldn't keep her out of the kitchen.'

'And from what I've tasted she's not wasted any of those years.' He smiled warmly.

'Glad, get Alfie a cuppa then come back in here, will you?' Nellie gave her friend a meaningful look.

'But—'

'Just do it, for gawd's sake!'

Gladys huffed and got up to do as she was told. 'I don't know why I put up with that woman,' she grumbled. 'Who does she think she is, orderin' me about like that?'

'Glad, you know you don't mean that,' Marianne said placatingly. The truth was, Gladys would do anything for Nellie. Gladys's husband had been killed during the last war. Unfortunately, they'd only married the day before he went away, and she'd been left destitute when the landlord had thrown her out of the rooms they'd just moved into. Nellie had seen Gladys sleeping under one of the market stalls, and brought her in and fed her. And there she'd stayed until after the war when Nellie had somehow managed to browbeat the local MP into looking into the injustice and making sure she got her pension. She'd even lent her money to get her flower stall up and running.

'Hmph. Maybe not, but still . . .'

'Oh, hush your moaning, Glad, and get out here, will you?'

Alfie sat down in the seat just vacated by Gladys and smiled. 'Are they always like that?'

'Everyone's like that around my mother, hadn't you noticed?'

'She's not like that with me. Should I be flattered?'

'Give it time. She won't play nice for long.'

'By the way, Marianne' – Nellie's head poked through the hatch – 'postman brought this earlier.' She threw an envelope at Marianne. 'Looks official. Hope you're not in trouble?'

Marianne looked curiously at the brown envelope with the neatly printed label.

Alfie nodded at her. 'Go ahead. I can see you're dying to open it.'

She hesitated a moment; she was curious, but at the same time she wanted to talk to Alfie. Glancing up through her lashes, she took the time to examine him. Khaki suited him, she reflected, noting the shirt and the tie tightly knotted around the neck. His dark blonde hair was neatly combed and when he looked at her with his bright brown eyes, she could swear they softened. She felt the urge to stroke his cheek, which was freshly shaved and smooth, but she resisted. Instead she smiled at him briefly and turned her attention back to the envelope. Picking up a knife, she slit it neatly across the top and scanned the contents. Her brow creased in confusion. Who the hell was Henry Fanshawe? And what did it mean about *his* child? Was someone playing a cruel trick on her? But who would do something like that?

Suddenly the realisation hit her like a sledgehammer. *This* was Donny's father? How did he even know about her son? He'd left so quickly, and she hadn't even known she was pregnant until Donny arrived. Had he been here? Had he spoken to any of them? Her mother, perhaps?

Oh God, her mother . . . She felt sick. Dropping the letter, she put her hand over her mouth and rushed out into the backyard, getting to the privy just in time before her meagre breakfast of tea and toast reappeared.

Finally, with nothing more left in her stomach, she rose and rinsed her mouth at the small sink. Her hands were trembling, and she felt as if she might pass out.

When she re-emerged, Alfie was standing outside the door, staring down at the letter with a frown. He looked up guiltily as she came out and Marianne realised he'd been reading it. What on earth must he think of her?

'Are you ill? Do you need me to get your mother?' he asked anxiously.

The thought of her mother discovering what was in the letter almost sent her back into the privy. She'd *never* forgive her!

'I'm fine.' She snatched the paper from his hand and marched back into the kitchen.

Alfie trailed after her, looking confused.

Didn't he have *anything* to say? He must have read it. Or was he so disgusted with her that he thought it best to say nothing?

She turned to him impatiently. If he didn't want to say anything, she needed him to leave. 'I expect you need to be off soon. Thanks so much for coming by.' She held out her hand, which Alfie took. He looked upset. Well, so was she. 'Good luck with everything.'

She turned and fled up the stairs to the second floor and locked herself in the bathroom, where she sat on the toilet, holding the letter in a trembling hand.

She couldn't understand how this had happened. Henry Fanshawe? The man she'd met had been called Gerald. And if this really was Gerald, why was he suddenly so interested? He'd always known where she lived but he hadn't got in touch in over ten years. And what could she do? How could she fix this without her mother finding out? She shook her head. That was the least of her worries. The question she should be asking was how could she fix this without losing Donny?

She read the letter again.

Carter & Billing Ltd.
Randolph House
Burgate
Canterbury

8 September 1939

Dear Miss Castle,

Regarding legal custody of Master Donald Castle

It has come to our client Mr Henry Fanshawe's attention that following carnal relations with said client in 1928, you conceived and bore a child without informing our client.

It is our considered and professional opinion that the best interests of the child would be served if custody were to be granted to our client, considering his financial stability, access to society and the promise of a share in a profitable family business should said progeny be taken into his care.

Therefore, having advised our client that he has a strong case to seek custody under the Guardianship of Infants Act (1925), he has instructed us to take action to that effect.

If you do not reply to this letter within seven days, then legal proceedings will begin forthwith.

Yours etc . . .

Without informing his client? How the hell could she have informed him when he hadn't even given her his real name? As if it wasn't bad enough that he'd seduced her and left her to face the consequences, he'd lied about *everything*. God, she was a fool! A wave of humiliation threatened to overwhelm Marianne and she blinked away the tears as she read through the devastating words again. *Carnal relations.* It all sounded so cold and sordid. But she supposed as far as *their client* was concerned it hadn't meant anything at all. He'd seduced her so easily. All it had taken was a couple of walks along the cliffs, a cup of tea and a slice of cake. She'd thought he was the most wonderful human being she'd ever met: so handsome and worldly, and so *interested* in everything about her. And no one ever showed an interest in her. She was just the cook; the surrogate mother; the one her younger brothers and sisters came to for comfort. But who comforted her? It certainly wasn't Nellie.

Marianne's mind wandered back to those dark days. Just a year or so earlier, their father had died, leaving them all shocked, traumatised and confused. She and Rodney had had to look after their siblings; Nellie had been no use. She'd taken to her room, refusing to speak to anyone except Jasper. And with Rodney needing to go to school, it had been Marianne – with Jasper and Gladys's help – who'd kept the café open and looked after her brothers and sisters, while also trying to deal with her own grief. None of them had known their father really. He'd crouched in that living room for years, while they'd all tiptoed around him, wary of disturbing him in case it brought on one of his terrifying rages where he'd shout and scream before collapsing in tears.

Sometimes on these occasions, Jasper would take Donald back to his own house and look after him, giving the family some relief, but at others, Nellie would guide him to their bedroom and sit with him for hours, holding him while he wept. Then, when he'd died so suddenly, it was Nellie who took to her room. Lying in the dark, refusing to leave, until finally one day she'd emerged, brimming with anger and determination, and life had returned to something resembling normality. But the damage had been done. None of them had come out of the experience unscathed. The difference was Marianne was the one they clung to when the memories of that time became too much. She'd had no one to turn to aside from Rodney, who had buried himself in his schoolwork, his one goal being to become an officer in the navy.

It was no wonder, then, she reflected, that when Gerald – or Henry, or whatever his name was – came along to order a cake for his mother's birthday, she'd been ripe for the plucking. She'd spent hours on that cake, creating a little garden on the top from marzipan and rice paper to try to impress him.

When he'd invited her to have a cup of tea with him, she'd been so thrilled she hadn't considered refusing for a minute. It had been the first time she could remember that anyone had paid special attention to *her*. Who had admired *her*. And she'd fallen for it hook, line and sinker.

She buried her face in her hands, her heart breaking for the young, naïve girl who so desperately wanted some love and attention that she'd allowed herself to be seduced by the first handsome stranger who smiled at her. She couldn't regret it because it had given her Donny . . . But now it looked like she might lose even him. And once her mother found out, she might well lose her too.

She should never have told her mother that she'd been attacked. Nor given her a false name. She'd chosen the name of a poor lad she'd read about in the paper who had been killed in a traffic accident – she'd thought as he was dead the lie could never be uncovered. Unfortunately for Marianne, the boy's family were known to her mother, and Nellie had refused to speak to them again. Every action has a consequence, she thought grimly. And Marianne had ruined a perfectly civil friendship with a woman who was already suffering the loss of her child.

There was a knock on the door.

'Marianne! We're leaving.' It was Jimmy.

Reluctantly she opened the door and Jimmy scanned her face anxiously. 'Hey, what's wrong?'

She shook her head. 'Nothing. It's nothing. I'm just sad you're all leaving.'

He took her face in his hands and wiped the tears away with his thumbs. 'Don't worry about us. We'll be all right.' Jimmy pulled her in for a hug, and she inhaled the familiar scent of him. How she longed to confide in him, but she couldn't. The last thing he needed was to be worrying about her when he was meant to be concentrating on staying alive.

Jimmy kissed the top of her head. 'See you soon, sis. Take care.'

Bert took his place, enfolding her in a huge bear hug. 'Be careful, won't you, Bert? Don't do anything reckless.'

He laughed. 'I can't promise that, love. But I'll be home again. Don't worry about us.' He stared down at her face. 'I don't know what's wrong, but chin up, eh? Things will work out, they always do.' Then, like Jimmy, he kissed the top of her head before turning and running down the stairs.

Marianne shut the door and leant against it, more tears flowing down her face. She felt as if her world was falling apart again. She dropped her chin to her chest and took a deep breath. It was no use hiding away crying. She couldn't allow herself to be intimidated by this man. Donny was *her* son and hers alone, and she would fight to the death anyone who tried to take him away from her. An idea came to her, providing a sliver of hope. There was perhaps one person who might be able to help.

She washed her face and looked at herself in the mirror. Her eyes were red and swollen, but at least the tears had stopped.

Running down the stairs, she went into the kitchen, keeping her face averted. 'Mum, I need to go out. The steak and kidney pies are ready to warm in the oven for lunch. And Gladys can make the mash and sandwiches, can't she?'

Her mother huffed. 'It's not very convenient.'

'Mum, when do I ever ask for time off? I need to get out.'

Nellie looked closely at her daughter's face. 'What's up, love? If you're worried about the boys, then you're not the only one, but we just have to keep going. Nothing else for it.'

'I know.' Nellie's gentle tone made her long to confide in her. Her mother was always so *certain* of everything. So good at taking control and making people do what she wanted. But there was no way Marianne could talk to her about this. This was one problem she would have to sort out on her own.

Marianne strode purposefully up Castle Hill, praying she'd be able to get word to Marge. Before joining the Wrens, Marge had worked as a secretary at a solicitor's office in the town. Even if she couldn't advise, she could certainly ask her old boss if he could help; Marge had always said he was kind.

It was a cold, drizzly autumn day, and the trees that lined either side of the road dripped steadily on to her, soaking her hair. She'd run out in such a hurry that not only had she forgotten her coat, but her gas mask too. In the distance, she heard the rumble of aircraft. She looked up, but she couldn't see anything through the canopy above her. A military van rushed past her far too close and Marianne stumbled into the undergrowth by the side of the road, tripping over a branch and falling on to her backside.

For a moment she sat listening to the sounds of war around her, and for the first time, she felt real fear. Somehow, in the kitchen, she felt protected, distanced from all the drama. Their basement was just a few steps away if she needed to take cover, and though she heard the planes and the occasional explosion from the Channel, she was cocooned in her safe little world. She couldn't believe she'd taken it all so lightly. She needed to open her eyes if she was going to keep Donny safe. Hugging her knees, she stayed where she was, suddenly too scared to move.

Finally, she rose, uncomfortably aware of how wet her skirt was. She pulled her cardigan more tightly around herself and resumed the long walk up the hill. Near the castle she reached a checkpoint where she was told to turn around and go back. Producing her identity card, she explained she was visiting her brother at the castle with urgent family news – she figured that Rodney's rank would more likely get her through, and she was right. With a cheery salute, the guard allowed her to pass.

Sneaking past the garage at the bottom of Constable's Road, she peeked over at the forecourt and spotted Edie, head bent over the bonnet of a truck. She smiled briefly. She did admire her sister; she'd discovered her passion for engines early and followed that path no matter the discrimination she faced for being a woman.

Marianne was stopped again as she wound her way up the road, the castle's ancient grey walls looming over her.

'No further, love. ID, please.'

Marianne dutifully showed her identity card. This time she explained how she needed to see one of the Wrens on an important family matter. The man looked at her suspiciously.

'Could you at least ring through to the Wrens communication room and leave a message for Margaret Atkinson? Tell her Marianne Castle urgently needs to see her on an important family matter.' There were tears in Marianne's eyes, and he relented.

'Oh, all right.' Sighing, the man disappeared into his box, where he relayed the message through his walkie talkie. 'Right, wait there where I can see you.' He pointed to a patch of grass beside the sentry box.

Obediently Marianne stood to the side, watching the activity as trucks came and went, and soldiers marched down from the barracks on their way to the docks. Finally Marge's blue-clad figure appeared, running down towards her, waving. Marianne rushed to greet her, but the sentry stopped her abruptly, thrusting his gun out at waist-height.

'Leave off, Frank.'

'Can't be too careful, Marge.'

Marianne turned to him. 'You know her? But you made out you'd never heard of her.'

'Well, I ain't never heard of a Margaret Atkinson. But if you'd said Marge, I'd 'ave known sooner. Everyone knows Marge.' He winked at Marge, who laughed her throaty laugh.

'Careful, Frank. A girl could get offended.' She took Marianne's hand and led her down the road a little. 'Hey, what's all this about? I thought someone must have died.' She searched her face anxiously. 'From the look of you, maybe someone has.'

'Oh, Marge. Something terrible's happened.' She fished in her pocket and wordlessly handed her the letter from the solicitor.

Marge scanned it quickly, a frown forming between her brows. 'What the hell is this all about? I thought his dad was dead? Who's Henry Fanshawe?'

Marianne hung her head miserably. 'I don't know who he is. He *says* he's Donny's dad, but I only knew that man as Gerald, he didn't give me a surname. And . . . well, Mum was going on and on about making the man marry me. And so . . . I told her a boy forced himself on me and that he was dead. I even gave her a name. I thought she'd throw me out if she knew the truth – that I'd gone and slept with a man I hardly knew, like a common tart . . . And now . . . If this man really is Donny's dad . . . I just don't know. It only happened once and I never saw him again after . . . But . . . Oh God, what if it's true? What if he really is his dad? Maybe he saw him. Don looks so like him that he might have realised . . . Can he really take him away?'

Marge huffed out a breath and read through the letter again. 'As to whether he can take him away . . .' She sighed. 'Mr Wainwright's dealt with a few cases like this, and in almost every one, the judge plumped for the wealthiest parent, considering *that* to be in the child's best interests. And, of course, the mother – and it was *always* the mother – couldn't fight it cos she had no money. But hey, first he's got to prove it. And I can't see how he can do that, unless . . . Donny really does look like him?'

Marianne nodded miserably. 'Spitting image if this man really is him. But it must be. Why else would he be doing this?'

'What do you want me to do?'

'Can you ask Mr Wainwright if he'll help?'

Marge lit a cigarette and thought for a moment. 'All right, I'll telephone Mr W. He's such a love, I'm sure he will. I'll send you a message with a time and date. Or I could run down and give the message to Edie? I'll say it's a meeting with me so she doesn't cotton on to anything.'

Marianne threw her arms around her friend's neck. 'Oh, thank you, thank you!' She burst into tears and Marge put her arm around her, patting her back.

'Hey, it'll be all right. You are *not* going to lose Donny, all right? Not if I have anything to say about it. And I reckon Rodders would help too, if you'd just let him.'

Marianne shook her head. 'No! I can't speak to Rodney about this. He'll never forgive me for lying. You know what he's like.'

'Hmm. You might be surprised. He's a stickler, but he's a loyal stickler. Think about it. He's a good person to have on your side.'

Marianne drew back and looked at her friend in surprise. 'Since when have you had a good word to say about Rodney?'

Marge smiled. 'He's not so bad, really. And he'd do anything for his family.' She threw the cigarette on the ground and looked at her watch. 'Blimey. Better get going or old Molloy will have me on report.' Giving

Marianne a swift kiss, Marge jogged back up to the castle.

'Oy, Marge!' the sentry shouted up to her. 'Fancy a drink sometime?'

Marge turned around, laughing. 'You should be so lucky, Frank!' Then carried on running.

Shaking her head and wishing she had half the confidence her friend did with the opposite sex, Marianne turned and ran down the road, feeling if not relieved, at least reassured that she wasn't on her own.

Chapter 14

Edie was lying under a green army transport truck, trying to tighten some bolts, when she heard a very loud, very posh voice ring out.

'Excuse me! I need some help!'

Assuming Mr Pearson would deal with her, Edie stayed where she was. Soon, though, Mr Pearson's head peered at her under the chassis. 'Umm, Edie. There's a woman wants to speak to you.' He looked uncomfortable and, puzzled, Edie pushed her way out and blinked up at him enquiringly. He gestured weakly towards the forecourt and she turned her head to see who it was.

A beautiful, platinum-haired woman strode over to her, her smart, maroon high-heeled shoes clicking on the concrete. Her hair was perfectly curled and a small dark green hat was perched on the side of her head. Underneath her unbuttoned fur coat, Edie could see a tailored dress in dark green with a slim skirt that reached to mid-calf.

'You!' She pointed down at Edie, who stared at her blankly.

'Stand up, I want to talk to you, you tart!'

Edie blanched and looked over at Mr Pearson, who looked away. Slowly, she rose to her feet.

'I'm sorry, I don't think we've met?'

The woman was standing in front of her, arms crossed, her eyes scathing as she looked Edie up and down. They could not have looked more different, Edie thought self-consciously as she adjusted her headscarf.

'What the hell did my husband see in a dirty little scrubber like you? I mean, look at you!'

Edie was getting more confused by the minute. 'I'm very sorry, but I don't think I know you or your husband.'

'Don't know him? Well, well. Not just a filthy whore but a liar too.'

Edie stepped back in shock. 'I-I-I don't know what you're talking about.'

'And stupid as well! He really is scraping the barrel.'

'I promise you, I don't know who you mean.'

The woman looked over at Mr Pearson, who was shuffling from foot to foot, not sure whether to leave them to it or stay to protect Edie from this mad-woman. 'Does she lie to you too? You should dismiss her immediately. You can't have a nasty, lying, filthy SLUT working for you!' She screamed the last few words directly into Edie's face, so close that flecks of spittle landed on her cheeks. Edie, her mouth hanging open in shock, wiped them away, unaware that her hand left a trail of dirt across her face.

The woman fished in her bag and took out a compact. Opening it, she held the mirror towards Edie. 'Just look at yourself! You disgust me! Sneaking around, sleeping with other women's husbands. Well, I've got news for you, he's already moved on to the next.' She laughed at Edie's shocked expression. 'What? Did you think you were the only one? He's got a string of women around Kent all happy to spread their legs for him.' She put her finger to her chin. 'Let me see … how many have there been now?' Mockingly she held up her hand and started to count on her gloved fingers. 'Oh look! I seem to have run out of fingers. Believe me, there's nothing special about you!'

Edie felt a surge of anger. 'Look, I don't know who you are, and I can promise you I am *not* sleeping with anyone's husband! And if he's cheating, then perhaps you need to take a look at yourself. All the fancy clothes in the world can't hide the fact that you're a nasty cow!' Breathing heavily, she turned away. Lily would have been proud of her. Perhaps she was more like her mother than she realised.

A hand grabbed her shoulder and whirled her around. 'So it wasn't you simpering and giggling upstairs at Elizabeth Crescent?'

Edie paled at her words. 'But …'

'I know very well it was you. Do you know how? I *heard* you. And then I found your filthy overalls at the foot of the stairs.'

Edie's mind went back to the day they'd heard someone in the house.

'My husband's told me all about the woman who fixes his motorbike and suddenly it all made sense.'

Edie's thoughts whirled. There was only one man she knew with a motorbike. 'His motorbike? D-d-do you mean Robert Stafford,' she stammered, desperately hoping there'd been a terrible mistake.

'Oh, is that what he's calling himself these days?' she sneered. 'I can assure you his name is *not* Robert Stafford.'

Over her shoulder, Edie suddenly saw Marianne's face staring at her in puzzlement.

'Edie. What's going on? Who's this?'

She closed her eyes, praying for the ground to open up and swallow her.

The woman whirled around. 'Who the hell are you? Don't tell me you're another one!'

'Another what?'

'Another one of my husband's *women*,' she spat the word out.

Marianne looked over at Edie again. 'Edie?'

It was too much for Edie. The reality of what she'd just learnt, and the fact that she had been so horribly humiliated in front of not just her boss but also

194

her sister, caused her to whirl around and run into the office.

There was a tense, awkward silence, until finally Mr Pearson spoke up. 'I think you'd better leave, madam. You've caused quite enough upset. And kindly tell your husband to take his business elsewhere. Good day to you.'

'You can tell him yourself. I won't be speaking to him any time soon.'

As the woman marched to her car, Marianne watched in bemusement. She shook her head. Surely not. She didn't believe it. She knew Edie had been seeing *someone*, but a married man? There was no way Edie would do that. But then she remembered how easily she had been seduced all those years ago. How could she blame Edie for falling for a man's lies, when she'd done exactly the same?

She could hear her sister's heartbroken sobs coming from the open door of the office. Oh God. Poor Edie.

Marianne walked slowly over to the office. She had no idea how she could possibly make it better for her sister. But she would try. Edie was always so hard on herself that even being told off by her mother for a minor transgression used to send her into a deep depression. But this? She knew Edie would blame herself.

Stopping by the door, Marianne took a deep breath, trying to compose herself, then walked in. Edie was standing hunched over the desk, her shoulders shaking.

Marianne grasped her arms and pulled her around into a hug. Her sister was nearly a head taller than her, but she didn't resist and dropped her head on to Marianne's shoulder and wept as she had when she was a confused little girl who'd just lost her father.

Mr Pearson hovered in the doorway uncertainly. When Marianne raised her eyes to his, he gave her an enquiring look and she shook her head. He got the message and disappeared to the tiny kitchen, and soon Marianne heard the welcome sounds of tea being made.

'Hey, Edie. Look at me,' she said gently after a while.

Edie shook her head.

'Ah, love. Whatever's happened, you know I'll never think badly of you. Come on, look at me.' She pushed Edie back and took hold of her shoulders. Edie refused to meet her eyes, instead rubbing the tears away with the palms of her hands, smearing more grease across her face in the process.

'Oh, sweetheart. Come on. Tell me what's happened. Is this about the man you were seeing?'

Edie nodded miserably. 'I didn't know. I promise I didn't know. I would never . . .'

'I know you wouldn't, love. He deceived you and it's not your fault.'

'I should have realised. Mr Pearson warned me. But he never said he was married. It was a lie . . . It was all a lie, and I thought . . . I thought . . .' She dissolved into tears again and Marianne led her to one of the two chairs by the wall and sat down beside her.

'Listen to me, Edie. None of this is your fault. It's *his*. God, if I could get my hands on him! And how *dare* that woman come here and insult you. If anyone knows what her husband's like it's her! How could she take it out on you?'

Mr Pearson came through then with a tray and three mugs of tea. He handed one to Marianne, then tried to give one to Edie, who refused to look at him.

'Come on, Edie. I put plenty of sugar in. You need this, love.'

'Do you want me to leave?' she asked in a small voice.

'Leave?' He gave a short burst of laughter. 'And how would I manage without you? Look around you. The forecourt's packed and you an' me are the only people working. You're staying put if I have to lock you in.'

She looked up at him then and took his hand. 'Oh, thank you. And I'm sorry. I should have listened to you.'

Mr Pearson squeezed her hand. 'Well, I wish I could say I've not made mistakes in my life, but then I wouldn't be human. Now, come on, drink your tea, then I need you back out there.' He looked over at Marianne. 'I'll leave you to it, then. Ten minutes is all you're getting, mind. Then I'll be back in here to drag her back to work.'

The sisters sat in silence after he'd left, drinking their tea. Finally, Edie spoke. 'I feel like such a fool. How could I have been taken in? Maybe deep down I knew he wasn't right, that's why I didn't want you to know about him.'

'It's not your fault, Edie. If anyone knows about making mistakes, it's me. And yours isn't so bad, really, provided there's not likely to be any consequences . . . ?'

She left the question hanging, but Edie knew what she was asking.

'No. It's all right. He was careful.' She blushed.

Marianne knew from experience that that didn't always mean anything, but the last thing she wanted to do was worry Edie, so she just nodded.

'Good. But if you feel strange or unwell, come and talk to me.'

Edie gave a short laugh. 'And what will you do about it? Look, I'm not pregnant, all right?'

'Fine.' Marianne finished her tea and stood up. 'I need to get back.' Looking down at her sister's bent head, her heart contracted. 'Don't blame yourself. Men like that are clever. You won't be the only one he's deceived.'

'And that's meant to make me feel better? Well, it doesn't. If anything, it makes me feel worse.' Suddenly Edie looked at her sharply. 'What the hell are you doing up here anyway? You never leave the café!'

Marianne looked away. 'Oh, Marge left her lipstick in the flat on Saturday, and you know Marge . . . Can't live without it.' She laughed unconvincingly.

'You could have waited and I'd have brought it tomorrow.'

'I needed some air,' she said evasively. 'Anyway, never mind that, I'm more worried about you.'

'Well, don't be. I've been through worse. We all have.' Edie scrubbed at her eyes and stood up, squaring her shoulders. 'And if I want to keep this job, then I'd better get to it.'

Marianne sighed. There was nothing she could say that would make her sister feel better. Time was the only thing that would help, and even then there was no guarantee. Not with Edie, who always brooded over everything.

'I'll see you later, all right?'

Edie nodded, but as Marianne reached the door, she called out, 'Marianne! Don't tell anyone about this, will you? Not Lily and especially not Mum.'

'Don't worry. I won't breathe a word. But I'm always here if you need me, Edie. You know that, don't you?'

Edie gave her a weak smile. 'I'll be all right. Don't worry about me.'

Marianne nodded briefly and left, but as she made her way back down towards the town, her mind was in turmoil. For a while, her sister's problems had pushed her own worries aside. But now they all came rushing back. Edie wasn't the only one who needed to keep secrets; somehow she was going to have to keep behaving as if nothing had happened, because the last thing she needed was her mother asking questions.

$$\infty$$

Nellie slammed down her knife and fork and looked around the small table in the living room. The meal had passed mostly in silence, the only noise being the sound of the wireless burbling quietly in the corner. Lily had gulped down her food, then excused herself to go upstairs to do her homework, while Donny had shovelled his food down in two minutes flat and was now sitting staring hungrily at his mother's plate. Nellie looked at her two daughters. Marianne was pale as a ghost while Edie's eyes were red and swollen; she'd clearly been crying.

'Are you two going to tell me what's going on? You disappear for hours, Marianne, leaving me in the lurch today, while you' – she pointed her knife at Edie – 'have been sitting there with a face like a slapped arse. So, come on, spit it out.'

Nellie saw Marianne shoot a swift glance in Edie's direction, but Edie ignored her. *Something* was definitely up between these two, and she intended to get to the bottom of it.

'Well? You haven't touched your food, and if there's one thing I can't abide it's waste. Food'll be scarce enough once rationing comes in.'

'I'll eat it if they don't want it,' Donny said eagerly.

200

'May as well, Don. Way those two are poking and prodding at it anyone would think it's poisoned.' She passed Marianne's plate of cold meat and bubble and squeak made with the leftovers from lunch the day before to Donny and he tipped the food on to his plate.

'I'm just feeling a bit tired, is all,' Marianne said weakly. 'And I'm worried about the boys.'

'Tired? Is that what you call it these days? You must take me for a fool. No, you girls are hiding something, and I want to know what it is. Well?' She glared at Edie.

Edie refused to meet her eyes and instead pushed her chair back and stood up. 'Just leave it, will you, Mum.'

Nellie stared at her daughter's swollen eyes. Edie had always been the most emotional of her children, and the most difficult to read. But unless she was very much mistaken, that was the face of a girl who'd just had her heart broken.

'Has this got anything to do with that man you've been mooning over? The one you think I don't know about.'

At Edie's startled expression, Nellie huffed. 'Like I thought. It's always a man.' She paused then. 'You're not bloody pregnant are you?'

'Mum!' Edie glanced at Donny, whose cheeks were bulging as he chewed his food, listening intently to this fascinating adult conversation.

'Well?'

'No, I'm not pregnant! I'm not stupid.' She shot a look at Marianne and grimaced. 'Sorry.'

Marianne gave her a small smile and shrugged.

'So he's dropped you, has he? Perhaps if you'd introduced him to your family then he'd have taken you a bit more seriously.'

'If he'd met you, he'd probably have run off sooner.' Edie threw her napkin on the table. 'And that's what I'm going to do. I need my privacy, so I'm moving out.'

Nellie stared at her daughter with her mouth open. 'Moving out? Where to?'

'To the garage. The flat above it has two bedrooms and as Mr P. needs me seven days a week at the moment. It'll be easier all round if I just stay there.'

'You will do no such thing! Living with an unmarried man, indeed. It'd be different if his wife was still alive. But she's not. So, you are staying here. I won't have people whispering about my daughter.'

'Really, Mum? It wouldn't be the first time, would it?'

'Exactly. And I won't have it again. We've had enough scandal in this family, and what with the war, I want you where I know you're safe.'

'Don't you think she's old enough to decide for herself, Mum?' Marianne stepped in to back her sister up. She understood perfectly why Edie felt she needed to go.

'She's nineteen years old! And until she's twenty-one or married, my word is final. She stays.'

'No, Mum. You can't make me stay, and *my* decision is final. I'm packing my bag and I'll leave in the morning. I'm sorry.' With that, Edie turned and left the room, running up the stairs and slamming the door of her bedroom.

'But why does Auntie Edie have to go?' Donny piped up. 'I hate this war! There's hardly anyone left as most of my friends have gone to Wales ...' Donny's lip trembled.

'Would you like to go to Wales, Don?' A thought had suddenly occurred to Marianne. Much as she hated the idea, if he left Dover, then that man couldn't take him away from her.

'NO! I *told* you, Mum. If you make me go, then I'll just run away.'

'If your mum says you have to go, then I'm afraid you'll have to go, Don. But not yet.' Nellie patted his hand reassuringly. 'Your mum will only send you away if there's real danger for you here.'

'NO! I'm *not going*!'

Marianne put her hand to her head. She couldn't take much more today. 'Donny, I promise not to send you away unless there's a very good reason to. How about that?'

'Not even then, Mum. Unless you come too.'

'We'll see.'

The chimes of Big Ben rang out for the seven o'clock news and Nellie hushed her family. The news was sacrosanct, and no matter what was being discussed, it was put on hold until the broadcast was finished. Even a momentous announcement like the one Edie had just made would have to wait.

Nellie nodded in approval on hearing that Canada had declared war on Germany, but then the newsreader reported that Warsaw was surrounded by the Nazis with little hope of driving them away. She shook her head. It could so easily happen here; if the Nazis managed to defeat France it would leave just a small body of water between them and her family. And with her children spread out around the country, how could she keep them all safe?

'Did you hear that, Donny? Those poor people in Poland don't stand a chance. And if there ever comes a time when the Nazis are on our doorstep, then you'll have no choice. I will drag you to Wales myself if it means keeping you safe, do you hear me?'

Donny nodded reluctantly, but then he grinned. 'But no way will that happen, Gran. Not with *our* soldiers, so I don't think you should worry.'

'That's what we all—'

'Mum!' Marianne interrupted her sharply. She didn't need Donny being frightened by stories of what happened in the previous war again. There were enough threats to their safety without imagining more. But the threat wasn't just from the Nazis. It was from someone who even now was plotting to take Donny away from her.

Chapter 15

November roared in with storms and rain, and everyone's mood became fractious. Though for most of the country, the war had barely made an impact, in Dover it was very different. Explosions in the Channel were commonplace as ships were blown up by either mines or German submarines and the activity above the town was becoming more intense as the RAF endeavoured to keep the navy safe at sea.

One morning, during breakfast, Donny came rattling down the stairs, his schoolbag on his back.

'Hurry up, love. You'll be late. And don't forget, I want you to come home the minute school is finished. Do you hear me?'

'Why do I have to keep coming home so early, Mum?'

'Just do as I say.' Marianne turned back to the stove and flipped an egg with a practiced hand.

Ever since the harrowing week in September after war was declared, Marianne had been on tenterhooks. Marge had been as good as her word and arranged for her to see Mr Wainwright soon after they'd spoken.

He'd been kind and reassuring, and had written a letter to Henry Fanshawe's solicitor demanding proof of paternity, but they'd not heard a word since. Sometimes Marianne wondered if she'd dreamt the whole thing, but then she'd take out the letter and a shiver of fear would run through her. It had been nearly two months now, so why hadn't he replied? Maybe he'd decided not to bother after all, she thought hopefully. But in her heart she knew it was unlikely. Why would he go to all that trouble to begin with if he didn't intend to follow through with his threat? It felt, sometimes, as if he were playing with her.

Lily came down the stairs then, her dark blue woollen coat buttoned up. 'Ready, Don? Let's go!'

Donny followed her through to the café, where Freddie was stuffing a currant bun into his mouth while he waited for his friend.

'Bye, Gran,' Don said as he trailed after the other two.

'See you, poppet. Have a good day.'

He didn't reply, and Nellie shook her head and looked at Jasper, who was eating breakfast at his usual table. 'I don't know what's up with everyone lately. Even Donny's miserable. Edie's not visited since she left and Marianne's jumpy as a cat on a hot tin roof.'

'War, Nell. That's what's up with everyone. It might seem like nothing's happening, but us Dovorians know better. And don't forget, it was only the other night that Don saw that ship blow up. That shook him really bad.'

Nellie sighed. 'Poor lad was in a right state. I'm starting to think he should be sent off. It's not right for him to see all that.' She turned her head. 'What do you think, Marianne?'

Marianne, who was putting some plates on the hatch, looked up, not having heard a word of the conversation. 'What?'

'Ach, never mind. We'll talk later.' Nellie turned to a soldier who was standing patiently at the counter. 'Bacon sarnies, is it? Coming right up!'

⁂

Henry parked by the covered market, his eyes on the café door. The windows were steamed up so he couldn't see inside, but he watched as a steady stream of people came and went, some clutching paper-wrapped sandwiches, while others stayed inside for longer. They were clearly doing a roaring trade, he thought resentfully, while he was struggling to make ends meet, what with the IOU that was being called in, his wife wanting a divorce and both his houses mortgaged to the hilt and requisitioned by the army so he couldn't even sell them.

He'd never had to worry about money before. Fanshawes was the largest brewery in Kent and his family was worth a fortune. But his father had stopped paying the generous allowance Henry relied on to fund his lavish lifestyle when Elspeth had miscarried in August – as if it was his fault she'd got drunk and fallen down the stairs! But worse, much worse, was the fact that his dad had cut him out of his will as well – punishment for his debauched lifestyle, apparently. He knew his brother Rupert was behind this; his dad had always been a soft touch. Which is why he hadn't shut the door entirely and had left half of the business in trust to any son Henry might have. But with Elspeth being told she couldn't have any more children, his only hope of getting anything now rested with this guttersnipe of a boy. It had been a stroke of good fortune that he'd chanced upon him, and that the boy was the spit of him. At the time he hadn't realised just how lucky, of course. Not until Elspeth lost their baby and his dad changed his will.

That's when the game got serious and he'd resorted to legal action. He'd thought everything would have been sorted by now. How was he to know the little cook wouldn't be as easily intimidated as he'd assumed. From his vague memories of her, she'd been a timid little thing. Boring too, but it had passed a couple of afternoons. But since the initial letter he hadn't been able to pay the lawyers to continue working for him, so he was left with only one option. He needed to charm his way into the boy's affections and convince him that he'd have a much better life with him. Shouldn't be too hard, he thought dismissively, staring at the café. What boy could refuse the chance to live in an enormous house and be given anything he could ever wish for? But if that didn't work . . .

Well, it had to. He'd run out of time. If only he hadn't decided to go on that hunting trip to Scotland with his friends. He'd not only have done something about this problem sooner, he'd be a sight better off as well – gambling with his rich friends was never a good idea and he'd robbed Peter to pay Paul. And now there were some very unpleasant people demanding repayment, so he needed to disappear and let things calm down for a bit. But he wasn't leaving without sending a message to the cook. She needed to know that he wasn't giving up, and what's more, he'd enjoy seeing her squirm.

A little after eight, the boy and his friend came outside, accompanied by the beautiful blonde girl he'd seen the last time he'd visited. The girl paused and said goodbye, before walking down Castle Street, while the boys turned right and scampered the other way, their gas masks bouncing on their backs.

Henry watched them for a moment, then refocused on the café. He needed the place to be quieter before he went over there. He sat down on the steps and lit a cigarette, oblivious to the cold.

An hour later, he crossed the square, opened the backyard gate and slipped inside. A window looked into the scullery where a woman wearing a flowered headscarf and bright red apron was washing dishes. Luckily her head was bent over her task, so she didn't spot him, and he ducked down as he moved to the door. It opened easily, and he peered in, inhaling the smell of frying bacon, sausages and eggs. A short corridor had three doors leading off it. To his left was the scullery, next to which was another door – to the basement, he presumed – and through the open door on the right he could see floor-to-ceiling shelves crowded with butter, packets of flour and sugar. Several loaves of bread wrapped in white paper sat on the lowest shelf. Beyond the larder, the short corridor opened up into the kitchen, and at the large range against the left-hand wall stood the boy's mother.

He stared at her back with curiosity and some anger. What had he ever seen in a little frump like her? he wondered. And how dare she demand proof of paternity? If she'd just capitulated as he'd expected, this would all be sorted now and he'd be living his old comfortable life, with his son safely installed and the promise of getting a share of Fanshawes as soon as his old dad dropped off his perch. Which, judging by the state of him, wouldn't be long. He felt a surge of anger towards the woman. Well, she'd get her just deserts soon, but in the meantime, he was going to leave her in no doubt about what he wanted.

The woman with the headscarf came out of the scullery. 'Right, that lot's done.' She took her apron off. 'I'm off up the butcher for some mince. What else do we need?'

The woman at the stove fished in her pocket and handed her a note, mumbling something he didn't hear.

Henry ducked back out onto the street, carefully closing the gate behind him. Finally, the older woman, wearing a mauve coat and a yellow felt hat, came out carrying a string bag, her gas mask slung across her shoulder and a large black bag hanging from the crook of her arm. As she disappeared around the corner, he went back in and peeked through the scullery window. His grey eyes met the shocked hazel gaze of the boy's mother.

Chapter 16

A cake tin under her arm, Lily puffed up Castle Hill, pausing to catch her breath as she reached the garage.

'Morning, Tom. How's tricks?' she asked the soldier standing sentry.

'All right, Lily.' The man gave her a cheeky grin and a salute. She'd been up here so often over the last few weeks she no longer had to show her identity card.

As she approached the garage, she could see her sister was hard at work already, holding a spanner down to a hand poking out from under the chassis of a truck.

'Edie!' she called. 'Any chance of a cup of tea?' She came over and peered inside the open bonnet.

'Oh, hello, Lil. Give me a mo.'

Five minutes later, Lily followed her sister into the office. 'I don't know how you know one bit of an engine from the other.'

'And I don't know why you want to be a nurse.' She shuddered. 'All that blood.'

Lily put the tin she'd been carrying on the table. 'Fruit cake. Marianne baked it first thing.'

'How is everyone?'

Lily paused for a moment. 'You know, ever since that day you decided to leave home, something's been up with Marianne, but she won't talk to me or Mum. She's jumpy, nervous and she's lost weight. In fact, you don't look any better. What's going on?'

Edie looked away evasively.

'For goodness' sake, Edie! I've been coming up here for weeks to make sure you're all right. "Give her time," I thought. "She'll come round." But not a word. You don't even visit. Don't you think we deserve an explanation? And what has all this got to do with Marianne?'

Edie's eyes filled with tears. 'I think she hates me,' she whispered.

'Course she doesn't. She's visited loads.'

'Only with you. Never on her own. You know what she's like. She always has to do the right thing, so she comes because she feels she should.' Edie suddenly burst into tears. 'I feel so ashamed.'

Alarmed, Lily put her arm around Edie's shoulder. 'Why?'

Edie just shook her head and squeezed her eyes tight shut.

Lily slammed her hand on the desk. 'Right! That's it! Either you tell me what's going on or I stop coming. I've had enough of you two going around with faces like wet weekends.' She walked towards the door, then turned. 'Well?'

Edie sighed and nodded. 'All right, I suppose you deserve an explanation, but don't tell Mum. And promise you won't hate me.'

'I could never hate you, you daft ha'p'orth. You're my bleeding sister.'

Before she said any more, Edie went into the kitchen to make tea, then the sisters sat at the desk and, between sobs, Edie told her about Robert.

By the end, Lily's mouth was hanging open. 'You were' – she flapped her hand expressively – 'with a married man?! And his wife found out?! Hells bells and buckets of gore!' She sat back in the seat with a huff. 'What a dirty, yellow-bellied rat!'

Edie stared at her for a moment, then suddenly she started to laugh. 'Yellow-bellied rat?' She giggled some more. 'Where did you hear that?'

Lily shrugged sheepishly. 'James Cagney in *Taxi!* I've always wanted to have a reason to say it.' She started to laugh as well but stopped abruptly as the door between the office and the garage thumped open. Looking up, Lily was surprised to see a young, brown-haired man in overalls standing in the doorway, his cold gaze fixed on her sister.

'Did I just hear that right?'

Edie paled, staring at the man in shock.

'And you're laughing?' he said with disbelief.

Lily jumped up. 'Hang on a minute! I bet you're not such a bloody saint yourself, so don't go around judging others!'

'Leave it, Lil.' Edie stood up and walked towards the man. 'And you should mind your own business,' she hissed, before shoving him aside and slamming out of the door.

'Who the hell are you?' The man glared at Lily.

'Her sister.' She folded her arms across her chest. 'Who the hell are *you*?'

'I'm Bill. Not that it's any of *your* business.'

'Oh, so you're the famous Bill,' Lily said sneeringly.

'What's that supposed to mean?'

'I always thought *you* were her secret boyfriend.' She looked him up and down. In his blue overalls with his brown hair falling over his face, he really was quite handsome, but his holier-than-thou attitude infuriated Lily. 'But now I can see why she always insisted you weren't.'

Bill stared at her wordlessly for a moment, shook his head and followed Edie outside.

Sighing, Lily picked up the empty cake tin and stuffed it back in her bag. Who'd have thought her sister would get caught up with a married man? What with Marianne and her shady past, and Edie up to all sorts, her reputation as the rebellious sister was seriously under threat.

Suddenly she became aware of shouting outside. If that man was giving Edie a hard time, she'd have something to say about it.

She threw open the door to see Edie and Bill both staring up at the sky, their mouths hanging open. She followed their gaze and her heart started beating faster as she saw a Spitfire, smoke pouring out of it, flying towards them. It was making a loud stuttering noise, as though the pilot was desperately trying to restart the engine, and it was flying so low, it was skimming over the trees. Loud yells from the castle made her whip her head around to see the sentries running down the hill towards them, waving their arms.

'It's going to come down on the garage! Run!'

Their words jolted Lily into action and she leapt at the other two. 'Come on! We've got to get out of here!'

Bill snapped to attention, and catching both their arms, he pulled them down on to the concrete.

'Keep your heads down!' he yelled over the noise. Then he stood up and stared at the approaching craft, shouting, 'Keep the nose up, man. Come on, nose up!' As if the pilot could hear a word he said.

It felt like the plane was just above them now, and Lily didn't dare look, terrified she would see the its nose diving straight towards them. She crawled over to her sister and put her arm around her.

'I'm scared,' she whispered.

Edie pulled her in tight. 'Me too.' But Lily could barely hear her over the noise as the plane whined ever closer.

Chapter 17

Marianne froze and the colour drained from her face as she stared at the man looking in through the window, his wheat-gold hair flopping over his forehead, his grey eyes mocking. No! It couldn't be! On some level she'd half expected him to come, but as the weeks had passed and she'd heard no more from him or his lawyer, she'd prayed that he'd given up. But now here he was . . . For a moment she stood stock-still, shock coursing through her, her stomach in knots. But then suddenly she was furious! He was as handsome as she remembered, but that no longer impressed her, and she'd be damned if she'd let him come in here and intimidate her. It felt as if a valve had been released and all the pent-up tension of the last few weeks came rushing out. She flew out of the scullery, hands dripping soap suds, and rushed into the yard.

The man stood with his hands in his pockets, a wide grin on his beautiful face. 'Hello, darling. Long time, no see.'

'Get out now!' she said in a low, dangerous voice.

'But, darling, I just came to see my boy. Is that too much to ask? The bond between father and son is sacrosanct.' He shook his head at her. 'It was very wrong of you to keep him from me.'

'How could I have told you? Far as I was concerned you were called *Gerald*! Then suddenly you turn up here, write me notes and then threaten to take my son away! Why didn't you just try to talk to me?'

'What would have been the fun in that?' He smirked. 'Anyway, I thought you might not be . . . receptive. After all, as you say, I did rather disappear from your life. And perhaps I wasn't entirely truthful. But now I know about him, I just want to see my boy, darling. Surely you can understand that.' He looked around the yard. 'I don't suppose your sister's here?' He grinned at her.

'My sister? What do you mean?'

'Although, having caught sight of the youngest one, perhaps I should try for a hat trick.'

Marianne stared at him, bemused, trying to make sense of what he was saying.

'Imagine my surprise,' he drawled, 'when I saw my sweet little mechanic running around the market square with a boy who looked exactly like me. The hair fooled me for a moment, but when he came up to me and I saw his eyes, you could have knocked me down with a feather.' He tsked. 'You really should have told me, you know.'

Marianne frowned. Was he saying . . . ? Suddenly the penny dropped.

'It was you? *You're* the married man Edie's been seeing?'

Oh God! Edie would be even more devastated if she ever learnt that the man she'd fallen for was not only married, but also Donny's father! She shook her head as she tried to digest this information. How much damage could one man wreak in a family?

He held his hand up. 'Guilty as charged.' He sniggered. 'I gather my wife has made her displeasure known, which has rather put the kibosh on my entertaining game. I must admit, I hadn't intended for my little affair with Edie to go on longer than the first time. But then, well, when I discovered that she was *your* sister and my boy's aunt, I found it all rather titillating. I ask myself whether I would have continued if it was you.' He looked her up and down disparagingly. 'Probably not,' he said with a sneer.

Marianne felt herself shrivel a little inside, but she fought down the lump that had risen in her throat. She would *not* let this man affect her. Not when he'd broken not just her own heart but her sister's too. And it would be over her dead body that she allowed him to have anything to do with Donny.

'I'm sorry.' He smiled at her. 'That was uncalled for and not true. As I recall, you were utterly charming. Didn't you bake me the most delicious cake?'

Marianne narrowed her eyes at him.

'Yes, you did. It was an absolute marvel.'

'I'm glad your mother liked it.'

'Mother? It wasn't for my mother. She'd been dead for years at that stage. No, it was for my fiancée's birthday.' He grinned at her.

Marianne swallowed back her reaction. He was engaged to another woman while she'd been starry-eyed, believing she'd found the love of her life. Even after eleven years, that hurt. It had nothing to do with wanting him, though. No, it was because she had never forgotten how, for those few short days, she'd felt special, as if she really mattered. She hadn't expected to feel like that again, but at least she'd felt it once. But now he'd taken even that from her. He'd barely spared her a thought, whereas she'd spent years nursing the futile dream that one day he'd walk back into the café, sweep her into his arms and tell her he had never stopped thinking about her.

But she still couldn't understand why he'd behaved as he had. 'So why all the shady behaviour? It was you, wasn't it, who sent the note and the roses? Why?'

'I'm sorry about all the silly games.' He smiled at her ingratiatingly. 'I don't know . . . It was just such a deliciously naughty situation that I couldn't help myself. I see now that I was very, very wrong.' He gave her a regretful look from beneath his lashes. 'All I want now is to talk to my son just once before

I go off and fight. Just in case . . .' He shrugged and looked away.

She raised her eyebrows at him. 'You've joined up?'

'I leave tomorrow, so this might be the only chance I have.'

Marianne stared at him for a very long time. He looked so sincere and his grey eyes – so like Donny's – were soft and pleading. He really thought she'd let him anywhere near her son? Risking not only his heart, but also putting Edie in an even more awful position. And after everything he'd just said! Her breathing went shallow, her heart started pumping faster, and she could feel a flush of heat rising up her neck as a picture of her sister's distraught face and Henry's wife's furious one flashed into her head. How dare he think she was so stupid that just one smile from him would make her do anything he wanted. She would never, ever let this man near her son. He'd lied and cheated and hurt her and two other women – and those were just the ones she knew about. He was a compulsive liar who seemed to relish causing turmoil.

Mistaking her silence for acquiescence, Henry held his hand out to her as his smile broadened. 'I knew you'd—'

Marianne let out a shout of anger and smacked his hand away, putting her hands on his chest and shoving him towards the gate with all the strength she could muster. 'You must think I'm still the same naïve fool I was all those years ago.'

He stumbled back, shocked.

'Well, I'm not,' she continued, fury, outrage and hurt warring within her. 'You're nothing but a nasty, dirty, lying toe-rag. I was *sixteen*! You took advantage of me; you *lied* to me, and you left me to face the consequences. And you broke my sister's heart as well as your wife's. Do you really think I'd let you anywhere near *my* son?!' She laughed bitterly. 'You're not fit to lick his boots. So get out. Before I call the policeman who's sitting just inside to come and arrest you for harassment.' She shoved him harder and he stumbled out of the gate.

Recovering himself, Henry grabbed Marianne hard by the upper arms and shook her. 'Listen . . .' He paused. 'Whatever your name is. You have no idea how much money my family has. If I decide I want my son, then I will get him. And there's nothing you can do about it.'

She laughed humourlessly. 'You don't even remember my name, do you? You got me pregnant then just forgot all about me. Well, no amount of money in the world is enough to part me from my child. So get out of my sight! If you come near me again, or go within a mile of Donny, I'll have you arrested.'

They were so intent on their argument that they didn't notice the plane stuttering overhead, nor the tall, rotund figure wearing a blue uniform who ran up to them, put his arm around the man's neck and pulled him away.

'You need me to take him to the police, Marianne?' Jasper said, keeping his arm around the younger man's throat. 'It'd be my pleasure.'

Marianne shook her head, immediately conscious that if Jasper found out who this was, he would be bound to tell her mother. 'Thanks, Jasper, but he was just leaving. Weren't you?'

'You sure? Because from where I was standing it looked very like he was about to do you harm. A woman half your size an' all.' He tightened his grip and gave the man a violent shake before releasing him and shoving him away. 'You'd better go then, *mate*. And don't let me catch you hanging around here again!'

'All right, all right. I'm going,' Henry choked out, stumbling towards the square.

'And if I ever see you around here again, you won't be getting off so lightly,' Jasper boomed threateningly.

Henry stared hard at Marianne. 'You haven't heard the last of this.' His eyes were as cold and threatening as the sea on a stormy winter's day. 'I will be back.'

Marianne shuddered at the malice in his expression and wrapped her arms around herself as she watched him stride across the square. Jasper put his arm around her and she leant against him gratefully as her legs started to shake. They stood in silence until Henry had rounded the corner, then Jasper cleared his throat uncomfortably.

'Who the hell was that? And what's he got to do with your Don?'

Marianne shook her head. 'He's got *nothing* to do with my Don.'

'Has Don said something to you about him? Is he one of them perverts?'

Marianne hesitated. She wanted to say yes, but the lies were adding up and she couldn't do that. Not even to Henry. Because no matter how much she wished it wasn't so, he was Donny's father.

Finally, she shook her head. 'No.'

'You're sure, love? If he's one of them, you say the word and I'll get a mob together soon enough. We don't want those types around here.'

'No. Honestly, Jasper, it's not that.'

'What then, love? I can see he's upset you.'

She owed him some sort of explanation, so she gave him the only one she could. 'That's the man who broke Edie's heart.'

'What? Him? What's she doing with a posh prat like that?' He shook his head. 'If I'd known I'd have given him the hiding he deserves.'

Nellie came around the corner then and jumped at the sight of them.

'What's going on here?'

Marianne sent Jasper a pleading look and he gave a faint wink.

'Nothing, Nell. Just thought I'd pop in for a quick chat.'

Nellie eyed him suspiciously. 'In the yard? And what are you doing out here, Marianne?'

'She was watchin' that plane.' He looked up at the trail of smoke in the sky. Suddenly there was a loud boom from the direction of the castle and they all jumped.

'Gordon Bennett!' Jasper exclaimed. 'Don't say it's crashed into the castle!'

Nellie had gone pale. 'Or the garage,' she whispered. 'Oh God! Not the garage!' She dropped her bags and started to run up the hill, followed closely by Jasper.

Marianne followed but Nellie turned to her. 'Go back and take care of the café! There's no point all of us going!'

Marianne saw the sense in this, but her heart was in her mouth as she watched her mother lumbering awkwardly away. Please God let nothing have happened to her sisters.

Chapter 18

Lily felt Bill's body drop on top of them just as a loud boom made the ground shake. Hot air swept over them and Lily opened her eyes and tried to lift her head to see what was happening.

'Keep your head down,' Bill growled out before starting to cough.

Beside her she could feel Edie shaking as she choked. Lily held her breath and tried to rise up again.

'I said keep down!'

'I want to see if anyone's hurt!' she screamed.

With an effort she managed to roll from beneath Bill, and pulling her coat over her nose she looked up at the garage. The chimney had been torn off, and bricks and roof tiles were scattered over the forecourt, but somehow the pilot had managed to get enough elevation to avoid crashing straight into the building. Behind the garage, a large plume of black smoke was rising into the air. She started to run towards it, joining the soldiers who had already made it to the waist-high wire fence that bordered the field.

Bill skidded to a halt next to her, choking and cursing as he looked at the fallen plane.

'Keep back!' one of the soldiers shouted.

Lily didn't listen. She was desperate to see if she could help the pilot, she might not be a nurse yet, but she'd learned a lot about first aid by volunteering at the hospital. The nose of the plane was smouldering, but the engine hadn't exploded yet, so they might be able to get him out. She scrambled over the wire fence, tearing her skirt as she came down on the other side. Beside her Bill helped her up and they ran towards the plane.

They had made it to within a couple of hundred yards when they were driven back by another whoosh of hot air, as the engine exploded. Bill and Lily were thrown to the ground, and they lay for a moment panting, arms over their heads.

Risking a peep into the smoke, Lily let out a sob. 'He'd never have survived that!'

Beside her Bill whispered, 'That's Pete's plane. I was working on it just the other day. I told them it wasn't ready before I left to come here. Why was he even flying it?'

Lily looked over to him and all her earlier anger disappeared as she saw the look of total devastation on his face. There was nothing she could say, so she put her arm around him and together they watched as the plane was devoured by the flames, leaving the wings and tail incongruously intact, as though once the fire was out, it would be taking off again.

Tears were streaming down Bill's face, but she wasn't sure whether it was the smoke or grief. 'It's not your fault, Bill.'

'And how would you know that? It's *my* responsibility to make sure the planes are safe. *Mine!* So, who else would you blame, eh?' He glared at her angrily.

'But you told them, Bill. This is *not* your fault.'

He shook his head and stood up, then held his hand down to help Lily to her feet. They staggered back to the fence where the soldiers were standing silently, their caps held over their chests. Beside them, Edie was watching, her green eyes wide, her face smudged with soot.

One of the soldiers shook his head. 'That pilot had some skill, eh? I don't know how he managed to miss the garage. I was sure he'd smash straight into it. You could all have been killed. He saved your lives.'

Bill nodded. 'Pete was one of the best,' he murmured. 'I need to get back to Hawkinge. Do you reckon one of your lot could take me?'

'Edie!'

Lily turned her head to see Rodney running towards them. He looked frantic. Just behind him was Marge, running as though her life depended on it.

Rodney skidded to a stop in front of Edie and pulled her into his arms. 'Thank God!'

He looked over at Lily and held an arm out to her too. 'And you're here!' He swallowed and pulled her in tight to his side. 'Jesus! When I heard a plane had crashed into the garage, I thought . . .' He closed his eyes.

Marge came up then and put her arms around all of them. She was panting and coughing from her unaccustomed run. 'Oh my God! Never bloody make me that scared again!'

Lily gave a slight laugh, relishing the feel of her brother's arms around her. She ribbed him mercilessly for being pompous, but Rodney always managed to make her feel safe. 'It was hardly our fault, Marge.'

Marge half laughed, half cried. 'Poor Rodders nearly had a heart attack when he heard. It just so happened we were on a break in the canteen together, so here we are.'

'Well, as you can see, we're all right.' Edie looked sadly over at the smoking plane. 'I wish we could say the same for the pilot.'

They stood silently for a moment, contemplating the burning wreckage. They were interrupted by Bill, who cleared his throat.

'I need to get to Hawkinge. Tell Uncle Sid I'm sorry I had to leave.' He looked at the damage to the garage and shook his head. 'Of all days to have to go to the dentist . . .'

Rodney pulled away from his sisters. 'I've got to get back. Come with me,' he said to Bill. 'I'll find someone to take you. And you two,' he said, looking at Lily and Edie sternly. 'For God's sake stay out of trouble.' With a last hug, he walked away with Bill.

Marge stepped back from the girls too, wiping her eyes. 'I'd better go as well.' She gave each of them a kiss before, with a wave at the two soldiers, she made her way slowly back up the hill.

In the distance they could hear the frantic ringing of a fire engine, and soon a swarm of men had cut down the fence and started to hose down the plane.

Lily took Edie's arm. 'Come on, sis. There's nothing more we can do here.'

Wordlessly, Edie allowed Lily to lead her back to the office, where she slumped down on a chair and put her head in her hands, her shoulders shaking with sobs.

Lily sat beside her. 'This makes it all seem so real, doesn't it?'

Edie nodded. 'How many more will die like that? Burnt to a crisp in a plane? Oh, the poor man! It makes everything else seem so ... insignificant.' She sniffed and wiped her nose with her sleeve.

Lily got up and went to the kitchen, where she made some more tea, spooning plenty of sugar into the milky brew, though her hands were shaking so much the countertop was covered in milk and sugar by the time she'd finished.

Bringing the tea back, she handed one of the tin mugs to Edie and they sat in silence for a while, listening to the shouts of the firemen and the hiss of the water as it hit the flames.

Suddenly, Edie said, 'Nothing matters anymore . . . Robert, his wife . . . I don't even care that Bill hates me.'

Lily sighed with annoyance; she'd had more than enough of her sister's self-pity. 'He doesn't hate you, Edie. No one does. You've got to stop thinking everything's about you. Mum misses you, Marianne misses you, Donny misses you. And *I* miss you. Can you please stop sulking and at least come and visit? Look what's just happened! None of us know what's around the corner, so you've got to stop being so selfish and try to appreciate what you've got. Us. Your family. Mum. We're not perfect but we're here and we love you. Any one of us could be killed at any moment. What if a bomb drops on the café? We'd all be gone and you'd forever regret the fact that you didn't see us more.'

Edie looked at her sister in disbelief. 'Selfish? Me? Coming from you, that's rich!'

Lily was too tired and too shocked to argue. She held up her hands. 'Suit yourself. But don't come running to me when you find you've got no family left!' She stood up with a huff. 'I have to go; Mum'll have heard the explosion and be beside herself.' She walked to the door, then turned. 'Did you even think about that?'

'Of course I did! And anyway, if I had no family, then I couldn't run to you, could I? Stupid!' Edie said, trying

232

to lighten the mood. 'Tell Mum I'll be home soon. Maybe on Sunday.'

'Good! And make friends with that yummy man. Or let me make friends with him.' She managed to muster a grin, though in truth she was still feeling shaky and scared. But she'd be blowed if she'd show it.

Edie managed a small smile back. 'Thanks for coming, Lil. You were so brave just then. I was a gibbering wreck, and yet you ran straight towards that plane.'

Lily shrugged and walked out of the door on wobbly legs. The whole experience had made her feel as though the war was creeping closer and it scared her rigid.

∽

Nellie puffed up the hill, her heart beating fast. She wasn't sure she'd be able to keep going much longer. But her girls! She'd known her boys were in danger, but she'd never imagined she'd have to worry about her girls like this.

Jasper tugged on her arm. 'Nellie, you'll give yourself a heart attack if you don't slow down.'

'I can't slow down! What if . . . ?' She left the words unsaid, instead bending over as she tried to catch her breath.

'Nell, it don't matter when we get there. What's done is done, and if you kill yourself on the way up there, then where would we all be?'

Nellie nodded, seeing the sense, but it wasn't just the unaccustomed exercise that was making her breathless. It was the thought of Lily and Edie, crushed beneath a burning plane. She turned away as nausea overcame her.

Jasper's strong arms held her up, as they so often had in the past, and she leant her head against his side as she spluttered into the undergrowth. Finally she stood up straight and wiped her mouth on her mauve coat, the cheerful colour seeming to mock her. If anything had happened to her girls, she didn't think she'd ever be able to wear bright colours again.

She drew in a deep breath, squared her shoulders and looked at Jasper. 'Come on, then. Let's stop this dilly-dallying!' She marched on, her head high. Whatever was at the top of the hill, she'd find a way to cope. She always did.

They were only halfway up when they saw a familiar figure walking towards them, her bright blonde hair shining out like a beacon of hope.

'Lily!' Nellie screamed.

Beside her Jasper gasped, 'Oh, thank God! Thank God!' as he started to sprint up the hill. As soon as he reached Lily, he caught her in his arms and squeezed her tightly against him, pushing her head under his arm and roughly stroking her hair. 'Jesus, girl! You nearly gave us all a heart attack. Where's Edie?'

'She's fine. She's fine. The plane missed the garage. But the pilot's dead.' Lily burst into tears just as Nellie reached them, and, dragging her daughter from Jasper's grasp, she held on to her as if her life depended on it. Lily was several inches taller than Nellie, and she rested her head on her mother's yellow hat, her shoulders shaking as Jasper's long arms encircled them both.

Chapter 19

Although Marianne and Gladys tried to keep things running as normal, neither of them could concentrate on anything while they waited for Nellie and Jasper to return. The café was buzzing with news of the crash and the reports all differed. Some said it had crashed into the garage, while others insisted it had managed to avoid the building and come down in the wheat fields beyond. Others still insisted it had landed on the castle.

The worry of this, on top of her fear of what Henry would do next, meant that Marianne managed to burn the pies for lunch and slice her finger open while she was chopping potatoes. Finally, she gave up and sat down at the small table under the window.

'I can't go on, Gladys,' she said. 'I just can't.'

Gladys put a consoling arm around her shoulders. 'Come on, girl. Chin up. They'll be back soon. We just have to keep putting one foot in front of the other till we know what's what. Life can't just stop.'

As she said this the back door burst open and Marianne jumped up as her mother, Lily and Jasper walked in. She ran to them. 'Where's Edie? What's happened?'

'All right, all right, keep your hair on. Get us all a cuppa, will you?' Nellie said gruffly, before striding through to the café, where the customers looked up at her expectantly.

For the next half an hour or so she and Lily regaled everyone with what had happened, while Marianne stood at the hatch listening. Finally, Nellie stood and raised her teacup. 'A brave man lost his life today, and somehow, even though he knew he was going down, he managed to make sure no one else was hurt. So I want to raise a toast.' She looked around the café and waited as everyone stood up, each holding a teacup or glass. 'May your soul rest in peace. Thank you for sparing my girls. Go with the angels.' Nellie choked a little on the last words, but no one seemed to notice as they repeated, 'Rest in peace.'

∞

As the café settled back to normal and Lily went upstairs to rest, Marianne's thoughts once again turned to Henry. She just wished she knew what he was playing at. Maybe then she'd know how to protect herself and her son. And what about Edie? How was she going to hide the fact that the man she thought she'd fallen in love with was her nephew's father? Marianne shook

237

her head. She really couldn't think about that. The most important thing right now was keeping Donny safe. She wouldn't put it past Henry to wait for him outside the school. The thought made her catch her breath. What if he took him? How could she ever get him back if he did that? He'd said himself his family was rich and could give Donny so much more than she ever could, so what chance would she have against them? Her stomach churned. She *had* to get to the school before the end of the day and she would walk Donny home herself. She'd do it every day if she needed to.

Keeping one eye on the clock, Marianne somehow managed to get through the next couple of hours. She needed to be ready to leave the minute it got close to home time so she could run up and make sure Donny returned safely.

As the lunchtime stragglers began to leave at around two forty-five, Marianne threw off her apron and put on her coat.

'Where are you going?' Nellie had seen her through the hatch. 'As if I haven't had enough worry today without you doing a disappearing act as well!'

'Got to go out, Mum. Won't be a tick.'

'But—'

Marianne didn't hear her; she was already dashing out of the back door. She ran up Cannon Street and then up Folkestone Road, until she stopped, puffing, outside the grey stone building that housed Donny's school.

The children were streaming out, the boys pushing and shoving each other, while the girls held hands and skipped down the road.

Spotting Freddie, she ran up and grabbed him by the shoulders. 'Where's Donny?'

Startled, he looked down the road. 'He was talkin' to that fella with the motorbike. And the man said he'd take him home. Lucky thing. I wish I could get a ride on that bike.'

'Which direction did he go?' Marianne's grip on Freddie's shoulders tightened.

Freddie looked puzzled as he tried to shrug her off. 'Down there, course. He's taking him home.'

She was too late! Marianne felt nausea swirl in her stomach as she turned and ran back towards town. Maybe he'd just dropped him at the café. Maybe she was worrying over nothing. Just as she turned into High Street, the air raid siren began to wail and she glanced up at the sky. It went off so frequently that people rarely took any notice of it anymore, but after the tragic events of the morning, everyone was feeling jittery and she noticed many people hurrying to shelters. But Marianne kept on running, ignoring the voice shouting behind her to get to safety.

Dashing into the café, she found it deserted, although the tables were littered with plates of half-eaten food and cups of tea. They must all have gone to the basement. Heart in her mouth, she ran down the narrow aisle between the tables, not noticing as she sent a cup and saucer crashing to the ground.

Shoving open the door to the basement, she could hear singing, Nellie's tuneless voice rising above the others as they belted out: 'Waiting at the Church'. Hurtling down the steps, she skidded to a stop as she saw a group of about ten people sitting around the large room. The singing stopped abruptly as they all looked up at her in surprise. And there, on a chair by the table, sat Henry with Donny beside him. Marianne's heart seemed to stop beating as Henry gave her a mocking smile.

'Mum!' Donny leapt up and ran over to her. 'Jasper made everyone come down here and this man gave me a ride home on his bike!'

'Where the bleeding heck have you been?' Nellie said reprovingly.

'I went up to the school, Don. And you weren't there. I was worried sick.' She looked over at Henry, who was watching her intently. Bending close to Donny's ear, she whispered, 'What have I told you about talking to strangers? I'll be dealing with you later.'

'But—'

She held up a warning finger and shook her head. 'Later.'

Then, taking his hand, she dragged him over to sit on one of the cushions by the wall. 'Don't let me stop you. It sounded lovely.' She forced a smile.

Looking around, she spotted Daisy sitting next to Lily. Both were staring at her strangely, as was Nellie, whose gaze was flicking between her, Donny and Henry, a puzzled frown drawing her brows together.

'Daisy! What are you doing here?' Marianne tried to speak casually but her voice came out unnaturally high.

'Just popped in to see you. Imagine my surprise when your mum told me you weren't here. That's got to be a first.' She looked questioningly at her.

'I'm not tied to the stove, you know. I do get out sometimes. I went up to the school to fetch Don.'

'You've not fetched him since his first day when he was five. What brought that on?' Lily asked.

Marianne shrugged, her eyes flicking to Henry, who was smiling smugly as he watched the interaction.

'Come on, everyone, who's for a song?' he said, grinning evilly at her. 'How about "Come Home, Father"?'

Marianne shuddered at the look Henry shot her as he said 'Father'. She just wished she knew what he was playing at. If he was joining up, then why would he bother with Donny now?

'Gordon Bennett, why do you want to sing that gloomy old song?' Nellie exclaimed. 'You want a game of cards, Don? Perhaps your new friend could play with us. What did you say your name was?' Nellie looked at Henry as Don leapt up to join them at the table. His gran didn't often offer to play cards with him.

'Henry Fanshawe.'

'What, of Fanshawe's Breweries?' Daisy piped up. 'We serve your beer. Good stuff. What are you doing here?'

'Oh, just passing through, visiting old friends.' His eyes slid towards Marianne. 'Happened to stop outside the school for a quick fag and this little lad hijacked me. When he said he lived here I thought I'd drop him back.'

Marianne's stomach roiled at the thought of him standing in wait outside the school.

'Come on then, Don. Best of three Go Fish. Mr Fanshawe, do you like cards?' Nellie asked.

'You could say that.' He grinned. 'In fact, you might say that I like nothing better. So come on, Donny, my lad, let's see what you're made of. Who knows, you might find you have a talent for it. Maybe it runs in the blood.' He shot another sly smile at Marianne.

Nellie hadn't missed a thing, and she cleared her throat. 'Get dealing then.'

Marianne watched helplessly as her son played cards with his father. Every second was torture as she noticed more and more similarities between the two. The different hair colour distracted you at first from the fact that their features were so similar. Even the way they held their heads was the same. Oh God! Would her mother guess? She was far too sharp. She had to find a way to throw her off the scent.

For the next half hour, Henry thoroughly charmed the other occupants of the basement with jokes and card tricks, and to make matters worse, Donny seemed to have been the most beguiled, constantly asking questions and finding every joke Henry told hilarious.

As soon as the all-clear sounded, Marianne ran up the stairs and stood by the basement door, her back to the kitchen, waiting for Henry to exit.

As he stepped out – the last to leave – he held his hand out to Marianne. 'It's been an absolute pleasure, Miss Castle,' he said with a slimy grin. 'And can I say what a fine boy you have? I very much hope I see you both again soon.'

'Get out!' she hissed. 'Get out and don't come back. I don't want you within a mile of my son, do you understand?'

'Ah, but does Donny feel the same? I have a feeling that soon he'll be desperate to be by his old dad's side.' He leant forward and gave her a peck on the cheek. 'I will get my way. You can be assured of that,' he whispered.

He moved around her and smiled charmingly at Nellie, who had been hovering behind her daughter. 'Thank you so much for your hospitality, Mrs Castle. Obviously I wish it could have been under different circumstances, but I shall carry the memory of this past hour with me to France.'

'Goodbye, Mr Fanshawe. And good luck.' Nellie watched Henry as he left, then turned to Marianne. 'Are you going to tell me what's going on? Because sure as eggs is eggs, that man is not what he seems. And why does he look so familiar?'

Marianne had thought of little else but what to tell her mother since she'd seen him sitting in the basement, and she had come to the conclusion that the only way she could throw her mother off the scent was to betray her sister. She hated to do it, but desperate times called for desperate measures.

'That, Mum,' she said fiercely, 'is the toe-rag who broke our Edie's heart, and I want you to promise if he ever comes into the café again, you will throw him out.'

Chapter 20

The weeks following Henry's appearance at the café were torture for Marianne. Every time Donny left the house, her stomach was in knots. She didn't trust for a moment that Henry had disappeared from their lives, but if she tried to stop her son from rambling around Dover as he usually did, she knew she'd be faced with a barrage of questions she couldn't answer. In addition to this, she worried that Edie, who was visiting more now since the incident with the downed Spitfire, would notice Donny's resemblance to the man who had broken her heart. She was determined that no one else would find out that Donny's father was alive and well, and threatening, for whatever reason, to take her son away from her. None of them would ever forgive her for lying to them – especially her mother. And as for Edie, to know that Henry had found it amusing to toy with her simply because she was Marianne's sister would be even more devastating.

The only consolation was that her explanation of who Henry was had distracted her mother to such an extent that she hadn't asked any further questions. She'd also instructed Gladys and Lily to watch out for the man, telling them to lock him in the basement should they ever see him again so she could throttle him at her leisure.

By the time the annual market square Christmas party came around in mid-December, Marianne decided to try to put thoughts of Henry to the back of her mind – she didn't want him ruining Christmas on top of everything else, and the party was always a big event for the café. Today, she needed to concentrate on making sure everybody had fun, particularly the children.

∞

'Help yourselves!' Nellie stood behind a trestle table that had been set up outside the café. It was piled with plates of mince pies, biscuits decorated with tiny angels and holly – Marianne's work, of course – and a huge Christmas cake, which had been topped with white icing and decorated with a large yellow star.

Nellie stamped her feet and rubbed her gloved hands together in an attempt to keep warm. She didn't mind the cold, though; at least it wasn't raining. She sniffed the air appreciatively. From the table outside the Turners' grocery shop opposite came a whiff of cinnamon and cloves from the large vat of mulled cider that was bubbling gently on a primus stove. This, mixed with the scent of mince pies and gingerbread drifting from the open door of the café, brought back memories of other market square Christmases. It was wonderful to see that, despite the war, some things never changed. Even Rodney and Edie had come to help out. Nellie glanced behind her and laughed. The window had been festooned with tinsel, and Donny and Freddie, assisted by two of their school friends, were standing on a table sticking yet more up. When he saw his grandmother watching, Donny grinned cheekily at her. She winked back and gave him a thumbs up. The more sparkle the better as far as she was concerned.

Behind them, children crowded around the tables; it was one of Nellie's hard and fast rules that on this one day of the year, no adults were allowed in the café. Today was children's day and their task was to decorate the room. The end result was always a glorious, colourful mess. Some of the children sat at the tables drawing pictures or making Christmas cards – many of which ended up on the café walls – while others were painstakingly cutting strips of coloured paper to make long paper chains, which would later be slung across the ceiling. In the centre of the room, Rodney was holding up a tiny girl while she hung a large red paper bell on the light fitting. And behind them, Nellie could see Marianne setting yet another tray of gingerbread out on the counter to sit next to the piles of mince pies and biscuits.

Around the Christmas tree in the centre of the square, the church choir was enthusiastically singing 'God Rest Ye Merry, Gentlemen', managing to almost drown out the hubbub coming from the stalls set up around them. The covered market was shut on this very special Advent Sunday, and the market traders had moved outside, their stalls sheltered by red and white striped awnings. Daisy presided over her second-hand clothes stall, Lily and Edie were selling Marianne's homemade sweets and biscuits, while the other stalls sold everything from small gifts to hot soup. This year, to add to the throng, there were crowds of servicemen and women in khaki, blue and even the light blue of the RAF.

It was Nellie's favourite day of the year. The day that the people of Dover came together, and though they could not have lights on the tree this year, nevertheless, the atmosphere was merry and optimistic.

December had been a relatively quiet month; there were still regular explosions out in the Channel, and planes flew over them daily, but the air raid warnings had not been as frequent, and today it was as if the townsfolk had decided to put their worries aside. They were all well aware that with rationing due to come into force in January, this time next year they'd not have the luxury of all this food, so it was their last chance to eat and drink whatever they liked. Soon the hard times would be here, but not today. It was an attitude Nellie thoroughly approved of.

'Afternoon, Mrs C.'

Nellie snapped out of her reverie and smiled with pleasure. 'Marge! Long time, no see. How're you getting on?'

'Oh, you know, long hours sitting at a desk, rarely seeing the daylight, and really awful food. But other than that it's all right.' She took a sip from the cup of mulled cider she'd got from Reenie outside the grocery. 'Is Marianne in? I need a word.'

'Go through. Perhaps you can find out what on earth is going on with the girl. Something's not right, there. I was hoping today of all days she'd snap out of it, but no, she's as tense and jumpy as ever.'

Marge smiled. 'I'll do my best.'

Pushing her way through the crowd of children, Marge shouted over to Donny, 'Oy, Don, any more tinsel and we won't be able to see out of the window!'

'That's the whole point, Auntie Marge,' he threw back cheekily.

Rodney, smart and buttoned-up as always in his navy blue uniform, looked up from the paper chain he was helping to make, and coloured slightly.

'Hello, Marge. If I'd known you were coming we could have walked down together.'

Marge rolled her eyes at him. 'Of course you knew I was coming. I'm hurt, Rodders, honestly hurt that you didn't want to walk with me.'

'No, it's not that ... it's just I walked with Edie. Thought if I collected her she couldn't back out.'

'Good. I saw her a moment ago at the stall looking far too thin and pale. What's up with her?'

Rodney shrugged. 'Who knows? You women are a mystery to me.'

Marianne came out of the kitchen then, bearing yet another tray of mince pies and whipping the empty one off the counter.

'Marge! Fancy a cuppa?' she said delightedly. How she'd needed to see her old friend in the past couple of weeks.

'You read my mind, love.'

They went through to the kitchen and Marge sat down at the table, eyeing her friend suspiciously while Marianne busied herself with spooning tea into the pot and filling the large kettle. Like her sister, Marianne had lost weight and looked tense.

'Right, want to tell me what's going on? I presume you've still not heard any more from you-know-who since the last time I saw you.'

Marge made a point of popping in for tea on her days off every couple of weeks, and so she knew Marianne hadn't had a response to Mr Wainwright's letter. But she didn't know Henry had visited the café and talked to Donny, nor that he'd been having an affair with Edie. The memory of the awful day when Henry had turned up still made Marianne sick with anxiety. She prayed the army had sent him far, far away and she never had to see him again.

Marianne shook her head and glanced over to the kitchen door. 'Later. Daisy and Reenie are coming at six.'

'They know?'

'No. But I'm going to tell them. I need them to look out for Donny whenever they can. I can't do this on my own.' Marianne's face creased and she felt on the verge of tears. She was living in a nightmare; not knowing what Henry might do next was driving her mad.

'Look out for him? Why? What's happened?'

Again Marianne shook her head, nodding her head at the open kitchen door. 'Later.'

Marge nodded her understanding and changed the subject. 'So, I have leave at Christmas, but with Mum and Dad off in Wales, and my sister moved to York-shire with that no-good husband, I wonder if . . . ?'

'Oh, yes! Please come! It's going to be a full house: Rodney, obviously, Jasper; the Turners and the Perkins. It'll be fun! I want to fill the place to distract Mum from the fact that the boys have said they won't be able to get home for Christmas.'

Marge smiled. 'Perfect. I can't wait. Speaking of which, have you heard anything from that delicious trumpeter?'

With everything that had been going on, Marianne had tried not to think about Alfie. When the boys men-tioned him in the couple of letters they'd received, it brought back the memory of the warmth he'd stirred in her. He had been so kind and funny, and he'd been wonderful with Donny. But he'd had no right to read her very private letter and now he knew her darkest secrets – secrets that he might let slip to her brothers at any moment. In addition, his lack of reaction had upset her, and she refused to acknowledge how contradictory her feelings were.

'No. He's not the man I thought he was. But probably more to the point – I think he realised I wasn't the woman he thought *I* was. Just as well we found out sooner rather than later.'

'What did he do?'

Marianne explained what had happened when Alfie had picked up Henry's letter.

'And you're telling me this is the reason you're refusing to write to a gorgeous man who seemed to really like you? Maybe he just didn't know what to say. After all, he knows nothing about your past, and he was probably waiting for you to explain. And when you clearly didn't want to, he thought it best not to ask. Which I think is very sensible.'

Marianne shrugged sulkily. 'How can you know that? You weren't there.'

'For goodness' sake, Marianne, at some point you're going to have to forgive yourself. You haven't done anything wrong, and yet you still creep around like you have to apologise to the world. No wonder people take advantage of you. You spend your life in this kitchen, desperately trying to make up for the fact that you were young, unhappy and innocent, and someone took advantage of you. You have *nothing* to be ashamed of.'

Marianne gave a short laugh. 'Well, there are several people who would disagree with you. The Smiths, for instance. They won't even let Donny play with Davey.'

Marge made a dismissive gesture. 'Nobody takes any notice of Horace Smith. Why can't you realise you never notice that most people love you? They always know they can count on you. And they love Donny. So please, get over this stupid idea that you're some sort of scarlet woman and write a bloody letter to the lovely trumpeter. You have to give yourself a chance at happiness at some point, you know.'

Marianne wiped her eyes. She knew her friend was right and what she'd said about Alfie not knowing what to say was probably true. If she was honest, she'd probably used that as an excuse to back away from him. Because she hadn't ever forgiven herself. She adored Donny, but the price she'd paid for her stupid mistake had been a heavy one. Anyway, it was too late to start writing to Alfie now. And frankly, if he'd really been interested, he could have written to her. No, relationships were something she needed to steer clear of. Especially now she had the spectre of Henry hanging over her.

Marge stood up and gave her a hug. 'Hey, I'm sorry, love. I didn't mean to upset you, but you do know I'm right, don't you? As always.'

Marianne laughed. Marge was so forceful and confident, she wished she could be more like her. She never shied away from telling the truth, much like her mother, but unlike Nellie, Marge knew when to hold back.

They were interrupted by a loud voice shouting, 'Ho ho ho, and what do we have here?'

The children started to squeal and Marianne smiled. 'Sounds like Jasper's arrived.'

'Right, that's my cue to get out of here. I'll see you later.' Marge moved to the back door while Marianne went into the café to watch as Jasper, resplendent in a bright red suit with a white fur collar, a red hat and a huge fake beard, came in through the front door with a silver dustbin on his shoulder.

'Make way, everyone,' Rodney shouted. 'Let Father Christmas in or you won't get your presents.' He shooed some children away so Jasper had room to sit by the counter.

Jasper edged his way into the crowded room and heaved the bin to the ground with a thump, causing a little cloud of sawdust to fall to the floor. He stared around at the excited faces with a twinkle in his eye. 'Have you all been good children?' he boomed.

A chorus of 'Yes' answered him. At the door, more children were being ushered in by Nellie.

Jasper reached into his pocket and produced a list – prepared by Marianne, Nellie and Donny the night before, as they tried to ensure that each child was mentioned. 'Paul!' He looked at a little boy of about five, who was bouncing excitedly by his knee. 'It says here that you've been feeding the chickens every day, and helping your mother bring in the coal. Good work, boy. Violet.' A small girl, her eyes bright with excitement, raised her hand. 'The elves tell me that you've been helping your mother with your baby brother. Well done.'

And so it went on. At the counter, Marianne beckoned to Donny and he pushed his way over, whispering the names of children who'd been left off the list as she hastily scribbled them down. For each child she tried to come up with a word of praise based on what she or Donny knew about them and their family. She handed the note to Jasper.

Finally, after Jasper had read through the list and looked around to make sure he hadn't forgotten anyone, the children were allowed to step forward and dig into the sawdust to find a present. Crayons, toy soldiers and cars, small dolls and packs of cards had all been painstakingly wrapped in newspaper by the family and Jasper the night before. It was a tedious task, but it was always worth the effort as they watched the children – some of whom would probably not get any other presents that Christmas – excitedly tear off the paper.

Once each child had a present, Nellie, who had been standing in the doorway with a huge grin on her face, clapped her hands. 'Time for Pin the Tail on the Donkey,' she cried, as the noise levels rose again.

Daisy always drew them a large paper donkey to stick on the kitchen door, and soon the room was filled with more excited laughter as the children queued up for their turns. Jasper officiated, tying one of Nellie's colourful scarves over the eyes of the child at the head of the queue. The winner was a small boy wearing a frayed jersey and shorts, whom Rodney lifted up, directing his grubby little hand to exactly the right place as the other children groaned and shouted, 'Not fair!' The boy beamed around at the crowd as he snatched his prize – a colouring book – from Nellie's hand.

'What do you say, Charlie?' Nellie asked reprovingly.

The little boy looked ashamed. 'Sorry, Mrs Castle. Thank you, Mrs Castle,' he lisped.

Nellie smiled at him and stroked his cheek. 'Good boy. Now go and enjoy yourself.'

For the rest of the afternoon, the children ran riot while their parents gravitated to one of the many nearby pubs. Until at three thirty, the party started to wind down. In previous years, it would have gone on until well into the evening, but mindful of the blackout, this year they had started earlier. Gradually, the café emptied as children were called to go home. Donny left too, excited at the prospect of staying with Freddie for the night.

Once the café had been tidied, Nellie looked around at the room, festooned with tinsel, paper chains and the large paper bell hanging from the light fitting. On the wall were dozens of pictures that the children had drawn. 'Well, now, this is more like it. I wish we could keep it like this all the time.' She sat down at the table with a groan. 'Anyone going to make us a cuppa?'

Jasper, still in his Father Christmas outfit, took off his jacket and slumped down beside her. 'I can't move another muscle. Me ears are ringing from all that screeching.'

'You love it, Jasper,' Lily said, placing an affectionate arm around his shoulder.

'I do. But once a year's enough for me. Them kids could drive the Nazis away with their noise alone.'

Marianne came through with a large tray stacked with cups, saucers and mince pies, and the family sat down around a table.

'What time do you have to get back, Rod?' Nellie asked, biting into a mince pie with relish.

'I'll just have this tea, then I need to make my way. You coming with me, Edie, or staying?'

'I'll walk with you. I've an early start in the morning.'

Nellie looked disgruntled. 'Why can't you just stay here? After what happened, I don't like to have you out of my sight—'

'Mum,' Edie cut her off. 'Please don't. I'll be back in a couple of weeks for Christmas.'

Nellie sighed. 'I don't have the energy to argue right now, but it's a crying shame you feel you have to live away from your family. It's not right. In my day, a girl didn't leave home until she was married.'

'Times are changing, Mum. And lots of girls are living away from home now. Look at Marge.'

'That's different. Marge is old.'

Marianne spluttered, 'She's the same age as me!'

'Exactly.'

Rodney looked over at Marianne's outraged expression and laughed. 'Leave it out, Mum.'

'Well, it's true. Marge should be married with a couple of kids, not living in a tunnel typing messages. You should and all.' She looked at Marianne. 'But seems unlikely now, I suppose. As for you, Lily, don't you get any ideas.'

'Don't worry, Mum. When I start at the hospital, I'll be staying here. They like to keep the nurses' home for people who have nowhere else to go.'

Nellie finished her cup of tea. 'Right, I'm going to leave you lot to it.' She rested a hand on Jasper's shoulder. 'See you tomorrow, Jasper?'

'You can count on it, Nell. He rose. 'I need to get back an' all. I'm on duty later.' He took his jacket from the back of the chair and, kissing Nellie swiftly on the cheek, made his way out into the dark.

It was the signal for the end of the day, and once the cups and saucers had been washed and everyone else had left, Marianne began preparations for her friends' visit. It had been a wonderful day, she reflected, as she laid out the plates of sandwiches she'd prepared earlier. And just for a while, she had forgotten about her worries and the feeling of impending doom that seemed to hang over her like a cloud. But now the worry came crashing back down. She just hoped her friends could help her find a way out of it.

Chapter 21

'Helloo!' a merry voice called out, just as Marianne was pouring more water into the teapot. She poked her head through the hatch.

'You're first, Daisy. Sit down and I'll bring you some tea.'

'Not for me, thanks. Some water would be nice.' Daisy appeared in the kitchen.

'Are you all right?' Marianne studied her friend's face. She looked as beautiful as she always did, but her dark green jersey highlighted the pallor of her face, and there were dark shadows under her bright blue eyes.

'I'm fine. Just a bit tired. It's been a long day and I'm missing Stan.'

'Have you heard from him?'

She smiled. 'He tries to write every day.' She sighed. 'But I'd prefer him to be here.'

'Don't tell Mum that! We've only had a couple of letters from the boys, and one of those was just to let us know that they won't be here for Christmas. She's spitting. Reckons they don't care about us.'

Marge and Reenie arrived then. The two were so different – Marge so tall and striking in her navy blue uniform, her red hair curled back from her face, and Reenie, solid and strong, wearing her customary slacks and sweater, and a man's donkey jacket, her curly blonde hair tied back with a scarf.

Reenie held up a bottle of cider and grinned at them. 'I thought we could all do with a little drink.'

'Not half.' Marge sank dramatically into a chair beside Daisy. 'Oh, it's good to have the old gang back together. I mean, I'm only up the road, but I feel I never see you.'

'How is it up there?'

'Busy. Stressful. But also ... exciting. Does that sound bad?'

'I could do with less excitement, to be honest,' Marianne said ruefully.

The cider fizzed as Reenie opened it. 'Oh, me too. All the explosions and planes are playing havoc with my nerves. Still, at least it's been a bit quieter lately.' She poured the golden liquid into the glasses. 'Anyway, cheers, everyone.'

They raised their glasses, clinking them together before taking large gulps. Daisy, Marianne noticed, only took a small sip before placing the glass back on the table.

'What's with you, Dais?' Reenie asked.

Daisy coloured and smiled. 'I have some news ... I'm going to have a baby. At last! Should be some time

261

in June. But now I can't stomach the taste of alcohol, or tea, come to that.'

Marianne squealed and the other two put their arms around her. 'Oh, that's good news. Stan must be beside himself, after all these years of trying.'

Daisy shook her head. 'I haven't told him. He's got enough to think about without worrying about me. But he's home for Christmas.' She beamed. 'It'll be the best present I can give him.'

'Oh, Daisy.' Marianne had tears in her eyes. 'That is the nicest news I've heard for weeks.'

'I know, but I keep crying and I feel sick all the time. And bringing a baby into the world now feels . . . scary. What if something happens to Stan?' She put her hand on her stomach. 'Poor baby. Being born into this madness.'

'Nonsense! It'll have the best mother in the world. What more does it need?' Marge put her hand over Daisy's.

Daisy sniffed and wiped her eyes. 'See what I mean? I've turned into a watering pot. Mavis says it's cos of the baby. I am happy, I promise.'

'I think this warrants another toast.' Marge held up her glass. 'To mothers, babies and lovers.'

Marianne raised her eyebrows at her. 'You have a lover?'

'Not at the moment.' She winked. 'What about you, Reens?'

'As if. Anyway, I don't have time for men. I have my Dig for Victory committee to organise, so I've too much to do as it is. But Marianne, what about Alfie?'

'There's nothing to tell. I only met him a couple of times.'

'But I thought after he walked you home that time . . . ?'

'Like I said, we've only met a couple of times. I expect the only time I'll see him is when he collects his trumpet and that'll be the last of it.'

'But he was so nice. He seemed like just the bloke for you. Has he written to you?'

'No, and there's no reason why he should. Anyway, girls . . .' Marianne hesitated and looked at Marge, who nodded at her encouragingly. 'I wanted to get you all together because I need your help with something—'

Before she could say more, there was a banging at the café door.

'Open up! I know you're in there. Open the door!'

Startled, the girls looked at the door and then at each other.

'Who the hell could that be?' Marge went to the front and peered around the blackout curtain, then jumped back.

'I saw you! Open the bloody door before I smash it in!'

Marge looked back at Marianne. 'Who the hell is this woman? She sounds posh.'

Marianne paled as the voice triggered an awful memory. She leapt up, her hand over her mouth.

'Marianne?' Marge looked concerned. 'What the hell is this all about?'

'Don't let her in,' she whispered. 'She mustn't come in.'

Nellie came through the door then, followed by Lily.

'What the hell is all this racket? Who's at the door?'

Marianne stared at her mother, her eyes wide with shock, but no words came to her.

'Only one way to find out.' Nellie tutted, heading for the door.

'No, Mum! Don't let her in!'

Nellie ignored her and the noise of the bolts being drawn back reverberated through Marianne like hammer blows.

As soon as the door opened, a slim woman with platinum blonde hair pushed her way past Nellie; her eyes flicked scornfully over the haphazard decorations, then she turned her attention to the women, who were looking at her in surprise.

Marianne's stomach dropped. It was just as she'd feared. Standing before her, dressed in a stylish blue woollen dress belted at her trim waist, a fur coat hanging open and high-heeled lace-up shoes, was Henry's wife.

'Which one of you is it? Who's the slut who thinks they can get money from my family?'

Nellie bristled. 'Who do you think you are? I have no idea what your game is or why you've come to *my* home to insult *my* friends and family, but you need to leave.' She caught hold of the woman's fur-clad arm and tried to hustle her back towards the door. But the woman was at least a head taller than Nellie and she wouldn't budge.

She looked first at Marge, her gaze running over her red hair and then down over her uniform. 'Well, it's not you,' she sneered. 'Brassy red-heads have never been his type.'

Marge gasped with outrage and looked over at Marianne, her eyes questioning. Marianne didn't look at her; her horrified gaze was fixed firmly on the elegant woman. Had she found out about Donny? Or was this about Edie again? She prayed it was the latter, but she knew in her heart of hearts she was wrong. She shot a glance at her mother, who was still wearing the bright red dress covered in green swirls that she always wore for the Christmas party. Her hair, though, was now in curlers and covered with its customary colourful scarf – bright blue and pink today.

The woman looked at Reenie then, her eyes drifting over her briefly, before looking away dismissively. Lily was standing at the kitchen door, mouth open with shock. Wearing a red jersey and blue pleated skirt, and with her blonde hair glowing under the light, she looked beautiful.

The woman pointed at her. 'I'd have thought it might be you, but you're too young.' Then she looked at Daisy and her eyes spat fury. 'You! It's you, isn't it? I don't know what lies you told my husband to convince him that your bastard is his, but let me tell you now, I am not as gullible as he is.'

Daisy gasped. 'What are you talking about?'

Nellie's face turned an unflattering shade of red, clashing violently with her dress, as her fury at this intrusion mounted.

The woman looked at her and laughed. 'And I suppose you're the grandmother. God, as if a child brought up in this' – her hand gestured around the room – 'could even begin to fit in with a family like ours.'

'Right, that's it. Out!' Nellie once again grabbed her arm, this time aided by Marge on her other side. But the woman managed to wrench free from their grasp, stalking towards the table and putting her face close to Daisy's.

'You really thought you could get away with it, didn't you? Well, the Fanshawes might be rich, but they're not stupid.'

Nellie fell back at that as comprehension dawned. 'Fanshawe?' She looked over at Marianne, who quailed at the expression on her mother's face. She'd clearly remembered the man in the basement that day – the man whom she'd told her had been having an affair with Edie.

266

Daisy, meanwhile, leant away from the woman, a frown of recognition on her face as she heard the name.

Reenie leapt forward and pulled the woman away from her. 'Leave her alone! She's pregnant and she doesn't need you frightening her.'

The woman paled. 'Pregnant?' She glanced at Daisy's flat stomach. 'It better not be another of my husband's bastards or I swear to God, you will never live another peaceful day in your life.'

Daisy finally managed to move, and though she was small, she was tough, and she slapped the woman hard around the face, forcing her to stagger back, her hand flying to her cheek and her eyes watering from the blow. Daisy pointed a finger in her face. 'You'd better do as you've been told and get out of here. And the next time you want to fling your filthy insults at someone, check your facts! This is my *husband's* baby.' She held up her left hand, her wedding ring flashing in the light. 'If your husband is Henry Fanshawe, then I've met him. And I promise you, I wouldn't touch that sleazy bastard if he was the last man on earth! Now, do as the lady asked and get out!' She flung out her arm, pointing towards the door.

Mrs Fanshawe, though, was bubbling with rage and she wasn't leaving until she'd said her piece. 'So you do know him.' she said in a dangerous tone.

Quivering with fear, Marianne stepped forward. 'I think it's me you need to talk to,' she said quietly.

The woman turned, her gaze raking over Marianne from top to bottom. 'You?' She laughed scornfully. 'It was you my husband was playing around with when he was engaged to me? Oh, now I really have seen everything. All I can say is you must have changed a lot in the last ten years, because he wouldn't go near you now!' And then she flew at Marianne, her arm raised.

But Marge was too quick and caught her around the waist. 'That's enough!'

Marianne gestured to Marge to let her go. 'It's all right. Perhaps it's for the best if we talk.' She looked around at her friends: Marge holding tightly to Mrs Fanshawe; Reenie, open-mouthed in shock, and standing protectively in front of Daisy, who looked ready to scratch Mrs Fanshawe's eyes out. 'I'm so sorry you had to see this. But could you all leave us now? You too, Mum and Lily. This is between me and her.'

Marge reluctantly let go of her captive and the three women collected their coats and gas masks. Each gave Marianne a sympathetic smile as they left. 'Let us know you're all right, won't you, love? I'll fill everyone in,' Marge said.

Marianne nodded slightly, though she didn't look at them.

As soon as the door shut, a tense silence descended, and the four remaining women stood as though frozen. Marianne and Mrs Fanshawe had not taken their eyes off each other, while Nellie stood by the door with her arms crossed, breathing heavily. Finally, Lily went to stand beside her sister and put a reassuring hand on her arm. Marianne tore her gaze away long enough to smile briefly at her, then she nodded towards the kitchen door.

'Please go, Lil. And you, Mum.'

'I'm not going anywhere until I get the truth.' Nellie stabbed a finger at her oldest daughter. 'You have been lying to me for years. To all of us. To Donny, to your sisters, your brothers. How could you? How could you keep something like this from me? But most of all, from your boy? Didn't he have a right to know? All those times he asked. All the insults he's had to endure. And for what? For your stupid, stubborn pride! What happened, Marianne? Did that Fanshawe bloke even know about Don? Or did you lie because you weren't sure whose baby it was?' She threw her hands up in the air. 'I never thought I'd see the day when my own daughter, who I've stood by through thick and thin, would turn out to be such a lying, ungrateful little cow!'

Tears started to run down Marianne's face. There was nothing she could say to defend herself; every word was true. She shook her head. 'It wasn't like that, Mum. I'm sorry I lied, but I didn't even know his name.'

Nellie stalked up to her. 'You didn't know his name? What happened? You just fancied a bit of how's your father and grabbed the nearest man?'

'No! No . . . he . . . he told me his name was Gerald and he was so nice to me. I was sixteen, Mum. I didn't know anything. I suppose I felt . . .' She sniffed, trying to hold back her tears. 'I felt lonely. Unnoticed. I just wanted . . . I just wanted to feel special.'

'Oh, so it's my fault, is it? Me, who has worked her fingers to the bone looking after all of you! Me, who's given you a living, looked after you, loved you, helped you raise your son!' Nellie's voice was trembling with emotion and she shook her head. 'How could you? How could you do this to me? To Donny?'

'Come on, Mum . . . Don't be so hard on her. Can't you listen to what she's just said?'

'Don't be so hard on her? How the hell would *you* know? You were seven! What do you even know about how it was for me? The neighbours who smirked at me. Who just *loved* the fact that Nellie Castle had got her comeuppance. And *my* daughter did that. The daughter I loved, cared for, worried about. Well, no more! That's it. From now on, you're on your own, Marianne! And as for you' – she turned her heated gaze on Mrs Fanshawe, who'd been watching the exchange with a faint smirk on her lips – 'if I ever see you within a mile of this café again, I'll give you such a hiding, you'll wish you'd never been born!' Nellie whirled around and stormed back to the kitchen, wrenching open the door and stomping up the stairs. Her heavy footsteps could be heard as they stamped across the living room, causing the paper bell to sway cheerfully above their heads.

'Well,' the hateful woman said, 'that's answered a few of my questions. Looks like your goose has been well and truly cooked.' She cackled humourlessly.

'How did you . . . ?'

The woman gave her a scornful glare. 'How did I find out? He sent an oh so touching letter to his father. I don't know what you said to convince him the brat is his, but rest assured, if you ever, *ever* bring that mongrel near the Fanshawes, you'll regret it. I don't care what my husband says.'

Lily stalked over to Mrs Fanshawe and put her face close to hers. 'Listen to me, you stuck-up bitch. Your husband is the one who needs to stay away from *us*. He's nothing but a filthy swine. He seduced and deceived Marianne when she was *sixteen* and engaged to you. What does that say about *you*, eh? And I don't care if your name's bloody Windsor—' She stopped abruptly and looked over at Marianne as the realisation of when she'd seen Henry Fanshawe before and what Marianne had said about him suddenly hit her. 'Your bloody husband can't seem to stay away from us, can he? It's not just Marianne—'

'Lily!' Marianne managed to come out of her shocked stupor long enough to stop her sister from saying any more. The last thing Marianne needed was for Mrs Fanshawe to recognise her from the day at the garage.

But she was too late as the woman looked at her sharply, then back at Lily. 'What? What are you saying? *You've* also . . . ?'

Lily looked away sulkily. 'No. Nothing.'

'Oh my God.' She put a hand to her mouth. 'I've seen you before.' She stared at Marianne. 'At the garage.' She closed her eyes and swallowed, and despite her own misery, Marianne felt a stirring of sympathy for the woman. After all, she was as much a victim of Henry as she and Edie were.

'What is this? A family of whores?! Does your mother pimp you out to the highest bidder? Is that it? And you think our family would want anything to do with a child that comes from this sort of perverted household! Well, this is what I think of all of you!' She spat and the spittle landed on the front of Marianne's cardigan.

Marianne stepped back in disgust while Lily moved forward, grabbed the woman by her shoulders and pushed her none too gently to the door. Opening it, she shoved her outside into the total darkness of the square, yelling, 'I hope you fall into the bloody docks, you stupid bitch!' Then she came back in, bolted the door and, running over to her sister, held her tight as Marianne sobbed into her shoulder.

When her sobs finally subsided, Marianne insisted Lily go to bed. Her sister left with reluctance and only after she'd extracted a promise from Marianne to wake her if she needed anything. It was strange, Marianne thought. For so long, she had been the one to take care of Lily, but her sister was growing into a confident and kind young woman, and suddenly their roles had been reversed.

She sat for a long while in the dark, nursing a cold cup of tea. The decorations around the room felt like a travesty and the happy atmosphere of the afternoon seemed a very long way away now.

She took a deep, shuddering breath, wondering how on earth she was going to face her mother, and terrified about what she might do or say. She knew Nellie would never throw her out on the street – she wouldn't do that to Donny – but she fully expected that she would make her life so miserable that she might be forced to find somewhere else to live. But would that be the end of the world? She could always find a job as a cook somewhere – maybe even up at the castle. The problem was she refused to go anywhere without Donny, and she didn't want to disrupt his life any more than necessary, so if she could find a way to stay, she would. She needed to gather her courage and try to make her mother understand why she'd lied.

Thank God neither Donny nor Edie had been here to witness this awful humiliation. It would have been worse for Donny, of course, to hear the vile things that woman had said about her – and him. And how would he feel knowing he'd met his father without realising? Should she have told him then? She wasn't sure he'd be very understanding about her lies. But he loved her. Surely he'd forgive her eventually.

Her mother, however, was a different kettle of fish. Nellie could harbour a grudge like no one else. And worse, Marianne knew she was hurt. And Nellie in pain was always at her most dangerous. The years when Marianne's father had been alive had taught them all that.

A knock on the café door made Marianne jump. Please don't say she's back, Marianne thought to herself. But when she went to the door, Jasper was standing outside, holding a torch up to his face. She sighed with relief. He was probably the only person she could bear to see right now.

'Have we got light showing, Jasper?'

'Just wanted to check everything was all right here,' he said through the door. 'Found a woman outside earlier, and she looked a bit the worse for wear. Wondered if she'd come from here?'

Marianne reached up and opened the bolts on the door and ushered him inside, then went straight through to the kitchen to put the kettle on the stove. Jasper followed, sensing tension from the stiff set of Marianne's shoulders.

'What's happened?' he asked anxiously. 'Is Don all right?'

'Course.' Her hand shook as she measured a spoonful of tea into the teapot, spilling most of it on the table. Jasper gently took the spoon and did it for her.

'Tell me,' he said quietly, with no trace of his usual jocular tone.

Pouring water into the pot, Marianne carried it back into the café and put it on a table, gesturing for Jasper to sit.

He did as he was asked, his gaze never leaving Marianne's face as she busied herself with setting out the cups and saucers. Finally, she sat back and sighed, rubbing at her eyes, then, taking a deep breath, she told him everything: from how she met Henry and why she lied, to the solicitor's letter and him turning up here out of the blue. Finally, she explained that the woman outside was Henry's wife, a woman who had been engaged to Henry around the time Donny had been conceived, and who wanted to make it clear that she wanted nothing to do with her husband's son.

By the end of the story Marianne was weeping and, unable to look at the man she loved more than she'd ever loved her own father, she laid her head on her arms on the table.

For a moment, Jasper sat in stunned silence, then he let out a long, low whistle. 'So you're telling me that prat I caught in the yard with you that time – that's Donny's dad?'

She nodded.

'What on earth did you see in that posh ponce? I mean, I can see he's handsome but dear oh dear, he was . . . Hang on, didn't you tell me that was the man who ditched Edie?'

She nodded again.

He gave another low whistle. 'What a tangle. And Edie doesn't know that the man is Don's . . . ?'

Marianne sat up and straightened her shoulders. 'No. And I don't want her to know. She's so hard on herself she'd probably blame herself for that too.'

He shook his head slightly at that. 'This man sounds like a thorough bad'un. He deserves to be horsewhipped for what he's done to you and Edie, *and* that poor heartbroken woman out there. But you Castles are tight. One way or another, you'll come through this.'

'Will *you* speak to Mum?' she asked hopefully. If anyone could talk her mother around, it was Jasper.

He shook his head. 'Oh no. I'm not getting involved in that fight. You did wrong to lie, and Nellie deserves a full apology. It won't be easy, mind. You know your mum – she's not going to accept it any time soon.'

Marianne hung her head, knowing he was right, but wishing he'd do what he used to when they were children and he felt Nellie was being unnecessarily harsh. She only appreciated it now she was older, but they had all counted on him in so many ways.

'Please.' She gave it one last try, looking up through her wet lashes with a pleading expression.

He smiled gently. 'Nope. Not for all the tea in China.'

'What do you suggest then?'

Jasper was quiet as he sipped his tea, deep in thought. Finally, he put his cup down and wiped his moustache. 'Here's what you have to do, Marianne.' He paused and she waited with bated breath, praying he had a solution that would help her earn her mother's forgiveness, and at the same time keep the truth from Donny and Edie.

'You need to tell the whole truth and nothing but the truth to everyone.' He held up a finger. 'And I mean *everyone*, mind. You can't tell your mum some of the truth, and keep hiding it from Edie. Nor can you tell your mum and Edie, and not let your Don know. It's not fair, and as you've discovered, no good has ever come from a lie. Lies are like weeds: they grow and grow, until eventually they overwhelm everything and no one knows what the truth looks like anymore.'

'But I can't,' she whispered. 'Everyone will hate me.'

He got up and put his arm around Marianne's shoulders. 'Hey, hey, it'll be all right in the end, you'll see. But this is the only way.'

Marianne sighed and nodded. 'You're right, but I . . . I'm scared. Scared none of them will ever forgive me.'

'I know, love. But this lie has been like a rotten tooth that you've refused to have pulled cos it'll hurt. You know very well that if the tooth comes out, the wound will heal and the pain will stop. But if you leave it festering, it will never stop hurting.'

Marianne grimaced at his analogy, but there was no other option for her, and first thing tomorrow she'd talk to her mother. If she'd let her.

Chapter 22

Marianne rolled out some pastry for a rhubarb pie, one ear on the conversation in the café. It had been nearly a week now since that dreadful night and still her mother wasn't talking to her. She wasn't talking much to anyone, and the regulars had started to stay away, tired of her bad temper. The only person she still treated with affection was Donny, who was clearly bemused by the strained atmosphere.

The previous evening Marianne had escaped with Reenie and visited Daisy at the Royal Oak, but even that had done nothing to lift her spirits. Daisy, although clearly still suffering from sickness, was overflowing with happiness. Stan was due back in a few days and she couldn't wait to tell him about her pregnancy. Marianne was pleased for her friend, but she couldn't help comparing their two situations. Daisy's baby would be brought up with two loving parents and would never have to endure some of the insults that her lovely little boy had. How she wished she could know what it felt like: to be expecting a child knowing that it would be loved and secure, and that no one would judge.

As well as this, Daisy would be part of that little community of mothers, she thought wistfully; the ones who chatted in the square while the little ones played. Who looked after each other's children when one of them was sick. She remembered, once, trying to join in with a group of older women, all of whom had toddlers the same age as Donny, and they'd turned away and walked off. June Perkins – Reenie's sister and Freddie's mother – had smiled tightly at her. 'You can't blame us, Marianne,' she'd said. 'They reckon you might steal their husbands if you get too close.' Then she'd called to Freddie and walked off.

The visit to see Daisy had ended up with Marianne feeling more depressed than she had before, and Reenie, deeply concerned for her friend, had promised to come round to the café to check up on her. Marianne had tried to dissuade her – for some reason her mother had decided that her friends had been in on the secret and therefore were just as much to blame for her lies.

'Your mother is all mouth and no trousers. I'm not scared of her,' Reenie had said with a dismissive tut.

If only that was true, Marianne thought. As a general rule she would have agreed, but not this time.

The bell above the front door tinkled and she heard her mother say, 'What do you want?'

'Just popping in to see Marianne, Mrs C.' It was Reenie.

'Well, you can turn around and go right back out.'

Hearing her mother's strident voice, Marianne poked her head through the hatch and, catching her friend's eye, she pointed behind her, indicating that Reenie should come to the back door.

Her friend nodded slightly. Before she left, though, she had a parting shot for Nellie. 'Look, Mrs Castle, why don't you talk to her? Maybe try to understand why she acted the way she did.'

'Easy for you to say. You're not the one who's been kept in the dark all these years. No, worse: *lied* to.'

'It was as much a surprise to us as it was to you.'

'Oh, I don't think so. I know you girls – you tell each other everything. Been laughing about it, has she? About getting one over on her old mum? Maybe you've *all* been laughing. Well, I tell you now, Reenie Turner, you and your little group are no longer welcome here.' She pointed to the door.

Reenie looked around the café furtively. Luckily it wasn't too busy, but even so her cheeks burnt with humiliation. 'You might be able to intimidate your family, but you have no power over me. And if you still want to have a daughter or a grandson after all this, then you should go a bit easier on Marianne.'

'Go easy?! EASY!'

Around them, the half a dozen or so customers gave up all pretence of not listening and turned to watch.

281

'I've done *nothing* but go easy on that girl all her life! And this is how she repays me? With lies. LIES! Everything was a lie, and you knew! So get out now!' Nellie marched over and stared bullishly up into Reenie's face.

Jasper walked in at that moment. He'd taken to popping in and out of the café several times a day, leaving his apprentice in charge of the forge, well aware that at some point Nellie's rage and upset was going to bubble over and explode. He'd been hoping to be there when it did, and by the looks of it, he'd come just in time.

'All right, Nellie,' he said. 'No need to scare off all the customers.'

'And you can stay out of it, Jasper Cane. This is family business, and you are *not* part of the family!'

Jasper ignored her and instead took Reenie's arm and steered her swiftly to the door. 'Best leave for now, Reenie. She'll come around, but give her a few days, eh?'

Reenie sighed and nodded. But once out of the café, she ran around to the back gate and slipped through. Marianne met her at the door.

'You all right, love?' Reenie looked at her friend's pale face and puffy eyes.

Marianne shook her head, but smiled bravely. 'Not really. I keep telling myself she'll calm down enough for me to talk to her, but it's been a week now. Poor Donny can't work out what's going on. He's spending most of his time over at the Perkins' to get away from the atmosphere.'

'Well, you know where I am if you need a bolthole. Don't let her bully you.'

'I won't. But this is all my fault and I can't really blame Mum this time.'

'Bollocks to that.' Reenie rolled her eyes. 'Your mum needs to learn to calm down and listen once in a while instead of always going off at the deep end.'

'I told you to get out!' Nellie stood at the kitchen door, her eyes spitting fury at the two women.

Reenie gave her a mocking salute, then with a last meaningful look at Marianne, she left.

If Marianne had hoped that her mother would say something to her, then she was disappointed. Nellie gave her a long, furious glare and turned away.

'Glad, tell my daughter not to let anyone in at the back door in future, will you?' she called over to her old friend. 'With her track record, Christ knows who she'll let in next.'

Marianne's heart sank. She'd known this was going to be hard, but if her mother kept on like this, then she wasn't sure she'd be able to live here much longer.

Jasper stood by the counter. 'Nellie, for gawd's sake, it's nearly Christmas. What happened to peace and goodwill?'

'And what happened to honour your father and mother? I thought I told you to leave. And while you're at it, you can shove your peace and goodwill somewhere the sun doesn't shine.'

The door opened and a couple of soldiers walked in.

'Afternoon, Mrs C.' one of the soldiers said in a broad Irish accent, giving her a cheerful salute. 'You wouldn't have some grub for a couple of hungry soldiers now, would you?'

He was a regular, and usually Nellie was happy to banter with him. But his salute felt as mocking as Reenie's and suddenly she snapped. Looking around at the avid faces gawking at her, she flung her arm out and pointed to the door.

'Everyone out!' she screamed. 'Out! Bunch of nosy parkers. I bet you'll be out there gossiping about the crazy Castles soon as you've finished. Well, I won't have it. So GET OUT! ALL OF YOU!'

There was a stunned silence, and Gladys put her hand on her friend's arm. 'Nellie, that's enough. Why don't you go upstairs, eh? Me and Marianne can manage.'

'I want them out! Now!' Nellie was almost in tears as her frustration and rage bubbled over.

Jasper stepped up and, taking Nellie's arm, he man-handled her towards the stairs, passing a pale and shaken Marianne as he went. She made to follow but he shook his head at her, and she stepped back and sank, trembling, into the kitchen chair.

∞

Upstairs, Jasper levelled a disapproving look at Nellie. 'You need to calm down and pull yourself together, Nell.'

'And you need to leave, Jasper. You seem to think you can tell me how to run my family, but this is *my* business, not yours. These are *my* children!' She stabbed her finger at him.

Jasper swallowed but stood his ground. They weren't his children, but God, how he wished they were.

'Nellie, you need to think very carefully about what you're doing. You're driving your Marianne away, and mark my words, she'll leave if you keep on like this. Then who will be here for you? Just Lily, and it won't be long before she's gone and you'll be a sad, lonely old woman with no one to blame but yourself.'

'I know exactly who I'd blame, and it wouldn't be myself. It'd be that treacherous daughter of mine. All these years, Jasper. All these years . . .' She sank down into her favourite armchair, her pink woollen cardigan clashing violently with the red and purple flowers of the upholstery.

Jasper's heart ached for her, but he couldn't soften. Kneeling in front of her, he put his hands over hers and held on to them tightly.

'Listen to me, love. That girl is at sixes and sevens. She told a lie and she's sorry. But think about it: if she hadn't lied, what would you have done?'

'I'd have looked after her and Donny just the same. She knows that.'

'Does she? Do you remember how you were in the days after Donny's birth? Shouting at the poor girl, demanding answers. She was only just seventeen, love!'

'I was eighteen when I had Rodney. What's that got to do with anything?'

'You were married, Nell. Safe, secure, living here with Donald, all above board and respectable.'

'Which, if Marianne hadn't been such a fool, she could have had too.'

'Oh, Nell. Come on. That girl's been helping you run this place since she was fourteen, as well as helping you look after the other kids. They love you, Nell, but it's Marianne they run to when they're in trouble. But where does she run, eh? Where was her soft place to land when she was in trouble?'

'What are you implying?'

'I'm not implying anything. I just want you to try to look at this from the point of view of a scared seventeen-year-old whose mother can be very ... forceful. Look, when Don was born, it was only a couple of years after Donald died, wasn't it? You were all still in shock and mourning.'

She snorted. 'Oh, I mourned for that man in the year after he returned from the war. By the time he died, my tears had been dry a long time.'

'Maybe yours had. Had Marianne's? Had the other children's?'

She shook her head and sighed. 'How would I know? I wouldn't let them talk about it. To anyone. But why does that excuse Marianne lying to me? Oh, the getting pregnant part I understand perfectly – she fell prey to a scoundrel, and she won't be the last. But I'm her mum. I might be harsh at times, but doesn't she know I'd pull down the moon and cook it for my kids if they wanted me to? And yet she's played me for a fool all these years. And then there's that poor, poor woman.'

Jasper was puzzled for a moment. 'Who?'

'Marianne told me that Donny's dad was Cyril Baker. You know the Bakers? Live up near Connaught Park. I knew his mum. Even went to that poor lad's funeral and paid my respects. But when Marianne told me . . . When she told me it was him, and that he'd forced himself on her . . . Well, next time I saw her I looked the other way and I've not said a word to her since. So you see, Jasper, it's not all about me, it's about that poor, grieving mother as well.'

Jasper shook his head. 'It's not, Nell so stop trying to justify your behaviour. Yes, that's dreadful, but it's not why you've been raging for a whole week, is it? And did you never think, if that lad really had been the father, that you were depriving that woman of her grandson? A little something of her son to hold on to.'

'After what Marianne said he'd done? And she begged me not to say anything, so I promised. And I kept my word. Thank God I did! How would that poor woman feel now if I had to tell her Don wasn't her grandson? She'd be bereaved all over again.'

Jasper had to concede she had a point. As he'd told Marianne, just one lie could grow and spread until it completely obscured the truth.

'Marianne's made a dreadful mistake, but it's time to forgive her. Christmas is next week and you can't spoil it. Think, Nell. Every minute you get to spend with your family is precious. Us old-timers know that better than anyone. You think those air raid warnings are just for fun? Soon enough the bombs'll fall, so don't waste the time we have in bitterness and anger, love. You'll only regret it.'

Nellie sat for a while, her eyes downcast, her hands clasped in Jasper's strong grip. The silence stretched, but Jasper kept quiet, watching Nellie's face carefully for signs that she was softening. She looked up at him finally and opened her mouth, but before she could say a word, the air raid siren started to wail outside. It was the first time in days and he chuckled softly. 'God is listening, Nell. It's a sign that he agrees with me.'

She sighed and smiled ruefully, pulling her hand from his and reaching out to stroke his cheek in an uncharacteristically affectionate gesture. 'Where would I be without you, eh, Jasper?'

Jasper grinned, putting his large, warm hand over her small, plump one. 'Gawd only knows. But I doubt you'd like it.'

'This doesn't mean I'm not still furious, mind.'

'I know, love. But you need to let her apologise and explain. Then you can enjoy this Christmas with your family.'

Suddenly she stood up. 'Oy, shouldn't you be out there pestering people to get off the streets?'

He shook his head. 'I'm not on duty. But come on, as your friendly local ARP warden, I should probably evacuate everyone to the basement.'

Nellie stood and listened for a moment. 'I don't hear the ack-acks, so no point.'

'Oh no you don't. Get down there now before I arrest you.' He pushed her over to the door, giving her ample backside, clothed in a bright yellow and black checked skirt, a little pat.

'Hands off!' She turned back and gave his hand a smack, but she was smiling slightly and Jasper breathed an inward sigh of relief. The clouds were clearing. Now all he had to do was encourage Marianne to take advantage of the blue skies.

❦

The basement was cold and damp, despite the little oil heater, and Nellie shivered as she looked around the room: six customers, plus Gladys and Marianne. Lily was helping out at the hospital again now the school holidays had started. That girl was going to make a very fine and dedicated nurse, she thought proudly. The place had gone silent the minute she stepped in and she felt a slight flush of shame rise to her cheeks. When would she learn to control her temper and keep her family business private? Donald had always told her that her temper would be the death of him. She smiled faintly at the memory. Bless his heart, she'd driven the poor man around the bend and then the war had finished the job. She shook the melancholy thought away.

She felt Jasper's solid presence behind her, warming her back. 'I think you need to say sorry,' he whispered.

She turned and frowned at him. But he was right. Again. Drawing a deep breath, she said, 'Just to say, I'm sorry. I've been like a bear with a sore head, but I'm back to meself now, so if I've offended anyone, then you have my permission to call me a foolish old woman.' There was laughter from the people huddled in their coats around the table.

'You're one foolish woman,' the Irish soldier said to her. 'And you're lucky your daughter's such a grand cook, else you'd not be seeing me again.'

'Fair enough.'

Gladys piped up. 'Nellie Castle, you are a foolish old woman, and don't expect me to put up with that sort of behaviour again. Next time, I'll walk.'

'With your bunions, I doubt you'd get far.' Nellie snorted.

She looked at the others, but they just smiled and shook their heads. Finally, her gaze rested on Marianne, but her daughter refused to look at her.

'All right, then. That's your lot. And if any of you ever call me that again, you'll regret it. Anyone for a game of rummy?'

She sat down at the table, Jasper by her side, and started to shuffle some cards.

Soon the atmosphere relaxed, as people smoked, drank tea, played cards and chatted while they waited for the all-clear. None of them expected there to be a raid. So far, aside from a mine exploding on the beach, the worst that had happened in Dover was a stray anti-aircraft shell striking a street up near the hospital.

After half an hour, the all-clear sounded and the little group headed back upstairs. Only Marianne remained where she was, huddled in a blanket on a cushion beside the wall. She hated the way her mother could just swan in, apologise and suddenly be everyone's best friend again. She wasn't sure she could forgive her so easily. And she wasn't sure she wanted to cook anymore today. Let her mother do it for once, she thought, as she laid her head against the wall and closed her eyes. All she wanted to do was sleep, and maybe when she woke up she would find this had all been a nightmare.

At the sound of footsteps on the stairs, she opened her eyes, but she didn't raise her head. She knew who it was and she wasn't inclined to give them her attention. Her shoulders were taken in a gentle grasp, but she shrugged the hands away. Finally, fingers under her chin tilted her head back and she stared into her mother's eyes.

Nellie was looking sad and remorseful, but Marianne refused to react.

'Marianne, my love, I'm sorry. I'm ready to listen now if you want to explain.'

Marianne shook her head. 'Is there any point, Mum? I've already tried so many times, but you rant and you shout and you treat me no better than a piece of dirt.'

'I said I'm sorry, and I mean it, but don't try to pretend you're entirely blameless. Have you any idea what it was like hearing the truth from that stuck-up cow? Well?'

Marianne looked away. 'It wasn't so great for me either.'

'But you knew! None of this was a shock to you.'

'I never wanted you to know. I was too ashamed.' Marianne covered her eyes and Nellie pulled her to her.

'I know, love. But it doesn't make it right. I'm ready to listen now, though. Will you tell me?'

Marianne stared at her mother for a long time, trying to gauge her sincerity. She seemed to mean it, but she knew that whatever she told her could come back to haunt her the next time her mother's temper was roused.

'Do you promise never to throw this back in my face? I need a solemn promise, Mum. Because I'm telling you now, if you ever behave like you have this past week again, I'm leaving and taking Donny with me.'

Her mother nodded. 'I'll do my best.'

'That's not good enough. I need a solemn promise. I can't live in fear of you holding this against me.'

Her mother sighed. 'Like I said, I'll do my best. But you know sometimes I speak before I think.'

'You have to change then,' Marianne said. 'Because I meant what I just said. I *will* leave.'

Nellie sighed and gave a small nod. 'All right. I promise.'

'That man,' Marianne whispered. 'I never told you because I didn't know his full name.' She gave a short, bitter laugh. 'And as it turns out, I didn't even know his first name either. But I thought you'd think I was some sort of tart for sleeping with someone I hardly even knew.' She closed her eyes. 'I mean even *more* of a tart.'

'I never thought that, love. But you have to admit, Don's arrival was a shock. To all of us.'

'I'm sorry I lied. I was young and terrified and I'd just had a baby thrust into my life. And, to be honest, I was suffering from a broken heart. I really thought I loved him, Mum. I would never have . . . you know, otherwise. I wish I hadn't lied. I wish with all my heart

I'd just been brave and told you the truth, but I didn't have the strength.'

'I see that now. But I'm going to have to find a way to make it up to Mrs Baker. That poor woman didn't deserve me blanking her the way I did.'

Marianne looked away, feeling sick over the way she'd used that poor dead boy. Then she took a deep breath. Jasper had told her to tell Nellie everything, and after the last few days, she thought it would be best. 'There's more,' she whispered, then paused, trying to gather her courage. 'I've seen Mrs Fanshawe before.'

'What? When?'

'Up at the garage. She confronted Edie about her affair with Henry.'

Nellie jumped up and began to pace. 'She knew about that!'

Marianne nodded. 'She heard them, figured it out. It was awful, Mum. The things she said to Edie . . . That's why Edie's stayed away. She's too humiliated and she never wanted you to know she'd been with a married man.'

'No, I bet she didn't! Of all the stupid—'

'Mum, stop it. You promised to listen, so listen. You know very well she didn't know he was married. The man used a false name with her as well and . . . and she has no idea that he's also Donny's father. I just can't tell her. Jasper says I should come clean to everyone – Donny included – but I just . . . I just don't think it's a good idea.'

Nellie stopped pacing. 'Ooh, if I could have five minutes alone in a room with that scoundrel. What he's done to my girls.'

'But what should I do? Should I tell her?'

'Don't you dare! I want that girl home, and this will drive her further away. As for Donny . . . well, I think maybe not right now. If this Fanshawe bloke has joined up, then let's leave it. Maybe . . .' She stopped, unwilling to wish anyone dead, however tempting.

Marianne nodded, relieved. 'I won't then. But can we be friends again, Mum? I've missed you.'

Nellie held her arms open and Marianne stood and rushed into them. They stood for a long time, Nellie smoothing her daughter's hair. Finally, she drew back. 'I'll be calm for now. But that man has messed with one too many Castle women, and if he ever dares show his face again, he'll wish he'd never been born.'

Chapter 23

Christmas Eve, 1939

In the week following Nellie's now infamous explosion of rage, it was as if something had been released within her and she entered fully into the Christmas spirit. Every customer who came in was given a complimentary mince pie. 'Take it while you still can, Flossie,' she told a woman sitting at a table with two small children, who were looking with large, hungry eyes at the food being consumed around them. Their mother had brought them in to get warm, and she had only managed to muster enough money for a cup of tea and a glass of milk for each of the children. The woman shook her head, looking embarrassed.

'They're on the house, love.' She knew that Flossie had been having a hard time since her husband had left her and her two children almost destitute. 'And if you hang on a mo, I'll get you a couple more to keep for your dinner tomorrow.'

When the woman still hesitated, Nellie said, 'Go on, rationing'll be upon us before you know it.' She leant close to the woman's ear. 'Just so you know, love, if you're ever in need, you can always pop in here. We often have leftovers. That applies for *after* rationing too.' She gave her a wink and tapped her nose.

The woman smiled gratefully at her. Nellie had a fearsome reputation within the community, but everyone knew that if you were in trouble, her door was always open. Just as long as you didn't take the Michael.

Roger Humphreys was seated at a table nearby, buttoned tightly into his police uniform, and he turned to frown at Nellie. 'Mrs Castle, I hope you don't mean what I think you mean,' he said reprovingly. 'The constabulary have been warned that once rationing comes into force, then we need to keep a sharp lookout for nefarious goings-on.'

'Nefairy what?' Nellie laughed. 'Well, you've got nothing to fear here, Rog. There are no fairies in this house! I don't stand for that sort of thing under my roof.'

Marianne caught the last of the conversation as she put some plates on the hatch and her thoughts immediately turned to Jimmy. After her experience the previous week, she prayed nothing like that would ever happen to her brother.

Roger wagged his finger at Nellie. 'You know what I mean, Mrs Castle. I have it on good authority that people are already stockpiling rationed goods to sell on the black market.'

'I wouldn't know about that, Rog. The only things we stockpile in here are nosy customers who listen to other people's conversations.'

There were several muffled chuckles from the customers at the other tables, and Nellie grinned at the policeman. 'See? I think that just proved my point.'

Roger's face flushed angrily and he stood up abruptly, gulping the last of his tea. 'You have been warned. I'll be keeping a close eye on Castle's from now on. That goes for all of you.' He looked around the room, then craned his neck to the side to see if he could spot Marianne, but she had hastily ducked out of sight as soon as he'd stood up. She'd managed to avoid Roger these past few months and she intended to keep it that way.

Nellie snorted. 'Oh, get out, you interfering old busybody. What business is it of yours if I choose to help a neighbour with a bit of food?'

With a last baleful look at the woman, he left.

'Good riddance to him,' Phyllis Perkins said from the corner table where she was having a quick fag and a cup of tea with Ethel Turner from the grocery. 'He's been sniffing around us as well. Cheeky bugger! Perkins has always stayed on the right side of the law, and always will.'

'He's been tryin' to check out our stocks of beer. Reckons it's not legit. Brian nearly smacked him one.' Ethel smacked her hand on the table to illustrate her point.

'Well, if he's keeping an eye on us, we'll return the favour and keep an eye on him. Anybody sees him sneaking around where he's no business to be, let us know, and I'll do the same.'

'Good idea, Nell. I'm up for that.'

'We'll show the police they can't mess with us.'

Outside it began to snow and Nellie sighed. 'Just look at this . . . Our poor boys out in France. Apparently it's the coldest winter they've had for years. And there they are tramping around with nothing to do. What the hell is this war all about, eh? When will Chamberlain see that you can't just send an army out and hope the Nazis give up. If he declared war, why isn't he fighting it? Have you heard what's happened to those poor people in Poland? And still he sits on his hands, waiting to see what happens. No, only way to beat them is to attack.' She shook her head. 'Say what you like about Hitler, but he doesn't hang about. Why can't they see that?'

'Speaking of which, Nell, where are your boys? I thought you said they'd be back for Christmas.' Ethel asked.

'No. Not this time. Daisy's Stan's made it back, but my boys apparently haven't managed to get leave. Maybe in the new year. It'll be the first Christmas without them. Still, Rodney'll be here. That's something, I suppose,' she said mournfully. The absence of the boys was the only thorn in Nellie's good cheer. 'Anyway, my friends, finish up, if you don't mind. It's gone three, and I'm closing early.'

While the customers started to get up, drinking the last of their tea and stubbing out their cigarettes, Nellie went through to the kitchen, found a string bag and disappeared into the pantry, scanning the shelves and taking a spare loaf of bread and a couple of cans of tinned meat. She popped in a few muddy potatoes and some carrots and parsnips. Finally she found a foil-wrapped ginger cake that Marianne had made earlier and added it to the haul.

'Mum! That's for tomorrow!'

'Oh, hush. We've got plenty, but I have a feeling those Priests don't have more than a bit of stale bread and cheese for their Christmas dinner. Here, we don't have a few lumps of coal going spare, do we?'

Marianne went out to the backyard to the coal bunker and shovelled some coal into a sack. She handed it to her mother, who nodded in satisfaction and took the lot out to the café. Flossie Priest was kneeling in front of her little boy, buttoning up his threadbare coat.

'Here you go, love. And you have a merry Christmas.'

The woman looked at the bags with tears in her eyes. 'I don't want no charity.'

'Not charity. A Christmas present. There's a nice bit of ginger cake in there, an' all. Take it, I'll be offended otherwise.' She thrust the bags into the woman's hands. 'Have a merry Christmas, love.' She ruffled the children's hair, then turned and went back into the kitchen.

Watching, Marianne marvelled at her mother. On the one hand she could be a temperamental tyrant, but on the other, there was no one better than Nellie to have by your side when you were in trouble.

Smiling, she turned and began the laborious process of cleaning up the kitchen in readiness for the feast she needed to prepare for the following day.

Christmas Day dawned snowy and cold, and Marianne was up early preparing the enormous goose that the Turners had provided as their contribution to the lunch. She'd made the Christmas cake and Christmas pudding weeks before, and the cake now stood, resplendent on a cake stand, covered with white icing and decorated with a marzipan Christmas tree with tiny parcels – toffees that she'd made and coated in colourful icing – underneath. She'd also baked huge batches of mince pies that now stood on a plate in the pantry, decorated with little stars and dusted with icing sugar.

Reenie had delivered a sack of potatoes, plus carrots, parsnips and Brussels sprouts from her allotment a couple of days before, and the previous night, Marianne, Nellie and Lily had sat around the kitchen table preparing it all. It had been a convivial evening: Nellie had opened a bottle of sherry and they had listened to the carols on the radio. Out in the café, Donny had been tasked with cleaning the floor and pushing all the tables together, which he then covered with an enormous red cloth, arranging fifteen chairs around it before laying the table with their best crockery and some crackers that Jasper had given them.

Now, after going to church and opening their presents, everything was prepared. The goose was in the oven, emitting delicious smells, the spuds were ready to stick in later, the café looked beautiful and Christmassy, and, despite the absence of Bert and Jimmy, Marianne felt a surge of hope that maybe the next year wouldn't be so bad.

Just then, Marge, Rodney and Edie rushed in through the front door, their coats covered with snow.

'Christ! Should have taken Donny's toboggan with me to the castle, I could have hopped on and slid all the way down Castle Hill,' Rodney exclaimed, shaking the snow off himself.

'That's a sight I'd pay to see,' Marge remarked. 'I never had you down as the tobogganing sort – too much risk of losing control.'

'That's because you don't know everything about me,' Rodney said sharply.

Donny, who'd been idling at the kitchen table, kicking his feet and moaning about being bored, leapt on this. 'Can me and Fred go tobogganing later, Mum? Can we?'

Marianne rolled her eyes and went to give Rodney a kiss. 'We'll see,' she said.

'That means yes!' Donny did a little dance of joy.

'That means we'll see,' she said sternly.

The door opened again and Jasper appeared. 'Merry Christmas!' he boomed, dumping a bottle of sherry and a colourfully wrapped present on to the table. 'This looks very nice,' he said, gesturing at the table.

'I did it!' Donny said proudly. 'Don't you think I should be allowed to go tobogganing as a reward?'

Jasper laughed and ruffled his hair. 'I do, son. And I'll join you. Champion tobogganer back in my day. Slid all the way down the cliffs to the sea one year.'

'You never!'

'I did.' He winked.

'Land's sake, Jasper Cane, don't put ideas into the boy's head.' Nellie appeared and glanced at the present on the table. 'That for me?'

'It is, madam. Made by my own fair hands.'

Nellie snatched it up, tearing at the paper as eagerly as a child. She gasped as she saw what he'd made. Two wrought-iron candlesticks shaped like roses, so the candle would sit in the centre of the petals.

'You are an artist, Jasper Cane. A true artist,' she whispered.

Jasper shrugged modestly. 'Just a little sideline of mine. Folk don't have much call for decorative iron-work in Dover. Still, glad you like them.'

She placed one at either end of the table and ordered Donny to find candles. 'They're, perfect,' she said as she lit the candles. 'Just what we needed. Sometimes, Jasper, I find it hard to be annoyed with you.' She gave him a cheeky wink.

'And sometimes, Nellie Castle, I'm reminded that you're not all bad. Now, who's for a sherry?'

By one o'clock the rest of the guests had arrived and were sitting at the table. They clapped with admiration as Marianne carried in the huge plate with the goose resting in the centre, surrounded by golden roast potatoes and balls of stuffing. There were dishes of carrots, parsnips and Brussels sprouts, and jugs of steaming gravy and white sauce. The Turners had also brought some ginger ale and bottles of beer, and drinks were poured and a toast was made.

'To peace!' Rodney called out, and everyone raised their glasses.

'Do you remember Christmas Eve 1914?' Ethel Turner glanced around at the older guests.

'Aunt Ethel!' Reenie knew what was coming; she told this story every year.

'How could I forget?' Phyllis Perkins said. 'First bomb to drop on English soil, and just a few doors down from my parents' house. Broke all their windows.'

'They got cut to ribbons by the glass, didn't they, Gran!' Freddie interjected with bloodthirsty glee. He too had heard this story countless times.

'Fred, not at the dinner table,' his father, Wilf, admonished.

Nellie nodded. 'We hadn't even realised that planes could drop bombs. Terrified, we were, and now it's about to start all over again. It might be peaceful enough now, but mark my words, this is the calm before the storm, so we may as well try to enjoy it.'

There was silence around the table; Nellie's speech had ruined the happy atmosphere. Marianne took a gulp of her drink, suddenly not feeling hungry.

But their spirits couldn't be dampened for long with Freddie and Donny around. Wilf and Marge both gave bellows of surprise at the same time. Marge bent down to look under the table. 'Why you . . .' She laughed, pulling out a giggling Freddie, who was holding a piece of holly. He'd been prickling her legs with it, while on the other side, Donny had stuck a holly leaf down Wilf's sock.

'Donny!' Rodney roared. 'Apologise immediately to our guests. Can't you learn to sit down and be quiet for once in your life?'

'Oh, stop being such an old misery, Rod, there's no harm done. Come, you.' Marge started to tickle Freddie.

Beside her, Rodney muttered in her ear, 'It would be helpful if you would not undermine my authority. The boys will never learn otherwise.'

She looked at him in disbelief and snorted. 'Undermine your authority?' She said loud enough for the entire table to hear. 'We're not at the castle now, Rodney. Stop being so stuffy, for God's sake.'

Rodney's cheeks flushed with anger, and Marianne smiled at him sympathetically. Poor old Rodney, no matter how he tried, he couldn't quite shake off his pomposity.

Despite this interruption, the rest of the meal passed merrily, and at three o'clock, as everyone was polishing off the last of the Christmas pudding, Nellie stood.

'Time for quiet, everyone. The King's due to make his broadcast in two minutes.' She switched on the wireless as the table came to a hush.

By the end, many of them had tears in their eyes as everyone stood for the National Anthem. But their singing was interrupted by the door banging open. Cold air and snow blew into the café, making Lily exclaim, 'What the . . . ?'

As one, everyone turned to see Bert and Alfie standing in the doorway, grinning.

'Afternoon all. Room for a couple of little ones?' Bert said.

In the general noise and excitement, Marianne didn't move. Her gaze was fixed on Alfie, who, along with Bert, was in the centre of the excited group. He looked up and their eyes met. She looked away hastily as the memory of the last time she saw him rushed back into her mind.

'I hope you don't mind, Mrs Castle? The others volunteered to stay behind, and I was missing my trumpet, so

I couldn't resist the chance to say hello to it. We should have got back two days ago, but the bloody weather held up the trains.'

'Mind?' Nellie was so ecstatic to see her youngest son that she would have welcomed the devil himself. 'The more the merrier. Come on in. And, as you're here, you may as well make yourself useful. Can you play Christmas carols on the trumpet?'

'You name it, I'll play it.'

Donny was already moving to the back of the café, eager to see the trumpet again. Marianne had forbidden him to touch it, but he'd still snuck down there every so often and tried to blow on it.

'No playing until you've eaten, though,' Nellie said. 'That is a hard and fast rule in the Castle house.'

The rest of the afternoon sped by in a blur of laughter and music. Alfie played a host of Christmas carols in a style none of them had ever heard before, and the group did their best to keep up with him. Finally, though, it was time for people to leave, while the family cleared away the mess and washed up.

It had been a wonderful day, despite her discomfort at Alfie's arrival. Luckily, he'd been so busy playing, she hadn't had to talk to him. But now he stood beside her with a tea towel in his hand, and while the rest of the family bustled around, chatting and laughing, the silence in the scullery could have been cut with a knife.

Alfie cleared his throat. 'Marianne . . .'

When she didn't say anything, he touched her arm. 'Marianne. I hope you don't mind that I'm here.'

'Why should I mind?'

'Well . . . I . . . I feel I offended you in some way last time. And . . . I don't know what I did. But whatever it was, I'm sorry.'

She turned to him, her eyes wide with disbelief. 'You don't know what you did?'

'No.'

His apology annoyed her. He'd read a very private letter, and then said nothing. How could he not know what he'd done?

'You didn't do anything,' she said dismissively. 'And of course I don't mind that you're here. I told you you were always welcome, and I meant it.'

Alfie was silent for a moment, then he cleared his throat again. 'But you seem so . . . angry with me.'

'No. I'm not angry with you,' Marianne said shortly.

'Right. Right.' He clearly didn't believe her. 'Then perhaps to prove you're not angry with me, you'd like to go for a walk tomorrow?'

Marianne was silent for a long time. He might have been able to charm everyone else, and she had to admit, he'd really made the afternoon special, but that didn't mean she trusted him and she certainly didn't want to spend any more time with him than necessary.

She turned to face him. 'I'm sorry, but I'll be very busy tomorrow. Maybe you could go with Lily or Edie?'

Alfie's eyes flashed with disappointment and he turned away, stacking a plate on to the shelf. 'Or maybe I asked you because it was *you* I wanted to go with.' He sounded confused and a little cross.

'Oh. Well. Like I said, maybe someone else would be better.' Marianne kept her back turned.

At that moment, Donny waltzed into the scullery then. 'Mr Lomax,' he piped.

'Hey, haven't I told you to call me Alfie?'

Donny grinned. He never called any adults by their first names – apart from his family and Jasper, and he didn't count. 'Are you going to stay with us?'

'Well, I hope I can. Your Uncle Bert said it would be all right, and so did your gran. You don't mind, do you?'

Marianne knew this was directed more at her than at Donny.

'No, of course not. I already told you we're happy to have you,' she said sharply.

Oblivious to his mother's tone, Donny gave a little cheer. 'How long are you staying?'

'Just a few nights, then me and your uncle have to get back to France.'

'Do you think . . . ?' He hesitated, shifting from foot to foot. Marianne turned to watch her son, pretty sure she knew what was coming.

Alfie was looking at Donny expectantly, but when he still didn't seem able to say anything, he helped him out. 'You want some more trumpet lessons?'

'Can I? I want to be able to play like you!'

'Well, to reach my dizzy heights, you'll need to practise every day. But tell you what, I'll teach you what I can before I leave, how's that? At least I can show you how to blow into it properly.'

Donny threw down his tea towel and rushed into the café, where the trumpet was sitting on the counter. He brought it back and held it out to Alfie hopefully. 'Can we start right now?'

'Donny, he's been playing all afternoon, let him rest for a bit.' Marianne glanced at Alfie apologetically.

'First, we need to finish helping your mum. Then, if you've been very good, I'll give you your first lesson. How's that?'

'Really? I'll be good, I promise.' Donny put the trumpet back, picked up his tea towel and started drying with an energy she'd never seen him apply to his chores before.

Alfie was as good as his word, and by Boxing Day, Donny could just about manage to play 'Twinkle, Twinkle, Little Star'. But the noise coming from the basement was driving Marianne mad as she worked in the kitchen. Even now, when Alfie had gone for a drink at the Oak with Bert, Donny was still playing, determined to master the instrument.

The back door opened and Alfie and Bert walked in.

'All right, sis? Surprised you can stand it down here with that racket,' Bert said good-humouredly. 'Maybe you need to get out of the house for a bit of peace. Hey, Alf, perhaps you and Marianne should go for a little stroll?'

Marianne whirled around at his words, her eyes shooting daggers at her brother. 'I'm fine where I am, thanks. It's far too cold to walk.'

Alfie looked uncomfortable.

'Oh, come on, sis. Get your coat on and get a bit of fresh air.'

'I *said* I don't want to, Bert.' Avoiding looking at Alfie, she turned away and continued with her task of chopping vegetables for the soup she was making for dinner.

She heard the sound of Bert slapping Alfie on the shoulder as he said playfully, 'Never mind, mate. Better luck next time, eh? You couldn't make us a cuppa, could you, Marianne?'

Marianne narrowed her eyes but didn't respond. Her brother knew exactly how to rile her.

Bert sighed. 'Ah well. Come on, Alf. Let's go upstairs and get warm.'

Marianne heard Bert's footsteps moving away. What was her brother playing at? And what had Alfie said to him about her? She jumped as a hand touched her shoulder.

'Sorry about that. I promise I didn't encourage Bert to say that. I know you're not keen, but he seems to want to throw us together.'

'Yes, well,' she snapped without looking at him, 'he should know better.'

There was a brief silence, then Alfie sighed and followed Bert up the stairs, leaving Marianne feeling unaccountably depressed.

∽

On the day after Boxing Day, Marianne was making some toffee for the New Year party the mayor was organising for the children at the town hall, while in the basement Alfie was giving the insatiable Donny yet another lesson. The noise stopped and she breathed a sigh of relief.

Alfie emerged from the basement and sniffed appreciatively. 'Something smells good.'

'Toffee for the kids,' she said shortly.

Donny skidded in after him, still holding the blasted trumpet. 'Ooh toffee! Can I have some?'

'No, you can't. It's for the party.'

'Mum, do you want to hear what I can play?'

Marianne sighed and beside her Alfie laughed softly. 'It'll get better, I promise.'

'Oh, go on, then.'

There followed an ear-splitting few minutes as Donny showed off a far from perfect 'Twinkle, Twinkle, Little Star' and then followed it up with an even worse 'London's Burning'. Marianne forced herself to smile encouragingly, but it wasn't easy. Finally, he finished and looked at her expectantly.

'That was marvellous, Donny. Well done,' she said. 'You'll be as good as Alfie in no time.'

'Can we do some more, Alfie?'

'I think that's enough,' Marianne said. 'This is meant to be a rest time for Alfie. Go upstairs and play with something else.'

'Please?' he said, looking at Alfie with a winning smile.

'Later, mate. I think I need a cup of tea first. Why don't you run down and practise without me?'

Donny ran off, slamming the basement door behind him.

In the face of Alfie's patience and good humour, Marianne couldn't deny that her feelings towards him were softening slightly. She shook herself. Just because he was nice to Donny didn't mean he could be trusted. He clearly had an ulterior motive, though for the life of her she couldn't understand why he seemed to be persisting with her. There were plenty of other women who'd be delighted to spend time with him. She wasn't going to encourage him, but the least she could do was be polite when he was being so kind to her son.

'I'll put the kettle on.' It was as much of an apology as she could muster. 'And I'm sorry about Donny. Just tell him no if you're not up to any more lessons.'

Alfie smiled at her. 'I don't mind. Truth is, I'm having the time of my life. I spend most Christmases working. Always lots of parties and nightclubs to play at.

Usually on Christmas Day I'm in some damp boarding house sharing a bit of dry turkey with John.'

Marianne's soft heart melted a little. She hated the idea of people being lonely at Christmas. 'Well, it's about time you had a proper Christmas then, so I'm glad Bert brought you. I'm just sorry my son has monopolised your time.' She placed the tea on the table beside him.

'I'm glad too,' he said. 'Thank you for looking after me so well. And I'm sorry again if I offended you in any way last time I was here.'

Marianne smiled briefly and turned back to the pot of bubbling sugar on the range.

'Your Don's a smasher,' Alfie said, changing the subject. 'Bright as a button and lively as a cricket.'

Marianne laughed. 'The boy never stops. None of us can keep up with him and he's constantly in trouble with Roger.'

'Ah yes, your friendly local bobby. I think he probably just wants to have an excuse to see you. And I can't blame him. If I was him, I'd probably do the same.'

Flustered, Marianne picked up the pot and poured the bubbling toffee mixture into a tin she had prepared.

'Sorry, I didn't mean to embarrass you.'

She carefully carried the tin to the pantry to leave it to set, then returned, looking at Alfie out of the corner of her eye. His khaki shirt was unbuttoned at his throat and she could see a little smattering of hair poking out. She averted her eyes quickly, hoping he hadn't noticed, but when she looked at his face, it was clear he had, as he was staring at her, his eyes warm, smiling slightly. He always seemed to be smiling, she realised. And knowing a little about what a difficult childhood he'd had, and how alone he seemed in the world, it made her feel slightly ashamed of her coldness towards him.

'Why don't you stop for a moment and have a cup of tea with me?' he asked.

'Later. Just got to wash these pots, then make some fudge.'

'I can see where Donny gets it from.'

She looked at him, frowning. 'Gets what?'

'His energy. He never stops and neither, it seems, do you.'

She laughed. 'Difference being, I don't have a choice.'

'Course you do, Marianne. Come on, sit down, have a little break.'

She hesitated, but seeing the warm smile on his face and the hope in his eyes, she relented. 'Oh, all right, but you'll have to help me catch up.'

She poured herself a cup of tea and they sat in silence for a while, before Alfie said, 'Thank you, by the way.'

'You've already said that.'

'Yes, I have, haven't I?' He was quiet again.

Finally, Marianne cleared her throat and broke the silence. 'How is it? In France, I mean. Has there been any fighting?'

'No. Mostly we're just cold. And bored. Which is why I miss my trumpet. I've organised a choir and we sing, we march, we shiver ... To be honest, it just feels like we're on a really bad camping holiday. With guns.'

She laughed. 'And the French people? Are they happy to see you?'

'They're all right. It's hard to remember that there's a real threat out there. And we're just a bunch of men who've had a few months shooting practice and have done a bit of marching, but are we really fighting men? I don't know. Time will tell, I suppose.'

'Are you frightened?'

He thought about this for a moment. 'No, not the stomach-churning terror you might get if someone was actually shooting at you. But it's the threat of it. You can never completely relax, which is why I like to sing with the men. It takes everybody's minds off what might be coming. So many of them have dads, uncles, brothers who died or were horribly injured during the last war. I suppose we're not the same as they were when they went off to fight last time. We know what can happen. Sometimes, I look around at everyone's faces and wonder . . .' He stopped and shook his head. 'This is morbid, let's not talk about it anymore.'

Without realising she was doing it, as Alfie was talking, Marianne had put her hand over his. He looked at their hands for a moment, then shifted his so his fingers curled around hers. 'Will you write to me this time?' He smiled self-deprecatingly. 'Sorry, I sound a bit pathetic. You don't have to.'

Marianne felt guilty. Maybe she'd misjudged him. She needed to think of him as one of her brothers, and show him the same affection she gave them. 'If you want me to.'

'I'll try to write back, but it might not be very often. Writing's not really my strong point.' He grinned. 'Used to get me into terrible trouble at school.'

'I promise not to get offended then.'

An ear-splitting screech from the trumpet in the basement made Marianne wince.

Alfie laughed. 'This has been one of the best Christmases I've ever had. A real family Christmas.'

'You're always welcome here. And Donny loves you.'

He laughed. 'He loves my trumpet, you mean. It's good to know that it has someone to look after it properly while I'm away.'

'I reckon it would manage. It's not a person you know.'

'It is to me.'

Footsteps clattered down the steps and Marianne hastily withdrew her hand from Alfie's and stood up. Lily burst in, followed closely by Bert and Edie – who had agreed to stay for a few days, much to Nellie's delight. They had their coats on and, without pausing, Lily went to the basement door and opened it.

'Don! Stop that infernal racket and get up here! Time for a snowball fight.' She turned. 'Come on, you two, get your coats on.'

Donny was out of the cellar in a flash, running up to the apartment to get his coat. Marianne opened her mouth to refuse, but Alfie caught her hand, pulling her along as he followed Donny upstairs.

'No excuses! Time for some fun!'

∞

Alfie and Marianne were the last to emerge onto the square where a raucous snowball fight was already in full swing. Before long, Wilf and Freddie joined, as did Reenie and Jasper, who looked comical in an enormous woolly hat and scarf that Nellie had knitted him for Christmas. Nellie, meanwhile, looked on from the window upstairs in their apartment.

At one point, Bert tackled Marianne to the ground, pushing a snowball in her face. Squealing, she fought him off, only to have Donny leap on her. He landed right in the middle of her chest, and for a moment she was unable to breathe. Alfie pulled him off, and Donny ran around and leapt on to his back. Laughing, Alfie grabbed his legs and raced around the square, whooping at the top of his voice. Not wanting to be left out, Freddie jumped on to his dad's back and the two men ran across the square, egged on by the crowd around them.

Marianne stayed sitting on the ground, watching them, a strange ache in her heart. Finally, Alfie ran up to her and dropped Don to the ground. 'Enough,' he pleaded. 'Have mercy.'

Don pushed him and he slipped and landed with a thud beside her. He was laughing so much that tears were pouring down his reddened cheeks. He turned his head towards Marianne and he looked so funny with the snow stuck to his stubble that she couldn't resist leaning over and wiping his face.

'You look like Father Christmas.'

He returned the favour, brushing the snow from her hair. 'And you look like the snow queen.' Then he caught her mittened hand and yanked her down beside him. Thumping him, Marianne giggled and tried to get up, but he pulled her back, and they lay for a moment, face to face, giggling like children.

'Oy! Love birds! Leave it out,' Lily yelled at them.

It was as if Lily's words had thrown a bucket of cold water over Marianne, and she scrambled up, flustered. She needed to get away before she made a fool of herself.

'Hot chocolate and mince pies for everyone in fifteen minutes!' she yelled. Then she ran to the sanctuary of her kitchen, pulling off her coat and mittens as she went.

It wasn't long before the café was full, and Donny once again persuaded poor Alfie to play a few tunes.

He didn't seem to mind, though; he was in his element when he played. Marianne watched surreptitiously, and though Alfie tried to catch her eye, she refused to look at him, bustling back and forth, making sure everyone had enough to eat. Once she was certain everyone was happy, she went upstairs, ignoring her mother's pointed look as she hurried up the second flight of stairs to her room.

What was wrong with her? she wondered. Hadn't she promised herself she would not be charmed? But somehow Alfie had managed to worm his way under her defences. Had she misjudged him? Or was she being played for a fool again? She sat down at the dressing table and stared at herself in the mirror. Her chestnut hair was damp, her cheeks rosy from the cold and her hazel eyes sparkled. For just a moment, she thought she looked pretty. But then she shook her head and stood up, throwing herself down on the bed in annoyance. She was being ridiculous; she needed to remember all the reasons why getting close to Alfie was a very bad idea.

∽

The next morning the men had to leave early. Marianne got up to see them off, making them an enormous breakfast of sausage, egg, fried bread and bacon. Afterwards, Bert went upstairs to collect the kit bags while Alfie came over and stood beside Marianne as she wiped down the kitchen table. A tense silence stretched between them, and finally Alfie took the cloth from Marianne's hands and turned her towards him.

'Marianne, will you look at me?'

She glanced up, blushing, and he smiled and took her hands. 'I know I've said it before, but this has been the happiest Christmas I can remember. Thank you.'

He bent close and kissed her lips. Shocked, Marianne stood still for a moment, but then Alfie pulled her closer and the warmth of his arms and the delicious scent of him made her relax, and she reached her arms around his neck and kissed him back. What was the use of pretending anymore? And surely one kiss couldn't do any harm.

Bert's footsteps sounded on the stairs and Alfie stepped back, his eyes intense. 'Remember your promise. Write to me.'

Wordlessly, she nodded, and he smiled and squeezed her hands. 'Thank you.'

Bert arrived and, taking in the situation at one glance, he grinned. 'And about time too. Shame we have to leave.'

Nellie and the others appeared behind them, and after a round of loud and emotional farewells, the two men went out into the snowy morning. Marianne and Nellie followed them to the door and watched as they walked down King Street towards the docks. When they reached the corner, they both turned and waved.

Marianne waved back, and then they were gone. The lump in her throat seemed to be choking her, and she could feel tears gathering in her eyes. Beside her Nellie was sniffing, and Marianne caught her mother's hand, squeezing it.

Nellie looked at her daughter, noting her devastated expression, and nodded. 'So that's how it is, is it? I'd be careful, if I was you. Guard your heart, girl. You don't want to find yourself in trouble again.'

Marianne wiped her face. 'Don't worry, Mum, I've learnt my lesson. I won't be making a fool of myself again.'

Chapter 24

March 1940

'Gordon Bennett! Don't tell me another ship's gone down,' Nellie exclaimed as a series of deep booms rattled the windows of the café.

This had been happening more and more recently, and with the news that a German plane had crashed over near Deal the other day, it felt to everyone as if the phoney war was finally coming to an end. On top of that, food was becoming harder to get. Rationing had only been in force for a few weeks, but already the queues outside the shops made food shopping a time-consuming chore. For now, the café was exempt, but Nellie had warned Marianne that she doubted it would last.

'Don't worry, love, I've got my feelers out, and I reckon we'll be all right. Just adjust the recipes a bit, cook more veggies and less meat, and cut down on the sweets and cakes, and we should be fine.' She'd nodded in satisfaction. She wasn't about to tell her daughter about the very interesting conversation she'd had with a friend of Jasper's in the Oak before Christmas. He'd told her he knew of someone who might be able to help them out a bit in the future, and after her run-in with Roger, she was all the more determined to make sure they had a good supply.

Marianne stopped rolling the pastry and listened, but there was no sound of an aircraft and the ack-ack guns were quiet, so she continued with her job. She added a bit of butter, reflecting that she should probably have found another way to moisten it. She'd seen some recipes in magazines that suggested using potatoes to make the pastry, and she resolved to try one of them for the next pie she made. Reenie was keeping them well-supplied with potatoes from the large allotments off Adrian Street, so if it turned out well, she was certain she'd be able to come up with some interesting dishes.

Gladys came into the kitchen with orders for the potato and leek soup that was simmering on the range, and while Marianne ladled it into bowls, the other woman reached into her pocket.

'Postie left it earlier, but I forgot in the rush.' She held out an envelope.

Marianne's first thought was that Alfie had written to her at last, and she smiled with pleasure as she reached over to take it. She'd written twice, but had still not received anything in return, and though she'd tried not to feel offended, she found she did. Her stomach dropped as she realised this was not the usual envelope used by the forces. This looked official. The last time she'd been handed a letter like this, her life had been turned upside down. Since the upheaval before Christmas, she'd done her best to put the drama with Henry out of her mind. If he really had joined up, then surely nothing more could happen. Alternatively, perhaps his wife's furious objections to Donny meant that he'd decided not to bother trying to get custody anymore. But the sight of the brown envelope brought it all back again. Please God, don't let Henry be back and trying to take Donny from her again.

She snatched it from the other woman and stared at the neat writing on the front.

'Here, you all right, love?' Gladys asked. 'Is that from that lovely trumpeter of yours?'

'I'm fine, Glad. And no, it's not from Alfie.' Marianne stuffed the letter in her apron pocket and forced a smile. 'I'll take a look at it later when my hands aren't so floury.'

For the rest of the day, Marianne felt as if the letter was burning a hole in her pocket, and every time her hand brushed down the front of her apron, the envelope rustled, causing her heart to lurch again.

By the evening, once the kitchen had been cleaned and she was sitting at the table with a cup of tea, she knew she couldn't put it off any longer. Pulling the envelope out of her apron pocket, she stared at it for a long time. The postmark said Folkestone. She didn't know anyone in Folkestone, did she?

Her mother came in then and looked at the letter curiously. 'Aren't you going to open it?'

Marianne shook her head. 'I'm scared, Mum. What if it's from Henry or the solicitors again?'

'Give it here.' Nellie snatched it from her hand. 'Whatever it is, it's not going away. Best get it over with.' She ripped the envelope open and took out a single sheet of paper. Scanning it quickly, she thumped into her seat and handed it over to Marianne without a word.

Her mother's reaction made Marianne even more anxious, and she took the paper gingerly, her heart starting to thud.

Ernest Fanshawe, Esq.
The Gables
Hawkinge

15 March 1940

Dear Miss Castle,
It is with great regret that I write to inform you that my son, Henry, has been pronounced missing, presumed dead, in France. The details are sketchy as he was not

with the Expeditionary Force, but had apparently been engaged in covert activities. We may never know exactly what happened.

Before he left, Henry sent me a letter informing me that he has a son. One he wasn't aware of until very recently. It was a shock, I must confess, but, in deference to my daughter-in-law, Henry's wife, who has found the news hard to accept, I have not been in contact before.

But now, on receipt of this terrible news, it is my fervent wish to meet the boy. Would you be so kind as to visit me at the above address? My health prevents me from travelling, otherwise I would, of course, have visited you at your café.

If this is not convenient, then perhaps my son, Rupert, can drive to Dover and bring him to me? I will expect to see you on Sunday 24th March.

Yours sincerely,
Ernest Fanshawe

Marianne let out a gasp. 'Henry's dead,' she murmured. To her eternal shame, she felt a small stab of relief at the news, but not for long, as her thoughts turned to Donny. She looked up at her mother, the mix of emotions clear on her face. 'Mum, what am I going to do?'

It seemed Mr Fanshawe was insistent about the visit, and she couldn't deny him this link to his dead son.

The man must be devastated. But how on earth was she going to explain this to Donny?

'Seems to me you don't have a choice. We'll have to go, otherwise if that man comes and takes Donny, who knows if we'll ever see him again.'

'But . . . this means I'm going to have to tell Donny about Henry!'

Nellie nodded, her expression grim. 'And you need to think about Edie.'

'Oh God! Edie! How will she feel about all this? She'll be heartbroken.'

'I hate to say it, love, but you made your bed, so you'd better go lie in it. Secrets have a way of coming out and biting you on the behind when you least expect it. But if that man thinks he has a chance of getting Donny, then I'll put him straight.'

Marianne looked up at her hopefully. 'Will you come with me?'

'As if I'd let you go alone. Who knows what that posh lot have up their sleeves.' She paused for a moment. 'You don't reckon that woman will be there, do you?'

Marianne paled at the thought of having to confront Henry's wife again. 'Blimey, I hope not. First I need to think about how I'm going to tell Don.'

'Tell me what?' Donny piped up from the doorway. Marianne had forgotten he was in the café, sweeping the floor. She stared at him, her heart full. Somehow he'd managed to get some crumbs in his mop of unruly dark hair, his sleeveless sweater had a hole in it and his shirt was poking out underneath.

'Nothing, Don. I was just wondering whether you wanted to show me your favourite spying spot up on Western Heights? Maybe we can go tomorrow.'

'You want to go and sit and watch the ships and planes with me?' Donny sounded sceptical.

Marianne nodded. 'I really do.'

'All right. I suppose I could take you to the cave,' he said. 'I could build a fire and we could watch the ships through my binoculars. But what about school?'

'How about you skip school tomorrow and help me and your gran out in the café?'

'What about the walk and watching the ships and planes?'

'After that.'

'Yay!' Donny did a little dance, then dashed into the scullery to put the broom away. 'Can I go play the trumpet till dinnertime?'

'Gawd, if you're going down to make a racket, I'm going up for some peace and quiet!' Nellie heaved herself out of the chair and made for the stairs, swiftly followed by Marianne. Tonight she'd let Donny do whatever he wanted, because by tomorrow he might not want to speak to her again for a long, long time.

The following day was cold and blustery as Donny and Marianne made their way along Marine Parade. The sea to their left was choppy and grey, and dotted with ships of all sizes. Some had guns, while others were smaller and sat lower in the water.

'That one over there's a minesweeper,' Donny told her knowledgeably, pointing at a small ship in the distance.

'How do you know?'

'Cos I seen it yesterday, and that means it's just sailing around the Channel sweeping up the mines to keep the big ships safe.' He held his binoculars to his eyes. 'I hope it don't blow up. I seen four of them blow now.'

Marianne shivered. 'I don't want to watch, Don. Come on.'

'It's all right, Mum. Lily said the sailors get rescued.'

Lily had lied, she knew, but she wasn't going to tell Don that.

'Even so. Come on, I'm freezing and I want to see your cave.'

They walked up Snargate Street and clambered up the steep bank, until Donny pointed out a small opening, half hidden by grass. They crawled in while Donny set about lighting the kindling that he and his friends had left there. Soon he had a fire burning and he sat beside it, looking out over the docks through his binoculars. He crawled out further as a squadron of planes flew overhead.

'Hurricanes,' he said. 'Wonder what they're doing? Probably on reconsance.'

'What?'

'Reconsance. That's when they fly around looking at stuff and then come back to tell everyone else.'

This made Marianne smile. 'Reconnaissance,' she said.

'That's what I said.' He lay on his back, his feet in the cave and binoculars pointing at the sky.

Marianne cleared her throat. Her stomach was in knots but it was time to tell Donny the truth.

'Don, I need to speak to you, come back inside.'

'What?' He sat up. He had grass in his hair and Marianne brushed it off while she tried to find the right words. She'd been thinking about how to tell him all night, and as far as she could see, the only way was to be completely truthful. The problem was she just didn't know where to start.

'I've got to tell you something about your father, Don.'

Donny dropped his binoculars and sat up straighter. 'But I thought he was dead.'

Marianne took a deep breath. 'I've done a very bad thing, darling. I told a lie and now I need to tell you the truth.'

'You lied? What about?' Donny's eyes were round with astonishment.

She reached for his hand. 'When I had you, I was so surprised and it had been so long since I'd seen your dad, that I told your gran a dreadful lie.'

He pulled his hands away from her. 'You lied? About my dad?' Donny's tone was incredulous.

'I told your gran he was dead. But Don, he wasn't.'

'I've actually had a dad all this time?' His voice had gone up an octave. 'So I could have played with Davey and not had people say mean things?'

'No, sweetheart. No, that would still have happened because your dad didn't want to marry me. But I'm so sorry. I'm so, so sorry for lying to you. Can you forgive me?'

'He didn't want to marry you? But why? *I* would.'

She kissed him on his tousled head and rested her face there for a while. 'Thank you, love. That's wonderful to hear.'

Donny was quiet for a moment. 'But maybe I don't want to marry you anymore,' he said in a small voice. 'You should *never* have lied to me. And as for him, why didn't he come and find me? Didn't he like me? Is that why he didn't want to marry you?'

Marianne swallowed the lump in her throat. 'He didn't know about you. And I didn't know where to find him to tell him. And then . . . then he found you.'

'When? When did he find me?'

'Do you remember Mr Fanshawe with the motorbike?'

Donny nodded.

'He's your father, love. And he ... well, he wanted you to go and live with him, but he thought maybe it would be nice to speak to you first.'

Donny's face flushed with anger. 'The man with the motorbike is my dad and you didn't *tell* me? Why didn't *he* tell me? Why do grown-ups always lie?'

'I'm so sorry, Don.' She tried to draw him in for a hug, but he pulled out of her reach.

'Where is he? I want to go and see him NOW!' He was screaming in her face. 'And when I see him, I'm going to tell him he should have said something. He should have married you, and he shouldn't have pretended to be a stranger when he wasn't. He's a liar and I DON'T want to live with him. I want to live at the café, like always. Even if you did lie too,' he added as an afterthought.

'Oh, love. You can't live with him anyway. You see, he went to France and ... and ...' She could hardly bear to snatch his father from him just as he'd discovered his existence. 'He's been declared missing, presumed dead, love.'

'He really is dead now? Is that another lie?'

Marianne shook her head. 'I promise you, Don, this is the truth. You see, his father wrote a letter to tell me.'

Donny's eyes widened. 'I have a granddad too? Like Fred does and all my other friends?'

Marianne nodded. 'Yes. He says he'd like you to visit him. Would you like that?'

'Does that mean I have another gran? And maybe more uncles and aunts?'

'I don't know, love. But we'll find out if we go.'

Donny's chest was heaving with emotion as he thought about her words. 'My dad was alive and now he's dead,' he murmured. 'All this time.' He clenched his fists and gazed out towards the sea as he tried to come to terms with his mother's news. Finally, he looked at her, his beautiful grey eyes so like his father's. 'I liked Mr Fanshawe when he let me ride on his motorbike, but perhaps he wasn't a nice man. He didn't want to marry you and I heard you tell Gran that he's the reason Auntie Edie left home. Is that true? How could he make Auntie Edie leave home?'

Oh God, Marianne thought. She hadn't realised he'd cottoned on to that.

'You see,' she said carefully, 'the reason he found you was because he became friends with Auntie Edie when she mended his motorbike. Then one day he brought her home and saw you.' She stroked his face. 'You look so very like him, love, that when he saw me as well he realised that . . .' She paused, unsure how to continue.

'But why did that make Auntie Edie leave home?' he persisted.

'I think he made her sad when they had an argument.'

Donny narrowed his eyes at her. 'I think you're lying. Auntie Edie never argues with anyone apart from Gran and Auntie Lily. And why would that make her leave?' A sudden thought occurred to him. 'Was it cos of me? Cos she was cross that he's my dad?'

'Oh no! No, of course not. It was because she was sad and wanted to be by herself for a bit. And it's easier for her to stay at the garage to work.'

'You're lying again! I don't believe *anything* you say anymore. And I *do* want to see my grandfather. Maybe he'll tell me the truth!' Donny scrambled out of the cave and set off at a run down the hill.

Marianne crawled awkwardly to the opening. 'Where are you going, Don?'

He turned briefly. 'I'm going to ask Auntie Edie why she left; I bet she won't lie to me.'

'No! Donny, don't do that!' Marianne called desperately. Oh God, poor Edie. She shouldn't learn the truth from her nephew.

Donny ignored Marianne, scampering down the hill like a mountain goat. There was no way Marianne would be able to catch him; she just had to hope she could reach the garage before too much damage was done.

Chapter 25

Edie was in the bathroom washing her hands when Mr Pearson knocked on the door. 'Edie, young Donald's here. Says he wants to speak to you. Seems to be in a state.'

Edie came out and was almost flattened as Donny's small body slammed against her and he wound his arms around her waist.

'Donny? Hey, Donny, what's this? Has something happened?'

He shook his head against her stomach and she raised her hand to smooth down his hair. She looked up at Mr Pearson. 'Sorry,' she mouthed.

'Fifteen minutes.' He sighed.

Edie manoeuvred Donny to the chair, then sat him on her lap.

'Now, Don, what's happened? This isn't like you.'

He looked up at her and she could see he'd been crying. There were dirty smudges on his cheeks and his eyelashes were spiky. 'I want to ask you something and you have to promise that you won't lie.'

Puzzled, she nodded.

'Why won't you live with us anymore?'

She hesitated.

'Is it cos of me?'

'Why would I leave because of you, silly? If anything, I would stay because of you. You're my favourite person in the world, don't you know that?'

'I don't think that's true, is it? Mum says you left cos you argued with the man who's turned out to be my dad. If *that's* true, then you must have left because of me.'

Edie stared at him, speechless.

'Donny, I promise you I don't know what you're talking about. What man? And I thought your dad was dead?'

Donny searched her face. 'Did you? She lied to you as well? Anyway, my dad is dead now. He was alive, but now he's dead in France.'

Edie gasped. 'What? Who lied? What are you talking about? Who is your dad?'

His face crumpled a little. 'Why can't anyone tell the truth? *He* lied as well, and tricked me into thinking he was just a friendly man. And Mum lied cos she *knew* he was my dad and didn't say. And I bet Auntie Lily and Gran have been lying too.' His voice had been rising during this speech and his breathing was becoming ragged.

Edie stroked his back in an effort to soothe him, but she was still mystified. 'Who did I argue with, Don?'

He sniffed and rubbed his nose with the sleeve of his duffle coat. 'The man with the motorbike. Mr F . . . Fansomething.'

Edie paled as she finally grasped what he was talking about. 'Mr Fanshawe?'

'Yeah. Him, with the bike that you mended. He gave me a ride and we sat in the basement with Gran and Auntie Lily and Mum . . . He even played cards with me and he *never* said anything. And now he's dead and Gran's a liar and Mum's a liar!' Donny leapt up and started to pace around the small office. 'Are you lying too?'

'Are you saying that Mr Fanshawe is dead? And that he was your father and everyone knows?' Edie could hardly take it all in. Her heart hurt at the thought that the man she'd loved so much, and who she'd thought had loved her, was dead. But . . . if he really was Donny's father, that meant that he and Marianne . . . Edie's stomach heaved and she doubled up, putting a hand to her mouth in case she was sick. What an utter fool she was. Had he known when he'd met her that she was Marianne's sister? Had he known about Donny then too? Was it all a big joke to him, seducing the younger sister? She closed her eyes. As if it wasn't bad enough that she'd been sleeping with a married man . . . She felt dirty. But also, an overwhelming grief. Henry had been so full of life. She thought of the evenings they'd spent together, and the times they'd sped through the countryside on his bike, her arms clasped around his waist, head pressed into his warm back . . . She didn't know whether to scream with hurt and anger or weep with sorrow.

But of course she could do neither. Not while Donny needed comforting.

'Except me!' Donny shouted. 'And I'm the one who should know the most and now I have a granddad who wants to see me, and I bet he lies to me too.'

'You're going to the Fanshawes' house? To see your granddad?'

He nodded.

'Ah, my poor boy. How confusing this must be for you.' She reached out and caught his hand. 'Come here, and I will tell you the truth as far as I can.'

'Promise?'

She swallowed the lump in her throat. 'I promise, love. Come on.' Pulling him close so he stood between her knees, she looked up into his face. 'I didn't know, Don. That Mr Fanshawe was your father. I had no idea, I promise you. And he *is* the reason I left, in one way. You see, I thought he loved me, but it turned out he didn't, and that made me very sad. But I promise you this: if I'd have known he was your dad, I would have told you and I would never ever *ever* have become such good friends with him. His wife was very cross and she came to see me, and I felt sad, Don. I felt I needed to be away from everyone to think about what had happened, and so I came to live here. I miss you every single day. Nothing you could say or do would drive me away from you. Do you understand, sweetheart?'

Donny had been listening intently, staring into her eyes, and at her words he smiled sweetly, although his eyes were still clouded with confusion. 'I'm glad, Auntie Edie. Cos I love you too. Will you come home now?'

She shook her head.

Seeing the tears in her eyes, Donny put his arms around her neck. 'I don't think they lied to be mean, though. I think they didn't want you and me to be upset. But they did lie and now they've made us more upset than we would have been. I'm sorry.'

The tears Edie had been holding back started to flow freely then, and she hugged her nephew tight to her, keeping her face turned away. They might have hidden the truth for all the best reasons, but finding out like this had made her feel a hundred times worse. Would she ever be able to get over this betrayal? Now it wasn't just Henry who'd betrayed her, but her sisters and mother as well. And on top of that, there was the grief . . . Her shoulders shook, and Donny started to rub her back to comfort her in an imitation of her own actions just a few minutes before.

They were in this position when the door burst open and Marianne stumbled in, huffing and puffing as though her lungs were about to burst.

'Gawd, I had trouble getting through the checkpoint today. Those soldiers must be new. How'd you manage it, Don?' she gasped.

He sniffed. 'All the soldiers know me, Mum,' he said, though there was no smile on his face.

Edie had risen at her sister's entrance and was standing stiffly by the desk, wiping her face. 'Well?' she said, blinking back her tears. 'It seems you've got something to tell me.'

Marianne looked over to her son, who was staring between the two women. 'Don, could you wait outside, love? I need to speak to Auntie Edie in private.'

'But why can't I stay? Why do you all think I'm a baby? Auntie Edie's told me the truth, Mum, and you lied to her too!'

'Please, Don. Outside. I won't be long.'

Donny slumped towards the door. 'I'll go, but you've still got a lot of explaining to do!' he said as he slammed the door.

Marianne almost smiled at that. How many times had she said that to him? But her sister's furious expression was enough to drive all the humour away.

'I'm sorry, Edie. I never wanted you to find out like this.'

Edie snorted. 'You never wanted me to find out at all, you mean. You've been lying through your teeth for the whole of Donny's life! How could you not have told me? Didn't I have a right to know just what

341

a dreadful mistake I'd made? As if I didn't feel bad enough – what with that woman coming around spitting her insults. And now this . . . Why didn't you tell me? Did you think I couldn't cope? Poor, sensitive Edie, let's not let her in on the big secret in case she cries! Is that it?'

Marianne shook her head mutely, although that's exactly what she'd thought, and now she felt ashamed. Edie wasn't a child anymore. If she was brutally honest with herself, she had used protecting Edie as an excuse to protect *herself*.

'It was wrong of me. Jasper told me I should—'

'Even Jasper knows?! And you thought this would make me feel better? I feel like even more of a fool. Who else knows? Mum? How she's forgiven you for lying all these years, I can't imagine. Lily? And Rodney? Have you written to Jim and Bert to let them know too? Perhaps you've even told Alfie!'

Marianne shook her head. 'No! It wasn't like that! I didn't want anyone to know. I didn't know myself until he turned up at the café one day. I swear before that I didn't have a clue! But . . .' She hesitated. 'Edie, I think he must have seen Don when he dropped you off one day. Can you see now how alike they look?'

'So it's my fault? Is that what you're saying? I should have been looking out for any possible similarities between my lover and my nephew! I mean, what girl doesn't?' She threw up her hands. 'Don says you're going to see Henry's father.'

Marianne nodded. 'I don't think we have a choice. He says he's going to send his other son around to collect us otherwise.'

'Will *she* be there?'

Marianne shrugged. 'I blooming hope not.'

Edie sighed and took off her scarf, combing her fingers through the long brown strands. 'I feel I need to apologise to her.'

'What?'

'To that woman. Henry's wife. I've done her a terrible wrong and I need to apologise. And now he's dead' – her voice cracked as she said that, and Marianne put a comforting arm on her shoulder – 'he'll never get the chance to make it up to her, so . . .'

'That's the worst idea I've ever heard. She'd probably scratch your eyes out.' Marianne explained what had happened on the night of the Christmas party. 'But you've done nothing wrong, Edie. *He's* the one who did wrong. He deceived us all.'

'That poor woman. First she finds out about me, then she finds out her husband has a child conceived when she was engaged to him. And then he dies . . .' She shook her head, her anger suddenly overwhelming her. 'If I knew where it was, I'd dance on his bloody grave!'

'You don't mean that. That's Donny's father you're talking about.'

'Oh, now it matters, does it? Yet you've spent his life pretending he doesn't exist. You're a hypocrite and a coward, Marianne. You knowingly lied, and then cried and said sorry when it came out. Well, you've managed to hurt *everyone*, and right now I don't want you here, so please leave.'

Marianne stared at her in shock. Her sensitive sister had become hard over the past months, and she was partly to blame. Finally she nodded, and without saying another word she left.

As soon as her sister had gone, Edie slumped down in the chair and sat staring into space. Everything was such a mess. All she'd done was fall in love, and somehow it had unleashed a chain of events that had alienated her from her family and destroyed her peace of mind. Well, she wouldn't be making that mistake again.

'Ready to work, Edie?' Mr Pearson called through the door.

'Yup. Be right there.' She scrubbed at her face, removing the last of the tears and tying her headscarf back around her head.

Mr Pearson's expression was sympathetic when she returned and he handed her a spanner. 'Get those nuts off the wheels over there.' He gestured towards a Humber.

'Righto.' She took the spanner and walked over to the car.

'You know, Edie, doing this job, you realise there's not much that can't be fixed. Sometimes it just takes a bit of time and patience. Do you get what I mean?'

She looked over at him the tears springing to her eyes again. 'And sometimes you just have to accept that some things can never be fixed,' she said grimly as she got to work.

Chapter 26

Marianne sat silently beside her son as the bus wound its way through rolling fields towards Folkestone. In contrast to her mood, the countryside looked beautiful under the weak March sun. On one side the wheat gleamed dark green, rippling slightly in the wind, while on the hillside to the left, sheep grazed on the bright green grass and lambs frolicked around their mothers. By the roadside little patches of purple and yellow shone out brightly as the crocuses pushed their way out of the cold earth. It had been a bitter winter, but days like today gave you hope that spring wasn't too far away. But what would spring bring? They'd been at war for months and yet it still felt as if the country was holding its collective breath, just waiting for the bombs to fall. The news last night had been full of the fact that a German plane had been shot down over Britain for the first time. Would it be the first of many? Her mother believed that it would. She shuddered at the thought. Everything was changing, and now Donny would have a new family. What if he decided he liked them better than her?

Nellie was sitting on the other side of the aisle, grim-faced and straight-backed. She was wearing her mauve coat and yellow hat, her big black handbag planted on her knee and her chin up, as though preparing to go into battle.

'Mum.' Donny tugged on her coat, pulling her from her gloomy thoughts. 'What if Mr Fanshawe doesn't like me?'

Since the day she'd told him about Henry and the emotional scene with Edie that had followed, he'd barely spoken to her – or any of them, for that matter. And she couldn't blame him. But right now, in his nervousness, he had clearly decided to end his self-imposed silence.

Marianne put her arm around her son. 'How could he not like you? He's going to be just as worried about you liking him, you know. Remember that and try not to worry.'

After nearly an hour of bouncing along the pot-holed road, their backs bumping uncomfortably on the hard wooden seats, the bus drove into Hawkinge and stopped outside a school – a pretty Victorian building with a red-tiled roof and honey-coloured bricks.

On the opposite side of the road, several men in light blue RAF uniform and wearing heavy flying jackets were standing outside a pub. Donny stared at them in fascination. 'They must be pilots,' he whispered. 'I wonder if they've ever seen me and Freddie waving?'

Marianne smiled distractedly. Mr Fanshawe had sent directions from the bus stop and told them it was around a twenty-minute walk, so they set off down the main street, which was lined with small terraced houses with neat gardens, and turned right at a sign pointing them in the direction of 'The Gables' – the Fanshawes' home.

Nellie was still silent, marching ahead with her bag over one arm and an umbrella in the other hand, but her steps slowed as the road turned into a hedge-lined mud track and she had to avoid the puddles left from the overnight rain. 'You'd think with all their money they'd do something about this road,' she moaned, skirting carefully around a large pothole full of dirty water.

Marianne didn't reply. The closer they got to the house, the more nervous she became. Finally, they reached some black wrought-iron gates, behind which a large Victorian house with weathered red bricks and mullioned windows stood at the end of a curved gravel drive. Around the house, the extensive lawn was perfectly manicured and bordered by well-kept rosebushes.

'Cor. Is my granddad rich or something?' Donny asked, his eyes round.

'He is that, Don. But that doesn't make him better than us. Remember that.' Nellie pushed at the gate and began to walk up the gravelled drive.

Once at the door, Donny reached up and banged the large brass knocker. The door was opened almost immediately by a bald, portly man wearing a smart three-piece suit. He'd clearly been waiting for them.

'Mr Fanshawe? Nellie Castle.' Nellie stuck out her hand and the man smiled.

'Goodness me, no. I'm Jones, the butler. And you must be young Master Donald.' He bent slightly at the waist and held out his hand. Donny took it as the man examined his face. 'My, you really do look like your dad when he was your age. You've got the same mischievous look in your eye.' His expression turned sad then and he cleared his throat.

Donny smiled uncertainly and the man straightened and ushered them in.

'So you're here then.' A sharp voice greeted them as they stepped through the door.

Marianne's heart sank as she looked up to see Mrs Fanshawe standing on the wooden staircase directly in front of them. She looked as elegant as usual in a white blouse and blue skirt, a pink cardigan thrown casually over her shoulders. The woman had always been slim, but she looked almost skeletal, and her face was pale despite the cosmetics.

'I didn't expect you'd be able to resist. I mean, look at this place.' She gestured around her at the paintings on the walls, the striped, expensive-looking wallpaper and the patterned rugs on the polished parquet floor. 'It's a far cry from your little caff, isn't it? And your sort are always on the make.'

Nellie bristled. 'Believe me, I wouldn't touch your family with a bargepole if I had a choice. But I know my duty. Unlike some I could mention. Now go and crawl back into your hole and leave us decent folk to introduce this young man to his grandfather. The sooner we do, the sooner we can leave.'

Jones cleared his throat uncomfortably. 'Follow me, please.'

He led them into a book-lined study to the left of the front door, where an old man was sitting by a roaring fire, a blue tartan blanket over his knees. As soon as he saw them, he beckoned them in eagerly.

'Come in, come in. Let me see you, young man.'

Donny hovered by the door until Marianne gave him a little shove. He moved over the thick-piled blue carpet and stopped in front of the old man's chair. Mr Fanshawe took Donny's hand and gazed at his face for a long time, his expression rapt. Finally, he put his right hand up and stroked his cheek.

'I wasn't sure, you know. But now . . . Look at you. So like your father.' He looked over at Marianne and Nellie with tears in his eyes, and Marianne's heart went out to him. No matter what Henry had done, his father must have loved him.

'Thank you, ladies, for bringing him. Do come over and we'll have tea. Cook's baked a Victoria sponge. I expect you'd like that, wouldn't you, Donald?'

The table beside him held a tray full of pretty flower-patterned cups and saucers and a large teapot. In front of him, on another table, stood a cake, dusted with icing sugar.

'My name's Donny,' he said sulkily. 'And I like cake. But I 'spect it won't be as good as my mum's.'

'Donny,' Marianne gasped, reddening at his rude tone.

Mr Fanshawe laughed. 'Quite all right, dear. I believe I've had the pleasure of tasting one of your cakes and he's right. I doubt Cook, for all her talents, could make anything to compare. Now, I have some photographs to show to young Donny here of his dad when he was younger, and then perhaps we can have a nice chat and get to know each other.'

Nellie smiled grimly at him. 'Nice to see that *some* people in this family are polite, at least. Gawd knows your son didn't inherit your manners. And as for your daughter-in-law . . .'

Mr Fanshawe's smile slipped. 'I can only apologise on my son's behalf. He was always rash and impulsive and prone to getting into scrapes. But he was my son.' His voice cracked and Nellie's expression softened as she nodded.

'And please, you must forgive poor Elspeth. She's been having a hard time of it and . . . well, she lost her own baby in the summer and now she's lost her home to the army, and—'

'Ernest!' Marianne turned to see Elspeth Fanshawe standing in the doorway, her eyes blazing.

Mr Fanshawe looked shamefaced and cleared his throat. 'Yes, well. Please sit down. Mrs Castle, would you mind pouring for me? I'm afraid my hands aren't what they used to be.'

While Nellie went over to the fireplace to join the other two, Marianne looked at Elspeth with sympathy. 'I'm so sorry to hear that,' she said sincerely.

'Are you?' The other woman's tone was bitter. 'Well, it doesn't matter because my husband had another child lined up to take my baby's place.' She looked over at Donny and, despite her anger, Marianne could see a longing in her eyes. On impulse, she placed her hand on Elspeth's arm.

'Of course I am. I'm just sorry to have intruded on your grief like this.'

Elspeth shook her hand off and hissed, 'My grief? What do you know about grief? My husband and baby are both gone, which is convenient for you. But let me tell you, even if they were alive, I wouldn't have that cuckoo anywhere near me. Now go and play happy families with Ernest. But I'll be watching you, and if you and your despicable family dare try to take advantage of him, you will live to regret it. And know this: that boy will *never* be welcome in my household.' She turned and stalked out of the room.

Mr Fanshawe had been watching the exchange out of the corner of his eye and he gave Marianne an apologetic smile and beckoned her over. 'Take no notice, dear. She's still grieving hard for Henry, especially after . . . Well, it'll take some time for her to return to herself.'

'I don't know who you think you're fooling, Mr Fanshawe,' Nellie said. 'That woman's bitterness will destroy her, if she's not careful. And I won't have our Don bearing the brunt of it.'

Elspeth stood on the stairs and watched the little group leave the house. The boy ignored her, while the older woman in the garish clothes turned to give her an evil glare, but her gaze was fixed on Marianne. What could Henry have seen in her? She was dressed in a drab brown A-line skirt, a shapeless black jersey covered her top half, making her look dumpy, and the coat she was wearing was an abomination. The best she could say about her was that her hair was a pretty chestnut colour and her large hazel eyes and glowing skin gave her a wholesome look that some men might find appealing, but to Elspeth she just looked wet. And yet there she was holding Henry's son by the hand, welcomed into the family as though she was visiting royalty, while she, Elspeth, renowned for her beauty and style, was pitied and looked down on as the woman who not only couldn't hang on to her husband, but couldn't even have any children.

As though sensing her stare, the younger woman looked back at her and gave her a small, sympathetic smile. Elspéth scowled at her and turned to walk up the stairs, her back straight. She might have lost everything, but to have a woman like *that* pity her was almost more than she could bear.

Chapter 27

April 1940

It was midnight as Nellie pedalled furiously up Elms Hill, puffing and cursing. Behind her the bike trailer bounced noisily. She'd left the café furtively half an hour before, pushing the bike carefully through the dark streets, navigating from memory and the occasional glimmer of light from the moon when it shone out from behind the shifting clouds. The last thing she needed was Roger spotting her.

Once she reached Folkestone Road, she turned on the bicycle light and started to cycle, however, the dim, downward-facing light showed only the patch of road in front of her. She knew fields lay on either side, but she couldn't see them; she could have been cycling into hell for all she knew.

Not far now, though. Her heart was palpitating, not just from exertion, but from fear, and she knew she had to take a breather. She slowed to a stop and got off the bike, bending over as she tried to regain her breath. The last time she'd cycled further than the seafront had been before Lily had been born and she was a sight rounder than she'd been back in those days. Still, she'd noticed since rationing had begun and they'd all cut back on sugar and butter that her skirts had felt a little looser, so every cloud had a silver lining, she supposed.

She straightened and listened carefully. The road was quiet. Even the sky was quiet and she relished the peace. It wasn't easy to find these days. The noise from across the Channel was becoming incessant, and the number of planes whining above them had also increased. War was a bloody noisy business, she thought. On top of everything else.

She was headed for the Chequers pub in Hougham Without. A friend of Jasper's had let it slip one evening in the Oak that, in preparation for rationing, the landlord there had established a supply chain on the black market. She had no idea how he got hold of his goods, and she wasn't about to ask. All she knew was that as rationing tightened its grip and with even restaurants becoming subject to the cuts, she needed to find a way to keep the community fed, because it was only going to get worse. The market folk in Dover had never been rich, but they'd all got by somehow. And with the holidaymakers and passing traffic, they'd mostly managed well. But now everyone was leaving, businesses were closing and the holidaymakers were long gone. There were a lot of people struggling and she'd be damned if she didn't do her bit to keep people there. The war was already killing the town and not one bomb had fallen. God knew what would happen when they started. Which they would soon, Nellie was convinced of that.

Some weeks ago she'd walked up here and had a meeting with the landlord, and come to an agreement. She would come to him once a month to collect some supplies of flour, sugar and butter, and now, since meat rationing had started, she'd get a little of that too. Today she was after some minced beef that Marianne could make into small meat pies, which they could give out to those who looked like they needed them. She'd ask Donny to keep an eye on the children at school and let her know if any seemed hungry. Somehow, she'd find a way to keep the community together. She had to.

∽

Marianne looked up as her mother staggered into the kitchen at nine o'clock. Usually she was up and at the counter by seven, but yesterday she'd asked Gladys, Flossie – who Nellie had taken on to help out since Christmas – and Lily to handle breakfast without her. Lily had not been pleased. She'd be taking her exams in a few weeks and she couldn't afford to miss school. Once the exams were out of the way, she'd be helping at the hospital again while she waited for her results.

If they were good enough, she'd be enrolled as a trainee nurse by August.

'You all right, Mum?' Lily asked as her mother slumped down at the kitchen table and poured herself a cup of tea. Her head was still wrapped in the flowery scarf she used to cover her curlers at night and her eyes had huge dark circles under them.

'Why wouldn't I be?' Nellie snapped, taking a sip of tea and grimacing. She was trying her hardest to get used to drinking it without her usual three spoons of sugar, but it was an uphill struggle.

'Pardon me for being concerned.' Lily flounced out carrying a couple of plates loaded with fried eggs, mushrooms, tomatoes and fried bread. Bacon had been taken off the menu, although Marianne still managed to make the occasional cheese and bacon pie.

Nellie sighed and took another slurp of tea before heaving herself up and heading out to the café for another day's work. These midnight trips took more out of her than she liked to admit. Still, it had been a successful one: hidden carefully behind some empty boxes in the cold larder were packets of minced beef and down in the basement were the extra bags of sugar and flour. She'd disguised them rather cleverly, she thought, by draping a dark cloth over them and pushing them to the end of the basement where few people went. You wouldn't even know they were there unless you were looking. She might have to ask Jasper to build a special cupboard to put them into, just in case Roger became suspicious.

In the meantime, she needed to be her usual self. And that was hard when the weariness was dragging her down. She took her customary spot behind the counter, noting sadly that the proportion of service-men and women in the café now seemed larger, and there were fewer locals. Not that she didn't welcome them with open arms, but already the Corners had shut their hardware stall and the sweet shop had closed down. And that was to name but two. The market was no longer the bustling, crowded space it used to be, and it was breaking her heart.

She opened the paper, reading about the worsening situation in France with growing frustration.

'Have you seen this?' she shouted to no one in par-ticular. She waved the paper at the nearest table where a group of seamen were shovelling food into their mouths. 'Norway's been invaded! Churchill said we needed troops there, but did that bloody paper-waving coward listen? Months our troops have been hanging around doing nothing, and now look! It's a bloody farce, the whole thing, and if they're not careful, the Germans will have invaded France, killed our men, and be on their battleships headed in our direction before you can say Bob's your uncle!'

'Too right, Mrs C.' one of sailors said. 'There needs to be a change at the top, and hopefully it'll be

Churchill that takes over. Him and our admiral up at the castle seem to be the only ones who know what we have to do. At this rate we'll all be speaking German by Christmas.'

'And where will they invade first?' Nellie said indignantly. 'Right here, that's where. Well, if they think I'll ever serve any of their filthy German food, they've got another think coming. I'll blow the place up myself before that happens.'

The bell tinkled and Nellie glanced up. 'Well, well, look what the cat brought in,' she remarked snidely. Jasper had been busy with his ARP duties as well as keeping his ironmongery business going, so hadn't been around for nearly a week, and Nellie had missed him. 'Nice of you to bother to come and see us. I figured that now you get to march around town with an armband and a helmet telling people to shut their curtains that we weren't good enough for you.'

Jasper grinned. It was clear that he'd come straight from the forge this morning as he was wearing his workwear of checked shirt, baggy trousers held up with braces and big black boots. Walking up to the counter he planted a kiss on Nellie's cheek. 'Ah, Nellie, Nellie, Nellie. How could you have so little faith?' He grabbed her hand, pulled her from behind the counter and waltzed her through the narrow aisle between the tables, singing, 'Wait till the sun shines, Nellie. And the clouds go a-drifting by. We will be happy, Nellie. Don't you cry.'

Nellie tried to pull away; she was tired, she was angry and she wasn't in the mood for Jasper's cheer today. But then he looked down at her and gave her a sweet, sympathetic smile. He could tell she was tired and unhappy, and this was his way of trying to make her feel better. She gave him a reluctant smile in return, while around them, the customers broke into applause and whistles.

Jasper gave a little bow. 'Thank you, everyone. Now, Nellie, get us a cup of tea, love. I'm gasping. Been soldering all morning.'

Lily had already poured the tea and set it down on the table in front of Jasper. 'You missed your calling, Jasper. Quite a performer, aren't you?'

'Yes, in a freak show!' Nellie called. But she was still smiling and Gladys gave her a little wink.

Laughing, Lily collected some plates from a table and took them through to the kitchen. Marianne, watching from the hatch, shook her head. Thank God for Jasper. She was worried about her mother. She had lost weight and she seemed distracted and unhappy. She had also given Marianne hurried instructions about some meat pies she wanted her to bake, and told her not to tell anyone about it, which meant a late night for her, she supposed. It was clear that Nellie had found a source on the black market, and it made her anxious. She understood why she wanted to help the community in any way she could, but with Roger constantly snooping about, she was worried her mother might be caught. And she couldn't help anyone if she was behind bars.

∽

Much later, as Marianne cleared the kitchen in readiness for the lunch service, Nellie came in. 'Here, Marianne. A letter for you.' She held an envelope out to her with a raised eyebrow. 'Amount of letters you've received recently, I'm surprised the post office hasn't decided to open a branch in here.'

Marianne paled. So far the only letters she'd received had caused turmoil. Maybe the Fanshawes were going to demand custody now that his family were convinced that Donny was Henry's son. Since that initial meeting, they hadn't managed to get back to Folkestone. If she was honest, she probably *could* have, but she was reluctant. Mr Fanshawe was a sweet man, but she was worried if they visited too often, they might start pushing for Donny to stay there. And if Donny was familiar with them, then the courts might feel it would be in Donny's best interests to put him with the wealthier family.

She'd compromised by making Donny write to his grandfather every week, and though he protested, he dutifully sat down to write about his adventures. It was better than having to visit. He still hadn't really forgiven Marianne for lying about his father for all those years, nor had he come to terms with the fact that Henry was dead. He'd been withdrawn and quiet after their first visit, and had told her that he would prefer not to go again. He'd found sitting with the sad, sick old man uncomfortable, and the presence of Elspeth only made matters worse. He knew she hated him, and the feeling was mutual.

Lily snatched the letter from her mother's hand before Marianne had a chance to take it and examined the front. 'Well, it's not official. I can hardly read the writing, which is probably why it didn't get here sooner. I bet I know who it's from.' She slapped a hand over her heart. 'Oh, Alfie, can I blow on your trumpet?' She giggled as Marianne grabbed the letter from her, her face flushing and her heart beating faster. She'd written three letters to Alfie now, but received no reply. She'd tried to keep her disappointment under control, but if she was honest, she'd been hurt. Especially after the time they'd shared over Christmas. And their kiss.

Glancing at the others' curious expressions, she stuffed the envelope in her pocket. 'I'll read it later.'

Flossie poked her head out of the scullery. 'I didn't know you had a sweetheart, Marianne.' She grinned at her. 'Is he 'andsome?'

'I don't have a sweetheart,' Marianne said shortly. Why couldn't she get any privacy? She was starting to understand how Edie felt. *Perhaps I could go and live up at the garage too,* she though wistfully. *Then maybe I could receive a letter without every Tom, Dick and Harry wanting to know who it's from.*

"Scuse me for askin'," Flossie huffed, returning to the scullery and thumping the plates loudly onto the draining board.

Marianne ignored her. Instead she looked at the clock, counting the hours until she could read the letter in peace.

∽

It wasn't until eight o'clock that evening that Marianne finally got the chance of some privacy when she took sanctuary in the boys' room. Sitting down on one of the beds, she tore open the envelope and took the single page out, squinting as she tried to decipher the writing. Could this really be from Alfie? She spotted his name at the bottom, written carefully in block letters – like a child who had just learnt to write would do it.

Dere Maryan,

I am sory I hav not riten befaw. I hav been to scarred to rite. Now u can see wy. But I didn't want u to think i forgot u after you rote me yaw leters. Jon helped me to reed them. And so here I am swetting over a hot peace of paper. I know it woz long ago but thank u for Crissmas, for the food, for the larfs. It was the best I ever had and I think of it and u evry day. I hope I can come bak soon. I tawk betta than I rite as u can see.

I'm not like uther men and I neded to show u the sort of man I am so u never feel let down. I don't want to hide this from u. I did that once befor and ended with a broke hart. So this is me. Like I sed, I never was much good at skool. So its lucky I don't have to rite to many peeple.

But I wanted to say i think u are speshal, Maryan, and i hope u won't think less of me. Becoz i think of u like a shinning lite in my life, and remembering Crissmas warms my sole.

From Alfie

PS No one else nose I have this trubble sept for Jon. So keep it under your hat.

Beneath these words, he'd drawn a picture of her wearing her flowery apron and standing by the stove, one hand holding a spatula, the other holding her woolly hat on her head. She laughed; it was a very good likeness.

At the same time, her eyes were full of tears, and her heart was aching for him. How long had it taken him to write this letter? she wondered. And yet he'd done it for her and trusted her enough to show this side of himself.

Suddenly it hit her: he probably hadn't been able to read the letter from the solicitor that day, so no wonder the poor man had been bewildered at her behaviour. She closed her eyes and sighed. She felt dreadful for being so cruel to him. Seeing his vulnerabilities made her like him even more. He'd let her see a side to himself that he kept hidden behind his carefree smile. What strength he must have had to soldier on despite this difficulty. To become successful in his own right, without any help or support.

She held the letter to her chest, picturing his face: his warm smile, his merry brown eyes, and she thought about how patient and kind he was with Donny, the way he charmed Nellie, and how he had brought music and laughter to their Christmas. Oh dear, she thought. This was only going to end in heartbreak, whichever way she looked at it. He was facing an uncertain future in France, while she still had the threat of having her child snatched away from her. No, it wasn't a good idea, but it didn't mean she wouldn't write back to him. After the effort he'd put into this letter, she couldn't let him down like that.

She found a pen and paper in the chest of drawers, then sat on the bed, a book balanced on her knees as a makeshift desk. She was careful to write in large, clear letters, as she used to when Donny was learning to read. And she kept it short. She hated the thought that he wouldn't be able to read it.

Dear Alfie,
    Thank you for the letter. It made me smile. And of course I don't think less of you. If anything I think more.

I love the drawing. You dance, you sing, you play trumpet better than just about everyone, AND you can draw! Plus you make my mother laugh and Donny likes you almost as much as he likes his uncles. In fact, the trumpet means he probably likes you more. So it's only fair there's one thing you can't do.

Next time, just draw me a picture. I don't care what you send, I just need to know you and the others are safe.

From Marianne

Chapter 28

May 1940

By May, the news from France was getting increasingly grim. The only bright spot, according to Nellie, was that Churchill was at last in control. One Sunday in the middle of the month, Rodney had a rare afternoon off and came home for lunch. Marianne had hoped he'd bring Edie with him, but he came alone. She looked at him questioningly, shocked at how pale and thin he looked, his eyes black-ringed with exhaustion.

Catching her look, he shrugged. 'I asked but she said she was too busy.'

Marianne sighed with disappointment. Would her sister ever forgive her? They'd all been up to the garage on numerous occasions to try and talk to her but she refused to speak to anyone except Donny.

'Never mind, at least you're here.' Marianne took Rodney's arm, leading him to the kitchen table and pushing him into the chair. 'You look dreadful. If you don't start looking after yourself you're going to be no good to anyone.' She poured a cup of tea for him. 'Why don't you take this upstairs and have a lie-down? Lunch won't be ready for an hour.'

'That sounds like the best offer I've had in weeks. I think I will. Call me when it's ready.' He staggered to the stairs, his shoulders drooping.

Lily watched him go with a worried frown. 'He looks terrible. Do you think things are that bad?'

Marianne shrugged, but she suspected they were, and she was terrified to think about what might be happening in France. She worried for her brothers and Colin, of course, but, she realised guiltily, all her thoughts were usually centred on Alfie.

Following his first letter, he'd managed to send her another, which had contained several pictures. One was a cartoon of a group of bedraggled men standing in front of some tents with their mouths open, musical notes floating in the air above them. She recognised John and her brothers and Colin in the group. Alfie was standing in front of them, looking over his shoulder, grinning. Underneath he'd written: *The Alfie Lomax kwire sing show me the way to go home. I wish I wos with yew. xx*

He'd also drawn caricatures of Jimmy and Bert for Nellie, which she'd pinned to the wall in the living room, and one of Colin for his parents.

Nellie came down to the kitchen, pulling Marianne away from her thoughts. 'Rodney looks like he's been fighting the war on his own, poor lad,' she said. 'Shall we keep lunch for a bit and let him sleep?'

'Good idea, Mum. Think I'll whip up a cake for him to take back with him. He's too thin. I'll make it a big one so that he can share it.'

She got out the ingredients she needed and her largest tin. It would mean they'd be down on eggs, butter and sugar, and she pondered the problem.

'If you're worrying about the ingredients, don't. We'll manage.' Nellie winked.

Marianne thought of the bags of flour and sugar that her mother was hiding in the basement, which she dipped into whenever Nellie asked her to make a special batch of food for any families she heard of who were struggling. Tonight she was meant to be making some pies and bread to distribute tomorrow night. But if she was careful, she could make it all stretch.

By the time Rodney came down three hours later, she'd made a carrot cake. There were no decorations as she had no marzipan and the extra sugar for the icing would mean she had nothing left, but she doubted anyone would care.

Lunch was subdued. Rodney seemed disinclined to talk, but finally, he gave in to Nellie's barrage of questions.

'Mum, you know I can't say much about what we're doing. Just . . .' He swallowed. 'Things are getting hairy. I think we all have to be prepared for the worst.'

370

Donny, who had been sitting in silence, piped up, 'Are the Germans coming, Uncle Rod?'

'Not if we can help it.' He smiled at his nephew, but it was strained, and Marianne's stomach knotted. She pushed her trifle away, suddenly not hungry. She noticed the others seemed to feel the same. Only Donny continued eating, oblivious to the tension.

Rodney looked at Marianne. 'I think you really need to consider . . .' He nodded in Donny's direction.

She knew what he was referring to. The government had been calling for all children to be evacuated from towns they considered to be most at risk of bombing. Most of the children who had left at the beginning of the war had returned at Christmas and were still here, but she knew there was talk of them being sent away again. However, Donny had been so adamantly against the idea, and Marianne herself hadn't wanted to part with him, so she'd tried not to think about it. Mr Fanshawe had suggested Donny could go to relatives of his in the Cotswolds, but she would never contemplate that.

'Do you really think it's necessary?' she asked.

'I think you'd never forgive yourself if anything happened,' Rodney replied.

'He's right, Marianne,' Lily said. 'None of us would ever forgive ourselves.'

'Surely we can wait a bit longer before making a decision.' Marianne knew that Rodney wouldn't agree. He'd always been overcautious.

'I really think you need to do it. I'm serious. I can't say more, but it would be for the best.'

'For once, he's right,' Nellie agreed. 'At least that would be one worry off our minds.'

Marianne nodded reluctantly. 'I'll talk to him soon.'

'Talk to who about what?' Donny asked, scraping out his bowl noisily.

'Never you mind, Don. Aren't you meeting Freddie later?'

'Yes! I nearly forgot. Can I get down from the table, please, Mum?'

'Course you can. Have fun. And don't go anywhere you shouldn't.'

'Promise,' he shouted, as he grabbed his jacket and binoculars and dashed out of the door.

'Marianne.' Rodney was pointing at the coat rack. 'Gas mask.'

Picking it up, Marianne rushed to the door. 'Oy, Donny!'

Donny stopped and looked at her, and she held up the gas mask, swinging it back and forth. He ran and snatched it from her. 'Sorry, Mum.' He threw it over his head, then, with a quick, 'See you later,' he dashed off again.

She watched him until he'd disappeared around the corner with tears in her eyes. How was she going to tell him that she was sending him away? After the upheaval they'd just been through, she wasn't sure he'd forgive this new betrayal. She sighed. But better angry and safe than dead.

With this in mind, she went to talk to the headmistress at the school the next afternoon and reluctantly put his name down for evacuation, taking away a printed piece of paper with a list of what the children should take with them.

Walking back to the café, Marianne knew she'd made the right decision. It didn't make it any easier to bear, though, and feeling the need of a friendly face, she decided to visit Daisy. She hadn't seen her for a while, and it was only a month till she was due to give birth. Daisy had started helping out at the WVS's clothing depot, and Marianne guessed she'd probably be there now.

Hurrying down towards the seafront, Marianne jumped as an almighty explosion from the Channel made the ground shake. Looking down towards the sea in alarm, she saw a ship listing to the side. Her view of the horrifying scene was framed by the tall white buildings that stood on either side of New Bridge, and the smoke rising from the stricken vessel contrasted starkly with the bright blue of the spring sky. It was a grim image of war, and it made Marianne shiver.

'Let's pray that nobody's been badly hurt.' She turned to find the vicar of St Mary's, Reverend Johnson, standing beside her.

'I hope everyone's safe.'

The reverend sighed. 'I fear it's a sign of things to come. I'm already burying far more people than usual. Mostly sailors, of course. And recently I was called to the hospital to comfort a pilot who had crashed. I think I will be kept very busy in the coming months. Now tell me, how is young Donald? I often see him scampering around the town, but he never stops long enough for me to have a chat.'

'I've just been talking to Mrs Curtis about evacuation,' she said gloomily.

'It sounds like the wisest course of action.'

'I know it is, reverend. But . . .'

'You can't bear to send him away.' Reverend Johnson nodded. 'I understand. But a few months' separation must surely be better than a lifetime's?'

'You really think it could be that dangerous?'

'I know it could. I was an army pastor during the last war. I've seen what German invasion looks like. No one is safe, least of all young children.' He patted her on the shoulder. 'But ultimately this is for you to decide, and you must do as you think best. You are a good and loving mother, and I'm sure you'll make the right decision. If ever you need to speak to anyone, you know my door is always open.'

'Thank you, reverend. But I'm sure you won't have time for my petty worries. Let me return the favour . . .' She hesitated a moment. 'We've been making food for any in need, so if you hear of families who are struggling, please, let us know. If we can help, we will.'

The reverend nodded. 'I had heard some whispers. Thank you, my dear. I'll bear it in mind.'

Eastbrook Place had a terrace of large, white Georgian town houses, and the WVS had taken over a ground floor apartment to act as a clothing depot for the large amount of clothes that people were donating. Daisy was sitting in a chair busily darning a jumper, while two other women Marianne had never met grumbled as they sifted through piles of garments on a trestle table at the end of the room.

'What on earth are you doing here?' Daisy said as she saw Marianne standing in the doorway.

Marianne grinned at her. 'I could say the same to you. You should be at home with your feet up.'

'Nonsense. I need to keep busy and it keeps my mind off other things, especially at the moment when the news is so bad.'

Marianne nodded. 'I feel the same. I've been over at the school talking to Mrs Curtis.'

'Donny in trouble again?' Daisy asked, one eyebrow raised.

'Talking about evacuation.' Marianne sighed. 'I'm going to have to send him away, Dais. And it's breaking my heart. You got time for a chat?'

'Course I have.' Daisy stood up with some difficulty. 'Won't be a tick, Doris,' she said to one of the women at the table.

Outside, Daisy leant against the white stucco wall and lit a cigarette, rubbing her back. 'God, this little one doesn't half make me uncomfortable.'

Marianne studied Daisy closely. She was so small and delicate that her stomach looked enormous, standing out proudly under the flowered smock she was wearing. She put her hand out and stroked Daisy's bump. There was a thump against her palm and she giggled. 'Seems like a lively one.'

'Tell me about it! It never stops wriggling about.'

'Have you heard from Stan?'

Daisy nodded. 'Yes. He sounds so unhappy . . .' Tears filled her eyes suddenly. 'It's just not fair! We've wanted this for so long, this baby, but what if God thinks I don't deserve them both? What if, now he's granted this prayer, he thinks he has to take Stan in payment?'

'Daisy! Don't be silly. And since when have you ever worried about God?'

'Since I was about to have a baby in the middle of a war!' she wailed. 'Why couldn't I have had a baby when we first got married? Me and Stan would have been a proper family for all these years, and maybe not having him here wouldn't be so unbearable.'

Marianne put her arms around her friend and hugged her tightly. 'Ahh, Daisy, you'll cope with whatever comes, like you always do. You might be tiny, but you're strong as an ox and you and the baby will be just fine.'

Daisy sniffed against her shoulder. 'Do you think so?'

'I know so.'

Daisy straightened and mopped her eyes. 'Sorry. Everything gets on top of me sometimes. I've been thinking I'm going to have to leave Dover. I hate to do it, but so many people have already left, and what if there's an invasion like they're saying? I need to keep the baby safe.'

Marianne nodded. In many ways she was jealous of how easy this decision was for her friend. She would be going with her child, not sending it away to be looked after by strangers.

'You're right. I'll hate not having you close by, but you have to think of your safety first. Where will you go?'

'Derek's brother lives on a farm in Shillingford. It's perfect: not too far that I can't come back to visit, but less likely to be bombed cos it's just fields and orchards. I'm going to wait a little, see what happens, and then leave if things look like they're getting too hairy.' She looked at her watch. 'God, I'd better go.' She wiped her eyes and looked up at Marianne. 'Do I look like I've been crying?'

'You look as beautiful as always.' Marianne kissed her cheek affectionately. 'I'd better go myself. Take care of yourself, Dais, and don't overdo it.'

Daisy gave her one last hug, then turned and lumbered clumsily back into the building.

Suddenly the air raid siren screeched out and Daisy turned back to Marianne. 'Come on! Shelter's this way!' she shouted over the noise.

Around them, most people were staring up at the sky, then looking at each other questioningly. Was it worth interrupting the day yet again?

The sound of an explosion carried across the water, and to Marianne's horror she saw that a plane was spiralling down into the sea, smoke pouring from its tail.

'Oh god!' Daisy exclaimed. 'Another life lost.'

Doris came running out of the building and caught her arm. 'No time for that, come along and get to the shelter.'

Marianne refused. 'I have to get back. It'll only take me a few minutes to run home. We've got a basement, so we'll be fine.'

'Suit yourself, but you, young lady, need to come with us.'

Daisy looked back at Marianne as she was marched away by the older woman. 'See you soon,' she mouthed, before turning away.

Marianne hurried in the opposite direction. At least once Donny was safe in Wales she wouldn't have to worry about him every time the air raid warning went. The only trouble was, how on earth was she going to break the news to him?

Chapter 29

25 May 1940

As the end of May approached, all the talk in the café was of the growing emergency in France. The reality of what was happening was right on their doorstep. Above them there was the constant whine of planes, both German and British. In the Channel, they could sometimes hear the Luftwaffe firing bullets at the ships and it wasn't unusual to see the RAF engage them in dogfights above the sea. It was terrifying to watch, but the noise was worse.

Of the locals, one of the few who still turned up regular as clockwork in the café was Roger, who could be relied upon to be there early each morning for his breakfast, talking loudly to anyone who'd listen about what was going wrong with the war and how he would do it differently.

'I hear the army's retreating to Dunkirk,' he said on a morning when the activity across the Channel seemed to have intensified. 'But where will they go from there? Sitting ducks, that's what they are.'

'For God's sake, Roger, if you don't have anything useful to say, then get out!' Nellie was in no mood to listen to Roger this morning. She had hardly slept a wink the night before after listening to the news about the fall of Boulogne. Her anxiety was at fever pitch, and memories of the first war, when so many of her friends had died, were at the forefront of her mind.

Roger held his hands up as he called to Marianne through the hatch. 'Got a bacon sandwich for your friendly local bobby?' He smiled at her ingratiatingly.

Marianne cringed; the man had no sense of self-preservation.

'Roger Humphries, you have heard there's a war on, haven't you? And we haven't got any bacon.'

'But . . . the soldier going out had one . . .'

'That's right, but from what I can see you are not in the army,' Nellie said, hands on hips.

Roger looked baffled but shook his head.

'Are you in the navy?'

'Mrs Castle, what's the point of this?'

'Bacon butties,' she shouted, 'are for service personnel ONLY!'

'Since when?'

'Since I said so! You can have bread and butter, porridge or nothing!'

Marianne felt the need to intervene at this. 'Mum! Go upstairs. Gladys will be here soon and Lily will help until she arrives, but you need to calm down!'

'Calm down! *Calm down!* This man just said my Bert and Jimmy were sitting ducks! How bloody dare he! No one comes into my café and suggests my boys will be killed.'

She turned and stormed out of the front door, blindly pushing past Gladys as she came in to help with the morning shift.

Gladys stared after her in consternation. 'What the devil's that all about?'

Marianne sighed. 'Nothing. Mum's just worried, that's all. We all are.'

'That's no excuse for taking it out on me.' Roger puffed his chest out. 'I could have her arrested for that outburst.'

'Oh, listen to yourself, Roger,' Gladys said sharply. 'The woman's worried. And I have no doubt you didn't help much. Right. Tea, is it? Ah, Jasper, you wouldn't mind going to check on Nell would you? Roger's upset her.'

Jasper had just entered, but seeing the look on Gladys's face, and having spotted Nellie rushing blindly towards the seafront, he turned around straightaway and went after her.

Roger huffed and sat down, his face scarlet with indignation.

'I'll get your food.' Marianne hastily returned to the kitchen, where Donny was sitting eating a slice of bread.

Gladys came through. 'It's quiet in here this morning. Where is everyone?'

'No idea. One of the soldiers yesterday said they'd been told to stay at the barracks today. Something's happening, Glad. But God knows what.'

Roger followed behind them, much to Marianne's annoyance. 'The dock's teeming as well. Has been all night. Watched it as I did my rounds last night. Wouldn't surprise me if they're going to try to sail over and get the men. It's a fool's errand, if you ask me. What chance do they have against the Nazis?' he declared.

Marianne's face paled, but she ignored him, instead turning to poke at the eggs in the pan.

'Jesus, Roger, when will you learn to keep your trap shut?' Gladys rounded on him, shooing him back into the café and putting his tea on the table.

'Just saying it as I see it.'

'Well, don't. How many families do you know around here who have a boy over there?'

Roger gave the question careful consideration and started counting on his fingers.

'Oh, never mind.' Gladys rolled her eyes and stomped back to the kitchen. 'That man has the brain of a gnat. Why does he take everything so literally?'

Roger's voice carried through into the kitchen. 'Around forty. Possibly fifty, if you count the people flying. And should I count the people in the navy? That'll make it quite considerably more.'

Marianne and Gladys looked at each other, and for the first time in what felt like a very long while, Marianne felt her lips twitch. Gladys, on the other hand, let out a huge guffaw that turned into a coughing fit – she really shouldn't smoke so much.

Once they'd calmed down, Marianne's smile disappeared. 'Seriously, though, I just can't stop thinking about them all: Jimmy, Colin, Bert, Daisy's Stan and all the others . . .'

She didn't say Alfie, but Gladys knew. 'Your fella, Alfie, eh? Have you heard any more from him?'

'A bit.'

Donny piped up. 'I'm keeping the trumpet safe for him, so he'll definitely come back. He promised.'

'Good boy, Don. And how about you? How do you feel about your adventure? Only a few days now.'

Donny looked puzzled. 'What do you mean?'

Marianne stepped in hastily. 'She just means, you know . . .'

Realising her mistake, Gladys quickly said, 'Just ignore me, I'm being a silly old woman. Right, let's make the tea and butties and I'll get back out there.'

Donny looked at his mother. 'What did she mean, my own adventures?'

'I've no idea. She's just a bit confused at the moment.'

Donny looked at his mother sharply and noticed her reddened cheeks and nervous expression. He and his friends had been talking about the evacuation, and in school they had had assemblies about it to prepare them. 'Does she think I'm going to be evacuated?'

'Maybe that's it.' Marianne turned her back on her son and was alarmed to notice her hands were trembling.

'But I'm not, am I, Mum?'

It was no good, she couldn't lie to him when he asked a direct question, so she tried deflection. 'Let's you and me go for a little walk after breakfast.'

'But I've got school.'

'Well, I'll walk with you to school, then we can have a chat.'

All of a sudden, Donny slammed his chair back, sending it crashing to the floor. 'The only time you want to go for a walk is to give me bad news. I am NOT going to live with the Fanshawes. And I am NOT going anywhere else neither. You promised you'd never send me away! You said you loved me too much. That's what you said, Mum. But you lied *again*!'

Like his grandmother just a few minutes earlier, he rushed out through the café, knocking Roger's tea into his lap. Marianne ran after him, not noticing that she still had her apron on and the spatula in her hand.

Behind her, Roger was cursing as he tried to mop the hot tea with a napkin. 'If you ask me,' he growled to an apologetic Gladys, 'the lad should have been sent away months ago. What he puts his mother through.'

Lily had just come down the stairs ready to help out. 'If you ask me, Roger,' she hissed, 'you should have joined up months ago and put us all out of our misery.'

She went to the door and watched as her sister chased down the street, the spatula waving as she pumped her arms in an effort to keep up with her son.

'Donny! Don!' Marianne didn't care that she was probably making a spectacle of herself. But she was no match for a ten-year-old boy who spent his life running around, and she was soon puffing as she raced along the seafront, past the bandstand. Donny was a speck in the distance, but she knew where he'd go. Up to the little cave where she'd first told him about Henry. That conversation had ended exactly like this one – her chasing after him. And it had also precipitated a seemingly permanent alienation from her sister. Please God, don't let this alienate Donny, she thought.

Suddenly, in the distance, her mother and Jasper appeared. Jasper stuck out his big, beefy arm and caught Donny around the waist, and Marianne sobbed in relief. Donny's fists pummelled against Jasper's chest, but there was no way he'd be able to escape his iron grip.

'What's going on, Don?' she heard her mother say as she came closer.

'Did you know? Did you? I'm being sent away and Mum doesn't love me anymore!'

'Stuff and nonsense! Your mum couldn't love you more if she tried.'

'W-w-why is sh-sh-she sending me awaaaaay then?' he wailed.

Marianne arrived in front of them at that moment and, realising she was still holding her spatula, she threw it away with an annoyed curse. Then she grabbed Donny's shoulders and swung him around to face her.

'Sweetheart, please don't run away from me. Please don't.'

'I hate you!' Donny, who had allowed himself to be pulled into her chest, sniffled into her shoulder.

Marianne held him tightly, kissing his hair and murmuring comforting words.

'Donny,' Nellie said severely. 'Do you know where Uncle Bert and Uncle Jimmy and their friends are?'

Donny pointed over the sea to Calais; it was a clear day and plumes of smoke were visible, rising from the coast in the distance.

'And what do you see?'

'Not much.' He shrugged. 'Smoke.'

'No, I'll tell you what you see. You see danger. All that noise and smoke means that men are dying over there, Don. And do you know what? If I could only have sent your uncles away rather than having them over there with guns and bombs and smoke, then I would have done it, whether they hated me for it or not. And it would have been out of love, Don. Not hate. Love and fear and . . .' Her voice cracked and she looked away as

387

Jasper's arm went comfortingly around her shoulder, but she shrugged it off.

Donny looked at her, his eyes round and fearful. 'Do you think Uncle Bert and Uncle Jimmy are going to die?' He twisted his head to look up at his mother. 'And what about Alfie? He is coming back, isn't he?'

'We hope so, Donny.'

'I'll tell you what else that means, Don,' Nellie continued. 'It means the Nazis could invade us soon, and they are cruel, horrible people, and your mum loves you so much that she will do anything to keep you safe from that.'

'But, Gran, if they invade, I need to be here to help.'

'You're ten years old; what do you think you can do against a big Nazi soldier?'

'I'm nearly eleven, and I'm sneaky and quick. I could spy on them with my binoculars and find out all their secrets, and then I'd tell Uncle Rodney and he could tell someone else and I'd save everyone.'

Jasper smiled and put his hand on Donny's shoulder. 'Listen, mate. Your mum needs to know you're safe so she can feed all the soldiers and keep them fit and strong, all right? She'll visit, won't you, love?' He looked at Marianne.

'You won't be able to keep me away,' she said tearfully. 'And if it all calms down, then you can come home. You might only be gone for a few weeks.'

'But I can't leave Freddie!'

'His gran told me they'd be sending him too, love,' Nellie said. 'So will you go now?'

This was news to Marianne and she breathed a sigh of relief. That at least would make it easier.

Donny's shoulders dropped. 'All right,' he sighed.

Marianne tried to pull him back into her, but he shrugged her away. 'I need to get my satchel, so I'd better go now. Bye, Mum.' He walked off. He might have given in, but he clearly hadn't forgiven her.

She sighed and looked at her mother. 'Thanks, Mum.'

Nellie was gazing over the sea, a faraway look in her eyes. 'Yes, well, it's all true. You should have told him as soon as you'd decided. Putting off big decisions never helps anyone. Look at Chamberlain. If he hadn't sat on his hands for the last few months, dithering about what to do, then maybe our boys wouldn't be trapped over there with no hope of escape.' Like her grandson, she turned and marched away.

'Come on, love, let's get back. I could use a cup of tea.' Jasper took Marianne's arm.

She put her head on his shoulder. 'Do you think they'll make it, Jasper?' she asked.

'God willing. But there's nothing much we can do about it.'

'Is *anyone* doing anything about it?'

The whine of a squadron of Spitfires flying overhead drowned out his reply. They both stopped and tipped their heads, squinting into the sun as they watched the planes' progress across the sea, leaving long white vapour trails across the blue of the morning sky.

'I reckon those might have something to do with what they're doing about it,' he said. 'And those.' He pointed to the Eastern Docks beneath the castle and then the Western Docks just behind them. More and more ships seemed to have appeared and it was clear that something was afoot.

'It's the not knowing and the waiting that are the worst. It must be so much worse for the men over there, though. At least we're safe.'

'For now,' Jasper said in a grim tone.

Marianne looked at him sharply. Jasper was usually so good-humoured and optimistic that if he was feeling worried, it was probably worse than even she thought. 'Do you think I'm doing the right thing?'

'Yes, love, I do. All you can do now is show him how much you love him whenever you can. One thing I've learnt about war is that nothing is ever certain. Things can change in the blink of an eye. Lives lost, houses wrecked, limbs shattered . . .' He trailed off and Marianne squeezed his arm. He looked down at her affectionately. 'The only thing we can do during this ordeal, love, is to stand strong together, because if we don't, fear and hopelessness will creep in and we'll all be lost.'

Chapter 30

When Donny got home from school that afternoon, he refused to speak to his mother. Marianne had made him some of his favourite flapjacks, using far more of their precious golden syrup than she should have, but he didn't even look at them as he marched through the kitchen, throwing his satchel on a chair and wrenching open the door to the basement. Soon the familiar sound of him blowing tunelessly on the trumpet could be heard drifting into the kitchen.

'He'll come around,' Lily said sympathetically. She had just finished her final exams and was taking a week off before she started helping at the hospital again.

'I'm not sure he will. He can be stubborn.' Marianne sighed.

'Well, rather sulking and safe than dead, don't you think?'

'Yes, when you put it like that. But I don't want him to leave hating me.'

'He'll never hate you. He's just angry and feels powerless. You can't blame him for that. It's awful being a child sometimes.'

'Did you hate your childhood that much?' Marianne was surprised.

Lily shrugged. 'It was hardly fun and games, was it? It's awful to say, but things improved after Dad died, but then the guilt of thinking that . . . Anyway, forget that now. The important thing is to make sure Don is safe, and that's exactly what you're doing.'

There was a quick knock at the back door, and to Marianne's surprise, Daisy lumbered in. She looked stylish, even so late in her pregnancy, as she'd made a pretty pink and white striped cotton dress that floated around her like candyfloss.

'Sorry for barging in but we've got urgent business to discuss.'

'Who has?'

'All of us. So come along, we need to have a meeting.'

Daisy bustled out into the café, while Marianne looked at Lily, her eyebrows raised, and followed curiously.

There were still a few people sitting at the tables when they entered.

'Hello there, Perce.' Marianne recognised one of the regulars who was stationed up near the castle on the anti-aircraft guns.

He raised his teacup in her direction and smiled briefly. He looked as if he hadn't slept for weeks.

'Are you all right, love?' Marianne asked, concerned.

His companions looked up and shook their heads. They were all hollow-eyed and exhausted.

'We're meant to be resting, but we can't. It's sheer madness up there, so we came for a change of atmosphere, but we need to get back soon. We'll be on duty all night again and if it's anything like last night . . .' Perce trailed off, unwilling to say more.

Marianne patted his shoulder. 'Thank you for trying to keep us safe. Shoot the buggers down!'

'We're doing our best, love. We're doing our best.'

Nellie and Gladys were arranging chairs around a table, and Marianne was surprised to see Mary Guthrie – Colin's mother – already sitting there.

'Come on, you two,' Nellie said. 'Apparently we're needed for something.'

Marianne and Lily joined the others at the table, and once everyone was seated, Daisy looked around the group of curious faces. 'I don't suppose Edie's around, is she? I reckon she should come back if not. We need all the help we can get.'

'What's going on?' Gladys asked.

'I'll let you know as soon as you're all here. I'll be calling in on Reenie when she's back from the allotment as well.'

'Get on with it, Daisy, for the love of God,' Nellie said, turning the sign on the door to 'Closed'.

Perce and his friends made to stand, but she waved him back down. 'Take your time. And let us know if you need another cup, or some more food. You look like you could do with it.'

'Thanks, Mrs C.,' he said, puffing on his cigarette as if his life depended on it. 'Another cup would be nice. Then we'll head off.'

'Righto, just coming.' Gladys got up to get the teapot and also brought the flapjacks Donny had rejected and offered them to the men, who took them gratefully.

'On the house,' Nellie said. 'Right, Daisy, what's this all about?'

'You know I joined the WVS?'

'You never! That bunch of interfering old biddies. That Mrs Palmer's been sniffing around here trying to sign me up, but no way.' Nellie scowled.

'Well, they're coordinating all sorts of things for the war effort, and an urgent call's gone out. They need help at the docks and the train station over the next few days. They're expecting the first soldiers to arrive back from France early tomorrow morning. They've got mobile canteens at the docks and the station, and they need lots of people to help because they want to keep it manned twenty-four hours a day. Can you do it?'

Marianne gasped. 'They're bringing them back? How? There are thousands of them!'

394

'I don't know, that's all I've been told. We'll need clothes and first aid, and supplies to keep the canteen going – tea, milk, any sugar that you can spare. Some buns . . . Anything, just anything. I have no idea how many men there'll be, but we need to be prepared.'

Nellie stood up suddenly. 'We'll be there, Daisy. Anything we can do to help. And leave the rest with me. I'll get on to Beryl, Marjorie, that Liz who runs the fish and chip shop . . . Who else?'

'I can help with first aid,' Lily said.

'We also need a bit of help with the piles of clothes we've got to take to the station. We'll be offering the men clean, dry socks while we wash and mend their old ones to give to any more soldiers who make it back. I've volunteered to do that bit because it's something I can do sitting down.'

Nellie wrinkled her nose. 'No way I could handle a thousand men's smelly socks. Anyway, I can't darn for toffee.'

'Not to worry. You can just help man the feeding stations. And Mary, all the barracks round about are baking bread and buns, and the canteens up there will be making sandwiches, but there's always room for more. Is there anything your bakery can do for us with what you have?'

Mary nodded. 'We'll do our best. I'm sure we can stretch our supplies, and perhaps Marianne and Nellie, you could make some too. Between us we can make a few hundred buns by tomorrow morning if we work all night.'

'I'll try,' Marianne said. 'But I won't be able to make as many as David and Mary.' She glanced over at Nellie, who nodded, reading her thoughts. Their stash of contraband could be put to good use tonight. 'I reckon I could make a few score tonight, but I'll have to get my skates on.'

Daisy handed over the notepad to Marianne. 'Could you write that down here for me, and Mary, can you estimate how many you'll be able to do?'

Between them, Marianne and Mary thought they should be able to supply a couple of hundred buns. 'I'll pull in some extra people and we'll get a system going. But we'll need more supplies if this goes on too long,' Mary said.

Daisy nodded. 'I'll speak to Mrs Palmer, but maybe we won't need to. Depends how the army kitchens are managing.'

Donny, who had been hovering by the kitchen door, unnoticed by the women, piped up then, 'What can I do?'

Daisy looked at him reflectively. 'Perhaps you can help your mum make the food, Don.'

The bell above the door tinkled, and Mrs Palmer, the doctor's wife and chairwoman of the Dover WVS, walked in looking harried. She was carrying two large string shopping bags, which she dumped on one of the tables.

'Ah, Daisy,' she said. 'I see you're carrying out a planning meeting. Every household I've stopped at seems to be doing the same. Thank God for the Dover contingent; looks like we'll be in the thick of it.'

Nellie rolled her eyes. 'Aren't we the lucky ones.' She eyed the bag suspiciously. 'What's that?'

'I have here around a thousand postcards, and I need somebody to write them.'

Nellie snorted. 'Are you mad? What exactly are we going to write? "Wish you were here"?'

'If you'll let me explain, Mrs Castle. The army's been printing cards for the men to sign, but they're not sure they'll have enough, so I've been collecting thousands of the damn things, and if we're lucky, hopefully we'll need more. I was wondering if you could write "Arrived Safely" on each one, then we can give them to the men who make it back to sign and write their addresses, and we'll post them to their families. So, can you help?'

'With the best will in the world, Mrs Palmer,' Mary said, 'we'd love to help, but right now we're expected to make hundreds of buns, so I'm not sure we have time.'

'I can do it!' Donny leapt forward excitedly. 'I'll use my best handwriting.'

'Good lad.' Mrs Palmer smiled. 'I'll leave these with you then. Right, best be off. Can you bring them with you when you come for your shift at one of the feeding stations?'

'I can deliver them all!' Donny was almost jumping with excitement at the thought of being included. 'I can take the bike and trailer and cycle them down.'

'Donny, you'll be at school!'

'I'm not going and you can't make me! I want to help.'

'It would be a tremendous help, Marianne. I wouldn't normally condone children missing school, but this is a time of national emergency and we need all hands on deck.'

Perce and his friends stood up from the table behind them, startling the women, who'd forgotten they were there. 'Bless you, ladies,' he said. 'Between us all, we'll bring them home.'

'Stay safe, lads. And you know where we are if you need us,' Nellie said, giving them a gentle smile.

The soldiers strode out of the door with a new determination, closely followed by Mrs Palmer and Mary.

As soon as the door closed behind them, Nellie clapped her hands. 'Right then, we better get moving if we're going to bake enough buns to feed an army. Don, before you start, go and fetch your aunt, will you? Even she can't stay away for this.'

Donny nodded and raced off while the women went into the kitchen to start their mammoth task.

Edie arrived a little later and as she walked through the back door into the kitchen, Nellie went over and gave her a long, hard hug. 'Thank gawd you're here, my love. Will you be staying?' She looked at her daughter hopefully.

Edie pulled away, shaking her head, and looked around at her beloved family. Once, she could never have imagined living apart from them, but everything had changed and she wasn't sure she could ever come back.

She cleared her throat. 'I'm here for my brothers, and for all of the men in France. But that's not going to change the fact that I won't be moving back home.'

Nellie nodded and sighed. 'Fair enough, love. I understand your anger and wish things could be different. But here' – she tossed an apron at her – 'put this on and get started with the washing up, will you?'

∽

The women laboured through the night, while Donny sat at a table and painstakingly wrote hundreds of postcards, his tongue poking from the side of his mouth. Every so often, Marianne would place a cup of cocoa beside him, and he would absentmindedly drink it, sometimes dripping it onto the postcards. But she was sure that anyone receiving them wouldn't mind.

It was nearing midnight when Marianne peeked through the hatch. Donny was lying with his head on the table, the pen still loosely gripped in his hand and his fingers covered in ink. Tiptoeing out, she shook him gently by the shoulder. 'Come on, love, let's get you to bed.'

He looked up at her with sleepy eyes, not sure where he was for a moment, then he straightened. 'But I haven't finished!'

'It's all right, we'll finish them. Come on, now.'

He didn't protest as she guided him upstairs and helped him into bed fully clothed, pausing only to take his shoes off. She kissed him on the head and trailed back down to the kitchen, wishing that she, too, could sleep. She went to the table to clear away the post-cards and pack the finished ones into the bag, smiling as she saw how careful Donny had tried to be, but as he'd got more tired, his handwriting had deteriorated to a scrawl. She just prayed that soon her brothers and friends would be needing these as well. But she couldn't help worrying about Alfie. She thought about the one letter he had written to her – *Here I am sweating over a hot peace of paper* – and she swallowed a sob. That letter probably took him hours, so even if he did want to send a postcard, would he be able to write it?

Chapter 31

Very early the next morning, Marianne, Edie and Lily made their way over to the Western Docks train station. Lily was carrying the bag of postcards, while between them Edie and Marianne carried the buns.

The day was cloudy but calm, and in the dim light of dawn, they could see dozens of craft heading towards France on the grey water; only two were coming in the opposite direction. Looking west, Marianne could see that many of the boats had clearly left from other ports further along the coast, and if she looked behind her towards the castle, many more ships were amassed. Above them, planes were roaring across the Channel towards certain danger. Marianne said a prayer for the pilots; she could only imagine the fear that must be churning in their stomachs.

Though they were walking swiftly, they suddenly became aware of the sound of hundreds of marching feet behind them. Glancing around in surprise, the sisters saw a long line of khaki stretching all the way back to the Eastern Docks.

'Blimey!' Lily gasped. 'Are those the men?'

Looking closer, they noticed that they weren't marching in straight lines. Some of the men were straggling behind, their arms looped around comrades who were clearly too exhausted to move.

'There's hundreds of them,' Edie breathed in awe. 'Do you think Bert or Jimmy are among that lot?'

'Oh God, I hope so. Once we're there, keep your eyes open for anyone we know.' Marianne started to jog towards the station that was now only a few hundred yards ahead of them. Her sisters joined her and, after showing their papers to a couple of soldiers at the entrance, they ran inside.

The sight that met them was astonishing. Two of the four platforms had trains standing ready, steam rising up towards the high, vaulted roof. And everywhere they looked were hundreds of soldiers in khaki. Some were already aboard the trains, and more streamed down the length of the platforms, looking for a space. But despite the number of people, the place was eerily quiet. It was as if no one had the will to talk, and though there were shouted instructions and the echo of boots as the men tramped across the concourse, there was no homecoming joy here.

Lily spotted the first aid station towards the back against a brick wall and went over to offer her help, while Edie and Marianne went to the dark green WVS tea wagon, in front of which was a long trestle table loaded with several tea urns and jugs of milk. Standing behind the table, three women were busily pouring tea and handing out buns. There were also large steel jugs and tin cups, which others were taking along the platforms to hand out to the men.

'Ah, here you are.' Mrs Palmer greeted Marianne and Edie with a tired smile. 'And here are more buns. You are marvellous.' She handed the bags to a woman at the table. 'Right, girls, it's all fairly self-explanatory. Tea's being made in these urns. They need regular filling from the kettles in the van, so keep them heated. Buns are under here. One each only. Extra milk is in the van, and more should be delivered by and by. Just a splash, though. Unfortunately, there's no sugar to spare.' She looked around distractedly. 'If you need me, I'll usually be over at the entrance directing the men to either first aid, trains or canteen. Good luck.' She dashed off, and Marianne wondered how long the woman would be able to keep going. She looked dead on her feet.

The two girls moved behind the table, rolled up their sleeves and set about pouring tea into the cups that had been laid out in readiness. As the men continued to swarm in, Marianne was shocked at the state of them. Their uniforms were salt-stained from the sea and they looked exhausted. Many of them were wounded, with dirty, blood-stained bandages covering their injuries, and these men were whisked away to the first aid stations. There were also several men being carried in on stretchers from a ship that had just docked. They would either be put on a special hospital train or taken by ambulance to Casualty Hospital.

It was clear as the numbers in the station increased that there was no way all the soldiers could get to the table, so Marianne and a couple of the other women each took large metal jugs and walked down the platforms, pouring tea into the cups that had already been handed out, while Edie followed behind with a basketful of buns.

A soldier, who couldn't have been older than eighteen, took a cup with a shaky, blood-stained hand. Marianne glanced up at his face; it was deathly pale, and his eyes were red-rimmed.

'Is there anything I can do for you?' she asked. 'Have you filled in a postcard to send home?'

He stared at her blankly for a moment, then jerked his head, looking around in panic. 'Dad! Dad, where are you?'

An older man came up to him then and put his arm around his shoulders. 'All right, son, I've got you. You're safe now.' He pulled out a packet of cigarettes and lit one. 'Here, have a puff of that. Then how about you and me find a nice, quiet place to sit and drink our tea?'

The boy nodded meekly.

'Sorry about Ken, miss. It's too much for him . . .' His face crumpled for a moment. 'How we've let everyone down.'

'Is he your son?' Marianne asked, noting the resemblance between the pair.

He nodded. 'I couldn't let him come on his own, could I? His mum would never forgive me if something happened, so I joined up with him. He weren't too pleased about it at the time, but thank God I did.'

Seeing the despairing look in his eyes, and suddenly registering what he'd said earlier, Marianne placed a comforting arm on the man's shoulder. 'You've let nobody down. You're all heroes in our eyes. Now, take your boy and find a seat. You'll be home soon.'

The man nodded gratefully and shuffled away after his son. Marianne watched them with tears in her eyes. Suddenly she was jostled from behind and the jug of tea she'd been holding slipped from her hands, tipping its contents down the back of a nearby soldier.

The man looked around in alarm, but when he realised what had happened, he laughed and slapped his hands on his backside where the tea had spilt. His friends gathered around them, and for the first time since she'd arrived at the station, Marianne heard laughter.

''Ere, love, you wouldn't be able to wipe it off for me, would ya?' He gave her a cheeky wink.

'I'll do it, Dave.' One of the soldiers stepped up and gave him a whack on the backside, before rubbing at it.

'Oy!' The man shoved him. 'Geroff!'

Suddenly, the mood seemed to turn darker, and Marianne glanced behind her. Noticing what was happening, Edie hastily came forward.

'Buns, gentlemen.' She handed them out to the men, who looked sheepish.

'Sorry, luv, it's been a hell of a time. But you gave us the first laugh we've had in ages.' He held out his hand to his comrade. 'Sorry, mate.'

The other man slapped him on the back. 'Nothing to apologise for. Come on.' And with his arm around the man's shoulders, the group tipped their caps at the girls and moved off.

'Those poor men, I can't even begin to imagine what they've been through,' Marianne said as she bent down to pick up the jug.

A woman stopped in front of her. 'Well, well. Look at this. Is no man safe with you two around?'

Marianne recognised the cut-glass voice and her blood chilled. Raising her eyes slowly, she noted that the woman's slim legs were encased in high-quality stockings, and she was wearing a full-skirted turquoise cotton dress with little puff sleeves and a sweetheart neckline, which belted tightly at her waist. Her bright blue eyes matched the colour of her dress exactly and her lips were painted a dark red. Perched on top of her sleek, platinum blonde hair was a small straw hat, worn at a rakish angle. She looked as if she was on her way to tea at Claridge's, not passing out buns to a station full of shell-shocked and grimy men.

Feeling gauche and frumpy in her old brown skirt and white shirt, which was now covered in splashes of tea, Marianne stood and smiled uncertainly at Elspeth Fanshawe. Casting a swift glance at her sister, she saw that Edie couldn't take her eyes off the woman.

'Hello, Mrs Fanshawe. I didn't expect to see you here.' Marianne couldn't fathom what the woman was doing there. Shouldn't she be working closer to home?

'Really? Well, I expected to see you. Where there are men, the Castle girls are sure to be.' She looked at the tea stains on Marianne's blouse disparagingly. 'Seems you're rather prone to little *accidents*, aren't you?' She smiled at her contemptuously.

'And look at you!' She stared at Edie. 'I hardly recognised you without grease all over your face.' She moved closer. 'You might have been able to clean the dirt from your face, but you're still a filthy tart.' She turned abruptly and sauntered away.

'Hells bells. What is *she* doing here?' Marianne gasped.

Beside her Edie was silent and pale. 'She's right, though. I haven't felt clean since the day she came to the garage.' She walked away and offered a bun to the nearest group of soldiers.

Marianne stared after Edie in dismay. She hated the fact that her sister blamed herself for Henry's deception, and Elspeth Fanshawe's cruel words had destroyed any remaining pity she might have had for the woman. Sighing, she made her way back to the van to refill her jug.

∽

Marianne managed to avoid Elspeth for the rest of the morning by never standing for long at the table and spending most of her time walking up and down the platforms pouring tea. Edie employed the same strategy and as the day wore on, the station, though still busy, quietened down somewhat. Word had reached them that the men were only being evacuated at night as it was too dangerous during the day with the planes continually bombarding the beach and the ships. But even so, there were stragglers coming in, and many of the navy personnel popped by for a quick cup of tea before going back to the boats to prepare for the next deadly crossing.

Most of them were tight-lipped about what they'd seen, but occasionally one of the men clearly felt the need to talk. Marianne wished they wouldn't, because the tales of thousands upon thousands of soldiers trapped on the beach, taking cover in the dunes as best they could while bullets raked the sand at regular intervals, were hair-raising. According to one seaman, the number of dead was mounting, and it was hard to get the men to the ships. 'It takes so long, see. There's no proper jetty and the ships are too big to get close enough to the shore . . . There are thousands of the buggers. I just don't see how we're going to get them all off.' He had taken his cap off and was pushing his hands through his hair in agitation.

Nellie and Mavis joined them after lunch, and as soon as she arrived, Nellie leapt on Marianne and Edie. 'Any sign of the boys or their regiment?' she asked eagerly.

'Or Stan?' Mavis interjected hopefully.

Marianne shook her head dismally. 'But the men are being sent all over the place, Mum, so they might be taken to another port,' she said consolingly.

'Bloody war,' Mavis said, grabbing a teapot and filling some cups. 'Only way is to put your head down and keep going. Nothing else for it. Here, take this lot over to the first aid station and find your Lily. Then isn't it time for you to be getting off?'

Marianne nodded. 'Right, and then I'll try to find my truant son.'

The first aid station was manned by four nurses and a doctor, and between them they were either directing the walking wounded to a Red Cross train, treating minor injuries or directing stretcher-bearers to take the worst cases out to the ambulance for transfer to

Casualty Hospital. Lily, along with a few other volunteers, was helping to treat the less serious cases, and Marianne was impressed as she saw her sister bandaging a seaman's ankle with quick efficiency.

'Tea, folks. And knock-off time for you, Lil,' she said loudly, dumping the tray on a table.

Lily looked over to her. Though her hair was dishevelled, and her shirt and trousers looked filthy and blood-stained, her eyes were sparkling and she was clearly relishing the challenge.

A woman in a nurse's uniform approached. 'Yes, you need to get off, Lily, but do you think you could come back to help tonight? I'll be back at three a.m. and we've been told to expect even more men tomorrow.'

'I'd be happy to.'

The sister smiled. 'You've been a treasure today. I'm looking forward to when you finally start properly.'

'Really? Thanks ever so, sister. Fingers crossed my results are good.'

'Just a formality. You'll be one of us soon.'

She walked away and Lily patted the man whose ankle she had now finished bandaging. 'I think you should sit the next one out,' she said. 'You'll be no use to anyone if you can't walk properly.'

'Thanks, girl. But I can't. There's thousands counting on us and we're due back out in an hour. I'll manage now you've strapped it up. You know, I joined the ferry service cos I thought it would be a pleasant life.' He shook his head. 'But this . . . I ain't never seen anything like it. We're lucky to be alive. And then, after surviving dive bombers and fire, I fall down the gangplank.' He chuckled ruefully.

'It's because you're exhausted. You really should get some sleep.'

'Time enough to sleep when the lads are home safe.' The man got up and tried a few tentative steps. 'See? No bother. Thanks, love.' The girls watched him as he hobbled away, hoping he'd manage to stay safe.

Lily straightened her back and yawned loudly. 'Crikey, I could sleep on a washing line. I'll just say goodbye and meet you at the entrance.'

∽

Marianne was standing waiting for her sisters when a familiar little figure on a bike with a trailer bouncing along behind him came zooming up. The boy stopped by the soldiers standing guard at the entrance, got off the bike and, grinning up at them both, gave a smart salute. 'Donald Castle, reporting back for duty, sir.' He stamped his foot as he'd seen the soldiers parading through the town do.

The men saluted back, smiling. 'At ease, Private Castle. On you go.'

Donny got back on his bike and continued through. Marianne moved to stand in his path with her hand up.

'Halt!' she said.

Donny glanced up and a sheepish expression crossed his face. 'Oh, hello, Mum.'

'Hello, young man. And what do you think you've been doing?'

Donny looked behind him at the trailer, which was full of clothes. 'I've been doing my war work,' he said importantly.

'So I see, but I think it's time to get home now.' She held a bag up. 'I've got more postcards here, so there's war work you can do there.'

'But I prefer doing this.'

Behind him Freddie appeared. He had a heavy knapsack on his back and the basket at the front of the bike was full to the brim.

'Hello, Auntie Marianne. How are you?' he asked politely.

'Very well, thank you, Freddie. Donny's about to come home, though. You're welcome to come back with me if you want. Then you can help Don write the cards.'

Edie and Lily came up then. 'What's all this, then, Don? You been pilfering the washing lines again?'

'I have. So you better not hang your drawers out in the yard or I'll be bringing them here for the soldiers.'

'Why, you cheeky little monkey.' Lily laughed and threw a pair of socks at him.

'Go and deliver your cargo, Don, and meet us back at home. Bring any friends you like. The more we have to do this, the better.'

Along the seafront they were dismayed to see lines of injured men lying on stretchers. She'd thought that the station casualties were the worst of it, but it seemed that was just the tip of the iceberg. The sisters looked at each other in horror, and by unspoken agreement, they went along the line, checking for anyone they knew. But there was no one familiar. They weren't sure whether to be grateful or not.

As they neared New Bridge, the sisters' eyes were drawn to the opposite side of the Channel. Having been stuck in the noisy, echoing station all day, the faint but constant explosions and the drone of the planes had faded into the background, but now, out in the open, the grim reality of what the soldiers were facing hit them with full force as plumes of smoke could be seen rising from the coast of France.

'I just wish I knew where they were,' Edie said wistfully. 'And the other two. You must be worried about Alfie as well, Marianne.'

Marianne nodded. There was no point denying it. 'I am. Donny will be heartbroken if anything happens to him.'

'And not just Donny,' Edie commented. 'You know, there's no shame in admitting that you fell a bit in love with him when he stayed at Christmas. We all did. Even Mum!'

Marianne smiled sadly. 'Yes, everyone loves Alfie. He has the gift of making people happy.'

'Aha! You *have* fallen for him.' Lily put a comforting arm around Marianne's shoulders. 'And that's a good thing. It's about time you allowed yourself some happiness.'

'The last thing I need is to fall in love with a soldier who could get himself killed at any moment.'

Her sisters didn't reply to that, because they knew she was right, and silently they turned away from the terrifying sight across the water and headed for home.

∾

Marge took her headphones off and stretched her arms above her shoulders. Beside her, her colleague had nodded off with her head on her arms on the desk. She gave her a nudge and the girl sat up with a jolt, staring around her in bewilderment for a moment.

'You should get to bed, Sarah,' Marge said.

'I'd love to, but I've been told to stay until someone comes to relieve me, and with this madness going on, I think everyone's on duty.'

Marge yawned widely. She was right. Even though they were in the thick of the action, she had no idea what was happening outside. She didn't even know whether it was day or night. All she knew was that the messages she typed and passed on all related to ships going backwards and forwards across the Channel, and orders being sent to other ports and harbours along the coast. How successful the operation was, she couldn't say. For all they knew, the Nazis could be swarming over Dover right at this minute. She shuddered at the thought. If that happened, she knew that the castle was provisioned to withstand a six-week siege, but what of all her friends and family?

Static sounded through the headphones, the prelude to yet another order, and she wearily put them back on and positioned her fingers ready to type. Still, if she was feeling the pressure, she couldn't imagine how Admiral Ramsay was feeling. She'd seen him every so often striding purposefully through the tunnel rooms, throwing out words of encouragement and giving orders. The man was a dynamo, which was ironic, seeing as that was what the operation was called. She'd thought it was named for him, but one of the officers had told her it was actually the name of the generator in the room most of this was being plotted from.

Over the next couple of hours, Marge sat stoically, although her head was aching and the tips of her fingers had gone numb. She knew all the girls sitting at the rows of wooden desks were in the same position. But the messages did not stop coming. Sometimes the voices on the other end sounded as exhausted as she felt, but nevertheless, they all kept going, desperation and adrenaline fuelling them.

Carol Molloy came in then and clapped her hands. 'Hall, Baker, Merchant, Drew, Mount and Atkinson, time to knock off.'

With a sigh of relief, Marge took off her headphones and wearily plodded towards the door. The Wrens' underground dormitory was next to a small kitchen where the catering staff would leave them sandwiches and they could make tea. The women didn't speak as they trailed through the tunnels, but all around them the buzz of activity had not abated, and through the various doorways they could see hollow-eyed men and women bending over tables or typewriters.

She was so bone-weary that she hadn't noticed the other women had raced on ahead of her, and suddenly she crashed up against a hard chest. Stumbling back, she mumbled a sorry.

'Marge?'

Glancing up, she noticed that the man's uniform was immaculate and the tie was fastened tightly at the neck. There was only one man she knew who would never loosen his tie, even in the gravest of circumstances, and smiling wryly, she looked up. 'Hello, Rodney.' She frowned, unable to look away from his throat. She'd never noticed before how . . . *manly* it was.

Rodney was staring down at her anxiously. 'Are you all right? You look like you're about to faint.'

Marge flapped her hand dismissively, 'Oh, I'm fine. You know me, always on the go. I must say, though, you're looking smart as ever. Do you never relax, Rod?' On impulse, she reached up and tried to loosen his tie.

His hand came up and grasped her wrists. 'What the hell do you think you're doing?'

Rodney's face was going in and out of focus, and Marge was starting to feel dizzy. She realised then that not only had she been working for ... She tried to remember when she'd started work that day, but with no daylight to measure the time by, she could have been working for days, as far as she knew, and she hadn't had anything to eat and drink since she'd come on duty. There just hadn't been time.

She shrugged. 'You need to relax,' she slurred. 'Too uptight.' She felt her eyelids closing as she fell against the wall.

Rodney cursed and put his arm around her waist. It was surprisingly strong and felt deliciously warm.

'Have you been drinking?'

Her eyes blinked open indignantly. 'Yeah, we've been having a party. Shoulda joined us. It was fun.' She took his hand, intending to make him dance a few steps, but instead she slumped against his shoulder.

'Atkinson!' Carol Molloy's voice rang out down the corridor. 'What on earth are you playing at? Get to the dormitory at once, and come and see me tomorrow.'

Marge tried to raise her head but she couldn't, it was too heavy and her eyes wouldn't open. If it wasn't for Rodney holding her up, she would have collapsed on to the floor in a heap.

'Marge?' Rodney whispered urgently into her ear. 'Marge!' he tried again. He looked at her officer helplessly. 'I think she's suffering from exhaustion,' he told her. 'How long has she been on duty?'

The woman moved towards them and shrugged. 'Eighteen hours, I guess. Same as most of us.'

'Are you sure? That doesn't seem likely, given the state of her. Has she eaten?'

Carol Molloy frowned and thought for a moment. 'Oh no! One of them was sick so she volunteered to stay on after her shift until a replacement could take over . . .' The woman looked horrified.

'So . . . ?' Rodney was getting angry now.

'I don't think she's been off since she started yesterday,' she whispered. 'I forgot to send someone to relieve her.'

'So you're saying she's been working for twenty-four hours without a break?'

To her credit, Carol looked devastated. 'I don't know,' she said, her voice distracted. She put her hand to her head. 'How could I have forgotten? I've not had much sleep myself.'

'These women are in your care, and it's your duty to make sure they remain healthy and able to work.'

'I—'

Rodney sighed. 'It's all right, I understand. I'll take her back to the dormitory.' He swung Marge, who was still lolling against him, up into his arms and strode down the miles of whitewashed corridors towards the women's dormitory. He paused outside, wondering what to do. He couldn't just walk in, as they'd be preparing for bed, but Marge was not a small woman – if he was honest, he'd always admired her statuesque proportions – and his arms felt as though they might drop her at any moment. In desperation, he turned so that he could use Marge's feet to knock against the door and hopefully someone would open it for him. He swung her back gently, then nudged her feet on the door. There was no response. He tried again and still there was no response. Finally, he took a few steps back, then walked forward swiftly, banging her shoes on the door like a battering ram.

Eventually, a bad-tempered-looking woman wearing a dressing gown flung the door open.

'What the . . . ?'

Rodney gave her a charming smile. 'Can I come in?'

'What's up with Marge?' she said, her eyebrows raised in surprise.

'She appears to have fainted. You'd better let me in before I drop her. She's not light, you know.'

Marge's head raised from his shoulder then. 'Oy, don't be so rude, Rodders.' She looked at the girl in the doorway. 'Hullo, Jeannie. Let us in, would you?'

'Oh, so that woke you, but you couldn't manage to walk yourself,' Rodney said.

She grinned sleepily at him. 'What would be the fun in that? I never knew you were so strong.' She laid her head back on his shoulder with a sigh as, smiling slightly, Rodney pushed past Jeannie and laid Marge on the nearest empty bunk.

'Rest now, Marge, and next time try not to be such a bloody hero. We need everyone at full strength, all right?' He stroked his hand briefly over her red hair.

She turned her head and looked at him through half-closed eyes. 'Thanks, Rod,' she whispered. 'Sorry I'm always rude to you. You're all right, really.'

Suddenly aware of a host of curious eyes on him, Rodney looked around, embarrassed. Reddening, he nodded vaguely, before swiftly retreating.

'Well, well, well . . .' Jeanie came and stood beside her bunk. 'I didn't realise you and Rodney Castle . . . ?'

'Don't be ridiculous,' Marge murmured. 'He's a stuffy old boot.'

'Well, I wouldn't mind stuffing his boots, eh, girls?' Jeannie looked around with a wink and then started to laugh her deep, throaty laugh that never failed to set the others off. Before long the entire dormitory was in hysterics; they had reached a point of exhaustion and stress where coherent thought was no longer possible.

Marge was too tired to join in. Her eyes were already closed, but she could still smell Rodney's fresh, clean scent. How did he always manage to stay so clean? she wondered. And so warm and strong . . .

Chapter 32

Over the next few days the people of Dover worked tirelessly to help the returning soldiers. Many of them had thrown open their doors and taken in men who were too exhausted to travel any further, and most houses now had at least one soldier sleeping in their beds while the residents tiptoed around trying not to wake them. In addition, they donated their rations to the feeding stations, and somehow, together with the army catering, they were managing to give everyone who returned a cup of tea and a bun at least.

Despite the never-ending stream of men, however, they had also heard about the many deaths on the beaches and in the town of Dunkirk itself. It sounded like pure hell, and so many boats had been sunk that Nellie observed that it would be a miracle if they had a navy left by the end.

Every day, as more men poured off the ships, the number of casualties seemed to grow, and the stretchers bearing terribly injured men piled up on the dockside. Just the day before, they'd learnt that the ferry that had been the very first to come in had been sunk, although most of the crew and soldiers on-board had been rescued. The men on board a hospital ship that had taken a direct hit hadn't been so lucky, however.

'But which regiment were they all from?' Nellie was desperately asking every soldier she saw, but nobody knew and nothing they heard filled them with any hope.

For the women helping at the feeding stations, the days started to blend together. They would work an eight-hour shift, go home, sleep, then get up and start again – whether day or night, it made no difference. Gladys had agreed to run the café while the emergency was on-going, although the food served had become basic: sandwiches and soup was as much as she could manage, but the demand was high with all the soldiers passing through.

Donny, meanwhile, in an effort to convince Marianne to keep him at home, had made himself invaluable around the town, and he and Freddie had become familiar figures zipping up and down the seafront on their bikes, carrying messages and supplies of clothes.

⌁

Early in the morning of the first of June, Edie and Marianne were once again at the Western Docks, together with Reenie and Mavis.

'Mum!'

Marianne looked around in alarm at the sound of her son's voice.

Donny and Freddie were dashing towards her through the crowds, waving their arms. She rushed over to him, her heart in her mouth and only one thought running through her mind: *Please let them be safe! Please let them be safe!*

The other women paused in what they were doing, while Edie, who had been pouring more tea, dropped the cup she was holding under the urn, not caring as the hot liquid scalded her legs, and ran to join her sister.

Marianne grabbed Donny's shoulders. 'Is there news? Tell me quickly!'

Beside Donny, Freddie was hopping from foot to foot in agitation and looked to be bursting with news. 'It's my dad,' he burst out. 'He needs Auntie Reenie!'

'What?'

Freddie didn't reply; he'd spotted Reenie and raced over to her.

Reenie looked up in surprise when she saw her nephew. 'Fred? Has something happened?'

'My dad says to come home straightaway cos he needs you to drive him to his boat.'

'What?'

'He's going over to France to rescue the soldiers!' Freddie's voice rose with excitement.

Some of the soldiers around them looked at the boy in astonishment.

'What's he got? A bloody tanker? Don't see how he'll make much difference otherwise!'

'Is this some sort of joke, Fred?' Reenie gave him a stern look.

'It's not, I promise. They said anyone with a boat to please help. So he's going to go and fetch them back.'

Looking bemused and uncertain, Reenie stared at the other women.

'You get on, love,' Mavis said. 'We'll see you tomorrow.'

Donny was jumping up and down while Fred caught hold of his aunt's hand and pulled. 'Come *on*! We've got to go NOW!'

'All right, then! Come on,' she said urgently. And together the three of them pushed their way through the soldiers.

The people standing at the table – soldiers and women alike – stared after them. Some of the men were shaking their heads.

'I didn't like to say it, what with the lad just there, but Dunkirk's no place for fishermen and pleasure boats. Jesus wept.'

One of his comrades broke in, looking at his friend meaningfully. 'But they'll be all right, won't they, Pat? Nazis aren't interested in bombing a few little fishing boats.'

The other man was rubbing at his eyes, as if trying to erase the images. Looking down, he nodded. 'Course, they'll be fine.' He took a cup of tea and a bun and left the table without another word.

Marianne looked around at the other women, and she knew they were all thinking the same. If things were so desperate that they were sending out fishing boats, what chance did anyone have?

∽

Nellie practically fell into the café, making the bell tinkle wildly. It was nearly midday and she had been at the Eastern Docks since three a.m., serving tea while also searching the faces endlessly for a sight of her boys, but without success.

The strain of not knowing where they were was wearing on her. She knew she was being irritable and unreasonable, but she couldn't stop herself. She just needed to know they were safe.

'Nellie! You look like you're about to faint. Sit down for gawd's sake and I'll bring you a brew,' Gladys said anxiously, putting an arm around her friend's shoulder.

Nellie didn't protest and plonked down on the nearest chair. The table was occupied by a couple of soldiers, both of whom were sitting slumped over their tea, cigarettes burning unnoticed between their fingers. The ash from one was about to drop on to the table. Ordinarily, she'd have given the man a sharp rebuke, but she was too tired. Instead, she watched fascinated as the column of ash started to droop, hovered for a moment, then fell to the table, lying there like a sinister grey caterpillar. She shuddered.

'We got ashtrays, you know,' she said mildly.

The man looked up. His jaw was covered with stubble and his eyes were dark and haunted. At his hairline she noticed a nasty cut, which, though it had now scabbed, had left a trail of dried blood running down his cheek.

'Sorry, missus,' he said, swiping the ash on to the floor with his sleeve.

She chose not to comment on that. 'You made it,' she said. 'Shouldn't you be on your way?'

'We'll be leaving as soon as,' the other man replied. She assumed his hair was dark, though he was so filthy and unkempt it was hard to tell. 'Frank here just needed a sit down out of the crowds for a moment.'

'What regiment you with?'

'Second Battalion, Hampshire,' the man replied listlessly.

'Don't suppose you know anything about the Fifth Buffs?'

The man shook his head. 'Don't know anything about anything anymore.' He kept his eyes on the table, but the hand holding the cigarette started to shake.

The knot in Nellie's stomach, which had lodged there as soon as she understood what was happening in

France, tightened. She'd seen men in this state far too often in her life, not least her own husband.

'You should get off to your homes, lads,' she said gently. 'Your mums'll be frantic with worry. And your wives.'

The dark-haired man nodded. 'Just as soon as Frank's able, we'll move. Sorry if we're taking up space.' He looked at the smear of ash on the table. 'And making a mess.'

Nellie shook her head. 'Easily cleaned. You take as long as you need. In fact, if you want a lie-down, I got beds upstairs?'

'Sleep . . .' the injured man said dreamily. 'I'd like to sleep.' He sounded like a small boy.

She stood up decisively. 'Follow me, I'll take you up.'

The men rose silently and followed her through the kitchen, where she paused briefly. 'I'll make myself some tea upstairs, Glad. These two need a lie-down and so do I.'

Gladys looked at the men and nodded sympathetically. 'You all right, Nell?'

'Just tired. I'll be right as rain after forty winks. Thanks for looking after the place for me.'

'Tsk, as if I'd leave you in the lurch. Go on up and I'll see you later.'

The men followed Nellie up the two flights of stairs and she opened the door of the boys' room and looked sadly at the empty beds. She would give anything,

427

anything, to be directing her own two boys up here. Filthy, smelly, injured . . . she didn't care. She just wanted them here.

'Here you go, lads. There's a bathroom down the hall if you want a quick wash. Sleep as long as you need.'

The two men fell on to the beds and closed their eyes. 'Thanks,' the dark-haired man whispered.

'You're welcome, loves. See you later.'

She tiptoed away and stood outside the door for a long while, before sighing and making for the stairs. She'd gone only a few steps when she stopped as a tidal wave of grief crashed over her and, slumping down, she leant her head on the wall, her shoulders shaking. Putting her hand over her mouth in an attempt to stifle the noise, she sobbed, just as she had when her husband had returned from war, so changed she barely recognised him. Her tears had been shed in private then too. But this was worse. The thought of losing one of her sons . . . She couldn't stop the wail that came out of her mouth, and the noise kept on coming, though she stuffed her fist in her mouth and bit down hard in an attempt to distract herself from the pain in her heart.

Chapter 33

'Lily, come here a moment, will you?' Sister Sally Murphy called as she stood by a bed assessing a soldier's leg. It was clearly broken, and the poor man was doing his best to stifle his cries as Sally probed it gently.

'You'll need this set by a surgeon, I'm afraid. I'll get you some painkillers to take the edge off until you can go into surgery.' She wrote on the clipboard that was lying on the bed, then glanced up at Lily. 'Get him some aspirin and let Matron know he needs surgery.' She glanced at the watch pinned to her chest. 'You've been working for hours now, isn't it time you had a break?'

'I'm fine,' Lily said. She was too full of adrenaline to even consider resting.

'Well, once you've given this poor man his pills, I'm ordering you to take a break.'

Lily nodded and went in search of the painkillers. When she returned, she poured a cup of water and for the first time looked at the man in the bed properly. Her breath caught.

'Stan?' she said.

The man opened his eyes and tried to sit up, then winced and fell back panting, the sweat standing out on his brow.

'Lie still, Stan. Here.' She put the cup of water on the locker beside the bed and placed a strong arm around his shoulders. Lifting him gently, she said, 'Open up.'

He opened his mouth obediently and she popped the two aspirin into his mouth, then grabbing the cup, she held it to his lips as he took a gulp, grimacing at the bitter taste of the pills.

'There. You'll be all right, though that leg's a bit of a sight. Does Daisy know you're here?'

He shook his head. 'Don't think anyone's had a chance to tell her yet.' He looked up at Lily anxiously. 'Is she all right?'

'Of course she is. But this'll perk her up no end.'

Stan smiled with relief. 'Can you let her know I'm safe? I want to see her.'

'I'll do it soon as I'm finished here.' She laid a hand on his shoulder. 'I can't tell you how happy I am to see you! But . . . you didn't see anything of Jim, Bert and Colin, did you?' she asked.

He shook his head. 'It's chaos,' he said and closed his eyes. 'Bloody awful.'

Lily took his hand. 'All right, Stan. Rest now and I'll let Daisy know. She'll be with you before you know it.'

He smiled. 'Thanks, love. If I could just see her . . . just see her beautiful face.'

'I know. Leave it with me.'

She turned from the bed and went swiftly over to the sister. 'I think I'll head off now, if you don't mind. That man is the husband of a friend of mine and I want to let her know he's safe.'

Sister smiled. 'Good! Go home, get some rest and I'll see you tomorrow. You've done well, Lily.'

She grinned and turned, rushing through the ward towards the door.

Running as fast as she could, stopping only every so often to catch her breath, Lily reached Eastbrook Place. Leaning on the wall, she tried to compose herself before she went in. Finally, as her breathing slowed, she pushed open the door and looked around the room. A group of women was gathered by the wall on the far side. Suddenly a scream ripped through the room, reverberating off the walls, and Lily jumped.

'Daisy?' she shouted in alarm, running over to the women.

The group parted and Lily gasped at the sight of Daisy lying on a pile of blankets, her skirt hiked up above her thighs. One woman was sitting at her head, holding her hand, shouting encouragement.

'That's it, girl. Push now!'

Lily knelt down. 'Daisy! Oh my God, the baby's coming! But this is wonderful!'

Daisy looked up at her wildly and gave a bark of laughter. 'It . . . doesn't . . . feel . . . wonderful.' She fell back.

Another woman rushed in carrying a kettle full of hot water and a bowl.

'Hurry up, Sonia,' the woman sitting by Daisy's head shouted. 'Not long now, I reckon.'

'All right, all right, Vera. I'm here.' She hastily put the bowl and kettle on the floor and knelt between Daisy's legs.

'I want Stan,' Daisy wailed. 'Where's Stan?' The wail quickly became another scream as she succumbed again to the relentless contractions.

'Listen to me, Daisy. I've been at the hospital and—'

'Stan! He's dead, isn't he? Tell me he's not dead.' She was sobbing now.

'No! He's fine! I saw him and he's just got a broken leg. He's going to be fine, I promise.'

Around them, the women broke into a buzz of excited chatter, but Daisy couldn't take it in. Instead, she pulled her knees to her chest and started to groan.

Suddenly Sonia shouted, 'Hells bells, there's only a head!'

'Well, what did you expect? A blinking elephant?!' Vera muttered.

Lily laughed as poor Daisy alone carried on her battle.

'Pant for me, Dais. Small breaths. That's it. That's it. It's nearly here,' Sonia said.

Daisy fell back against Vera, who had moved behind her to support her back. She looked at Lily. 'What did you say?'

'Stan's fine. He's waiting for you!'

Daisy started to cry, then once again her tears turned into a long, deep moan as she concentrated on pushing.

Lily knelt beside Sonia and looked on in fascination. She'd never seen a baby being born before and she was eager to see how it was done. Half an hour later, Sonia shouted, 'Here it is!' as a slippery little body slid into her hands. Daisy fell back against Vera again and closed her eyes, while Lily burst into tears.

'It's a little girl!' she shouted. 'Looks like she's got your blonde hair.'

At that moment, the baby started to yell, and Sonia hastily cut the cord, wrapped her in a clean towel and handed her to Daisy, who grabbed the baby and stared down at her pink, angry face.

'Oh, she's perfect!' she breathed. 'Just like a little flower.'

Vera hugged Daisy to her chest, gazing down over her shoulder. 'She is that,' she said softly. 'What you going to call her?'

Daisy didn't seem to hear the question; she was too busy stroking her daughter's cheek and examining the tiny little starfish hands that were opening and shutting in agitation.

'Put her to the breast, girl,' Sonia said, unbuttoning Daisy's dress and pulling her bodice down. 'She needs a bit of food after all that work.'

Soon the cries stopped as the little mouth clamped on to her mother's nipple. Daisy looked up at Lily then, as if suddenly remembering what she'd said. 'Did you say something about Stan?' she said eagerly.

Lily's face was damp with tears, but she grinned widely. 'Stan's waiting for you, Dais. He needs an operation, but he'll live. He sends his love.'

It was too much, and as her baby suckled, Daisy's body was suddenly wracked with sobs. 'I'm ... I'm sorry,' she said after a while. 'I don't know why I'm crying when I don't think I've ever been happier.'

'We're all crying, love.' Vera wiped away a tear. 'What a day this is!'

Daisy groaned then and Sonia knelt again between her legs. 'That's it, love. Just a few more pushes, then we can clean you up and get you tucked up in your own bed.'

Daisy didn't seem to notice as the afterbirth slipped from her. Instead, she looked down at her precious baby. 'You'll meet your daddy soon, my sweet darling. Very soon.' She leant her head back on Vera and closed her eyes.

Chapter 34

2 June 1940

The news of Daisy's baby and Stan's safe return lifted spirits in the café the following morning, but nothing could completely disperse the cloud of worry that hung over the Castle women.

After lunch, Marianne made her way back to the docks. Lily had returned to the hospital and Nellie had decided to stay at the café – she wanted to be there in case the boys came home – but Marianne could see the strain she was under and knew her mother just couldn't take any more. Nellie was rarely quiet, but she had hardly said a word that day, not even when Gladys had dropped a tray full of plates. Instead she'd quietly got the mop and broom and helped her clear them up. Marianne had never thought she'd say it, but she wanted the old, blustering Nellie they all knew and loved back. Because if her mother lost her fighting spirit, what hope did the rest of them have?

Marianne's heart sank when she arrived at the feeding station to find the table manned not only by the usual crew, but also Elspeth Fanshawe, returning for the first time since their meeting a few days before.

Lucinda Tilbury, the mayor's wife, greeted her happily. 'Thank God you're here. We're overrun. Elspeth, love, will you and Marianne do the platform runs? There are so many men!' She looked around despairingly. 'How on earth are we ever going to get to them all?'

The station was crammed full of soldiers and the noise was deafening. According to the news, so far over 200,000 soldiers had been evacuated from France and it felt to Marianne as if they'd all passed through Dover. It was nothing short of a miracle, but why, among so many thousands of men, had her own brothers not returned? Alfie's face floated into her mind and she shut her eyes in despair at the thought that a man so full of life and laughter might not be returning to them.

'Chop chop, Marianne. No time for daydreaming when so many men need us.'

Marianne sighed. Elspeth made her feel horribly frumpy and inadequate. Today she was in another smart summer dress, with a little cardigan thrown stylishly over her shoulders, and high wedged sandals. Taking up a heavy jug of tea, Marianne followed obediently behind the other woman, who, of course, had chosen to take the buns and cups. Much easier and less messy.

As they walked back to the feeding station for a refill, Elspeth said, 'I hear your brothers are still missing. You must be terribly worried.'

Marianne couldn't tell from Elspeth's tone whether she meant what she said, so she didn't reply.

'And your brothers are ... ? Privates? Corporals? Well, no matter. No doubt they're doing their best.'

Marianne took a deep breath, refusing to rise to the bait. Reminding herself again that the woman had every reason to hate her.

When it was time for a break, Marianne gratefully made her way out of the station for some air. Elspeth followed her and leant against the wall, reaching into her bag to bring out a gold cigarette case. She fitted a cigarette into a long holder and stood against the wall, smoking elegantly, her face raised to the sky. There were several wolf whistles from the men, which she acknowledged with a flirtatious smile, but other than that she didn't say a word.

Marianne slumped down onto the ground, leaning her back against the wall. She wished the woman hadn't followed her, but seeing as she had, she felt she should say something.

'How's Mr Fanshawe?' she asked politely.

'As well as can be expected,' she replied coldly. 'Talking about his *grandson* non-stop. Looks like you might have fallen on your feet there.'

'Mrs Fanshawe, I know that you have every reason to hate our family, but I just wanted to say how sorry

I am about everything that's happened. Both Edie and I . . .' She paused, discouraged by the glint of fury in the other woman's eyes. Then she ploughed on. 'Edie and I had no idea. I was so young and it was so long ago. And Edie . . . if she'd known he was married she'd never—'

'I doubt that very much.' Elspeth raised a supercilious eyebrow.

'I was so sorry, too, to hear about . . .' She paused, trying to find the right words. 'Well, what happened to you. I understand how Donny's appearance must have upset you. I want you to know that we don't expect anything from your family.'

Elspeth threw her cigarette on the ground and crushed it under her heel. 'Good. Because you'll get nothing from us. Mr Fanshawe will be dead soon. And after that I never want to see or hear from you or your revolting little boy again. Understand?'

Marianne was on the verge of replying when her attention was caught by a voice shouting at her.

'Mum!' She glanced around to see Donny running towards her. 'Mum! Come quick. Uncle Jimmy and Uncle Bert are home!'

She jumped up and ran over to him. 'Are they all right? Have you seen them? Is Colin there? And John? Alfie?'

Donny shook his head. 'No. But they got a bus from Brighton!' He sounded utterly astonished by this fact. As if escaping from Dunkirk was nothing compared to this monumental achievement. 'It's taken them ages! They said they landed days ago!'

'But are they all right?'

'Yes!' He was hopping up and down now. 'You've got to come!'

Marianne looked around at Elspeth, who was frowning at Donny. 'If they're not hurt, then I think you should stay, Marianne. They'll still be there when you get back. And, frankly, we need all the help we can get.'

Donny hadn't noticed Elspeth before, but when he did he stopped suddenly, going quiet.

'Hello, boy.'

Donny didn't reply, dropping his gaze and shuffling his feet.

'Well? Are you going to say anything?' Elspeth said.

'I don't have nothing to say to you.'

'Donny.' Marianne gasped.

'Well, I don't. She don't like me and I don't like her.'

Elspeth snorted. 'We can all see the sort of upbringing this one's had. I think it best you keep him away from me.' She turned on her heel and stalked back into the station, head held high.

Marianne gave Donny a furious look and he kicked at the ground sullenly. 'Well, it's true. I don't like her.'

Marianne gave him a quick squeeze. What did it matter anyway, when her brothers were home safely?

'What did they say about the others, Don?'

'They didn't talk much. But Gran says it's because they're too tired and not to mind. She's made them go to bed.'

Marianne's heart sank. This could only mean that something terrible had happened to the other three. She put a hand to her mouth as nausea suddenly gripped her. 'And what about Freddie? Has he had any news of his dad?'

Reenie had come over to the café after taking Wilf to his boat and explained what was happening and how hundreds of small boats had gone across the Channel to help bring the men home.

Donny shook his head. 'But you mustn't worry, Mum. Mr Perkins is as brave as a lion, Freddie always says.'

She smiled and put her arms around her son, hugging him tightly to her. 'Go home, all right?' she whispered in his ear. 'Go and help your gran look after your uncles and I'll be back just as soon as I can.'

Donny nodded, then raced off into the crowd again.

Marianne stared after him. She was delighted at the news that Jimmy and Bert were safe, but now all her thoughts were centred on the other three. But mostly, it was Alfie she thought of. Just Alfie.

⁓

Nellie sat on a chair beside her sons' beds, listening to their quiet breathing. Every so often she'd get up

440

and stand over one of them, gazing down at their precious faces – covered in stubble and filthy, her sons had never looked better to her. After they'd walked through the door the three of them had stood, their arms around each other, and not a word had been said. When she'd looked up at their faces, Bert's had been grim and haunted, while Jimmy merely looked devastated, and she could tell he'd been crying. But it wasn't the time to question them, so she'd led them upstairs, taken off their boots and covered them with blankets. They'd been asleep before their heads even touched the pillows.

The door opened and she looked up as Jasper poked his head into the room and, seeing that the boys were still asleep, he crept in, carrying a cup of tea. 'I thought you might need this, Nell,' he whispered, his eyes searching her face anxiously.

Nellie smiled weakly and nodded her thanks, taking the tea and putting it on the floor by her feet.

'How are they? They said anything?'

'Not a word. But Jimmy keeps crying in his sleep, keeps calling Colin's name, and I don't know what to think. Is he dead? You know how close those two are. It'll be like losing a brother.'

Jasper shook his head sadly. 'Mary was here earlier. She heard they were back. Poor woman is frantic.'

Nellie sighed. 'God forgive me, but all I can think is: thank Christ I'm not her. I hate myself for it.'

'Ah, Nell Stop being so hard on yourself. Of course you're glad you're not her. And if the position was reversed, she'd feel the same. Truth be told, I've been having the same thoughts meself. You know I love these boys like they're my own.' He went over to Bert's bed and gazing down at him for a moment, put his hand out and smoothed his hair. He looked across at Nellie. 'Come on, Nell drink up and then come and get some food. You'll need your strength for the boys later.'

Nellie shifted over on the chair and patted the small space beside her. 'Sit with me for a moment, Jasper?'

He squeezed next to her and put his arm around her, while she leant her head on his shoulder, silent tears soaking his sleeve. Finally, she looked up. 'Right, then. No point sitting around moping. Let's leave these two to sleep in peace. You hungry?'

'Not really, love. But there's a boy down there doing his best to eat the café out of its supplies.' He smiled. 'And keeping his gob full of food is the only way I'm managing to stop him bringing out that infernal trumpet. He says if he blows on it loud enough maybe it'll bring the others back.'

Nellie laughed wistfully. 'Bless that lad. He'll be gone soon too. And then what? No men, no children, just a bunch of women and old men to keep the town going.'

'Well, as long as we've got you to tell us what to do, I'm sure we'll be fine.' He kissed her quickly on the head. 'Come on, old girl. Pack up your troubles and smile, eh?'

She nudged him. 'What have I told you about calling me old? Just because I'm feeling soft right now doesn't mean you can get away with it.'

'That's my girl.' Jasper took her hand and stood up, pulling her to her feet. 'One day, Nell, you and me . . .'

'You and me what, Jasper? There is no you and me, as you well know,' she said with a sniff, stalking out of the room.

Behind her Jasper chuckled, and with a last look at the sleeping men, he followed her down the stairs.

∞∞

A frantic banging on the café door brought Nellie staggering to the window. She stuck her head out and looked down.

'Mrs C.' She couldn't see who it was in the pitch black, but the voice told her it was Reenie. 'Let me in. It's Alfie. I just saw him at the station. They're taking him to the hospital. Get Marianne!'

Pushing the window down with a thump, Nellie ran up the stairs two at a time and burst into the girls' room. They sat up with a start, fearing the worst.

'Marianne, get up. Alfie's been taken to hospital.'

With a gasp, Marianne threw back the bedclothes and pulled on the skirt and jumper that were sitting on the chair beside her bed.

She found Reenie standing in the living room. 'Did you speak to him?' she asked urgently.

Reenie shook her head. 'He's unconscious.'

Marianne flew down the stairs towards the kitchen and, grabbing her gas mask from the hook at the bottom, ran out of the door without another word.

Reenie looked at Nellie. 'How are the boys?' she whispered.

Nellie shrugged. 'Hard to tell. I don't suppose . . . ? Colin?'

Reenie shook her head. 'Mary's been at the station asking everyone. So many of the regiment have made it back, but there's no sign of him. She doesn't know if he's alive or dead.' Reenie had tears in her eyes and Nellie put a comforting hand on her shoulder, but her heart was heavy. She'd known Colin since he was a baby, and he'd been in and out of the café with Jimmy as soon as he could walk. She'd looked on him like another son. He was such a lovely, gentle man, it was horrific to think of him dying in such violence.

Chapter 35

Although it was pitch black, Marianne knew the streets of Dover like the back of her hand and she ran the mile to the hospital without stopping.

Once there, she paused to catch her breath before entering through the large door. The corridors were full of soldiers, many of whom were still lying on stretchers, waiting for beds to be found. She rushed over to a nurse.

'I'm looking for a man called Alfie Lomax. He was brought in unconscious recently.'

The nurse looked at her watch pointedly. 'It's the middle of the night!'

Marianne ignored her and rushed down the corridor, her head turning from side to side as she searched for a sign of Alfie.

'Hey! Come back! I'll help you find him, but you can't just run around the hospital.'

'Really? Watch me!' Marianne went into a ward. Beds lined both sides of the room. She ran down one side, and then the other, and finally, in the middle of the room, she spotted what she thought was a familiar face. His head was swathed in bandages, his arm in a sling across his chest, and his eyes were closed. She walked over and put her hand on his.

'Alfie?' she whispered. He didn't respond, so she shook his hand gently. 'Alfie!' she said, louder this time.

He opened his eyes and stared at her, as if he didn't recognise her. Then he smiled, and it was the most beautiful thing she'd ever seen. 'Marianne?' he whispered. 'You're here?' He looked around, then stopped suddenly, as the memories came back to him. 'John?' he said frantically, then he fell back, as realisation hit him. 'Oh God! John! A bullet got him and there was so much blood. I tried . . . I tried to stop it.' Alfie swallowed. 'But he was gone.' And the man who she always associated with laughter and fun and kindness started to cry, tears pouring down his cheeks. 'Just gone . . .' he repeated.

Marianne gripped his hand tighter and with her other she stroked his cheek, as she tried to convey her feelings. 'I'm sorry, Alfie. I'm so sorry.'

Alfie shook his head, his expression bleak. 'There's no one left now.'

Marianne's heart broke for him, and she leant forward and brushed her lips over his cheek, surprised at how natural it felt to kiss him. 'Hush, my love. I'll stay here with you, and when you feel a bit better, you're coming home with me. You're not alone.'

He looked at her, his expression anguished. 'I am. All my memories . . . *All* of them, have John in them. He was my brother . . .' His face crumpled as more tears trickled down his cheeks.

'Oh, Alfie. Those memories – they're still with you, nothing can take them away. He'll always be your brother.'

Alfie shook his head and closed his eyes and not sure what else she could say, Marianne held tight to his hand until his breathing became regular. Then she put her head on the pillow beside his and fell asleep.

She was awakened by the matron shaking her shoulder. 'What do you think you're doing? Kindly leave the patients to rest and come back in visiting hours. Four till six.'

Marianne looked at her sleepily. 'I'm sorry, Matron. I heard he was here and couldn't wait.'

The woman's expression softened. 'As you can see, here he is. Now, get home and we'll take good care of him for you. He's had a nasty knock on the head and his arm's broken, but he'll recover. It's encouraging to see he's been talking to you. He'd not said a word since he was brought in. Been unconscious the whole time. Poor man.' She looked around the beds. 'Poor all of them, really. Now, go on, and we'll no doubt see you later.' She smiled and moved on.

Marianne gathered her things and leant down to whisper in Alfie's ear. 'Goodbye, Alfie. I'll see you soon.'

447

He opened his eyes and smiled sleepily at her. Unable to resist, she kissed him gently on the lips, but he'd already fallen back to sleep, so she tiptoed out.

∞

As the sun rose over the sea, and the dark pall of smoke rising from the beaches of France came into focus, Marge stood smoking a cigarette and contemplating the scene in front of her with a heavy heart. It had been a long and terrible few days, but finally it looked like things were drawing to a close. Word had it that tonight would be the last night of evacuations, and Marge felt nothing but relief. Though Anthony Eden had given a speech about their fighting spirit, everyone who had worked non-stop over the past week was too exhausted to feel euphoric. They just wanted to sleep.

Footsteps sounded behind her and she turned to see Rodney. She'd not seen him since he'd carried her to her bunk the other night, something Jeanie was still teasing her about.

'What are you doing here?'

'Just taking a breather, and I spotted you slipping out so thought I'd join you. How're you bearing up?' He studied her face for a moment. 'You look tired.'

Marge laughed. 'Well, I don't think I could look worse than you. I hope you get leave once all this has finished or I'm worried you might keel over.'

'I'll be all right. But yes, I'm going to go home soon. I got word earlier that Jim and Bert are home.' He smiled, his eyes lighting up in relief.

'Oh, that's wonderful.'

'I also heard Stan's home and Daisy had a little girl the other day.' Rodney paused, then sighed. 'Colin is missing.'

Marge gasped. 'Oh no. Not Colin.' Tears sprang to her eyes as she thought of her old friend. 'How do you know all this?'

He smiled sadly. 'I have my sources.'

She raised her eyebrows at him.

'He's ten years old and rides around the town on a bike as if he owns the place. He took it upon himself to deliver a note last night.'

'Where would we be without Donny, eh? And I gather he's being evacuated tomorrow?'

Rodney nodded. 'It's breaking Marianne's heart. And my mother's. But it's for the best.'

Marge gazed out towards France, as her mind filled with thoughts of Colin. She knew from all the messages that she had been relaying that many, many ships and lives had been lost. Knowing this, it shouldn't be such a shock that one of her own friends was among them. She knew too that many others would probably spend the rest of the war as prisoners. So while the country marvelled at the miracle they had pulled off, they also mourned the men who wouldn't come home, and preparations were already underway to repel an invasion. It was a strange feeling, she reflected, to celebrate a defeat, and she found she couldn't. Her shoulders sagged.

'Penny for them?' Rodney said.

'I was just wondering what the hell's to become of us all. Look how close they are. How are we going to keep them out?'

'Have a little faith, Marge. We've brought home over 300,000 men who were doomed to die, and if the Germans invade, we'll be on home territory. They won't get past.'

She smiled at him. 'It's not like you to be so optimistic.'

'Well, it's not like you to be so defeatist. Come on, let's get a cup of tea and get back to it. We're not finished here yet.'

Marge sighed. 'Lead on, then, Rodders!' She linked her arm through his and they strolled back in, her heart feeling a little lighter than it had. Who would have thought that *Rodney*, of all people, would manage to cheer her up?

∞

Nellie stirred as she heard movement from one of the beds beside her. After she'd been woken by Reenie, she'd not been able to settle, so she'd gone to lie down on Rodney's bed. She needed to be close to her sons.

She sat up and looked over. Bert was leaning up on his elbow.

'Mum?'

She smiled at him. 'Good morning, Bert. You hungry?'

He yawned and stretched. 'I could eat a horse. We didn't eat while we were on the beach and all I've had since is a bun.'

Nellie nodded knowingly. 'Oh, those blasted buns. We've been baking them non-stop since this whole mess started.' She glanced across at Jimmy and saw that his eyes were open and he was staring up at the ceiling. 'Jim? You want some breakfast?'

'No. I'm not hungry.'

Nellie looked over at Bert questioningly, but he just shook his head sadly.

'Right, then. I'll go down and get things started. Come down when you're ready. No rush.' She threw back her covers and padded over to the door, pausing briefly to look back at her two boys. Bert seemed all right, but Jim . . . She worried that the loss of Colin would have irrevocably changed him. She sighed. She knew exactly what that felt like, and she vowed to give him the space he needed to grieve for his friend.

Down in the kitchen, Marianne was already beginning on the breakfast. Gladys had arrived, and Edie and Lily were sitting at the table, drinking tea.

'How are they?' Marianne asked anxiously as she flipped some eggs in the frying pan.

'Bert's coming down, but Jim . . . Well, I think he needs a bit of time. Maybe we'll get some good news about Colin today.'

'God, I hope so,' Edie said sadly. 'Colin's such a lovely man.' Tears welled in her eyes. 'He's always been so kind to me . . .'

'Well, no point moping, there's still work to do,' Nellie said briskly. 'Marianne, are you down at the docks again today? Oh, I forgot! Alfie! How is he?'

'Confused, upset.' She sighed, her heart heavy. 'John's dead. He's devastated.'

'John!' Lily gasped. 'But he can't be. He was so full of life.'

'You'd better get used to this,' Nellie said. 'John and Colin might be the first, but they won't be the last.'

'Cheery words, Ma. Just right to get me ready for a day at the hospital.' Lily stood up. 'Anyway, I'd best be off. I'll check on Alfie as well, Marianne. And see you soon.'

'Is Alfie back?' a little voice piped up from the stairs. 'Can I see him? And can I see Uncle Bert and Uncle Jim?'

'You can see me, Don.' Bert's voice floated down from the top of the stairs. As he came into the kitchen, his sisters rushed to him, throwing their arms around him.

Bert laughed and put his arms around them in return. 'All right, girls? Did you miss me?' He sniffed.

'This place smells like heaven. Any bacon for me, Marianne?'

'You can eat our entire supply today if you want, Bert. Even Mum won't complain.'

Nellie smiled indulgently. 'The kitchen is yours, love. Eat until you're sick.'

Marianne poured him a cup of tea. 'Think I'll take one up to Jim.'

'Good idea. I think he needs you,' Bert said sadly. 'He won't talk to me or Mum.'

Marianne climbed the two flights of stairs and, after knocking briefly on the door, she went in and sat down on Jimmy's bed.

'Hello, Jimmy,' she said softly, planting a kiss on his cheek.

Jimmy didn't move, his gaze fixed on the ceiling.

'Jimmy?' she said softly. 'Drink this.'

He looked at her then and his face crumpled. 'Oh Marianne!' He sat up and flung his arms around his sister, resting his head on her shoulder.

Marianne held him quietly. There was nothing she could say to make him feel better. Finally, Jimmy sniffed and pulled away, rubbing his arm over his eyes.

'Do you want to tell me what happened?'

Jimmy shook his head. 'I don't even know. We were stuck in Dunkirk. We couldn't get to the beach because there were too many men, and Colin got shot in the arm. I got him to shelter, but . . . he was taken away by some medics and . . . the truck they put him in got hit. I tried to run to it, to get him out, but it exploded. Just went up in flames. He's dead, Marianne. No one could have survived that. And I don't know how I'm going to carry on without him! I don't even want to try.' He lay back again, once more staring up at the ceiling.

Marianne's eyes were full of tears. She had loved Colin, and not just for Jimmy's sake. She had seen how happy they made each other, how true and deep their love seemed to be, and the thought of never seeing him again tore at her soul.

Leaning forward, she put her head on her brother's chest and hugged him. 'Oh Jimmy. I'm so sorry.'

They lay silently for a while. Finally, Jimmy whispered, 'What am I going to do? How can I live without him?'

'You have to try, Jimmy. You have to try to carry on.'

Jimmy was quiet for a moment, then he murmured, 'I don't want to. I don't want to be in this life if Colin isn't with me. What's the point?' Then he took a deep breath and said, 'I've been thinking about Dad.'

Marianne held her breath, her heart full of dread.

'I've been thinking about how angry I've been with him all my life . . . And I realise I was wrong. I understand now why he did what he did. He just couldn't stand the pain anymore so he took the only way out he could. It wasn't his fault, was it?'

She shook her head. 'No, I don't think it was.'

'I feel so guilty. About how much I've hated him.'

'But you were a child! How could you have under-stood?'

'I've hated him all my life. I never knew him when he was a normal man. To me, he was just a strange, pathetic, shuffling figure. But now . . . I wish I could do the same.'

Marianne's throat was so tight, she couldn't say a word. The memory of the day their father had taken his own life was a raw wound at the centre of their family. But to think that Jim might want to do the same?

'And I . . . I feel that God's punishing me,' Jimmy continued. 'Punishing me for hating Dad. For loving Colin. For being *unnatural*.'

'Oh, Jimmy. You *can't* think like this. If you think this is God's punishment, then we're *all* being punished. But it's not that, is it? It's . . . it's just sheer madness. And if you start thinking all of this death is because of you . . . well, then you *will* end up like Dad, and I would never forgive you for that. Not ever, Jim! We all love you so much, and we *need* you. Mum needs you. Do you think she could go through something like that again? Do you think any of us could?'

Jimmy reached his hand out and stroked her hair. 'I know, I know. I just need to grieve. But people think I'm just sad because of the loss of my best friend, when really I'm mourning the love of my life. And it's wrong. I see that now. Our love was wrong and that's why he's been taken from me.'

'Love is never wrong, Jim. Please stop talking like this.'

He didn't reply, just shook his head, tears leaking from his eyes. Finally, he said, 'Is there any news of Alfie?'

'He's in hospital. But John's dead.'

Jimmy was silent for a moment. 'Poor Alfie. Those two were like brothers.'

'Will you come downstairs, Jimmy?'

'In a bit. I just need to think for a while.'

She nodded and got up. Jimmy caught her hand. 'Thank you, Marianne.'

'I'm always here to talk, Jim. I understand what you're going through, so come to me. Don't hold it in. And never think that what you and Colin shared was unnatural. I saw you two together. Your love was beautiful. How could it have been wrong?' She dropped a kiss on his forehead, then left the room, closing the door quietly behind her.

Jimmy continued to stare at the ceiling. No matter what Marianne said, he knew the truth. Colin had been taken from him because their love was sinful. His face crumpled at the thought, but he had to face the truth. If he allowed himself to live the way he wanted, who else would be taken in punishment? To protect his family and all those he held dear, he needed to change.

∞

For the rest of the day, Marianne bustled around the kitchen making bread and soup for the customers, and preparing a picnic for Donny and Freddie's train journey the following day. All the time she was aware of Jimmy upstairs torturing himself, blaming himself. But she had no idea how she could convince him this wasn't his fault. His traumatised mind was obsessed with the idea that he could have prevented Colin's death. She prayed fervently that maybe he was wrong. Maybe Colin had survived. But in her heart of hearts she knew that was a futile hope, and somehow she had to find a way to convince Jimmy that life was still worth living.

Donny sat disconsolately at the kitchen table, watching her and polishing Alfie's trumpet so it would be shiny for him when he came home. Every so often he'd lift it to his lips and give it a blow.

'Is it nearly time yet?' he asked for the hundredth time that day.

Marianne glanced at the clock. Lunchtime was nearly over, although given the traffic coming through Dover, it had made no difference. The café was constantly full.

'Soon, Don. Why don't you go and see Freddie?'

'I don't want to leave you, Mum. And I'll be seeing him all day tomorrow. Anyway, I 'spect he just wants to be with his dad.'

Marianne hadn't had a chance to see Wilf yet. According to his mother, he'd been in bed all day, and no one wanted to disturb him. Bert, meanwhile, had recovered well and had popped over to the Royal Oak to inspect the baby. Stan had also been discharged and the new parents were holed up in their rooms, being waited on hand and foot by a euphoric Mavis, who was full of news about her grandchild. Although, much to her disgust, the baby had been named Marguerite. Stan had discovered this meant daisy in French, and he'd been entranced by the idea of his two beautiful girls being named after the same flower.

⌒∞⌒

When four o'clock finally came around, Donny and Marianne could at last go to the hospital. They found Alfie fully dressed and sitting on a chair by the bed, his arm in a sling. Marianne was relieved to see that he looked much better, though his eyes were sad.

'Alfie!' Donny rushed over to him and swung the trumpet case that he'd insisted on bringing on to the bed.

'Hello there, mate. You been looking after her for me?' He nodded at the trumpet.

Donny clicked the case open and pulled the trumpet out reverently. 'I've polished it up good for you,' he said proudly. 'See?'

Alfie gasped in mock admiration. 'My, my. She's never been so spoilt. Just look at her, all shiny and contented. She obviously likes being with you.'

'She does. And I've been practising. Shall I show you?' He lifted it to his lips.

'Don! Not here, for goodness' sake.' Marianne pushed the trumpet down.

Donny glanced around. 'Sorry. Maybe when you come home then, Alfie?'

Marianne liked the way Donny thought of their home as Alfie's home.

'I'd like that, Don,' Alfie said softly.

'But you better hurry, cos I'm leaving tomorrow, and the trumpet's going to be all alone again.'

'Well then, I'd better see what I can do about getting myself out of here, hadn't I?' He looked at Marianne. 'They said I could go home this afternoon, and to take six weeks for the arm to heal. Do you think . . . ?'

'Of course you can! I wouldn't want you to go any-where else.' The thought of being able to look after Alfie warmed her. 'I think Jimmy would like having you there too.' She paused, then said sadly, 'Colin's dead.'

Alfie gasped, then shook his head. 'Colin,' he whispered. 'Such a good man.'

Donny had been listening and his eyes filled with tears. 'Is he really dead, Mum? And John?'

Marianne put her arm around him. 'I'm afraid so, love.'

Donny stared at the floor for a while. 'I'm really sorry about your friend, Alfie.' He sniffed. 'And Colin. He was nice.'

Alfie put his hand on Donny's head and rested it there for a while. 'Thank you, Donny. We'll all miss them.' He stood up. 'But we need to keep going, so how about we leave this place?'

Donny jumped up and took hold of Alfie's hand, almost pulling him to the door.

The walk took longer than usual as Alfie had to stop every so often to rest. Unusually, Donny stayed by his side, taking his arm when he seemed to be tiring. Finally, they made it to the café, where Gladys greeted them with a cry, giving Alfie a hug of welcome.

'Are we glad to see you, young man. Get upstairs, you look as though you could fall down. Bert's in the living room. Though Jim's still in bed.' She glanced over to Marianne and shook her head.

Alfie smiled his thanks and looked over to the counter, where Nellie was watching him, her face wreathed in smiles.

'You don't mind me staying, do you, Mrs Castle?'

'You're always welcome here, Alfie. And call me Nellie. If you're going to be one of my boys, I think Mrs Castle seems a bit formal, don't you?'

Marianne led him upstairs, where Bert was sitting listening to the wireless. He got up and clapped Alfie on the shoulder when he saw him.

'I'm sorry to hear about John,' he said sympathetically.

Alfie nodded. 'And I'm sorry about Colin.'

Bert smiled sadly. 'Two good men . . .' He shook his head. 'I think Jimmy would be pleased to see you. Why don't you go on up? You can have Rodney's bed.'

'I wouldn't mind a rest, if that's all right, Marianne?'

'Of course. I'll bring you both some tea. It's good to have you home.'

Alfie looked at her, his eyes moist. 'It's really good to be home,' he said finally, then turned and made his way slowly up the stairs.

Chapter 36

4 June 1940

Marianne woke when Donny crawled into bed with her. She stroked his hair as he lay quietly with his head on her chest. His silence told her more than words how he was feeling. She had no idea how she was going to manage without his sunny presence.

'Mum,' Donny whispered eventually. 'Please can I stay with you.'

She squeezed him tightly to her, inhaling his delicious scent. 'Oh, Don. I wish more than anything that you could. But it's going to be dangerous.'

'But who's going to keep you safe if I'm not here?'

'I have your gran, and you know how fierce she can be. Now, I got you a present.'

He sat up, distracted for a moment. 'What for?'

'Because I thought you'd like it. Something to make you remember home.' She reached under her bed and pulled out a parcel. Edie and Lily had woken by then, and Lily rose to open the blackout curtain. It was an overcast morning and, despite the early hour, the sound of countless people walking past and faint explosions from the sea drifted into the room through the open window.

'Morning, Donny. Are you excited?' Lily came over to give him a hug.

'No. How could I be? Everything's horrible.' He looked at the parcel, then set it aside with a sigh.

'Don't you want to open it?' Marianne asked, putting the parcel back in his hand.

He shook his head. 'I don't want it.'

She pulled him up on to her lap, cradling him as she had when he was small, his head on her shoulder. 'Hey. I know you don't want to go, and I wish you could stay, but I need you to stay safe so you can look after me when I'm old and grey. Go on, open your present.'

Donny sniffed and stared down at the parcel. Finally, his curiosity won out, and he ripped the paper off to find a small leather case. He opened it and gasped. It was the smallest trumpet he had ever seen. He pulled it out.

'It doesn't look like Alfie's,' he said, before putting it to his lips and blowing. A high-pitched screech came out, and Marianne winced.

'The man in the music shop said it was called a piccolo. And I thought, because it's small, it would be easier for you to play and also easier to carry on the train with you. This means you can keep practising.'

Donny stared at the instrument uncertainly. 'But why can't I have a trumpet like Alfie's?'

Marianne sighed. 'It's too big for you to take with you. So this will do in the meantime, don't you think?'

Nellie shuffled in then, holding a present of her own. She handed it over. 'I've got you something an' all, love.'

He opened it and found a book of trumpet music.

'See, now you can learn these tunes as well. Go on, give us a blow.'

Donny huffed and picked up the little piccolo. He blew tentatively and managed to play 'Twinkle, Twinkle, Little Star'. The noise soon brought everyone else into the room. Even Jimmy managed to rouse himself enough to come and see his nephew.

When Donny had finished, there was a round of applause.

'Oh, Don!' Alfie exclaimed. 'You really have been practising, and look at this piccolo! I've always wanted one of these.'

'Really? It looks like a girl's trumpet,' Donny said.

'Nonsense. There's no such thing as a boy's or girl's trumpet. Music is for everyone. Here, let me show you.'

He took it and, holding it awkwardly with his left hand, he began to play 'Pack Up Your Troubles', and soon everyone had joined in.

A reluctant smile broke out on Donny's face as he too began to sing.

'Come on, then. Tea and toast in the living room and then we have to get ready,' Marianne said. Though she was smiling, she was struggling to hold back her tears.

∽

By the time they were ready to leave for the station, the family mood was glum. Donny's little suitcase sat packed and ready by the living room door, together with his gas mask, his piccolo case, and a basket full of sandwiches and a small fruit cake.

'Come on, Don,' Marianne said reluctantly. She moved to the stairs, picking up the suitcase, while Bert grabbed the basket. Alfie and Jimmy followed behind them, while a disconsolate Donny thumped slowly down the stairs, carrying the piccolo case, his gas mask slung over his shoulder.

He hugged everyone in turn, then moved towards the door. 'I think I should go now. This is making me too sad. Take care, everyone.'

Nellie wiped a tear from her eye. 'You be good for whoever you end up with, lad. None of your shenanigans, please. And mind your manners.'

'I will, Gran. I promise.' He looked around at everyone. 'Look after Mum for me.' They nodded. He looked at Alfie. 'Will you come with us, Alfie?'

'If you'd like me to, of course I will.'

Marianne smiled gratefully at Alfie, glad she wouldn't have to walk home alone. She was surprised Donny wanted him there, but then he seemed to have developed a powerful affection for the man. She knew how he felt.

Wilf and Freddie were coming out of the fish shop as they left the café, and Donny ran over to his friend. They stood looking at each other solemnly.

'This is it, Fred. It's gonna be us against the world. Are you ready?'

He nodded.

'Let's go!'

The two boys ran on ahead as the three adults walked after them in silence, lost in their thoughts. Alfie caught Marianne's hand at one point and she looked up at him. He smiled. 'Are you all right?'

'Yes. This is for the best. Are *you* all right? I'm sorry I haven't been able to talk to you much since you've been here. It's just . . .'

'Hey, I know. And to answer your question: I'm bearing up. Your family is helping.'

She squeezed his hand. 'Good. You're one of us now, whether you like it or not.'

'Luckily I think I like it.' He returned the pressure.

The station was in chaos when they arrived. Soldiers were hanging around waiting for their trains, and over by one of the platforms, a large crowd of children, each with a suitcase and a gas mask, had gathered, while harassed-looking teachers attempted to keep them in order.

Freddie and Don spotted some of their friends and ran over to them, while Marianne went to greet the other parents.

At last, one of the teachers called out, 'Parents! Please say your goodbyes and then leave. The station is too crowded.'

Donny looked around. 'Mum!' he shouted, running over and throwing his arms around her waist.

She kissed the top of his head, then knelt in front of him. 'Listen, promise you'll be good, all right?'

'I promise, Mum. And thank you for my piccolo. I love it really. I'll play everyone tunes on the train.'

Marianne glanced up at Alfie and he winked at her, his shoulders shaking. 'How about you wait until you get to Wales? It might be a bit noisy for the teachers.'

'But I promised! I'm going to make it a party like Alfie did at Christmas.'

Deciding she'd leave the teachers to sort that one out, she hugged him again. 'All right. Now, give me a kiss.'

He kissed her, then looked at Alfie, holding out his hand. 'Goodbye, Alfie,' he said, giving him a manly handshake. 'Take care of yourself. And while you're staying, could you take care of Mum and make her laugh sometimes?'

'I'll do my best, mate.'

Donny nodded once, then disappeared into the crowd of children, while Alfie, his arm around Marianne's shoulders, steered her outside. She didn't say anything, feeling drained of all emotion. The last few days had tested them all to their limits, and now that it seemed it was all coming to an end, she just wanted to lie down and sleep for a week.

∽

Sipping from a hip flask, an unkempt man wearing a scruffy overcoat and broad-brimmed hat watched the couple leave. Who the hell was that man? he wondered. Had she got married? Well, what did it matter? It didn't alter the fact that the boy was his son, and the key to restoring his fortune.

He had no real plan in mind, other than to end his self-imposed exile. He'd spent far more time hiding away than he'd intended, but then he'd landed on his feet for a little while with a pretty young widow who ran a pub in London. He should have left sooner, but life had been very comfortable with her, and there had always been a plentiful supply of whisky. That was until her husband had returned from France . . . Turned out she was as much of a liar as he was.

Since then, he'd managed to gamble away the proceeds from selling his motorbike, and now he needed to return to the bosom of his family, boy in tow, and get back all that was rightfully his. He had no doubt he'd get it. His dad would be so happy he wasn't dead, he'd give him any-thing he wanted. And if he brought the boy as well, then even Rupert couldn't persuade his dad to cut him off.

He felt a rage burning deep within him as he thought about his brother. If it wasn't for him and his wife, as well as that damned little cook, he wouldn't be in this situation. He couldn't believe his life had spiralled out of control so quickly. He glared after the woman's departing back. Soon enough she'd learn what it was like to lose everything.

Chapter 37

Marge sat back with a sigh as Carol Molloy clapped her hands. 'Girls, I don't know what to say. I'm so proud of you. So . . .' She swallowed. 'What we've achieved is nothing short of miraculous. But our task is not finished! Boats are still coming in and we will continue as long as we can to help bring these men to safety. Now, those due a break, get off with you. The rest, it's back to work.'

Marge and Jeanie stood up, along with some of the other Wrens, and made their way through the tunnels to the canteen. When they got there the place was buzzing with excitement. Their exhaustion seemed to have been forgotten in the euphoria of the moment. More than 300,000 troops saved! When only ten days before, they thought they'd do well to rescue 30,000. But God, it had cost them, and the signs of strain were on everyone's faces – all of them pale from lack of sunlight, with eyes puffy and dark. Marge looked around at the tables and spotted Rodney. He saw her at the same time and smiled, beckoning her over. She grabbed Jeanie's hand and they went to sit with him and some of his colleagues.

The wireless was turned on and a voice called, 'Quiet, everyone! Churchill's about to make a statement!'

The room fell silent as they listened to the Prime Minister. There was a rumble of concern when he talked about the possibility of invasion.

Marge glanced at Rodney, who was, as always, perfectly groomed. He felt her gaze and looked over, smiling slightly as he put his hand over hers.

Jeanie, noticing, nudged Marge and winked, but she ignored her. She needed this reassurance right now. For who knew what they were going to face in the months to come?

She tuned in again to the broadcast.

'When Napoleon lay at Boulogne for a year with his flat-bottomed boats and his grand army, he was told by someone, "There are bitter weeds in England". There are certainly a great many more of them since the British Expeditionary Force returned.'

The room erupted into cheers at this and Marge laughed and squeezed Rodney's hand. He leant over and whispered in her ear, 'And I know where quite a few of those bitter weeds are living.'

Marge nudged him with her shoulder. 'I'm going to tell your mother you called her a bitter weed.'

'Who said I was talking about my mother?'

She giggled, then shushed him. Churchill's voice was rising and by the end of his speech the canteen was in uproar, as exhausted and relieved men and women cheered until they were hoarse. Marge didn't join in; neither did Rodney. Together they sat, their hands clasped tightly beneath the table, and watched as their colleagues let the stress of the past weeks out.

∽

It was a quiet group who sat in the living room that evening. With no Donny to liven things up, the Castle women, along with Alfie and Bert, sat listening to the wireless; Jimmy had gone back to bed. Marianne had pleaded with him to stay, but he'd shaken his head. 'I can't. I can't listen to talk of "miracles" when it couldn't feel less like one.'

Marianne stood up to follow him.

'Let him go, love. He needs time.' Nellie looked exhausted, and out of respect for Colin and John, she was wearing a black dress – her funeral outfit.

Marianne sat back down on the sofa underneath the window, between her sisters, and looked over at Bert, who was sitting at the small table, a plate of untouched sandwiches in front of him. Alfie, sitting opposite him, was sipping a cup of tea, his eyes fixed in the distance, his expression sad.

Marianne sighed. This was war, she realised. This frenetic activity, endless worry and exhaustion.

The familiar music of the news played and they listened as the newsreader introduced Churchill. As the Prime Minister spoke, images of the past few days played through Marianne's mind, and she saw again the thousands upon thousands of weary soldiers as they made their way to the trains. The people had cheered them, but in truth, few of the soldiers had been happy. Their overwhelming feeling was one of relief – and anxiety that they would soon be having to face the enemy all over again. Only this time with a greater understanding of what war was really like.

'We shall fight on the beaches, we shall fight on the landing grounds, we shall fight in the fields and in the streets. We shall fight in the hills. We shall *never* surrender.'

Goosebumps erupted along Marianne's arms and a shiver went down her spine as she clasped her sisters' hands, grateful that Edie didn't resist. These past few days had given her hope that perhaps they could at least try to be a family again. Although, she thought dismally, it would be a sadly depleted family, particularly now Donny had left.

Across the room Alfie drew in a deep breath, and Marianne saw him exchange a hard look with Bert; they, more than any of them, knew the cost of not surrendering. Nellie, meanwhile, was sitting up straighter. She too knew the cost of not surrendering. Would they all be paying an even higher price soon?

The broadcast ended and the room was silent for a moment. Eventually, Nellie got up and went to the small kitchen, bringing back a tray with a bottle of sherry and some glasses.

'Let's raise a toast.' She carefully poured out six glasses and handed them round. Then, standing, she raised her glass. 'God knows what the future holds, but if we stand together, we can get through anything.' She looked at Alfie and Bert. 'To you, boys, thank God you're home. And to you girls' – she looked at her daughters – 'let's just carry on. One foot in front of the other, that's how wars are won. I get the feeling that this one is just beginning, but, step by step, we'll get there in the end.'

Chapter 38

6 July 1940

It was a sad group that stood outside the café's plate-glass window. In front of them, the market square was bustling with servicemen and women, but the steps to the covered market were not as busy as they once had been. So many of the stalls had shut down as the market folk left to find safety. Every day brought stark reminders that they were on the front line. The harbour had been bombed twice already, and the air raid sirens had wailed mournfully across the town on more occasions than they could count, although as yet there had been no serious attacks on the town.

Marianne reached her arms up around her brother's neck. 'Take care, Jim.' She tried to pull him in tighter, but he reached up and pulled her hands away.

'I'll be fine,' he said tonelessly. Since their conversation when he'd first come home, Jimmy had retreated into himself. He spoke only when necessary, and rarely came out of his room. Now he was having to return to his regiment, and Marianne was terrified for him. He didn't seem to care about anything anymore, and his refusal to hug her back was hurtful. But it wasn't just her. Nellie, too, was rejected, and she stepped back with a disappointed look on her face. Jasper, however, wouldn't let him get away with this, and he pulled Jimmy's resisting body into a hug. 'Son, you have to come home for your mum, all right?'

Jim stepped back quickly and nodded once, before picking up his kit bag and striding down King Street towards the seafront.

Bert sighed and turned to Marianne. 'I'll give you a hug, sis, even if misery guts there won't.' He pulled Marianne into his arms.

'Watch out for him, won't you, Bert?' Marianne whispered.

He let her go and nodded, then he held out his hand to Alfie, who shook it awkwardly with his left hand.

'Good luck, mate.'

Bert tapped Alfie's plaster cast in response. 'If I were you, Alf, I'd keep this on as long as possible.' He winked. 'I'm tempted to get one myself.'

Alfie smiled. 'I'll be with you in a few weeks. Doubt they'll let me use this as an excuse to stay home for much longer.'

Then, hugging his mother, Gladys and Jasper in turn, Bert hurried after his brother. Nellie watched them until they turned the corner, tears in her eyes. Beside her, Jasper reached down and clasped her hand, giving it a squeeze. Nellie squeezed back, sighing, then went back inside.

Marianne stood a little while longer, praying that this wouldn't be the last sight she had of her brother.

'I'll go and get the bread, then.' Alfie drew her from her thoughts, holding up a string bag.

She nodded. 'Thanks, Alf. You don't mind?'

'I need to keep busy.' He smiled sadly.

Marianne was fully aware of this, and every day she found him small jobs to do to try and keep his mind off his grief, but it was only partially successful. Though he attempted to keep a smile on his face, she often caught him staring out of the window, his expression sombre.

As Alfie made his way up Cannon Street towards David and Mary's bakery, Marianne turned and went back inside. There was still no news of Colin, and though Jimmy was convinced he was dead, Mary refused to give up hope. It was all that was keeping her going.

Suddenly, a cacophony of bangs startled Marianne from her thoughts and she looked instinctively towards the sea. A plane spiralled down into the Channel, flames shooting from its tail. Above it, a Dornier turned sharply and headed towards the town, just as the air raid siren began to wail.

Heart in her mouth, Marianne turned and ran inside. She had never seen a German plane heading towards the town before and the sight of its great, dark shadow sent fear pounding through her.

'Everybody downstairs now! There's a plane headed our way!' she shouted.

Jasper jumped up, jammed his tin helmet onto his head and raced out of the door, blowing on his whistle.

Several passers-by rushed into the café and Marianne pointed towards the kitchen. Their basement had been listed in the local paper as one of the shelters people could go to during a raid.

Just as Marianne closed the door to the basement, an enormous crash made her scream in shock. This was the first time a bomb had fallen, and she hadn't been prepared for the noise.

Downstairs the room was silent as everyone sat, wide-eyed and pale, listening to the crashes coming from outside.

'Jesus, Mary, Mother of God,' an old woman murmured, fingering a rosary around her neck. 'Preserve us sinners in our hour of need.'

Nellie snorted. 'It'll take more than Jesus to keep us safe, Maud, I'm sorry to say.' She jumped as another crash made the floor shake and bits of plaster fell from the ceiling.

The old lady fell to her knees and started to keen. Nellie knelt beside her and pulled her close, stroking her wispy white hair. 'All right, Maud. All right. We're safe in here, love.'

Maud's wails quietened to a whimper, until finally she staggered up from the floor and allowed Nellie to guide her to a chair, where she sat shivering with fear. Nellie stayed beside her, an arm around her shoulders.

Marianne had taken a seat on a cushion by the wall and sat hugging her knees, feeling sick with fear. Alfie was out there somewhere. Had he got to safety in time? The thought of him losing his life after he'd managed to survive the carnage of Dunkirk was too much. Since he'd been staying with them, she'd come to rely on his presence. He was always happy to help and spent much of his time drying up dishes in the scullery. And now she couldn't imagine life without him around.

She put her head down and rested it on her knees, eyes squeezed tightly shut. 'Please keep him safe,' she murmured to herself. In her mind she could picture him as she'd first seen him, so merry and warm as he shook her hand. And then later, at the dance, arching his back as he played a high note on his trumpet, his cap falling off. She smiled at the memory of that night. But then the image expanded and she saw John, bouncing on the piano stool, his eyes alight with fun and mischief. Colin was there too, dancing with her and laughing as she stood on his toes.

Tears started to leak out of her eyes. She hadn't managed to cry properly yet. Either for Colin or John. But now the tears poured down her face as she cried silently, her shoulders shaking.

∞

At the hospital the staff had managed to get the patients down to the underground ward when the air raid siren sounded. It wasn't the first time they'd had to evacuate people downstairs, so they knew the drill, but this was the first time they were aware that there was a real threat, so the atmosphere was tense.

A massive crash that felt as if it couldn't be more than a few feet from the hospital made the walls shake. Everybody sat in silence, listening to the noise of bombardment and praying that their friends and family had got to safety.

When the all-clear sounded, the patients were left downstairs as the nursing staff went to assess the state of the hospital. Aside from broken glass, which was cleared up quickly while the caretaker set about boarding up the windows, there was no serious damage. Lily collapsed on a chair by the side of a bed, trying to control her trembling, as she pretended to sweep glass off a blanket.

'Lily, get off home now. I know you're worried about your family. We can manage here.' Matron had noticed her distress.

Pausing long enough only to collect her bag and gas mask from the cloakroom, Lily raced out of the hospital. The sight that met her eyes as she turned onto the road brought her to an abrupt halt. The air was grey with dust and the road in front of her had been reduced to rubble. A group of people was frantically digging through the ruins, while a little boy of about three was screaming in his mother's arms.

She looked closer. 'Flossie?'

Flossie turned a tear-streaked face towards her. 'Oh Lil. My room's gone! Whatever am I going to do?' she wailed.

Just then, Lily noticed Flossie's little girl cowering on the other side of her mother, clutching at her skirts.

'You're coming home with me. Come on.' She picked up the little girl. 'Hello there, Maureen. How do you fancy coming to the café?'

The little girl stared at her for a moment, then nodded. Shifting the girl to her left hip, Lily took Flossie's arm. 'Come on, Floss. Let's go. You need to get the children to safety.'

'But my things! We don't have much but how can I replace everything?'

'We can lend you stuff.' She urged the woman away and together the four of them stumbled over the rubble, heading for the café.

'Lily!'

Lily looked up to see Jasper, who was in a line of men moving the rubble.

'Is anyone hurt, Jasper?' She moved over to him swiftly.

Jasper shook his head sadly. 'We don't know yet, Lil. Most people got to safety, we think.' He chucked Maureen on the cheek. 'All right, my love. You go with Lily and she'll see you get a nice treat.'

The little girl sniffed and buried her face in Lily's shoulder. Flossie came up beside her then, and Jasper put a consoling hand on her shoulder. 'You go, love. I'll see what I can find for you.'

Flossie nodded tearfully, and they set off again.

As they were walking down High Street, she noticed Alfie coming towards her.

'Alfie!' she called.

He looked up and smiled with relief. 'You're safe! I heard the road near the hospital had been hit and I wanted to check you were all right. I'm on my way to help. Been sheltering in Woolworths. Tell Marianne I didn't manage to get the bread, will you? And don't worry. They say the market square's fine.'

'Thank God,' Lily gasped. 'Jasper's up there. But are you sure you should go?' She nodded at his arm.

'I've still got this one.' He grinned as he held up his left arm. 'I can't just sit in the café drinking tea, can I?'

'Go on, then. But be careful with that arm.'

'Yes, nurse.' He winked at her and carried on up the road.

By the time she fell into the café, Lily's arms felt as if they were about to drop off.

Nellie let out a loud exclamation. 'Land's sake! Get in, girl, get in.' She rushed over and took Maureen from Lily's arms. 'Oh, poor lamb. Here' – she put the little girl down – 'go through to the kitchen and Auntie Marianne will find you a nice bit of bread.'

'A bun?' the little girl said hopefully.

Nellie smiled. 'If you're very good, maybe we can find something. Go on now.' She looked up and went to help Flossie.

'Oh, love. Get upstairs and sit down. I'll bring you up some tea.'

Flossie nodded gratefully, tears in her eyes. 'Thanks, Mrs C. Ever so sorry about all this.'

'Don't be daft. And if you need somewhere to stay, you three can bunk down in the boys' room. There's only Alfie in there now, and he can use Donny's cubby hole.'

Flossie sniffed and walked through to the kitchen.

Nellie looked at Lily. 'You all right, love?' She put her arm around her youngest daughter, who was pale and dust-streaked.

Lily leant against her briefly, then straightened and nodded. 'I was just worried about you lot. But Union Road's been hit. Jasper's up there helping.'

'Oh, thank God.' Nellie raised a trembling hand to her brow and Lily knew her mother would have been desperate for news of him. 'Any news of Alf?'

'He's fine. I'll let Marianne know.'

Marianne looked up expectantly at the sound of footsteps, but her expression fell when she saw who it was.

Lily grinned at her. 'Glad to see you too, sis.'

'Sorry.' Marianne ran her hand through her hair. 'I thought . . .'

'Don't worry, I know. You're more worried about Alfie than you are about me.'

'No, of course not!' Marianne lied.

Lily laughed. 'It's all right. Anyway, you'll be happy to hear that he says sorry he didn't manage to get the bread.'

'He's all right?'

'Right as rain. Gone to help clear the rubble. Jasper's all right too. Now, come on, you.' She held out a hand to Maureen. 'Let's get you settled upstairs.'

∼∞∼

For the rest of the day, the café was full of people coming in to get some tea and talk about the air raid. Unsurprisingly, the residents were shell-shocked as the realisation that this was just the start began to sink in.

Nellie drew Marianne aside briefly. 'Do you think you can get some pies on the go, love? There's a bunch of people without homes to go to and the least we can do is get some food to them. Use the supplies.' She nodded her head towards the basement door.

Marianne nodded. 'I've got some spuds and carrots. There's a few leeks as well that Reenie brought around. I'll make turnovers – easier to eat without a knife and fork and they're tasty hot or cold.'

Nellie nodded approvingly. 'Perfect. Now, don't worry about anything else. Me and Glad will sort out the customers. Just do your best.'

As evening fell, Nellie packed the vegetable turnovers into tins, loaded up the bike trailer and set off. The homeless had taken shelter for the night in Dover College refectory, so she wobbled her way up High Street and made her way to Effingham Crescent. When she got there, a WVS catering van was parked outside the old medieval walls of the refectory and a small group of people was standing around it. Others were sitting on the grass, drinking tea and eating sandwiches. Behind them, the walls of the stately Victorian school building rose in splendour, its mullioned windows glinting in the setting sun. It was an idyllic scene, and if it wasn't for the desperate expressions on the faces of the people around her, it would have looked like a pleasant evening picnic.

Nellie stopped beside the van.

'Evenin' Mrs P.' she said. She and the doctor's wife had rarely seen eye to eye, but they'd called a truce during the emergency the previous month.

Mrs Palmer looked up and raised an eyebrow. 'Mrs Castle, what brings you here?'

Nellie gestured to the trailer. 'Brought some of Marianne's veggie turnovers. Thought they might help.'

The other woman came round and opened some of the tins. 'They smell delicious. But wherever did you get enough flour and butter for all of this?'

'Marianne can work wonders with a bit of flour and a dab of fat. Anyway, that pastry is made from potatoes.'

'Hmm. Well, we won't turn away food, provided it comes from a *legitimate* source.' She gave her a suspicious glare and Nellie bristled.

'Are you accusing me of something, Muriel Palmer?'

'Nothing at all. Just making our position clear.' Mrs Palmer placed the tins on the counter of the van, where a volunteer set about emptying them.

Nellie snatched the empty tins back. 'Well, if this is the thanks I get, next time I won't bother.' She got on her bike and wobbled off, muttering under her breath, 'Snotty-nosed cow!'

Chapter 39

20 July 1940

Alfie and Marianne walked down King Street together. After the terrible bombing raid just a couple of weeks before, there had been more attacks, but none so far had caused as much damage to the town. The harbour, however, was a different story.

Crossing over Marine Parade, they walked along the seafront for a little way towards the Western Docks, stopping by the railings to look out over the sea. In the distance, the smoking hulk of a warship listed to the side, and to their left under the castle, more smoke rose. The day before had seen a terrible bombing raid on the harbour, and several ships had been destroyed. They had sat in the basement of the café for what felt like hours while the explosions seemed to rock the very foundations of the building.

The sound of an aircraft droning towards them made them look up. It was hard to see anything as the sun was in their eyes, but it wasn't long before the ominous shape of a Messerschmitt appeared, heading straight for the town. Marianne grabbed Alfie's hand, trying to tug him towards Snargate Street, where she knew there was a tunnel shelter. But he held back.

'Look!' he shouted.

From behind them a Spitfire raced towards the other plane and Marianne covered her ears, watching with her heart in her mouth as the German plane, the swastika clearly visible on its tail, suddenly erupted in a ball of flames and circled down into the Channel. Despite the fact that this was the enemy, all Marianne could think as she watched it disappear into the water was that somewhere in Germany, a mother would soon be weeping for her little boy. Tears came to her eyes and she said a silent prayer for the fallen pilot.

Beside her Alfie put his arm around her shoulders. 'There's no choice, you know. It's either them or us.'

'I know. But ... none of it makes any sense. And soon that'll be you!'

Alfie had had his cast removed the day before and was due to return to his regiment in a couple of days.

'I'll be much safer than the men up there. Come on, let's go to this cave you keep telling me about.'

They walked further along the front, before scrambling up the hill. Memories of the last time she'd been here crowded in on Marianne, and she felt her chest ache. It was as if the invisible thread that attached

Donny to her heart was being pulled to its very limit, causing an actual physical pain.

They sat down together at the mouth of the cave, staring out again at the sea glistening blue in the sunshine. Alfie took Marianne's hand. 'You know, Marianne, this has been the best and worst of times for me. I'm not sure how I could have coped with John's death if it wasn't for you.'

'You must miss him,' she said, giving his hand a squeeze.

'Every day. He talks to me, you know. In my dreams.'

'What does he say?'

He turned and looked into her eyes. 'He says, "Alf, mate, you need to act fast, or you might lose the best thing that's ever happened to you."'

Marianne smiled uncertainly. 'He doesn't.'

'He does. I've been tiptoeing around you, Marianne, but now I'm about to leave, I have to say something. I can't go without telling you how I feel.'

Marianne tried to tug her hand away. She felt conflicted. What was the point? He would be away fighting, and she . . . well, she wasn't sure she was brave enough to love him back when at any moment she might lose him.

'I love you. And I love Donny. I wish I'd said something sooner. But I can't leave without asking. Will you marry me, Marianne? Soon as I'm back on my next leave? Or even now, if we can.' He laughed self-consciously. 'I don't want to wait.'

Marianne gazed at him with tears in her eyes.

'Marianne? You're making me nervous. Don't you feel the same as I do?'

She put her hand up and stroked his cheek. 'Oh, Alfie, I do. But . . . now isn't the time. If anything happened to you . . .'

'But what if it did? And we weren't even engaged? I'm not the only one in danger. If anything happened to you, I want people to know what you are to me. They need to know we love each other. Look at poor Jimmy. No one understands his grief because he was never able to shout about his love. I can't have that. *We* can't have that. We need to belong to each other so if anything does happen, at least we won't have wasted the time we do have.'

Marianne shook her head. 'I can't, Alfie. Not now. How can I get married without Donny being here?'

'We'll get married in Wales!' He grinned.

She gave a short laugh. 'Without my mother? She'd never talk to us again.' She looked down and picked up his hand, playing with his fingers. 'I can't do this now,' she whispered. 'Please don't ask me to.' She looked up at him, tears in her eyes. 'I need to know you'll be with me always before I marry you.'

'But I'd be with you always anyway. Just as you will always be with me.' He placed a hand over his heart. 'Right here.' He leant forward and kissed her deeply, and Marianne put her arms around his neck, pulling him in closer, wishing she was braver, wishing the world was at peace and she could be sure he'd always be there for her.

She pulled away. 'I'm sorry, Alfie.'

He nodded sadly. 'Is it because . . . ? Are you worried about the future, living with someone like me? I know I'm not the cleverest bloke, but I can still look after you. You never have to worry about that.'

'Oh, Alf, how can you think that? You don't have any limitations in my eyes.'

'So why, then?'

'It's too much of a risk. If we got married and I lost you . . . I can't think about it. And Donny . . . After everything he's been through with his father – and me . . .' She'd told him what had happened with Henry a few evenings before. 'He loves you, you know. And if he lost you . . .' She flapped her hand, unable to form the words. Her throat felt tight at the very thought that something might happen to Alfie. She stood up abruptly and brushed the grass off her skirt.

Alfie sighed. 'If you change your mind, you know where I am.'

'That's just the problem, Alfie. I won't. I won't even know whether you're alive, dead or lying wounded somewhere. I just can't live with the uncertainty.'

He stood up and took her hand. 'But life is uncertain. Even in peacetime.' He sighed at her stubborn expression and kissed her gently on the lips. 'I'll wait,

Marianne. I don't care how long it takes . . . One day, you will be my wife and Donny will be my son.'

She smiled. 'I hope so, Alfie. And one day, when things get better, I promise, my answer will be different.'

He sighed again. 'I'll just have to be satisfied with that, then.'

They said no more as they walked down the hill. By silent agreement they avoided the seafront, walking instead through the trees and down the long hill to the town.

As soon as Marianne pushed open the back door, Nellie came rushing into the kitchen, followed, rather surprisingly, by Mrs Palmer.

'Marianne!' Her mother looked absolutely devastated and her thoughts immediately turned to her brothers.

'What's happened, Mum? What's wrong?' She rushed towards her, grabbing at her arms.

'It's Donny!'

Marianne's blood ran cold and she rocked back on her feet, knocking into Alfie, whose arms went around her.

'Is he all right?' Alfie asked urgently, speaking for Marianne, who was unable to form any words.

Nellie shook her head wordlessly, and Marianne let out a moan of agony.

'He's fine as far as we know, Marianne,' Mrs Palmer said briskly, shooting a glare at Nellie.

Marianne raised her head, the vice that had been around her lungs easing slightly. 'What then?'

Mrs Palmer cleared her throat. 'It seems he's, uh . . . disappeared from his billet.'

Marianne stared at her in disbelief. 'Disappeared? What do you mean?'

'We received a telephone call from the WVS in the village they're staying in, and apparently young Donald went out the day before yesterday and hasn't returned.'

'What do you mean, hasn't returned? He's been missing for two days and they didn't think to say anything before?'

'Well . . . he's prone to wandering around, and they just assumed he'd come back soon enough. But his young friend Freddie has now told us that he went off with a man.'

'What man?!'

Mrs Palmer fished in her bag for a pad of paper and, placing a pair of rimless spectacles on her nose, she read from some notes. 'A tall, blonde-haired man, apparently.'

Marianne stared at her. 'Donny's been kidnapped?'

'Oh, my dear, I doubt it's anything quite so dramatic, but it seems he may be making his way back home.'

'But who . . . ?' The only tall, blonde-haired man she knew who might do something like that was dead. A feeling of dread started to rise within her. Wasn't he? 'Did Freddie say anything else about the man?'

'Apparently he called to Donny by name.' She looked at the pad again. 'I quote: "His voice sounded posh".' She took her spectacles off and looked around at the stunned faces. 'So clearly it's someone he knows. There's no cause for alarm. Hopefully he'll be back home before you know it.'

Marianne stepped towards her. 'No cause for alarm?' she shouted. 'He's gone off with some man and you say there's no cause for alarm!' She looked around wildly. 'Mum, we have to go to Hawkinge.'

'Hawkinge! Are you mad?' Slowly, though, the significance of what she said sunk in and Nellie dropped into a chair. 'But he's dead . . .'

'*Missing, presumed dead.* What if he never went away? He's not to be trusted. And what if we never get Donny back? What if the Fanshawes decide to keep him?!'

'Of course they won't. How could they?'

'Because the lawyer already said that it would be in Donny's best interests to live with them . . . They've got so much money, Mum. I can't fight them.'

'The Fanshawes? What on earth do they have to do with anything? And as for the family, well, Ernest Fanshawe is a highly respected man who does a lot for the local hospitals. Honestly, why would you think he'd take your son?' Mrs Palmer paused for a bit. 'Oh!' She looked at Marianne in shock. 'Donny—' She yelped as Nellie grasped her arm and marched her towards the café door.

'Thank you, Mrs Palmer. Very much obliged. And let's have a chat soon about the WVS. I'm sure you and I can come to some sort of arrangement about providing food. Unless . . .' She glowered at the other woman threateningly. 'You know I can't abide gossips.'

Mrs Palmer looked indignant. 'How dare you suggest I gossip!' She looked between Nellie and her daughter. 'But yes, I think between us we can come up with a plan to help the town. Good day to you.' She turned and walked away.

'Can someone tell me what's going on?' Alfie asked, looking bemused.

'Alfie, I need you to run across the road to Brian Turner and ask if we can use his van, and make sure he has enough petrol to get us to Hawkinge. I'll make good on it, tell him. Can you drive?' Nellie snapped.

'I can, as it happens, but . . . what's going on?'

Nellie pushed him towards the door. 'Later! Get going, for gawd's sake.'

Chapter 40

The three of them drove in tense silence along the country roads, winding between the yellow wheat fields towards Hawkinge. The signs had been removed from the roads, so Nellie navigated, and after a few wrong turns, they finally found themselves driving down Hawkinge high street, past the school they had stopped at when they got off the bus the last time they'd visited.

'Glad to see that even the rich people have to make some sacrifices,' Nellie remarked as they drove through the gap in the wall where the tall wrought-iron gates had once stood.

Alfie raced up the drive to the front door and brought the van to an abrupt stop. Marianne didn't even wait for him to switch off the engine before she jumped out and started hammering on the door.

Jones, the butler, opened the door and looked at them with an astonished expression on his face.

'Why, Mrs Castle, Miss Castle. And . . . ?'

'Is Mr Fanshawe in?' Nellie asked without preamble, shoving her way inside.

'Master Rupert and Mr Fanshawe are in the dining room with the ladies.' He gestured behind him.

Marianne ran in and sprinted down the corridor he'd indicated. Coming to a doorway on her right, she peered inside and found a large, airy room with lead-paned windows on two sides. Ignoring Jones's exclamations, she rushed in. At the table, Mr Fanshawe had dropped his fork and was looking at her in astonishment. A man, who looked disturbingly like Henry, leapt to his feet and rushed towards her. At the table, Elspeth and another woman, who were seated on either side of Mr Fanshawe, stared at her open-mouthed.

'Where is he?' she shouted. 'What have you done with my boy?'

'What the hell is the meaning of this?' Rupert Fanshawe's face was red with indignation.

'Donny. Where is Donny?' She looked at Mr Fanshawe, who was opening and closing his mouth, as if trying to get some words out.

Elspeth leapt up. 'What do you think you're doing? The man's sick. And we don't have your little brat. Why would we?' She gestured around. 'Unless you think we've locked him in the cellar?' she sniggered.

Alfie walked in then and tried to take charge of the situation. 'If everyone can calm down, I'll explain. It seems Marianne's son has gone missing from his billet in Wales and the description of the man who took him sounds remarkably like your son, Henry.' He looked over at Mr Fanshawe.

'What sort of sick joke is this? You know very well that Henry's dead!' Rupert exclaimed.

'Far as I remember, he was only *presumed* dead,' Nellie put in. 'And seems to me, thanks to your nonsense about wills and children and gawd knows what' – Nellie stabbed her finger at Mr Fanshawe – 'that he thinks as long as he has his son, then he can get his hands on half the company when you fall off your perch.'

'But . . . how did you know about that?'

'Does it matter? It's true, isn't it? And you never cottoned on to the fact that the only reason he gave two hoots about Donny was so he could get his filthy mitts on your money?'

Elspeth stood up then, her hand at her throat. 'Are you saying . . . ?' She swallowed. 'Are you implying that Henry is *alive*?'

'That's exactly what I'm implying. And he's nicked *my* grandson. What are you going to do about it?'

'But this is preposterous. Henry was doing covert work in France, so of course we've never had details of how he died. But why would he have lied?' Mr Fanshawe finally managed to splutter.

There was a silence as Nellie raised an eyebrow at him, then looked pointedly around the room.

'Oh God!' Elspeth put her hand to her head. 'The last time I saw Henry, he told me we were up to our necks in debt. He'd been gone for weeks before that, and that was always a sign he was gambling.' She slumped down in her chair. 'The bastard! The utter, utter bastard.'

'That's enough, Elspeth,' Rupert rapped out, looking at his father with concern.

Mr Fanshawe had gone deathly pale and Rupert gestured with his head to the other woman, whom Marianne presumed was his wife, to take him out. She rose obediently and wheeled her father-in-law out of the room.

Once they'd left, Rupert turned to Marianne. 'What contact did your son have with Henry before he died?'

'He's not dead.'

'How can you say that? He wrote to our father, told him that he'd been asked to go to France, but couldn't say much more. He spoke fluent French, so it didn't seem unlikely. Hang on. Elspeth got a telegram!'

He ran from the room, leaving Marianne staring at Elspeth, who was sitting with her head in her hands, sobbing softly. Marianne didn't have room in her heart to have sympathy for her anymore. After their time together during the Dunkirk evacuation, she realised that Elspeth, for all her suffering at the hands of her husband, was a nasty snob, and now she felt nothing for her.

Rupert returned holding a piece of paper. Silently, he handed it to Marianne.

Marianne took it and, with Nellie and Alfie reading over her shoulder, she read the few words on the telegram.

10 FEBRUARY 1939

. . . DEEPLY REGRET TO INFORM YOU THAT YOUR HUSBAND HENRY FANSHAWE IS MISSING PRESUMED DEAD ON OPERATION IN FRANCE. LETTER WILL FOLLOW.

Nellie let out a loud exclamation. 'Gone to France on an undercover operation, my foot! And what did this letter say?'

Both Elspeth and Rupert looked blank, and Nellie nodded. 'Didn't receive one, did you? Mark my words, this is a fake.' She snatched the paper from Marianne's trembling hand and threw it at Rupert.

'You think this is a lie?' Rupert's voice didn't have the bite Marianne would have expected; rather, he sounded resigned.

Elspeth spoke up then. 'I never truly believed it. It's just not Henry. He's always been a selfish sod, and he'd told me more than once he was going to get a medical certificate to get him out of joining up. And God knows he has enough friends in London who could fake a telegram. This is exactly the sort of stunt that bastard would pull. He probably thought he'd give it a bit of time and then come back from the dead, dragging his brat behind him. And Ernest would be so happy to see him, he'd give him anything. Well, I won't have it!'

'At least we agree on something,' Nellie snorted. 'Our boy will live with this family over my dead body.'

Rupert stood, deep in thought for a moment, then he looked at his sister-in-law and nodded sadly. 'I think you might be right.' He sighed. 'But where would he go, and why hasn't he come straight home?'

'He'll have gone off with some woman. Or he'll be holed up in some gambling den, leaving the boy to fend for himself.'

Marianne gasped. 'He'd leave him alone? But where?'

Elspeth thought for a moment. 'Folkestone. There's a club, in the basement of The Grand Hotel. He used to keep a room there. Claimed it was for when he was working at the brewery. Of course, it was where he took his filthy whores.' She threw Marianne a scathing glare. 'If you find him, tell him I never want to see him again.' She ran out of the room, unnecessarily shoving Marianne out of the way as she went.

Alfie steadied Marianne, then looked over at Rupert. 'Can you take us there?'

Rupert let out a deep breath. 'Yes, of course. I have a few words to say to him myself.' He shook his head. 'You know, I would have shared the company with him after Dad died if he'd proved himself. But now . . .' He stopped and looked at Marianne. 'Try not to worry. If he's in Folkestone, then we'll find your boy.'

'I want your promise that if we find him, then all talk of him coming to live here ends forever!' Nellie said fiercely.

'You'll get no complaints from me on that front. Now, come on. It's getting late.'

∞

Dusk was beginning to fall as Alfie drove them towards Folkestone. It wasn't far, and Rupert directed him expertly towards The Leas, where The Grand Hotel rose, stately and beautiful, it's many windows glinting in the evening sun. In front of it, a wide lawn stretched down to the concrete promenade, where the bandstand stood empty and forlorn. Out on the Channel, the scene looked very much like it did from Dover, with large grey warships looming into the distance.

They parked the van and leapt out, racing into the magnificent carpeted foyer, which was full of servicemen and women milling around. Without stopping, Rupert led them to the right of the long, mahogany reception desk and through a door that led down some steps and along a narrow corridor. From behind a door to their left, a woman was singing 'Somewhere Over the Rainbow', her voice so pure it raised goosebumps on Marianne's arms. Pushing open the door, Rupert went straight over to the bar, where a small redhead with heavy makeup and a low-cut top was serving drinks to a couple of men in RAF uniform.

'Rosie, have you seen Henry?' Rupert snapped without preamble. Clearly, he was well-acquainted with the place.

Rosie looked at him, then over his shoulder. Her gaze drifted dismissively over Marianne and Nellie, before lighting up as she spotted Alfie. She gave him a wink. 'Might 'ave,' she answered. 'What's it to you?'

Rupert seemed to sag at the confirmation that his brother was indeed alive. 'It's urgent. Where is he?'

She sniffed. 'Last I saw, he was blind drunk and being bundled out the door.'

'His room?'

She gave a short bark of laughter. 'No way. He ain't paid the bill for months and 'e's not allowed back till 'e does. Now, I got work to do.' She turned away to serve a soldier standing patiently at the bar.

'Did he have a boy with him?'

Rosie turned back, her eyebrows raised. 'A boy? Why would he have a boy? He's got his faults, but I never took him for a nonce.'

Marianne stepped forward. 'Please, please tell us where he might go?'

'Look, love, I ain't got no idea. All I know is the man's bad news. Now, please leave.' She looked over at a tall figure wearing a dark suit, who was standing at the end of the bar, and nodded at him.

The man stepped forward and, grasping hold of Rupert's arm, he led him and the rest of the group none too gently to the door.

'Well, where would he be if not here?' Nellie demanded sharply once they were back in the foyer. 'Where would he have taken Donny?'

'God knows. Look, you lot wait here and I'll go back to see if anyone else might know.' Before they could protest, Rupert headed back down the stairs.

Nellie marched up to the reception desk, where an elderly man presided. Like the barmaid, he looked her up and down, sneering slightly as he took in her bright pink dress, before turning his attention to some papers in front of him. But Nellie was not so easily ignored.

'Excuse me. Can you tell us where Henry Fanshawe is?'

'The gentleman you refer to is no longer welcome in this establishment, madam.' He sniffed. 'And if you take my advice, you won't make him welcome in yours.'

A disturbance at the front door caught their attention.

'Let me in, damn you. Don't you know who I am?'

Marianne and Nellie looked at each other, then dashed to the large revolving door at the front of the hotel. Henry was being shoved down the stone steps, but before they could reach him, he lost his balance and tumbled down, hitting his head as he fell to the ground. He lay on the ground, his eyes shut, and blood leaking from a gash on the side of his head.

'Quick! Get Rupert!' Marianne shouted to Alfie.

Alfie turned obediently and went back into the hotel, while Marianne knelt down beside Henry. He was a mess, his clothes unkempt and his hair dark with grease. The smell of alcohol emanating from him nearly made her choke. He was a far cry from the charming, dapper man she'd once known.

She slapped him in the face. 'Wake up!' she screamed down at him.

Henry didn't move, so, in desperation, Marianne put her arms under his shoulders and tried to make him sit up. But he was too heavy, and it was clear he was unconscious.

Nellie, meanwhile, had disappeared, but she soon returned carrying a bucket of icy water, which she threw unceremoniously in Henry's face. The man let out a yelp of protest as he opened his eyes and stared blearily at them. Then he groaned and, sitting up, he leant to one side and was violently sick.

'Ugh! Gawd's sake, the man's lost it!' Nellie shouted.

Marianne ignored her. 'Henry! Where's Donny? What have you done with him?'

Henry looked at them blankly, then shut his eyes.

505

'Henry! Where's your son?'

He opened his eyes. 'My son? What son?'

'Donny!'

His brow creased as he took her words in. 'Donny? I ... Donny! Where's Donny? I need him! My father ...' He shook his head, then lay back down and shut his eyes.

Rupert and Alfie came out then, and Rupert stood looking down at his brother with a pained expression.

'I've booked a room. Come on, let's get him inside.' Hoisting Henry on to his shoulder, he took him into the hotel and walked to the lift. As it cranked its way up, Marianne was shaking with fear and frustration.

'Someone must know where Donny is! Can't anyone help?'

Alfie put his arm around her shoulders. 'Let's get Henry to the room, then me and Rupert will go out again.' He looked over at Rupert. 'Any more luck with the barmaid?'

Rupert shook his head grimly. 'She used to be one of Henry's many women. Not sure she'd throw water on him if he was on fire now.'

Marianne's teeth started to chatter as she thought of Donny, alone and terrified somewhere in the town.

Once in the room, Rupert threw his brother onto the bed, then turned to the door once more. 'You two stay with him. He might remember something when he comes around. Come on.' He gestured to Alfie with his head and the two went out.

'Oh Mum!' Marianne started to sob as Nellie put her arms around her daughter. 'What are we going to do?'

'You and me are not going to stay here with this useless lump of flesh. If that barmaid knows something, then I'll get it out of her.'

Grabbing Marianne's hand, she tugged her to the door and before long they were hurtling down the stairs. They'd just reached the foyer when the air raid siren went off. Outside, the rat-a-tat-tat of the ack-ack guns could be heard coming from the direction of the seafront, as well as the whine of aircraft above them.

'Everyone downstairs!' The receptionist was already headed for the door to the lower rooms, and soon the staircase was crowded with people as they made their way to safety.

In the bar, the woman was still singing and people were drinking as if nothing was happening. The barmaid clapped her hands. 'Right, folks, form an orderly queue and we'll take your orders soon as we can.'

Nellie pushed her way to the front. 'Here's my order, young lady. I want information about my grandson's whereabouts!'

Rosie rolled her eyes. 'I told you, I don't know nothin' about no boy!'

'But you do know where that man's been staying.'

Rosie's eyes flickered and she looked away.

Nellie leant across the bar. 'Listen. Somewhere out there a young boy is all alone.' A loud crash and the sound of breaking glass reached them. 'You hear that? You got kids?'

'I got a kid. But I sent her to safety. Like you should have.'

'We did. And that man took him and left him somewhere. What if it was your girl, eh? And I was standing here, refusing to let you know where she was.'

Rosie dropped her eyes. Then she sighed. 'Look, all I know is 'e's been stayin' at Mrs Barker's place down near the docks.'

'Who's Mrs Barker?'

Rosie looked around furtively, then leant across the counter to whisper in Nellie's ear. 'She's a madam. Number three Clifton Gardens.'

'What?!' Nellie squawked. 'He's left my grandson in a brothel?'

'Shh, for gawd's sake. This is a respectable place.'

'How do I get there?

'Out of here. Turn left along The Leas a little way and it's on your left.'

Nellie whirled around and, grabbing Marianne's hand, hustled her out of the bar. Turning left, they ran to the end of the corridor, where they spotted a door that led outside. As soon as they pushed it open, the wailing of the siren was almost deafening. But far, far worse than that was the droning of the aircraft. Night had fallen and the moon was full. The sky looked heart-breakingly beautiful – a deep, royal blue with a myriad of golden stars glittering as far out into the horizon as they could see. But the beauty was marred by the shadows of wave after wave of planes flying towards them. For a split second they stopped and stared, transfixed by the sight. It was like a painting, Marianne thought. But then she gathered herself. Those planes were bringing almost certain death to the town and she wouldn't stop until she'd found her child.

'Come on!' She tugged at her mother's hand and set off at a run.

They ran along The Leas, doing their best not to look out to sea, where a ship was alight. Suddenly, a deafening explosion ahead of them caused them to stumble, and from the direction of the harbour bright orange flames lit up the sky. Nellie fell to her knees, and Marianne, panting with fear, grabbed her arm and pulled her up as they raced on, coughing in the smoke that blew towards them on the gentle breeze.

It was only thanks to the moon and the glow in the sky that they were able to find Clifton Gardens. They ran up the road. In the moonlight, the tall, white Georgian buildings looked neglected, with peeling paint and rotten window frames. Once there would have been iron railings in front of them, but these had all been removed for the war effort. On the pillar in front of a house on the left, a large '3' was prominently displayed, and together they staggered up the steps and banged urgently on the door.

Another explosion nearby had them both ducking down and covering their heads. Marianne couldn't help the sob of fear that escaped her.

'They're not going to answer,' Nellie shouted, trying the door. It opened and they found themselves in a dimly lit hallway with a red carpet and walls covered with flowered wallpaper. In front of them the same carpet ran up a narrow flight of stairs. Marianne ignored the stairs and raced down the corridor. In the wall on her right she found what she was looking for: a cupboard door. Opening it, she squinted inside, just as another explosion ripped through the night air and the hall light suddenly went out.

In the hush that followed the explosion, Marianne heard a whimper.

'Donny?'

'Who's that?' A harsh female voice rang out.

'Is there a little boy there?'

A torch was switched on and Marianne found herself face to face with a woman in her forties. No one would ever guess she was a madam as she wore no makeup and her greying blonde hair was scraped back into a bun. Beside her, curled into a ball with his head hiding in the woman's armpit, was Donny.

510

At the sound of his mother's voice, he looked out. 'Mum?' he gasped in disbelief. Then louder: 'Mum!' He tore himself away from the woman's side and rushed to his mother, winding his arms tightly around her neck as he burrowed into her.

'Shh.' Marianne stroked her son's hair as tears of relief poured down her face. 'Everything's all right now. You're safe.'

Nellie had crawled in behind Marianne and now the four of them sat crowded into the small space.

'Nellie Castle, as I live and breathe!' the other woman shouted.

Nellie squinted into the light. 'Who's that?'

The torch beam moved to the other woman's face and Nellie gasped. 'It never is! Is that really you, Hester Erskine? What are you doing here?'

'Hester Barker these days. And I could say the same for you!' The woman cackled. 'I didn't have you down as the sort to be in a place like this. Last I remember, you were cosied up with your Donald at the café.'

'And last I remember you were looking a sight plumper than normal, and then you disappeared. I thought you must have died or something.'

The other woman snorted. 'That nasty little worm Horace Smith knocked me up, then dropped me for being loose. And you know what people are like – soon as you step off the straight and narrow you may

511

as well be dead. Still, you do what you has to in life, ain't that right?'

'Well, I for one am glad to see you're alive and kicking. Never had much truck for the straight and narrow anyhow. And Horace Smith is a sanctimonious prig, ain't that right, Marianne?'

Marianne muttered an agreement as she held Donny to her, watching in astonishment as Nellie crawled over to the other woman and embraced her.

'Now, Nell.' The other woman pulled away. 'What's this boy to you? His name's Donny, so I can only assume he's your grandson. Bless him. He was dumped here by that no-good Fanshawe bloke and I done me best, but he's not been happy. If I'd known he was yours, I'd have got him back to you sooner.'

'That bastard kidnapped him. It's a long story, Hester. Another time, eh? But if you want to hear it you'll have to come to the café. No way I'm being seen dead in a place like this. No offence.'

'None taken.'

Marianne tuned them out as she leant back against the wall, Donny on her lap. Nothing else mattered to her. Her mother could come and work in the brothel for all she cared. Just as long as she had her son back.

'Mum,' Donny whispered. 'I'm sorry. When he turned up I told him he was meant to be dead and he said you'd lied cos you didn't want me to see him . . .'

Donny rubbed his nose against Marianne's shoulder. 'I was so angry I wanted to shout at you for lying again, so I went with him. But it doesn't matter now. I just want to go home.'

Marianne felt tears sliding down her own face. If she hadn't lied all those years ago, could this all have been avoided?

'Oh, love. I'm so sorry. But I didn't lie this time. We all thought he was dead. Even Mr Fanshawe.'

Donny was quiet for a moment, his head resting on his mother's chest. Finally, he whispered, 'I don't like my dad. He's drunk and he's rude and he's mean. And he lies *all* the time.'

'You never have to see him again. I promise.'

'I'd rather not have a dad at all than have one like him.'

She stroked his hair. 'Then we'll pretend he doesn't exist.'

'I think I see now. Why you lied.'

'That's not why I lied, Don. Your dad didn't used to be like this. What I did was wrong. But what he did was worse. And I promise you, love, I will never lie to you again. All right?'

Donny nodded, nestling back into his mother's arms, until eventually his breathing deepened and he fell asleep. While her mother and Hester chatted, Marianne leant her head back against the wall and closed her eyes, her heart at peace. Even her fear had

513

gone. Instead, she thought of Alfie, and how he had been more of a father to Donny in the short time he'd known him than even her own father had been to her. Why was she so scared? Alfie was right. Time was precious, and she wanted everyone to know that she loved him. She held Donny tighter as she thought about what the future could hold for her if she would just allow herself to live without fear. Not the fear of death that they all now had to contend with every day. But the fear of life. And love.

Chapter 41

An hour later the all-clear sounded and Marianne shook Donny awake. 'Come on, love. Time to go.'

He looked up at her and smiled. 'You really are here! I thought it was a dream.'

'No dream. You'll be staying with me forever if I get my way.' Her legs had gone to sleep from the weight of Donny sitting on them, and her shoulders felt stiff from holding her arms around him for so long, but despite this Marianne had never felt better in her life. As Donny moved away she crawled over to the door, pushed it open and stood up, holding on to the wall for support. Behind her Donny scampered out, followed by the two older women, who groaned as they stretched their cramped limbs.

Marianne turned to Hester and gave her a hug. 'Thank you! Thank you so much for taking care of him and keeping him safe, Mrs Barker.'

The other woman laughed. 'Well, bless me, what else could I do? He's a love, he really is. Reminded me a bit of my little lad, who's out on the submarines now – not so little anymore. And don't worry, soon as he got here I made sure to keep him far away from the *activities*.' She winked. 'If you know what I mean. Lucky for you we were shut tonight.'

Nellie saved Marianne from answering, much to her relief. 'I always knew you was a good 'un, Hester. If you're ever in Dover, come over to the café and our Marianne'll cook you a feast.'

'I'll hold you to that, Nell.' She chucked Donny under the chin. 'And you take care of your mum and gran, all right?'

'Thank you for looking after me, Mrs Barker,' Donny replied, shaking her hand.

Hester walked them to the front door. The smell of burning hit them the minute she opened it and they all put their hands over their mouths as they went down the stairs and walked to the end of the road. To their left, the harbour was on fire, and in the Channel, several ships were burning. Fire engine bells were ringing loudly in the distance.

Hester shook her head. 'I just pray everyone got to safety in time. Think I might take a walk down there, see if I can help. No doubt there'll be some waifs and strays that need a place to stay.' She turned left down the seafront, as the other three turned right. 'Goodbye! Maybe see you soon,' she called. And then she was gone.

Nellie shook her head. 'Bless my soul. I always did wonder what happened to her. Poor love. Still, Donny, here you are, safe and sound, praise God. Let's get you back to find Alfie and that Mr Fanshawe.'

'Alfie's here?' Donny sounded delighted.

'He's been helping us look for you.'

'I'd been wishing for him. I thought if only I had my piccolo I could blow it and he would come. But I didn't need it after all.'

Marianne squeezed his shoulders. 'Course you didn't, love. He'd always come and find you, if he could. Just like I would.'

'I wasn't allowed to play it in Wales,' he said sadly. 'Mrs Griffiths took it away and said I could have it back when I left. I wanted to leave there so bad, Mum. You're not going to send me back, are you?'

Marianne swallowed, hating to hear how unhappy he'd been. 'Never again, Donny. Never, ever again.'

He laid his head against her and they walked on in silence. Marianne was relieved to see that there had been no damage on this side of the town, all of the bombing seemed to have been concentrated at the harbour, which meant that Alfie was no doubt safe.

As they entered the lobby, Alfie came running over.

'Thank God!' He pulled Donny into his arms and hugged him close. Looking at Marianne over the boy's head, he held out his other arm, and Marianne moved into it without hesitation, hugging the two of them close.

Rupert appeared behind them. 'This is young Donald, I presume.'

Donny pulled away from Alfie and looked up at the man. He grimaced. 'Are you my uncle?'

'It seems I am.'

He stared at him for a while. 'You look just like my dad. And that's not a good thing.'

Rupert frowned. 'No, I imagine it's not in your eyes.' He looked over at Marianne. 'I've booked a suite for you all so you don't have to drive back immediately. In the meantime, I'll sit with my brother until he wakes up and then . . . I don't really know. But he won't bother you again. I have a feeling his mind's not quite right at the moment.' He sighed sadly. 'I wonder if it ever has been.'

'Thank you, but I'd rather get back.' Marianne looked at Alfie. 'Do you think you could drive?'

Alfie nodded. 'I'll give it a go. Should be just enough fuel to get us home. But with this latest attack, I'm not sure what the roads'll be like.'

'Please, Alf. I just need to get home.'

Alfie nodded in understanding. 'Come on, then. Reckon you can navigate, Nellie?'

'I'll give it my best.'

'I'll bid you goodbye, then,' Rupert said. He held his hand out to each of them in turn. 'I'm sorry we met in such bad circumstances, Donny. But please keep writing to your grandfather. He lives for your letters.'

Donny sighed. 'Do I have to, Mum?'

'I think it would be the kind thing to do, Donny.'

'All right.' Donny huffed and turned to go outside.

'Marianne,' Rupert said, as she was walking away. Marianne looked over her shoulder at him. 'I promise this will be the last you hear of Donny being taken away. I'll make sure of it. But encourage him to visit if you can. My father's heart is broken enough as it is.'

Marianne stared at him for a while. 'We'll see how he feels,' she said. 'Mr Fanshawe is not my concern and I'm not going to force Donny to do anything.'

Rupert nodded, then raised his hand in farewell and turned away, his shoulders drooping.

'Just goes to show,' Nellie remarked, 'that no matter how much money you have, it don't protect you from everything.'

∽

The drive back took far longer than when they'd driven during daylight. Mindful of the air raid, Alfie kept the headlights off and drove at a snail's pace through the country lanes, relying on the light of the moon. At one point, he turned off the road and drove straight into a field, while Nellie cursed him for being a fool.

In the back, Donny was lying with his head on Marianne's lap, fast asleep. She smiled faintly as she stroked her son's hair and listened to her mother. It seemed Alfie had well and truly been accepted into the family now. She'd known her mother's good behaviour around him couldn't last forever.

Some two hours after they'd left, they were finally driving down Folkestone Road. They stopped at a blockade, where a soldier demanded to know why they were driving in the middle of the night.

Nellie got out of the van and marched around to him. 'I thought I recognised your voice, Sergeant O'Malley,' she said. 'And if you must know, I've just rescued my grandson from a brothel, been caught in an air raid and now I'm on my way back to make sure I can open up the café in time for you to get your breakfast.'

The soldier stared at her in astonishment, then burst out laughing. 'Mrs C.! If I'd known it was you, I'd not have stopped ye. To be sure, if you weren't behind the counter at Castle's, I'd know the war was lost!'

He waved her towards the van. 'I'll see ye later. Cup of tea and porridge, if you don't mind.'

Nellie patted him on the arm. 'It'll be waiting for you, love. Much damage tonight?'

The man sobered. 'Aye. Ye'll find you might have to avoid Maison Dieu tonight. But the café's still standing.'

Nellie breathed a sigh of relief and got back in the van.

As they drove on, a thought suddenly occurred to Marianne.

'Mum, how did you know all that about the will and money?'

Nellie looked around at her and tapped the side of her nose. 'There's not many people around these parts that I don't know one way or another. And there's no secrets in a house with servants.'

'That doesn't answer my question.'

'Well, it's all I'm going to say on the matter.' Nellie chuckled smugly and turned back to stare out of the window in front of her.

A red glow was hovering over the Western Docks; it wasn't just Folkestone's harbour that had been hit. They carried on past Western Heights, the trees thankfully masking the sight of the burning docks. In the east, the first fingers of light were spreading on the horizon, making the castle stand out in stark relief against the rose-tinted sky, and Marianne realised wearily that breakfast would need to start in a couple of hours. She wasn't sure she'd manage it, but after another bombing raid, people would be counting on them. She'd just have to find the strength from somewhere.

Finally, the van stopped and they all got out. Beside her, Donny leant into her side, refusing to let her go, and she was more than happy with that. Alfie came up beside her and put an arm around her shoulders, and together they stood and looked at the café. The blackout curtains were pulled shut, and the 'C' and 's' of Castle's were obscured by the tape criss-crossing the window. But it had never looked better to her.

'Come on, let's get you inside.' Alfie urged her forward and they walked across the square and around to the back gate.

521

Nellie had gone in before them, and they could hear her loud voice exclaiming, 'What the devil are you three playing at?'

Marianne walked in to see both her sisters and Jasper sitting bleary-eyed at the kitchen table with cups of tea in front of them.

Lily jumped up when she saw Donny and ran towards him. 'Oh, thank God! Thank God!' She pulled him away from Marianne, hugging him tightly to her.

Edie was close behind, and once Lily had let him go, she knelt in front of Donny, smoothing the hair back from his face. 'Oh, Don! Am I glad to see you.' She kissed his cheek and held him close.

Donny pulled away and looked at his aunt. 'Have you moved back, Auntie Edie?'

She smiled. 'No, love. But Lily came running up to tell me you were missing and I couldn't leave her sitting on her own worrying about you, so I came to wait with her.'

'Will you be staying?'

She shook her head. 'I'm afraid not, love.'

Nellie shook her head sadly. 'Even after this? Even after nearly losing your nephew, you won't come home?'

'Oh, Mum, it's not that. I've done a lot of thinking over the past few months, and I realise that with everything going on I need to forgive and forget. But I need to be where I'm useful. Surely you can see that?'

Nellie slumped into a chair and Jasper went over to put his arm around her and kissed her on the hair. She leant her head into his side and sighed. 'Well, you need to do what you need to do, I suppose.'

Edie kissed her mother's cheek. 'Thanks, Mum.'

'Auntie Lily, you're not going to leave, are you?'

Lily ruffled Donny's hair. 'No, love. I'll be here. So there'll still be four of us. It's lucky you came back, really. We need you here to give us a hand.'

Donny nodded and yawned. 'I think I'd like to go to bed now. I'll tell you everything in the morning.'

Marianne took his hand and led him upstairs, followed by the others, who stood and watched as Donny got into bed, as if unable to let him out of their sight.

Finally, Marianne came out and shut the door. Edie and Lily hugged her in turn.

'We've got about one hour to sleep, I reckon.' Lily yawned. 'There wasn't much sleep to be had tonight anyway, what with the air raid.'

Nellie looked at Jasper and suddenly realised that his face was streaked with soot and he was wearing his navy blue ARP boilersuit. 'Shouldn't you be down at the harbour?'

'I was. But soon as I could I came here to check up on you lot, and when the girls told me you'd gone off to Folkestone, there was no way I could go home. You had me worried, girl. Don't do that to me again.'

Nellie patted his shoulder. 'As you can see, I'm right as rain. I just need forty winks before breakfast. I'll have a bowl of porridge waiting for you later. Extra honey.' She winked at him and he grinned and watched her as she went into her room and shut the door.

He went over and gave Marianne a hug. 'Thank God you're all safe.'

Marianne could clearly see the strain of the last few hours on Jasper's face, and for the first time she realised he looked older than his fifty years. 'Thank you, Jasper. For everything.' She put her arms around him, and he rested his head on her hair briefly, then stepped back and held his hand out to Alfie, who took it in a firm clasp. 'See you later, son.'

'See you, Jasper.' Alfie clapped him on the shoulder and Jasper turned and lumbered down the stairs.

Marianne looked at her sisters. 'You go on up, girls. I'll be there in a mo.'

They looked between her and Alfie and smiled slyly before retreating upstairs.

Marianne took Alfie's hand and pulled him into the living room, where they flopped down onto the sofa underneath the window. Marianne put her head on his shoulder.

'At last we're alone,' he whispered. 'I'm dying to hear the full story of what happened.' The journey had been so fraught that there hadn't been a chance yet to explain exactly how they'd found Donny.

Marianne told him and Alfie laughed at the strange coincidence of Nellie being acquainted with the madam at the brothel. Was there anyone she didn't know?

'She was nice, though, Hester Barker. I can see why she and Mum were friends once.'

She was quiet for a while, until finally she said, 'Something happened while I was sitting squashed in that cupboard under the stairs.'

Alfie stroked her hair. 'What was it?'

'I realised that I should stop being scared. And I don't mean scared of the war or the bombs.' She turned her head and looked up at him.

'What do you mean then? You know me, Marianne. I'm not all that clever, and I need things spelt out to me very clearly,' he said, looking serious.

She put her hand on his cheek. 'I mean that you were right. That time is precious and we shouldn't waste it being scared of what the future holds. It means, I'm saying yes.'

'To what exactly?' he asked carefully.

'To you, me and Donny being a family.'

An enormous grin broke out on Alfie's face and he leant his face down to hers, kissing her gently. 'Now you tell me. Just as I'm about to leave.'

Marianne nodded sadly. 'I'm sorry. But I'll be here when you get back. And you *will* get back. I refuse to believe anything else.'

He kissed her again and they stretched out on the sofa, Marianne's head on Alfie's chest, his arms around her. They were exhausted and even the effort of talking was too much right then; they were content just to be in each other's arms and feel the warmth of each other's bodies. Eventually, the rhythmic beating of Alfie's heart soothed Marianne to sleep.

∾

Bright sunlight hitting her face woke Marianne and she sat up with a gasp. She squinted over at the window. Donny had pulled back the blackout curtains and was now standing, his hair sticking up and his clothes filthy, staring with wide eyes at her and Alfie on the sofa.

She stood abruptly and smoothed down her skirt, just as Alfie began to stir, blinking at the sun.

'Morning, Mum! Morning, Alfie!'

Marianne cleared her throat and looked at Alfie, who grinned back at her.

'Why are you sleeping on the sofa together?'

Marianne blushed and looked at Alfie again. 'Well . . . umm . . . me and Alfie were so tired we couldn't even get upstairs.'

Donny stared at them, considering. 'According to my teachers, only mums and dads are allowed to sleep together.' He looked pointedly at the pair. 'So . . . that must mean that . . .' He gave a loud whoop. 'Alfie's going to be my dad!' He danced around, clapping his hands. 'And he's a lot better than my real one.'

'Donny!' Marianne's voice was sharp. 'Stop it.'

He stopped and looked at her. 'So he's not going to be my dad?'

'Well . . . Alfie?' Marianne looked at him pleadingly.

Alfie laughed and stood up, ruffling Donny's hair. 'We'll see, Don, eh? We'll see.'

'We'll see means yes!' he yelled, running over to Nellie's room. 'Gran! Gran, wake up! I've got a dad at last!'

After a pause, the door opened and Nellie poked her head out. Despite her exhaustion the night before, she'd managed to put her hair in curlers and she had her favourite bright orange and purple scarf wrapped around her head. She pulled her pink quilted dressing gown around her and squinted at her grandson, then came out and looked in the living room. Spotting Marianne and Alfie standing by the window looking sheepish, she grinned.

'Bless my soul, Donny, so you have!' She nodded at her daughter. 'And about time too. Come on, Don, let's me and you leave your mum and dad to talk some more and we'll get the breakfasts started, eh?'

Donny rushed over and hugged Marianne, and then, to Alfie's surprise, he threw his arms around his waist. 'This is what people do with their dads, isn't it, Alfie? I seen Fred do it all the time.'

'They do, Don. They really do,' Alfie said, squeezing the boy to him. He looked over Donnie's head and his eyes met Marianne's. Hers were full of tears, but she was smiling. He gestured with his head and she went over and put her arms around her two men, her heart full. She could hardly believe that after all these years of feeling worthless and unlovable, this wonderful man had come into her life. And no matter what happened in the months and years to come, whatever hardships and difficulties they faced, between Alfie and her family and their little community in the market square, they would find a way to get through it together.

She raised her head. Her mother was grinning at them, hands on hips, her dressing gown gaping open to show the bright yellow cotton nightdress underneath. Marianne smiled tearfully at her and Nellie nodded back, then turned and went downstairs to start the breakfast.

Acknowledgements

To begin with I would like to say thank you to Peter Holmes, my amazing father. He was born the year before World War II started and died suddenly on the very day the cover of this book was revealed. He and my equally fabulous mother, Anne, frequently regaled me with tales of their wartime childhoods, so thank you for those stories. My father never did see the cover, nor did he read any version of the book. But then, he preferred his fiction to have space ships or talking flowers, so I'm not sure it would have been his thing. But that didn't stop him being proud. I miss you, Daddy. Sleep well.

Next I would like to thank everyone else who helped me along the way.

To Teresa Chris, my agent, who encouraged me to write a book in the first place and for whom the term 'firm but fair' might have been invented – you were so right about my first draft! Thank you Claire Johnson-Creek and everyone at Bonnier Books UK for agreeing to publish me, and for keeping going despite the weird times we live in.

During my research I have read a lot about Dover during the war years, but the book I keep by my side while I am writing is Terry Sutton and Derek Leach's fascinating and comprehensive book, *Dover in the Second World War*. I'd be lost without it.

And finally a big thank you to my family and friends for listening patiently while I yabbered endlessly about my book. Especially Maddie, Sim and Olly, who are still bearing the brunt of this now. Thanks, guys, for not complaining, and for your creative plot ideas about aliens and dinosaurs. I'll bear them in mind for next time.

Welcome to the world of *Ginny Bell*!

Keep reading for more from Ginny Bell, to
discover a recipe that features in this novel
and to find out more about what
Ginny is doing next . . .

We'd also like to introduce you to MEMORY LANE,
our special community for the very best of saga
writing from authors you know and love, and
new ones we simply can't wait for you to
meet. Read on and join our club!

www.MemoryLane.club

Dear Reader,

Way back in 1984, I started studying for my A Levels in Dover. At the time, the town was quite rundown and the Channel Tunnel hadn't yet been built. My friends and I would rattle around between our favourite café – coincidentally right opposite where I now envisage Castle's Café to be – the beach, Western Heights and the Castle grounds. It's no surprise, then, that my characters tend to do the same!

What I didn't realise was that Dover was still suffering from the effects of being virtually demolished during the war, due to the relentless shelling it endured for four years. In addition, during that time, the town lost more than half its population, mostly due to evacuation, and even today it has still not quite recovered the numbers.

Not so long ago, when I was thinking about writing a wartime series, I visited Dover Castle and the wartime tunnels, and I was astonished to realise that I had lived there without ever truly understanding the role Dover played in World War II. Some further reading unearthed the existence of a restaurant called Igglesden and Graves that used to stand on the corner of Market Square and Castle Street (exactly where Castle's Café stands), and was a popular haunt for servicemen and women. I began to think about the person who would run it, and the formidable Nellie Castle and her six children started to take shape in my mind. But the books are not just about the Castles, they are about the community and its indomitable spirit in the face of almost unimaginable danger and destruction.

I have tried to stay true to the historical facts, but there are some inaccuracies. The most glaring of these is that Churchill's iconic 'Fight on the Beaches' speech was never broadcast on the radio. In fact, Churchill only recorded the speech for posterity in 1949. However, this is fiction, and I thought it was more dramatic to have my characters listening to his stirring words after the long days of struggle and worry they had just been through.

What I hope I have managed to portray accurately in *The Dover Café at War*, though, is how the people of Dover pulled together during the Dunkirk evacuation, putting their lives on hold to help the thousands and thousands of battle-weary soldiers who passed through the town. And in particular I hope that I have managed to do justice to the 'Dunkirk spirit' that somehow, against all the odds, got Britain and her allies through the war.

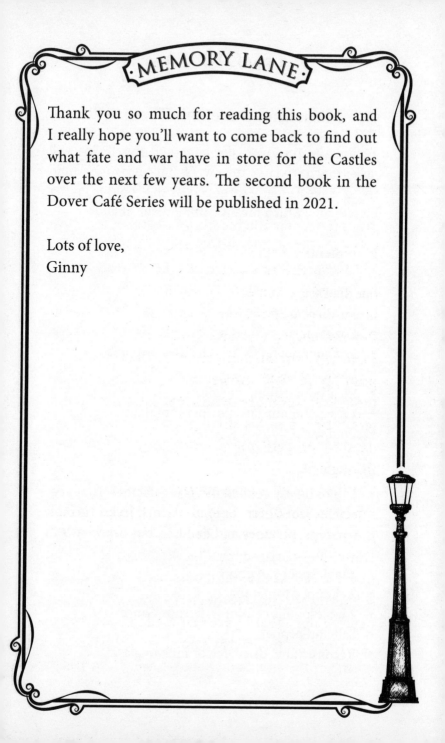

· MEMORY LANE ·

Thank you so much for reading this book, and I really hope you'll want to come back to find out what fate and war have in store for the Castles over the next few years. The second book in the Dover Café Series will be published in 2021.

Lots of love,
Ginny

Marianne's Vegetable Turnovers

Technically turnovers are large and this recipe will make four very large turnovers. But Marianne would try to make as many turnovers as she could from her ingredients, which meant cutting them small.

Ingredients

For the Pastry
- 4 oz mashed potatoes
- 4 oz flour
- 2 oz cooking fat (Marianne uses dripping)
- 1 teaspoon salt
- 1 teaspoon baking powder
- 1 teaspoon mustard powder (optional)
- Cold water

For the Filling
- 1 lb of lightly cooked diced vegetables – root vegetables work best (onions, carrots, leeks, turnips, parsnips, potatoes and swedes), but use what's in season
- 2 tablespoons of gravy
- 2 chopped tomatoes
- 2 tablespoons of Worcestershire Sauce
- Salt and pepper
- Reconstituted dried egg or milk to glaze

Method

To make the pastry: Sift the flour, baking powder, mustard powder and salt together then rub in the fat until combined. Mix in the mashed potatoes. Add a little water to bind, then knead until you have a soft dough.

Pre-heat the oven to 200°C (400°F) and grease a baking tray

Roll out the pastry and form into rounds, brushing the edges with a little egg or water

Mix the ingredients and gravy etc. together and put in the centre of each round or to one side, depending on where you intend to have the seam

Bring edges together and press between finger and thumb along the seam to seal

Make a slit or prick with a fork and brush with egg or milk

Place on a baking tray and cook for 20–30 minutes until golden brown

Serve hot or cold
Enjoy!

Look out for the next book in the Dover Café Series . . .

The Dover Café On The Front Line

As the Battle of Britain rages above Dover, and the
German guns across the Channel start to shell
the town, danger lurks around every corner.
But despite this, Lily Castle is happy to be
starting her nursing training at last.

When Lily is asked to help set up a secret military
hospital on the cliffs above Dover, she is thrilled.
That is until she realises that she will be working
with Dr Charlie Alexander, a man who at their
first meeting formed entirely the wrong
impression of her.

When a German pilot escapes from the hospital,
Lily is accused of helping him. With the only job
she's ever wanted in jeopardy, Lily must do
whatever she can to find out the truth.
And prove her innocence.

Coming in 2021

 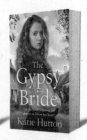